May these words weave glorious healing around, within, and through all.

The fates come full circle

Calling forth the spirit of love,

calling forth the innocent,

who shall try to override destiny.

The ancestors live in our bones.

This book is dedicated to my children. Susanne, who came into my life at a time when I needed to remember real love. She awakened within me the purest connection of mother and child, a connection beyond time and space. Tom, who came during a time of breakdown, awakening in me the joy and passion of living life as a creative expression of fearless adventure. George, my heart baby, came when I needed to remember my inner courage and the fierce love of Mother as healer. Awakening in me the timeless bond of mother and child to heal through a courageous love. Alex, came during a time when I needed to anchor in the stable and constant love found deep within the bones of life. He awakened in me the power of manifesting the heart's true calling. Brandon, who's arrival was an answer to a silent prayer. His life awakened in me the power to protect all that I hold dear, no matter what, and who's passing sent me farther into the truth that Love lives on, for it is where we come from and it is always where we return to. His essence reminds me that we can't get this wrong and our prayers are always answered, somehow and someway, because each and every soul is forever and ever loved, unconditionally and completely. Love is eternal and in infinity is where we truly exist. Remember that, live boldly and love big.

Chapter One

Britain Late 16th Century

The day was particularly heavy and it lay upon her like a thick blanket, comforting and soothing. She stared through the slit in the blood-red velvet curtain, past the etched glass pane, over the dull road, and into the smoky gray tendrils of limbs and boughs. The heaviness was otherworldly, vast and familiar. Her body shook as the coach hit rocks and rough patches on the well-worn path. With each bump her insides grew calmer as the coach traveled farther away from the estate walls and farther away from her well-kept life.

Keeping her eyes fixed on the forest that ran alongside her coach, she imagined an invisible veil, much like a wall, heralding the stopping point where the road ended and the forest began. As she stared, a faint voice beckoned her to enter into the forest. The soft voice told her to go past this wall and see for herself.

Squinting her eyes tightly she imagined who or what, called to her. The magic and mystery of such a question tightened in her belly. She kept her stare sure and steady, as shadows danced, the fog sang and the voice soothed her curious nature. After a time, she saw the flutter of wings darting merrily between the boughs and branches. Flickering sunlight, moist and vibrant cast a glow upon treasures forbidden. She sighed deeply. How would she ever be able to venture into the daring forest? The question was too much for her young mind to ponder. Sitting back against her seat with a thud, she turned her head downward and fiddled with her lace glove. Her face knotted up and matched the pull of regret within her belly. Life was quite laid out and in the broadest hope there was no room within its finely figured walls for her to adventure past the veil of the forest wall.

Elizabeth of Cumberland and her family lived perfectly tucked, hidden, and safely restricted within the walls of a lavish estate abutted against the edge of the forest. Estate walls were dull and flat, built by servant men to keep out the intruders and keep in secrets. With each passing year, the secrets grew stronger as did the deep longing for life beyond the walls. With each passing year, life seemed to both shove her out and hold her captive at the same time.

As the coach approached its destination, fog lifted and the familiar cacophony of sounds and scents from the bustling city drowned out the magical seduction of the forest. Not quite as mystical yet intriguing just the same, the city fully awakened her senses. Sitting upright in her seat, she restlessly waited for the first sighting of the market place. Forest imaginings left behind, Elizabeth strained to hear the calls of the merchants and laughter of the children scurrying to keep up with their mothers. Entering into the city, gave her a sense of hope, that someday she too would partake in a life far different from the one she presently lived. This new life included the forest, yes, but also the city, for it held a magic and a wonder almost as powerful.

The market place was not however, their destination. Nothing quite as exciting could call her family into the city square. The cathedral bells rang loudest of all and its spires were the final stop for the carriage. Standing tall in all its grandeur amidst the budding excitement of the city, the home of God stood perfectly coifed and guarded by saints, angels and gargoyles. As a very little girl she was intrigued by this immense stone creation and had many questions about the presence of such gruesome demons. She had however stopped noticing the gargoyles fierce stares, and the angels and saint's faraway looks, long ago when no one seemed as interested in

4

them as she. None of the adults seemed to know nor care, therefore, it was up to her to create the story that would suffice her curious mind. The immense stone gods were frozen in time, perched upon the cathedral to warn of the fear and doom that would befall each and every person who stepped foot inside. Yet, no one heeded the warning. They all went inside, listened to the sinister men deal fearsome messages, and then left to help spread these messages across the land through whatever merciless means necessary. The stone statues were lucky, for they did not ever have to enter into the walls of the cathedral, sit still and listen with pretend care, to the long winded old men waxing on about how dreadful everyone was, reminding all in attendance of the unworthiness of their souls and shouting about the various punishments of utmost horror that would befall them if they went against God, or the King.

This house of God was petrifying and the rants of the holy men questionable, as they spewed stories of hangings, burnings and beheadings of the heretics, most especially the Catholics and the witches. Elizabeth brought it to the attention of her father once. Father told her in a matter of fact way that witches were not real, they were the imagination of those who could find no other way to solve differences. And as far as the Catholics go, Father confirmed that Mother's family had been Catholic a few generations ago, but now they all attended the established church, the Church of the King, so presumably she was a saved soul. Father also assured her that she was untouchable. She was not sure what the untouchable part meant.

Being the thoughtful young girl, laden with common sense, she had taken her own counsel. Reaching into the depths of her being, she discovered a few satisfying answers of her own. God did not care if one were a Catholic or recusant or if one attended the new church, for she most certainly doubted that God lived in such a menacing place. She figured out, with the help of her eavesdropping skills, during the long evening gatherings Father held in his study, that it was the

5

kings and queens that were playing God and all the people that lived upon their lands were their flock. God was something else and somewhere else. Perhaps it was God who gave her the gift of common sense, which seemed quite possible. She did not dare speak of such knowing to anyone, not even Father, for she did know better than to defy authority, so she kept her understanding, knowing, and good common sense tucked safely inside, as best she could, for now.

When attending church services, she had found a way to use her imagination to ignore the stifling fear and trepidation that filled the air. She simply removed herself from all manner of praying to a god that she knew was not there and instead spent her time in a story of her own design. A well- developed imagination and keen mind assisted her through the depths of boredom that would surely overtake her if she did not do something to the contrary. The use of her imagination started thusly; scanning the church crowd she would find the most beautiful maiden present. Upon spotting her, she took in every detail of her gown, hair and jewels, naming each headpiece and color of fabric used. She entered in conversation with the maiden as if they were dear and trusted friends. They shared their deepest secrets, nothing was left out, not even their similar distaste for Sunday services. Her dear friend would then let her in on the juiciest, most scandalous secret ever; the name of her true love. Elizabeth would scan the rows and rows of seats looking for the most handsome young gentleman. This was a most difficult task for she could not let Father know she was looking around the Cathedral when she should have been praying. Luckily, Father was in his own world, either lost in thought, eyes closed, or staring blankly. Truth be told she was one of the only maidens who attended Sunday services anyway, for it was a place filled mostly with men and lads about to be men. Once she spotted the handsome lad of her best friend's affection she went on to imagine their life together, seeing their wedding festivities within her mind, deciding the number and names of their children and before she knew it service was over and she was free! This was indeed her most favorite game to play in the deep dank recesses of the city Cathedral and weekly service.

On that particular gray, heavy day as she and her father and brother traveled into the city, after catching the momentary glimpse of the forest fairies, she merrily became lost in the world of her own. This very morning, she had decided that on this day there would be a devilish twist in the game. Instead of finding the most beautiful maiden, she herself would play the part of the maiden in love. The thought sent a chill of excitement up her spine as she delightfully remembered the morning's events.

Elizabeth of Cumberland boldly decided that it was time for her to be a real maiden. She did not know quite what that meant, since there was no one in her life at the time that could help her with such things, yet she had declared today to be the day. To prove her determination and independence, she made a bold albeit cumbersome move. She shunned her servants help with any of the morning's dressing routines. She could not be bothered with the snooping and questioning from her Nanny Matilda or her dressing maid. If one servant was to know a thing, it was assured all would find out. No one need know that she would be going to cathedral as a maiden. Elizabeth was known for demanding her privacy, so she hoped her servants would not find her desire to dress herself this time to be too out of the ordinary.

"I am quite fine on my own!" she yelled as her maid knocked politely on the locked bed chamber door. Elizabeth had been trying to tie the ruffle under her neck for many a minute and it was not cooperating. She threw it under the bed in exasperation and instead opted for her second choice at defying the dress code of her father, via her dressing staff. Elizabeth rarely showed anger to her maids or any of the servants in the household, yet she so wanted to dress without the opinion of another for once in her life. She went to the door and whispered.

"I will dress myself today, Nell." She searched for the words that would make such a request plausible. "I'm not feeling well, wouldn't want you to catch ill." She whispered and coughed for good measure.

"Oh, my Mistress, would you like me to fetch ya some remedy? Would you like me to tell Master Cumberland you will not be attending services?" answered Nell.

"No, no, that will not be necessary. I shall drink the brew you left for me earlier and all will be well. Thank you Nell, that is all." Elizabeth waited until she heard the patter of footsteps trailing down the hall. She stared at the cold brew and laughed, congratulating herself on a job well done. She quite liked this precocious game she was playing. It suited her well and added much to her otherwise dowdy existence. Full of mischievous glee, she turned to the task at hand.

A small silver hand mirror that she had stolen from the dressing table of her mother would help assure the perfectly placed golden braids upon her head were still perfectly placed, after the tenuous ride into town. She tucked the mirror deep into her petticoats, smiling at the thought. A rush of heat ran through her belly. To steal from her mother, to hide the forbidden mirror, and to raise her petticoats in the holy prison was a true dare, punishable by exactly what, she was not sure, but punishable to say the least.

Elizabeth pulled the mirror out once more, and stared into its shimmery face. Heat from her fingers warmed the plain silver handle. Tarnish offset the shine of the precious metal and the one large ruby, inlaid delicately on its back, glistened in the early morning light. Holding the mirror

8

close, she stared at herself with curiosity. Her features were full, mouth and cheeks rosy and as much as she desired, she dare not use any of mother's white powder to hide her flaws. At least not quite yet, that would wait until next time. She had stolen a jar of the coveted white power, along with the mirror, and it lay hidden beneath the boards of her bed. Extending her arm, she continued to look over her reflection. Pushing up her bodice, she grimaced with a fanciful wish. "I wish this part of me was as full as my face." She whispered aloud. "Oh well, I shall have the look of a proper maiden someday. Mother is beautiful, and Father says I favor her."

Elizabeth's cheeks flushed hot as she recalled the time spent in secret, rummaging through Mother's jewelry and finery. No one could ever know of her escapades into the delight of Mother's chambers and she had become quite clever at entering into the dressing chambers unseen, carefully planning the caper when Nurse Beatrice was not doting over Mother's every move. Mother barely moved at all and spent most of her day neatly tucked in bed, barely visible among the clouds of blankets.

The touch and feel of the silky coolness, and rich softness of Mother's ball gowns took her to another place and time, when her now life-less Mother accepted callers and entertained guests donned in these fanciful and ever so beautiful pieces of fabric art. Elizabeth especially loved Mother's jewels, for she named each piece, and created a story as to how they came to be hiding away in Mother's jewelry cabinet. She believed each jewel as a gift from Father, in expression of his love for his one true love. The jewels were surely acquired on great jaunts upon the sea when Father was a successful sea merchant. Elizabeth could only surmise what life was like for her parents so very long ago. The mystery of both Father and Mother's past intrigued her to no end, but far be it for either of them to share any of the stories. She craved to know where she came from, and mostly, what life was like beyond the estate walls, yet she was left to her own imagination to weave the story of the history of her own flesh and blood.

Elizabeth found a way to weave together bits and pieces of her parent's past in spite of her family's tight lips, for her talents at thievery and eves dropping far surpassed any obligation she had to respectability and privacy. She was quite good, not only at slipping into her mother's dressing chamber, but also hiding in the most elusive of ways and listening to the conversations that passed between the loosed lipped adults of the estate. Her escapades and talent at thievery and mischief allowed her to artfully create a very real story about her mother and father and it had nothing whatsoever to do with the sleeping woman who lay alone in her bed chambers for days upon days. The mother of her present was surely not the mother of her past.

Today was the day that Elizabeth decided to step forward in her boldness, with or without her silent parent's consent or knowledge. Today was the day that she would be the maiden of the cathedral and today she just might find a young lad, soon to be gentleman who would catch her fancy, ask her to be his wife and take her to be the lady of her own estate. Yes, today was the perfect day, for she could feel true maidenhood was upon her and it would not be long until she would be choosing a mate. Her father would be the one to choose, with her consent of course and she wanted to be ready, for Father would surely want to know her preference when it came to matters of the heart.

Elizabeth sighed a great sigh as she was brought back from her musings of the morning, and continued to stare out the coach window. The grayness was truly oppressive today, yet failed to dampen her spirits. The forest was becoming thinner and the pine scent was giving way to the stinging odors of the approaching city. It would not be long before they arrived at their destination. Slowly clutching the hand mirror that hid under her petticoat, she readied herself, heart fluttering as she felt an unfamiliar stirring deep within her belly.

Elizabeth was startled at such an unfamiliar feeling and she started to wonder what could be the matter. Had she gone too far? Was she ready to enter the cathedral as a maiden? Sitting back, she forced her attention onto her brother Henry. He animatedly chatted with Father and Elizabeth stared at him with concern. Her thoughts easily diverted from her own discomfort and landed with familiar discord upon her ailing brother. She noticed that his skin had a slight ashen look, quite usual for a child with his weakened lungs. But was he more pale than usual? Was he laboring for breath? She watched him intently, as a mother watches her sleeping infant, noticing the rise and fall of his chest and noting the level of ease or difficulty in which his body took in air. She was satisfied that his breathing was sufficient and shifted her gaze to Father, who sat solemnly across from Henry. Father was still and quiet, properly dressed and handsome, the familiar faraway look frozen upon his face. Resting his hand upon the seat next to him, he clutched one of Mother's gloves as if Mother was really there. Mother was too ill to attend services again this week and Elizabeth could not remember a time when she was not too ill. In all her thirteen years, Mother had been ill. Father must have remembered Mother accompanying him to services, for why else would he hold her finely embroidered glove each and every Sunday? The glove looked like a lifeless ragdoll in Father's large hand, his knuckles white from the strength at which he clutched the delicate material. Mother was never there, yet her ghost always was.

Elizabeth pulled her gaze away from the lifeless remnant of her mother and settled her eyes upon Father. A bitter taste rose up from the depths of her belly and into her mouth as she took in the sadness. She drew her handkerchief up to cover her lips, just as the coach fiercely jolted and cries caught everyone's attention.

"No, no, we will not go with you!" Screams blasted through the thin walls of the coach. Horses whinnied and the coach tumbled with the movement.

Henry flew onto father's lap. Elizabeth slid off the seat, hit the side of the coach wall and landed on the floor in a heap of swirling petticoats. Jumping up, she pushed back the curtain to see where the screams came from before Father could stop her.

"No, leave us be!"

The cries came from a lad, who looked to be about her age. He stood tall and defiant in front of the shire reeve. Behind him stood a group of smaller children, huddling together and cowering in the presence of the shire and his men. The lad held his arms back, herding the little ones as they moved closer and closer together in a tight bundle as if they were a stack of kindling sticks ready for tying. Elizabeth counted five little ones, dirty and shoeless. Rags were their only protection on this cold spring morn. Grime covered their little faces, streaked at the places tears might fall.

"Lad, you and your little army are coming with us. Your devil ways are over now and forever!" The shire yelled and tried to pull the lad away from the children. The tall youngster was stronger than the shire thought, for his arm would not budge from the protective ring he had formed around the other children. The shire motioned to one of his monster men to help and Elizabeth watched in horror as the burliest, ugliest man she had ever seen waddled over and grabbed the lad's thin gangly arm and pulled hard. She heard the cracking of bones. The monster man did not stop; instead he swung the lad around by his broken arm and threw him into the cart.

"Run, run. Save yourselves!" shouted the lad to the others. The children however, stood frozen.

Elizabeth felt something rush up from somewhere deep inside of her. So deep, she thought it came from within the bowels of the earth itself and so powerful in its force, it seemed as if nothing would or could ever stop it from emerging. The bitter bile was evident upon her lips as she screamed.

"Great Mother, help these children NOW!"

All heads turned toward the coach. Elizabeth could feel the heat of the shire's furry directed towards her. Something was terribly, terribly wrong and now she felt as if she were a part of it. She did not however back down. She licked her tainted lips and spoke the cursed prayer aloud again.

"Great Mother, help them!"

The children did not run and the heavens did not open and scoop them up. The shire and his two men turned back to their crimes and proceeded to throw each child into the cart, binding them all together with a large rope. Now they did indeed look like kindling. Human kindling, ready for the fires. Before they could bind the oldest lad, he lifted his fractured arm and touched each one of the little children, as a father would touch his child after a fall or scrape. Elizabeth felt the sorrow and the love reconciling deep within her.

Father pulled Elizabeth away from the window. Closing the curtain tightly, he reprimanded her.

"Elizabeth, sit yourself down upon your seat. It is not proper for you to be staring." Father commanded with eyes lowered and lips pursed.

Elizabeth sat and stared at the blood red curtain. There was no place in her that could make sense of what she had witnessed. Her insides were torn apart and ached deeply. It was as if she herself was tied tightly to the bundle of children and their fate was her fate. The bitter taste in her mouth returned and was unbearable. She pulled out her handkerchief and spit into the embroidered family crest. She had to get the taste out of her mouth but it would not leave. She looked at her Father and a great shame and panic arose within her. He quickly turned away from her fierce glance. Her voice and spirit returned.

"But Father, those children…where is their mother…their father? Why is that shire treating them so? Did you not see?"

She demanded an answer as she peeked out the window to get another look. Father did not answer and refused to look at her. The carriage started moving again with a fury that matched her own. Elizabeth held onto the strap with one hand and kept her moist handkerchief closed tightly in the other. The curtain flounced open just enough for her to see the cart of dirty children following alongside their carriage. She stared at them and one small girl in particular caught her eye. This child looked to be about Henry's age. Elizabeth's eyes filled with tears and terror for the plight of this tiny child, yet she quickly wiped the tears, for the lass could see into the coach. Elizabeth forced a smile.

"Help us my lady!" the lass cried. "Help us please! They have hung our mama." Her eyes cried out to Elizabeth with more pain than she had ever witnessed. Elizabeth waved at the girl, hoping to ease her fright. Her wave caught the eye of the guard sitting with the children. He grabbed the little girl and started to beat her with his large fist.

"Shut up you little brat. How dare you burden the Cumberland family with your pleas."

The guard's booming voice made Elizabeth's ears ring as if he had shouted directly into her. The little girl cowered as the monster continued hitting her, blood oozing from her nose. The bitterness rose up within Elizabeth again, this time consuming her whole being. Swallowing hard, she yelled.

"Father...Father! Stop the carriage, we must help the children."

Elizabeth leapt up from her seat and sat hard upon her Father's hand, the one that still clutched Mother's glove. She swung the curtain open wide.

"Look Father. Look at what they are doing to that child. Why are they treating her so? You must do something!" Elizabeth cried.

Father turned quickly away from Elizabeth, but not quick enough. She saw the softening of his grey blue eyes.

"No Elizabeth, I will not look. I believe these young ruffians are the children of the thief who was hung last week. I am sure they will be hung too. The children of a thief are surely thieves themselves." The softness in his gaze turned to slate, as flat and cold as the words he spoke.

"Father, they are just children," Elizabeth cried softly, retreating back into her seat. Seeing Father in this confused state, his eyes saying one thing, his words another, wiped the rage from her heart and left her with a most frustrating sadness. She dared not look out the window again for fear of what she might see. The heaviness of the morning choked her and filled her with panic. She wanted to cry out to Father again, yet it was now her little brother who was in need.

Henry interrupted her despair with a deep cough that surely signaled a spell would follow. Wide eyed and panicked, Henry stared at her, the coughs and sputum erupting over the whole lot of them. He tried to hold it in but it burst through his puffed cheeks and the moistened air landed on Father. Father quickly pushed his handkerchief over Henry's mouth.

"Stop Father!" Elizabeth demanded. "You know very well that to hold his mouth shut during these spells will only aggravate him and cause his breath to weaken."

Elizabeth turned the despair for her father's complacency into what she knew best; caring for Henry. She was ready, always ready to care for her younger brother. She fumbled for a moment until she found the vile of medicine tucked neatly into the pocket inside her cloak. Henry was now in a full fit of coughing and wheezing, his hands grasping for the coach door. The spells always had him wanting to flee.

"Hold his hand Father and pull him slowly towards you. Do not cover him or upset him in any way." Elizabeth commanded. "Henry, come sit, I have your medicine."

Father held Henry tightly as he struggled to free himself. The coughing was weakening him fast. He was not listening and she had to act. Prying his mouth open, she emptied the vile and his medicine splashed onto his tongue. She knew how to do this, for she had done it hundreds of times before.

"Turn the carriage around." Yelled father to the driver.

The carriage stopped and reeled around. They were now heading back toward their estate. Elizabeth sat in silence, holding her brother's hand and stroking his hair. His body heaved until the calmness of his sister's touch and the effects of the medicine led him gently into a rhythmic breath. As they entered onto the road that ran next to the forest, Elizabeth muttered a quick prayer to the forest fairies to protect those children as well as her little brother. She then remembered the strange but familiar prayer that had burst from her being. *Mother in Heaven, save them.* She shouted the prayer over and over within the quiet of her mind as she stared into the forest and beyond its wall. She knew that she saw the faint glimmer of light. The light pulled, awakening and soothing something deep within her being.

*****

Elizabeth headed toward the kitchen to help Cookie bake the cakes for the week. Whispers from the pantry stopped her in her tracks.

"Yes, it was quite a sight, it was." said Cookie. "They were all five standing with the same look upon their grimy faces."

Elizabeth felt faint. She knew of what Cookie spoke. Cookie continued and Elizabeth went unnoticed.

"And the ropes went about their necks, nearly knocking the smallest ones over with the weight. Never a sight a mother would ever want to see, I tell you. They were all hung in a row, bodies dangling. Their faces went blue in a matter of minutes. I tell ya lassies, watching that, I prayed harder than I ever done, in hopes that the urchins were really the devil's children and the devil he 'self would save them. But, alas, he did not."

Cookie searched the shelves for some missing ingredient, her large body sweeping the remnants of the days baking onto the floor. Elizabeth saw the big wet tears fall from Cookie's face and disappear into the thatch along with the bits and pieces of crusts and herbs. Cookie swiped her feet, grinding in her tears and sending a pleasant and familiar scent of rosemary wafting upwards.

"It was told that their mother's screams could be heard for miles around when the last of her children were dead. It was told, yes that the witch herself rose up from her grave and screamed in grief."

"Is that true, Cookie? Did you hear it? Did you hear the mother's screams?" asked Annie, the laundry maid.

"No, me myself did not hear it. I only saw five dead children hanging. No one come to save them, no one to claim them."

Cookie's ample body moved fiercely as she opened the barrel and scooped generous amounts of flour into a bowl, sending powdery dust flying. Her voice rose as she continued.

"All the royalty sat and watched...all the bastards with the coin smiled as those babies hung. I saw that with me own eyes!"

Cookie's voice quieted as she leaned into the two servant girls as they attentively listened. Elizabeth squirmed nervously, not wanting to make a sound and be discovered. She was very good at moving undetected, yet the servants were also very good too. She gathered herself, froze in place, almost stopped her breath. and continued to listen.

"Anyone who has not the riches to defend themselves could be next. Anyone who lives as the peasants do must beware." Cookie gasped for air, the restraint of her voice made her bosom heave mightily. "Anyone who uses the old way is doomed! I hear the mother witch was caught birthing a babe. Now, we know that kind of thing happens still among the peasants, yet this wily witch had the gall to come to the aid of a Lady. She helped birth Lady Fortner's babe. And for that she was hung." The two servant girls backed away from Cookie in unison, both clutching their tiny bosoms in protection.

"But don't you worry yourselves, dears." Cookie consoled. "We are safe here, for Master Cumberland keeps us so. He may be one of them, a bastard…with riches, but he is…different…lost in his own misery. That keeps him right here with us. In a way, he is one of us."

The girl's eyes widened with mock horror at what Cookie had just said. They turned to each other with confused looks upon their faces. Cookie did not notice for she swung away from the girls and was nervously wiping clean a pantry shelf, over and over. Her back was turned towards the shocked servants, and her voice high and shrill. Then as quick as a pantry mouse, she turned and faced them. She bent down low to keep her bellowing voice safely tucked in her round cheeks. "Let me share with you my trick." She whispered. "Keep the Master well fed and treat him to a bit of humor when needed. Always do as he commands and…" Cookie's voice shot out from her throat as she straightened her spine. "Never, ever anger a man of the gold or a man of the cloth! You can't trust em and yee sure can't trust em angry."

Cookie's hands flew in the air, crumbs flying. The girls ducked as the dried bits and pieces of cakes, cookies and mouse droppings landed inside the crooks of their hair bonnets, down the ruffles of their corsets and into the pockets of their linen aprons.

Elizabeth stood frozen, hands trembling, as she took in the words *"they were all hung until they were blue"*. A vision of her father in the coach that day, with his ice cold stare, danced inside her head. Her belly felt as if a pile of rocks had found a home. Her body defied her and it was impossible for her to turn away from what she had just heard, until she felt a hand upon her shoulder. She still could not turn to see who had witnessed her spying on this very private horrific conversation. The hand pressed down harder.

"What are you doing here, child?" came the familiar voice of her nanny. She was one of them, the others, yet all her life Elizabeth trusted Matilda. At least to a point she did. Understanding seeped in. Elizabeth was truly alone inside this estate. She did not belong with her servants, Father, Mother or even Matilda. Who was she and where could she be safe? How could she be safe from a world that would murder innocent children and safe from people who could not or would not do anything about it? Elizabeth inhaled deeply and turned to face her nanny. She would carry on, she had to, she still had Henry, and Henry needed her.

"I am going to my bedchambers to finish my studies." She said.

Elizabeth inched passed Matilda and strode quickly down the halls, making a vow as she went. "As long as I shall live and however I might, I will protect the children. I shall find a way."

Chapter Two

Gregory of Cumberland stared out his study window. The view was quite pleasing, especially this time of year for the gardens were coming alive with the first signs of spring; tiny buds formed and a gentle pastel hue blanketed the landscape that sprawled beneath the window's cold glass pane. Crocus emerged and hyacinth unfolded, creating Spring's hushed vibrancy. Gregory took no notice, however, face vacant and mind cast into another time and place.

Each and every morning immediately after arising from another fitful night of slumber, Gregory retreated to his private study, threw open the window covering and stared blankly. The demons of the past called to him loudly as of late, and try as he might to get a moment's respite viewing the early spring scenery, the regrets pounced. There was only one way to silence the wail and stop the attacks. He must dutifully answer their call.

Silence and solitude were necessary for him to create the ritual that would soothe his tormented soul. Turning away from the window, he checked to be sure the doors into his study were secure from the inside. He guarded these doors with the heated and somewhat crazed passion of a Scottish warrior, for there could be no interruptions, while he took care of the demons. The ritual would commence as soon as he was sure he was completely alone. This solitary existence was not an easy feat, for it meant that he must denying himself the assistance of a Steward. Men of his standing, were never without the bothersome assistance of a man servant. Shifting nervously, he remembered the last of his Stewards, who's dismissal was exceptionally troublesome. Steward Johns had come highly recommended, of course, by way of the Duke of Winslow. The Duke, his father in law. He had to relieve Steward Johns of his duties, for he could not survive another prattling steward. It was hard enough that not t a week went by without a long lasting and just as long winded visit from the meddling Duke. His annoying mentions of finding a suitor for Elizabeth, were most unbearable. Gregory could not stomach the thought of his child being considered for marriage at such a tender age. She was a mere child, barely of courting age and would not be sold to the highest bidder. Gregory knew of no other way to insure the safety of his heirs than to be alone in his sorrows, and repent each day. It was his hope that this ritual of secret slashing, demon releasing, repentance, might restore a bit of his waning life force, and return him to the bold young man he once was.

On this particular morning as he prepared to calm the internal tormentors, his gaze turned toward the library shelves and fell upon the replica of his favorite sailing vessel. The model of the caravel designed and tested by Prince Henry was an exact replica of the one Gregory himself had last commanded. Prince Henry was brilliant and the caravel, a sea worthy masterpiece. Gregory so valued both the craft and craftsman, that he had named his only son after the royal heir. Gregory had hoped that he himself would be noted for his brilliance and success upon the high seas, yet that did not happen, and never would. He did not even hold out hope for his own son following in his footsteps, for there was not much hope alive within him now. Turning sharply, he shook his head to dislodge the gloom, as if his head were a rug on cleaning day and the gloom, tiny critters after a morsel.

Turning back to eye the caravel, Gregory touched the sails carefully, remembering the sway of the vessel, the movement of her body and the gentle rocking motion. In unison, his body followed memory and he too swayed with each side of his body catching the other in the exact moment. His entire being came alive on the sea and he had perfected a way to pay homage to its memory each morning in ritual. Gregory's fingers smoothed over the carving on the base of his wooden caravel. *"Jambe"* He whispered. *"Jambe"* he said aloud. The name his first Captain had given him.

The gentle rocking took him back many years to when he was a mere lad of sixteen. Purchasing his first sailing vessel with his inheritance, he hired the best crew he could scrounge up. This motley crew included the Captain Blaise and five other barely seaworthy men of various ages and rank.

"Tu as jambe! Amariner!" yelled Blaise each time he saw the young ship owner. Soon the name shortened to *Jambe*. Old, toothless, crippled, sun drenched Blaise had taught Gregory how to commandeer a ship and do it well. He could not have served under a more astute and learned seaman. Gregory bowed his head in memory and the depth of his respect for the sea filled his empty soul.

Inhaling deeply, the scent of the salty air mixed with the stench of life upon his sailing vessel filled his lungs. The aroma of filthy dirty men, rotting garbage and human waste drew together to remind him of the strong odor of home. The sea was his home, his paramour, his life. He drank in the memories, pushing them down onto his body in the same way one would take a lover after many months apart. The remembrance was his saving grace as well as his penance.

Continuing his morning ritual demanded that he go farther back in time. Backing away from the caravel and smoothing his trousers, he took a seat in a hard backed chair and held tightly onto the arms. Gregory recalled his father, the Earl of Cumberland. The Earl was a scoundrel and a cheat, squandering his share of the family fortune, taking his own life and leaving his only child Gregory to shoulder the burden and care for his widowed mother. Gregory was a mere lad of twelve, when this occurred, plenty old enough to own the shame of the Earl's legacy and the scorn of the family, and thus he did. Shortly after his father's death, Gregory and his mother were taken in by his father's parents. Gregory flinched slightly in the hard wooden chair remembering the just due. Removing his shoes, he held his hands out so that he could properly remember. Reliving the details of how the thick leather cat'o'ninetails slammed against his hands, forearms, and feet did help release the disgrace. Perhaps one day he would feel fully exonerated, so he remembered. He took himself back to the day the beatings started, he was old enough, his grandfather said, to properly own his share of his father's sins. Each day his grandfather sat him in a tall wooden chair, much like the one he sat in now, made him sit perfectly still and kept the nine tails coming until the blood ran.

"This is so you will never forget the sins of your father." Grandfather's words rang inside of his head bouncing back and forth within his skull, pounding out the rhythm of the life sentence. Each and every day Gregory sat and took in his punishment until the day his Grandfather died from failure of the heart. Gregory was extremely grateful. The day his grandfather died, was the one and only day Gregory believed in a god.

Gregory rose from his chair, rubbed his hands gently and opened the cabinet. Removing the decanter, he poured himself a small bit of spirits. Standing completely still, he took a long languishing sip reveling in the burning sensation. The liquid quenched his soul, if only for a moment. Gregory only ever drank enough for the sedation of the spirits to take him to the edge of where the demons frolicked in his mind, and not one sip farther. Setting the cup down next to his uneaten morning meal, his thoughts turned to his wife. A pleasant memory was next in line. Ordering the lingering pain of his shame to move aside, he went to his desk.

The pleasant memories were turning increasingly cold and damp as of late, as mysterious and fleeting as the last winter owl. What better than this, he thought as he pulled open his desk drawer and placed his hand upon his wife's pearl ring, to spark the scant warmth of my undying love? The talisman of a time long past, fit perfectly in the palm of his hand. Stroking the softness with his fingertips, he remembered. The gem was as big as a grouse egg and as smooth as a babe's cheek. Its suppleness aroused his deadened insides and transported him back in time to the day he met her, the day his fate was sealed and he came to be imprisoned in his drawing chambers instead of free on the open sea.

The Duke of Winslow owned a grand estate and had investments in every lucrative business in England. On the fated day, he had called all the most successful young sea merchants to his home, to discuss procurement for an expedition that was to set sail within the coming month; a quest that was sure to reap great rewards for all involved. Gregory arrived, his gate eager and sure. His exuberance would not be contained. All who were called were young and virile, with enough high sea quests under their belts to deem them worthy of an audience with the most influential Duke. It was a known fact that the Duke was looking to invest in the trading business and it was also well known that whomever he chose to do his bidding would more than likely become the richest and most influential man in Europe, behind the Duke of course. Gregory was the highest ranking of them all. He had been a sea captain for much longer than any of the other young men. Due to his Grandfather's demise, Gregory inherited the family fortune on his sixteenth birthday. He took every bit of the fortune and invested it in the shipping business and commandeered a fleet of trade vessels after apprenticing with a navigator under the watchful eye of Captain Blaise. A keen knack for knowing the business and a deep love for the sea, was indeed his destiny, he remembered with a smile, stroking the pearl.

The smile faded from his face as he carefully placed the ring onto his desk. Staring into its gloss he began speaking to the gem as if it could hear him.

"I saw you call to me from across the room. I saw you first, beautiful pearl. Then I saw her. She wore you well." A deep sigh erupted from his heart.

Picking up the ring, he pushed it onto his finger tip and waited for a response. One never came. He continued his remembrance. He entered into the estate and his gait slowed, not in an of his days had he seen a grand hall so lavish. It was befitting a King. Gaining his composure, he stood erect in his finest dress.

"Gregory Cumberland." His name boomed in the hallowed hall.

Gregory bowed, yet his gaze held steady. There, a few feet behind the Duke, in the far corner of the great hall, sat a young woman, elegantly donning many jewels. The sun shone in through the high windows at just the right angle, casting its glow upon the other fine jewels she wore, yet it was the pearl that caught his eye, the purity of it was spectacular.

"You were the loveliest pearl I had ever seen and the young woman… just as lovely." He continued his memories.

Gregory firmly shook the Duke's hand and tried to take his stare from the woman without avail. Her pull was enchanting and her spirit called to him. She looked both childlike and sensuous as she sat encumbered by mounds of billowy fabric. Strands of jewels adorned her neck and he caught sight of her soft bosom through the openings in the cloth that desperately tried to wrap her loveliness. A ring on every gloved finger sparkled and shone as she carefully whisked away stray strands of hair that had fallen onto her face.

Gregory did not know if he was more taken with the young woman or her jewels, but taken, he was. Transported to another time, he felt himself standing on the deck of his ship with nothing but miles of sea and this lovely woman. He had not known himself to be a romantic, nor a man who was easily taken in by feminine charm, for his lover was the sea, but this woman possessed him immediately. Pulling himself out of the trance he tried to gain his composure. Backing away from the Duke, did not help matters. The Duke pulled him closer, so close Gregory could smell his wine and mutton infused breath as it landed on his face.

"I see you have taken a fancy to my daughter, Gregory." The Duke spat as he talked and the heat of his words burned Gregory's eyes.

"I do not usually allow a gentleman to have the honor of meeting my daughter until I have known him for many a year, yet I can see the look of trust within your eyes and I feel it in your grip. I suppose it will not hurt for you two to have a brief conversation today," said the Duke as he pushed Gregory along towards the lovely maiden sitting with her jewels.

One part of Gregory's body sailed over to the woman and another part was left standing in the entryway of the great hall, his being fractured in two. The Duke motioned to one of his servants to bring a chair for Gregory while he made the formal introductions.

"Gregory of Cumberland, may I present to you, my daughter Charmaine. Charmaine, Gregory Cumberland."

The introduction sent chills up his spine. "It was then, I should have realized, it is then I should have known." Gregory spoke aloud into the shine of the pearl.

Touching Charmaine, drew him into her world. Sinking deeper into his chair, her mesmerizing voice drifted into his study, through his memories and opened the latch of his mind. Her voice was soft and low, whimsical and entertaining. As they spoke of nothing in particular, the sound from her lips danced into him, sending his body into waves of delight. She amused him with her animated ways and melodious tone. Gregory could not seem to get his bearings within her presence. He was caught in a place of senseless bliss as she captured his soul.

Picking up the pearl, he placed it securely in his palm and squeezed tighter and tighter, until the metal prongs dug deep into his flesh as he remembered what occurred next.

Gregory left the Winslow estate that day with a siren song alive in his heart. His mates had procured funding and he had fallen in love. He courted Charmaine for a mere three weeks before he approached the Duke for her hand in marriage. Time was of the essence, for even without the Duke's funding Gregory was scheduled to sail on the voyage that would have him absent from his love for almost one year's time. He needed to be assured that she would be his upon his return. There was something so very appealing about this woman and Gregory found her purity and innocence to be seductive and intriguing. She oftentimes made no sense, her words rambled and her gestures wild, but the oddities he had witnessed in the last three weeks merely lent themselves to the mystery. Gregory wanted more of her loveliness. He wanted to bed her and the only way he would do so, was for them to be properly betrothed. A meeting was set.

"I see Gregory. So you wish to wed my only daughter?" sneered the Duke.

Gregory was very sure of his conviction to wed Charmaine, yet as the Duke stared at him from across the broad dining table, he felt himself go weak. He had not felt the weight of this particular feeling since the days before his Grandfathers death. He straightened himself up, assuring himself that he wanted this woman more than anything and he would do whatever it took to prove himself worthy of her hand. Pushing his body upward, he leaned in closer to the Duke's putrid stare.

The Duke quickly stood up and walked over to Gregory. "I shall agree, on one condition." He whispered.

Gregory sat back in his chair, shocked that the Duke gave up his seat and wondering what was going on. This was not how he imagined this would go. Something was not right.

"Anything, my lord." he whispered back. Gregory lost his balance, even while sitting and found himself once again, fractured and floating, somewhere between the Dukes words and Charmaine's touch.

"You see, Gregory, if I agree, it shall be through a sworn blood oath, an oath that is forever binding. Do you understand?" The Duke did not wait for an answer and instead pulled out a long thin blade, from the inside of his tunic. Grabbing Gregory's left hand he pulled him close. Digging the blades curved edge into the fleshy part of Gregory's palm he drew a line, deep and cutting.

"You will care for my daughter, as she is, in her sickness, as she is. You will never speak of her illness to anyone, do you understand?" And with that, the Duke carefully, methodically drew another line and then another, deep into Gregory's flesh, marking his palm with a bloody letter W.

Gregory sat perfectly still, intent upon taking this pain and punishment, for he knew why he must. He too had a secret. He would be strong for his love and would carry her secret as well as his own. He would not flinch and would not be weak. Besides, Charmaine did not seem to be sick at all, perhaps a bit of the whimsy, but she seemed very healthy to him. He was sure the Duke simply had a flair for the dramatic. Gregory was so very, very pleased that the Duke would accept his request for betrothal.

"In return for my daughter's hand and your secrecy of the matters of her…shall we say…demons of the mind, you will always have all of your needs met. You shall have prestige and riches and will always be protected, but if you falter, just once by going against me, you shall be forever punished. I have my hand in every venture known to man at this time, now and always. I know who you are and where you come from. Do as I say, do as I command, and all will be well, defy me and I will not hesitate to destroy all that you love. Do we have a deal?" asked the Duke.

Gregory answered quickly. "Yes, my lord, we have a deal." That seemed a more than fair deal. He was eager to prove his worth to this man, whatever it took. He was overwhelmed with the opportunity to please his love and her father, for the Duke of Winslow had accepted him as his own flesh and blood. Finally, there was a way to redeem himself and to prove himself worthy and he would be allowed to spend the rest of his life with his beautiful Charmaine. More than a fair deal indeed.

That was then. Now, his heart was scarred and calloused over, just like the W upon his hand. Rubbing the scars on his hand always brought him back from his morning ritual of remembrance. Today, he rubbed the W so hard, that his skin started to burn and bleed. The old scars opened and tiny drops of shame, smeared over the pearl as he caressed it in his palm. The talisman would now remind him not just of the love he had for the woman that was, but how he defied his own destiny, and became a traitor to his spirit. Gregory never sailed again after that day.

The understanding of what had really occurred between he and the Duke was beginning to seep out of his bones and creep into his mind. A soft gentle knocking on his study door brought him fully present with the knowing and the deep, deep pain of the unspeakable betrayal.

"Father, I have brought your midday meal. May I come in?" asked Elizabeth.

Gregory threw the pearl ring back into the drawer and wrapped his raw hand in his kerchief. "Yes, my child, you may enter."

"Father, I have brought you your meal". His daughter slowly entered and set the tray down with a look of disapproval.

He knew why she looked at him so. He had not touched his morning meal, nor would he partake in this meal either. He had no appetite as of late, except for the brandy.

"May I sit with you for a moment today Father?" asked Elizabeth as she placed his meal upon his desk. I see that you did not touch your morning meal, and you are looking a bit thin and pale. Please partake in the meat pie that Cookie made for you, please!" begged Elizabeth as she approached her Father.

Gregory opened his arms and the handkerchief fell to the ground. He pulled his daughter in tight and hugged her with all his might. He needed to feel his child's aliveness. It fell upon him in all its innocent joy. As he hugged his dear Elizabeth, a tear fell from his face and melted into her golden hair. He watched it as it seeped into the tiny strands and silently disappeared pulling at his heart strings as it went. Gregory abruptly pulled back and straightened himself, trying to retain his cool demeanor. "It is time for you to leave me be." he uttered.

Elizabeth was staring in stunned silence. Gregory did not reach out to his child, for to do so, would surely pull her into his web of pain. He wanted to spare her the family curse. If he could. Elizabeth noticed the bloody rag on the floor. Gregory turned his back to his daughter and in a flash, said. "That is all Elizabeth. That is all for today."

Elizabeth did not argue with him, on this day as she usually did, yet still he waited with back turned until he knew she was gone. Striding to the window Gregory glared at the covering that blocked all manner of springtime renewal. "I shall not pass on my sins to my children. I shall not do to them what was done to me.

This declaration awoke the ghosts that lived within his heart, this room and his estate, thus changing the course of their lives forevermore.

Chapter Three

Elizabeth peered into the mirror on her dressing table, struggling over the last bit of French study before morning lessons. Her face contorted as she pronounced each syllable and still she was having trouble finding the proper way to move her tongue. So engrossed was she that she hadn't noticed Henry entering her bedchambers until he was upon her. She shooed him away in the direction of a pile of his toys strewn in the corner of her room, very close to the fire. He grabbed her leftover breakfast biscuits and began tinkering with the chess pieces, urging her to hurry and finish so he could beat her at a game. Elizabeth nodded her head and continued twisting cheeks and tongue, hoping to feel the vibration as her teachers had previously shown her.

"Merci, merrrrrr ci." The sound tickled her face and brought on a sudden sneeze. She reached out to grab a handkerchief to catch the sneeze when a piercing pain caught her on the back of her leg. Reeling from the pain of what felt like a hundred bee stings, she grabbed her skirts, turned and came face to face with Mother. A long thick bladed knife was clenched neatly in Mother's slender fingers. Fear gripped Elizabeth's mind. Something warm and moist bit the back of her leg. Reaching under her skirts, she felt the open wound oozing with her own blood. The room started to glare a fierce white and her head spun. Instinctively she drew in a deep breath. Somewhere nearby she could hear Henry crying.

"Henry!" She called out, yet her voice was but a whisper. She had to help him, get to him, somehow. His sobbing became louder.

"Henry", Elizabeth whispered again, forcing her voice out as best she could.

The vibration of her throat gave her strength and she shook herself free of the fear and fog. The outline of Henry's body appeared out of the right corner of her eye. Mother stood still, directly in front of her staring a cold, deadly, intent stare the knife tightly clasped in her hand. Elizabeth dare not look at Mother, for to do so would catch her in the spell of terror, but she could not help herself. Her head turned slightly and she looked.

"Give me the child Elizabeth." Mother's eyes were blood red, dripping fury. Elizabeth lowered her gaze, trying to remain calm as she spoke.

"What are you talking about Mother?' Elizabeth quietly asked, trying to control the shaking that altered each word. "I have no child here."

"Liar!" screamed Mother. "Give him to me! He is mine and I want him. He's been crying for me all night long and no one will help me… not even my own daughter! You can't have him Elizabeth, everyone wants my baby and you may not have him."

Hearing the senseless words pour from her mother brought back a memory. She remembered a time before this when Mother acted as if the devil were alive within her. The details were not in focus, yet she remembered the same words echoing through the halls of the estate.

"Mother, I will give you your baby. No one wants to take him from you!" Elizabeth looked directly into mother's reddened, crusted eyes.

"Yes they do, they all do!" Mother screamed and lurched toward Elizabeth. "They all want to take my baby from me. My baby needs me!"

With that Mother darted past Elizabeth and over to a hysterical Henry. She knelt beside him and picked him up in her arms never letting go of the knife.

"My baby, my baby" she cooed, trying to rock Henry back and forth in a suffocating embrace. "You are so hungry, little one, I shall feed you and you shall be safe."

Henry curled himself up tighter, trembling in fear. Mother clenched the knife, ever so close to Henry's throat, her knuckles turning a ghostly white. Elizabeth stared at them as questions flew in her mind. Where was Father? He had to be around somewhere, she thought. He never let Mother out of her room. She then remembered that he had gone to the city today. How had mother escaped her room and her nurse? Elizabeth was very alone in this situation and try as she might to make sense of what was happening, the only thing that rang true in her mind was that Mother would kill them both. The room started to swirl around her and her breath felt weak. Blood was soaking her undergarments. She had to save Henry. It was solely up to her.

"Mother may I hold the baby?" she asked softly.

"No, Elizabeth, he is too small for you to hold. I must feed him now. He is hungry. I have waited so long to feed him. He has been crying for me for hours…crying. Didn't you hear him? Why didn't you wake me? He is always crying for me and no one wakes me." Mother started moving more forcefully with each rock to and fro.

"You are an awful girl, Elizabeth. You are jealous of your baby brother. You should be ashamed. I must send you to that convent. Far, far, away! That is where you belong, far away. I will speak to your father about that first thing."

Elizabeth cringed at the thought of her mother wanting her gone. A familiar sadness welled up from deep within her being, along with a great burst of nausea. She had to be strong now and she swallowed hard. Noticing that Mother moved the knife away from Henry's throat to unbutton her blouse, Elizabeth saw her chance. Running toward her mother, she focused her entire being on that silver handle. She was just about to grab it, when Mother pulled it away.

"Stop!" she said. You may not take him. If I can't keep him no one will! You will not put me to sleep again before he is fed. Do you hear me?" And with those words mother readied to stab Henry. She held the knife over him as if she was Abraham killing his own son for God.

"Henry, stop her, stop her!" Elizabeth screamed. Henry awakened from his stupor and swung his arm out from under his chest. His hand met with the knife and blood seeped from the wound. Mother moved back just enough to enable Elizabeth to grab both of her arms from behind and wrench her away from Henry.

"Run Henry, run!" she yelled.

Henry rolled himself into a little ball, right out from under both Elizabeth and Mother and didn't stop rolling till he was nearly to the doorway, leaving a trail of his blood upon the fine Turkish rug. He jumped up, ran out the door and out of sight.

"Run Henry, run fast! Find Nurse Beatrice and tell her to come quick." Elizabeth pushed herself atop Mother, holding down both of her arms. Despite the pain radiating from her leg Elizabeth kept her focus on that knife. Mother refused to release the weapon and they were locked in a deadly standoff.

"You will regret this, you evil child. You have taken my baby away from me again. I will never forget this. You will die for it."

Elizabeth held on with all her might. Something came alive deep inside and she felt as if she had the strength of five robust horsemen. *Great Mother help me!* Elizabeth said it again and again in the silence of her mind. As suddenly as she attacked, Charmaine simply stopped fighting. Her arm went limp and the knife fell to the floor, her entire being lifeless. Scrambling, Elizabeth shot up, grabbed the knife and stood over her weakened Mother, wanting to slash at her body and tear into her flesh for causing such unbearable fear to her and her dear brother. Thoughts hurtled through her mind. How dare she hurt us, how dare she lay lifeless as if nothing had happened, how dare she cast blame upon me, how dare she! Raising up the knife she heard an unfamiliar voice come alive within her mind. She was not to allow the evil that destroyed her mother to destroy her too.

Elizabeth ran from the room, latching the door behind her. She must find Finding Henry and off she went, into the hallowed, dark and lonely halls to find her wounded brother. She must keep quiet as not to alarm the servants. She needed help, but Father had made it very clear that Mother's condition was not to be spoken of, ever. She would not break the silence, for the evil must be kept contained. Alone in her panic, she let its intensity fuel her as she padded down the long corridors. She entered into his bedchambers first. No one was about. She continued combing the halls. They were eerily quiet for the middle of the day. The sound of her naked feet echoed within the walls of her prison. Like the beating of a drum, her footsteps told of a terror that was both ancient and momentary.

Henry was nowhere to be found inside the walls of the estate. She ventured outside and took a deep sigh, breathing in the lighter air. She headed to the garden maze on the estate's easterly side. It was here that she found him, lying face down still rolled up in a ball like a newborn babe. His body gently moved and she recognized the signs of breath. Elizabeth should have known he would be here, for many a time they played in this safe and cozy hiding place. Carefully hiding the knife under a bush, so as never to be found, she could now tend to her brother. She held him for a few moments, yet he did not respond. His body moved rapidly now, trying to catch the air. Elizabeth knew he needed to rest so she patted his back and prayed, sending the prayers into his fragile body. As his breath calmed, she was able to assess his wound. His hand and wrist were cut, but the wound was more wide than deep and the bleeding was slow. Untying her sash, she bandaged the wound.

Elizabeth sighed. What to do next? It was then she remembered she too had been cut. Wrapping her arm around her long limbs, she felt the gash in her flesh. It stretched the width of the back of her leg, yet it too, was not deep. She took off her petticoat and carefully made a bandage and wrapped it gently about the cut. She was numb to any pain and decided she must find help.

"I shall go fetch Father and Dr. Fleish, Henry. I shall return as soon as I can." Henry did not respond so she kissed his head with a prayer and left.

Entering back into the estate through the stables, Elizabeth saw that Father's carriage had not yet returned. She would have to find someone to help with Henry's wound besides Dr. Fleish, so off to the Spicer's cove she went in search of Madeline. She would help, for she was the one who made the elixir for Henry to help soothe his lungs and calm his spells. Madeline knew everything there was to know about herbs and spices for confections as well as healing cuts, burns, scrapes and every malady one could think of. Madeline's demeanor always put Elizabeth immediately at ease. Quickening her pace she now knew that she not only needed Madeline's comforting presence, she too needed medicine. She was feeling incredibly weakened and light headed and knew a tonic would help her greatly. In order to get to Madeline, she had to pass her mother's chambers. Taking deep breaths, she started running ever so quietly. Nothing could have prepared her for what she saw as she entered the hall that took her past Mother's chambers. Nurse Beatrice lay slumped and lifeless, so close to Elizabeth that she could smell the odors of flesh and bone and blood as it penetrated the floorboards and the walls and forced its way into her nostrils. The smell of butchered animals lingered where it aught not be. Elizabeth vomited. Gathering every bit of energy she could, she ran back to Henry as fast as her weakened legs could take her. Mother's tiresome rage was taken out on Nurse Beatrice. For this Elizabeth was so very grateful and so utterly terrified.

Returning to the maze she found Henry as she had left him. For the rest of the afternoon, Elizabeth held him, soothing and comforting them both. They were safe, for now. They had to be. Sheer will and the fleeting knowing of some otherworldly power was all she had to ensure it was so. Henry slept peacefully in her arms yet she would find no peace in that beautiful maze that afternoon, for all the fear and confusion crept into her head and would not let her rest. She thought her mother to be so beautiful, so mysterious, despite her demons. What she saw in the blood of her mother's eyes and the slaughtered casualty of her tormented mind had changed everything.

Elizabeth made another vow that afternoon as she huddled with her brother. I must be strong and courageous for Henry and for Father, despite how much mother hates me. I will not think of this day again and maybe that will make it not so. If only those hurtful words her mother had spoken to her would stop ringing in her head. "You will die for this; you will die…"

***

As the sun was beginning to set and the cool dampness came to rest, Elizabeth heard the sounds of the carriage returning from the city. In a few moments time she heard her father approach.

"Come my children, come with me." He said as he bent to scoop up Henry.

Elizabeth started explaining what had happened, her vow to not think of it vanishing into a deep desire for Father's care and concern.

Father rose his hand up and said, "Shush". Holding Henry effortlessly in his strong arms, he motioned to Elizabeth to follow. He led them into his bedchambers and tucked them both into his bed. Father looked down at Elizabeth as she lay frozen in his bed.

"Elizabeth that there will be no talk of what occurred today."

Elizabeth looked up at him wide-eyed and sullenly nodded in agreement as she pulled Henry closer.

Elizabeth was drifting off to sleep still fighting demons that told her she was not safe. The darkness came up from within and engulfed her, no matter how hard she tried to think of good things, she feared she would always have remembrance of that day, for it was etched plainly upon her body. Dr. Fleish arrived and gently, without waking him, bandaged Henry's wound. Elizabeth did not say a word, instead she shut her eyes tight and feigned sleep. She did not want

Dr. Fleish to know of her wound, for she could not bear to have anyone touch her. She would seek Madeline's would help on the morrow.

Elizabeth's vow came to pass, for there was never talk of the incident and no mention of what had happened to Nurse Beatrice, a widow with no heirs. It all seemed so neat and tidy and finished. The cloak of fear wrapped tighter around the entire estate from that day forward, pulling its hood down over any outward glance.

Chapter Four

The years passed much as they had before the incident. Elizabeth spent most of her time caring for Father and Henry, doing her best to protect them all from Mother's evil sickness. Her vow to never mention the day was held true, but the day haunted her just the same. What does not get spoken, will come out somehow, as she was soon to discover.

Staying inside the estate and spending her days in study gave her plenty of distraction. Any thoughts of the freedom and magic that lay outside the walls, were fleeting. The walls were becoming thicker and viscid, much like the web of a giant monster spider. She must keep her distance from them, in order to be safe.

Except for the occasional Sunday visit to the cathedral, albeit far and few between after the incident, Elizabeth found her days stretched on, one after another in the same monotonously dreary way, until one day that too all changed. Time and age had a way of opening up the future, releasing the unspoken and bringing forth relief. Elizabeth was now of that age.

Towards the end of her sixteenth year, an unfamiliar and uncomfortable twinge grew deep within her belly. The curious feeling first occurred when she had occasion to enter into the city, and once inside the walls of her estate, it ceased. Within a mere week's time, as her seventeenth birthday approached, the twinge turned into a knot that tightened with discontent and was forever persistent. The clutching and binding began to overtake her whole being. Just when she could take no more, she thought to seek treatment for her ailment. Elizabeth had heard a few of the stable lads speak of the magic of Cook's concoctions after they had ingested a bit too much merriment. She doubted her troubles were from indulging in merriment but she surely did not trust Dr. Fleish to treat her for whatsoever it was that was wreaking painful havoc with her innards. She did not trust him, so Cookie it was!

"Cook?" asked Elizabeth hesitantly. "I have this terrible pain in my stomach that will not go away. Do you know a remedy?" she questioned.

Cook threw up her hands in mock dismay. "Why is it that you come to me, lassie? Are ya tryin to tell me that it's me cookin' that is doing the evil deed?" Cookie burst into gales of laughter.

Elizabeth looked about. The kitchen help kept to their work and no one seemed to turn a stare in their direction, nevertheless she lowered her voice to a barely audible hush. "No, not at all Cook, for I enjoy every morsel of the delicacies you prepare, it is just that I have such a pain and I heard…"

"Now, now, "Cook interrupt, bending her head until she touched Elizabeth with her moist brow. "I have something that will help just about anything. Is it your time to bleed? Is that the trouble?" Cook went to the pantry and took out some bottles.

"No, Cookie, it is not that. It is different. Here..." Elizabeth pointed to her upper torso, just below her bosom and stared at Cookie with wide eyes.

"Hmm…" muttered Cookie. She took out more bottles and mixed a bit of this and a bit of that into a mug. Adding a bit of brew, she winked at Elizabeth and motioned to her to drink it down quickly. Elizabeth did so readily and did not stop until the last drop was gone. It tasted a bit like honey and Elizabeth was fond of sweets. As quick as she drained the cup, the knot in her stomach grew stronger. The pain forced a contorted grimace upon her face and it felt as if her belly was bursting up into her throat. Shock and surprise exploded from her gut along with the loudest, longest belch she ever did hear. Elizabeth stood, eyes widened with bit of shame from the commotion that had blasted forth from her body, but she surely felt much better.

"Works every time", said Cookie, turning back to finish basting the meat on the fire.

"If that pain should happen to return, you know where to find me."

Elizabeth returned to Cookie several times over the next few weeks. Each time she belched louder than the last and the pain would go away for a bit, but after a while it seemed that even this never fail remedy was not working. One evening as she lay in her bed fitfully trying to sleep and pondering what to do about the upset within, she drifted off into a most lovely dream. She was inside the forest, completely and utterly alone, yet it was as if she was both watching herself from the outside and peering out from within. Her hair was long and flowing, not tied up in braids and her dress was light and simple, no fancy ties, buttons, chords or gems adorning the fabric. Looking down at her feet she could see she was wearing the most glorious satin slippers. She danced about the forest floor feeling the warm wind grace her gown as she went. This dream was so real and so comforting she did not want to awaken.

"I must go into the forest." The words flew from her belly and woke her from her slumber and she noticed the room was bright with the rising sun. "And, if I do not I will surely die of stomach poisoning or worse, I will blow up from belching."

"The forest?" Henry popped his head out from behind her dressing mirror.

"Henry, what are you doing in here? How dare you come and interrupt me while I sleep!" Yelling, she forcefully threw her night bonnet at him in hopes he would run out and leave her be.

Henry quickly dodged the headpiece, laughed and pointed his finger. "It's time for you to awaken, you lazy girl!" He teased. "It is almost midmorning!"

Elizabeth jumped out of her bed, ran over to her brother and pushed him out the door.

"Get out and stay out!" she yelled. Laughing she shut the door with a loud thud. Henry may be taller and heftier than me, but I am still his older sister, she thought.

"You may be my older sister…." He yelled as if hearing her silent words. "But I am smarter!". Henry laughed from the other side of the door, all the while pounding it in his joking manner.

Elizabeth smiled as she went to dress for the day. Today was a beautiful day. Her brother was well, his humor in full force and by the looks and sounds of him, his lungs were clear. She had dreamt of the cure for the incessant knotted rope that lived in her belly and she was ready to enact a plan.

All day long the soft seduction of the images in her dream pulled at her and when night approached she was ready to find out what was calling to her from the forest. It was a perfect eve, just days before her seventeenth birthday. A hush of excitement filled the air and the thrill of adventure enlivened her heart. Waiting until the light of the full moon was almost directly overhead helped ensure safe and secluded travels. She would not need a lantern when the moon was so full and bright. Finding her way without the use of a lantern would be best, but she would take one, just in case. This indeed was the perfect night for adventure. She quietly left her bedchambers, pattered down the halls, making a quiet joyful noise with each rhythmic step. One of the secret tunnel exits would give her journey the privacy she needed. She followed the passage out into the shadowy dark night.

The air was still and fresh and the rush of excitement chilled her body. The first step of the plan was to walk ahead on the slightly worn path and see where it might lead. She had seen the path many a time during the family outings into the city, yet never, ever had she stepped foot onto its mystery and wonder, until tonight. Pulling her cloak in a bit tighter around her body a flash of fear entered her mind. She noticed her arms were shaking, just a bit.

"Perhaps I should turn back before it's too late" she said aloud.

"Too late for what?"

The question came from somewhere between her mind and the forest wall. Elizabeth shook her head and threw back her cloak so that it hung precariously off her shoulders. The slightly worn path transformed before her eyes. It looked to her as if someone had put row upon row of luminaries along the edge of the path. She blinked a few times to be sure she saw correctly. Perhaps this is the answer for fear, she thought. I must follow this path and see what lay beyond. If I do not, then it truly shall be too late. She hurried her step as if she now knew exactly where she was going. Determination kept her gate sure and she trotted onward propelled by the force of the light that had awakened in her and on this path.

She kept on for what seemed no time at all. So intent was she that she did not realize that the path had ended. She came to her senses when before her stood a large boulder, its shiny smooth surface glowing in the moonlight. Elizabeth pressed herself up against its cool surface, taking in its boldness and welcome. Well, this was as good a place as any to rest… and perhaps throw off my cloak and dance she thought, haughtily. As her mind quieted, she heard a most beautiful melody. I must be hearing the music of angels, she thought. I cannot understand how I have not come into the forest before now, for it is so inviting, so captivating. Pushing herself away from the boulder she took an imaginary hand and began to dance. Twirling and dipping she danced to the other side of the boulder. What lay beyond the forest wall on the other side of the giant stone was more than she could ever have imagined. Elizabeth stood perfectly still, mouth agape staring at the most beautiful sight she had ever witnessed. Truly this must be a dream.

Immediately her stomach tightened and the dreaded knot made it perfectly clear to her that this was not a dream. She was very much alive and awake. Crouching down behind a fine row of saplings, gave her a much better vantage point to witness the incredible sight she happened upon. Stomach relaxing, she was now able to take in the scene. A small group of the most exquisite women, standing in a circle, dressed in robes of glistening blue fabric. The fabric seemed to be a part of their skin, or perhaps it was indeed their skin. And perhaps these were not women, but forest faeries, or angels! She could not look away and did not care to either. Inside the circle candles flickered in the still night air. Fifteen women, she counted quickly. One particular woman, garbed in white sat directly under the rays of the glorious full moon; her robe sparkled like snow upon the dell on a sunny afternoon. Careful to be ever so quiet, Elizabeth crept in past the row of young trees and knelt behind another boulder that was just high enough to keep her presence unseen. The woman in white sat with closed eyes, issuing a prayer, of the likes Elizabeth had never heard. All the same they drew her in, just as the path into the forest had called to her earlier that eve.

"...And the Goddess shall reign in Her beauty as we gather in Her gifts. This season is a time of quiet gestation, a time of joyful waiting. We thank you Goddess for the earth, the moon and the sun. We thank you for the time of winter slumber and the darkness that aids us in preparing our souls for peace and light to come."

Elizabeth didn't know quite what she was talking about, but the woman's words captivated her entire body. A comfort of deep warmth and belonging engulfed her being as she lay against the cool rock and watched the women's sacred ritual. This was the similar feeling she had experienced in her dream. She was watching herself and them from outside herself, yet somehow felt loved and warm and more safely at peace than ever. Were these women real? She wondered. Perhaps they are real forest faeries, or angels from heaven sent to dance on this lovely full moon eve. She could not tell, but from her hiding place, they seemed as real as she. She pinched herself continuously just to be sure. The pinching didn't change a thing. She still felt safe and warm and loved and strangely interwoven with these women.

Continuing her spying, she took in each and every moment. The presence of these creatures held her attention aloft. After the prayers, the women sat in silence, faces upturned they held hands and the light of the moon shone upon them. After what seemed like a very long time, they released their sacred hold on each other and started to rise. From behind them came little girls, dressed in brightly colored robes. The youths carried baskets of fruit and breads. They took the women in their midst and led them away into the depths of the forest. Elizabeth was mesmerized, still in her cocoon of love, taking in the magic and peace of what she had just witnessed. A dangerous sound quickly brought back to her surroundings. Something ominous was approaching.

Elizabeth stood upright in a start. The loud intrusive sound was coming from the path. The women made her feel safe and this sound gaining upon her was altogether different, for it blared of a threatening force. Quickly she crouched behind the boulder, but she feared it too late. She looked up and stared into the belly of a horse, dark and round. Throwing her head in her bosom, she hoped this monster would retreat.

"What are you doing out here maiden? Why are you crouched behind this rock like a scared animal?" An obtrusive, yet familiar voice demanded answers.

She knew that voice; it was the voice of James, The Earl of Hartford, who lived in the estate adjacent to her own. James was a robust and malevolently forceful man with wild black hair and shiny golden black eyes. His young wife had died in childbirth about one year ago leaving him childless and alone and unfortunately he made his unwelcome presence available to the family Cumberland quite often as of late. The Earl was a business associate of Grandfathers and she had known him since she was a mere lass, nevertheless Elizabeth did not like him at all. She was not one to view people as evil, but James of Hartford had just about earned the right to the title. There were rumors among the staff that he bedded another woman the day after his wife and child perished, and rumors aside, his crude manners and licentious glances always made her cower in shame. His mere presence sent a chill of foreboding misery down her spine.

"I was out for a stroll" Her head was still down as she muttered her answer.

"I don't believe you, my beautiful maiden. Did you see them? Were you with them?" he asked.

Elizabeth rose up in her full height suddenly angry with this untimely intrusion and insulted with his tone. How dare he call me his beautiful maiden, and how dare he interrupt my adventure. "You may address me as Lady, Sir."

She slowly looked up at the ostentatious offender and his brazen horse. The silvery light cast a shadow across his face, yet her gaze landed directly into his eyes. It was then she felt the hard slap of his demeanor land upon her heart and radiate down to her belly. Defiance rose up again and she pushed down all fear. At that very moment she knew why she was called here at this time and on this night. A cloak of protection arose from within her and reached out to embrace the lovely women of the forest. As she reached out in promise of protection to the strange women, she felt their love and protection hold her too. She drew her own cloak tightly around her body, closing off any access to her tender and radiant heart and stepped in closer to the horse and his rider. If wickedness had a smell, these two creatures carried it.

"Did you see them? Those devil worshippers, those witches!" James yelled, impatience arising in his voice. "I know they come out here to that spot right over there." he pointed to the clearing where the beautiful women had been standing just moments earlier.

"I have been trying to have them arrested for months. I just can't ever seem to get to them. They vanish every time. Devil's work is what they do and I will see to it that they are stopped and put to death, every last one of them!"

James then jumped down off his horse and stood very close to Elizabeth. She would not melt with shame this time, for there seemed a newborn courage within her that forced her to stand even taller. He was a tall man, yet at her full height she could almost see directly into his revolting face. It was then that she noticed he had his bow and arrow drawn. She lunged forward to throw him off balance. The sound of approaching horses startled them both and she tumbled into James' chest. The shire reeve and his men stopped their horses and Elizabeth righted herself. She could not bare the stench of him.

"Where are they sir? Asked the shire reeve looking around in wonder.

"They are gone." spat the Earl. He turned from Elizabeth, cursing under his breath and jumped back onto his horse, hitting her ever so slightly with his heavy woolen cloak. "She probably warned them off. For all I know this young one is their lookout." James sneered, looking down at Elizabeth.

"I don't know what you are talking about Sir James. I merely came out for a stroll on this fine evening. I have seen nothing out of the ordinary here, except you coming up behind me and frightening me so!"

James was about to respond when the shire broke in. "Lady Elizabeth, may I return you home this evening?" he asked. "I am sure your father would be fit, if he knew you, his beautiful young maiden, were out alone on this dark night. Coming out here on foot at this hour is unwise. You know we have been hearing rumors of witching activities in this area, or so says Sir James."

The shire gave an impatient look to James as he offered his hand to Elizabeth.

Elizabeth took his hand and pulled herself up onto his horse. She would allow him to escort her back to the estate. She trusted this shire reeve. He was not the same one who had arrested those innocent little children years before. He was the protector of this land, the upholder of the law, and he had always been kind to her and her family, besides she didn't want to be anywhere near Sir James any longer. She knew full well that it was he that was the only danger in this forest. Not even the wild dogs were more dangerous than this vile man.

"May I remind you who pays your salary?" grumbled James grabbing the shire's sleeve. "Those heretics are out there and we will find them. I will rejoice at their hanging when the time comes."

"Fine." answered the shire pulling away from James.

Elizabeth could feel his annoyance as well as a bit of fright she assumed, for James of Hartford called out fright in everyone. She held onto the shires back and readied to ride away from the wicked man.

"But, now it is time to return Lady Elizabeth home and I do believe I have a fine meal awaiting me at Brooker's Pub."

The shire slowly turned and put his steed into a gentle cadence, ensuring Elizabeth's comfort. James did not approach them, nor argue. Elizabeth said a silent prayer for the forest women, for their safety, just in case James had taken it upon himself to continue his search. She did not think they needed her prayers, but she uttered them nonetheless, for she again felt their well wishes coming directly to her. It comforted her greatly. They arrived back at the estate in no time, although they did not take the same path out that she had taken in. She saw no lighted lanterns along the way.

"I do not want to find you in the forest again, Lady Elizabeth. I will not mutter a word to your father if you promise me that you will not step outside these walls again. I would not want you getting caught in any hunter's snare." The Shire tipped his head and bid her goodnight.

"Yes Sir. Thank you for your kindness." smiled Elizabeth. Good thing the shire likes to relax at Brooker's Pub more than anything else, she thought, otherwise he would surely question her further.

Tomorrow eve and she would just have to be more careful than ever. The Earl of Hartford will not stand in her way and he will never, ever harm the women of the forest, she promised to protect them with all her will.

Elizabeth pretended to go into the gates, and waited for the shire to leave. When she was sure he was gone, she walked swiftly in a northerly direction. Long ago when Elizabeth's ancestors had first built the estate they had secret passages carved out of the earth in and around the living quarters. Elizabeth and Henry had discovered several of these passages when they were young children, and this allowed them to come and go as they pleased from one part of the estate to another, even within a home full of servants. It was best she exit and enter the estate through such clandestine means. These secret tunnels and entrances served as her only hoped for privacy and escape, until tonight. Tonight she had truly escaped, beyond the walls of the estate and into the forest.

Elizabeth slipped into the hidden entrance and lit the passageway lantern. I am free, she thought, I am free! Elizabeth skipped through the dark passageway, the shadows from the candlelight dancing merrily on the wall. The sounds of rats scurrying and the drapes of cobwebs bothered her not. If only for a few hours, she had partaken in something that demanded her heart soar. Her belly fluttered and felt incredibly light. She wound her way through the tunnel and into the kitchen. It was quiet and she hurried through, not stopping for a snack. She wanted nothing more than to crawl into bed and remember the night in every detail. Every detail except for the part with Sir James. Making her way to the bedchambers, she found Henry sitting outside the door

"What happened, Elizabeth? Why did you go without me? I thought I heard horses outside the gate. Why do you always have fun without me?" He asked jumping up and grabbing her shoulders.

"Henry! Shush! If you wake up the servants, we shall never get to go out.

"Nothing happened", she whispered, calming him down. "I simply was out walking on this beautiful night. A maiden needs time away from her annoying little brother sometimes. Now go and get some rest for if you do, I shall take you exploring tomorrow."

"Promise?" He asked. "Let's dress warmly and go to the creek to fish", he continued.

"Fine, said Elizabeth, "Now go to bed, Henry!" Her answer was laden with a faraway look.

"You promise we will go out tomorrow?" he demanded.

"Henry, I am very tired, please leave me be." She commanded.

Henry left stomping down the hall. She knew he was upset with her, but she did not care. He would have to be growing up now, she thought. He will not have me as his keeper all of his life. She entered her bed chamber and leaned against the heavy door. She never had a thought like that before. Henry needed her, forever. She had made a vow to always take care of him, but now something had changed. Something from deep within her was awakened and for the first time in her life she felt her destiny was not within the estate walls, nor did it include Father or even Henry. There was something else that called to her from the depths of her belly. What this something else was, she did not know, but it was out there, not here. Of this she was sure, as sure as she saw the ladies dancing in the forest this eve. Elizabeth slipped into bed and dreamt of the Ladies. They surrounded her, sang to her and offered her the baskets of fruit and flowers. She danced with them and laughed and laughed. Elizabeth had never felt so loved and protected and cared for as she did in the presence of the women, in the forest and here in her bedchambers. A great loyalty to these beautiful beings swelled within. They were to be a part of her destiny, this she was sure of.

As the nighttime dream continued, she found herself sitting with the one woman in white. This glorious Lady was sharing great stories of life and love, the words dancing from her mouth and landing in Elizabeth's heart. This was no ordinary Lady, there was something quite otherworldly about the way her presence came to life within this dream. Elizabeth knew she was dreaming, yet the woman's sweet fragrance danced along with her words. Lilacs and roses. Elizabeth was drawn into the magic. But then the mood changed. The woman's eyes of brown started sparkling with an ominous golden hue.

"Do not come to us until the next full moon. We are only safe at the full moon."

The woman insisted that Elizabeth agree. She sought to argue, even in her dream, for she did not know how she could stay away, but the woman was adamant. She held her hand up to Elizabeth's heart and showed her without words, what would happen if the women were found by James. The great boulder was sitting upon her heart and she could not breathe. The woman's eyes grew darker. Hanging, death, the gallows. She knew then that if these women were found, it would mean death for all of them, including her.

"Yes, my Lady." she solemnly answered." I shall do as you say."

Chapter Five

The Christmas season was once again upon the Cumberland estate. Gregory withdrew into his study as usual, hoping to find respite away from the merry comings and goings of the staff, as well as his children. The season was always one of celebratory fare, and Gregory, although not one to celebrate, saw to it to seize the opportunity to hold his yearly gala. He found it much easier to tolerate others at this time of year. The buzzing and humming of joyful activity could not help but enter into his being, if even for a few transient moments at a time.

Gregory stood alone in his study and smiled gently to himself remembering a scene he had stumbled upon this very morn. As he walked briskly to his study he happened upon Elizabeth. She was in the great hall, taking each and every candlestick and vase out of the credenza to help the young servant girl polish them up. He wanted to scold her at first, for that was not her duty, but he did not. He just watched her in action, as a deep pride welled up within. Elizabeth had become a beautiful young maiden. Some day, far in the future she would be running an estate of her own. Perhaps her future husband would come here and live, a kind and noble man would surely be the right fit for his Elizabeth. That particular thought brought stinging tears to his eyes as he walked over to his study window and pushed back the panels. He hoped a marriage was very far in the future. He needed more time to be around his children, for they were the only joy in his miserable life.

The view from this window was open and expansive and he gave thanks for the cold wind that whistled its way in through the cracks, its blast tempering the stifling, stinging air. He looked beyond the frost covered fields and past the tips of the forest trees. Perhaps Elizabeth would never marry and never go beyond these walls. As he gazed upon the vast expanse, a tear burned his eye. Nothing could stop his daughter from leaving him some day, for she had his blood running through her veins. She was much more like him than her mother, thank God. He sighed and closed his eyes. Yes, she had the adventurous, fearless spirit in her. As much as he would like to not believe that, he knew it to be true.

As Gregory thought of Elizabeth's adventurous spirit, memories of his days at sea inundated his mind. So much had happened upon God's waterways since he had last sailed. His Queen now owned the waterways. He held a certain gladness for his country's success at having secured the riches of the world, and even more so that it was against the cunning Spanish. He was never one to compete for world power, for his life blood ran quick only for the sea and to spend many a day within the bowels of one of her Majesty's ships gently rocking to sleep or viciously fighting for the life of his crew. He needed to be hiding among the grey mountains of water, lying in wait to pounce upon any enemy who dare try to take what they were both after. He needed to feel the bite of the harsh wind against his face and feel the sting and taste the blood upon his lips. Gregory looked down at his hands and saw the truth. He touched his lips and felt their smooth healthy surface. He was not a sailor any longer. He drew the window shut with a clash.

"Father?" The quiet knock upon the door startled him.

Gregory straightened his jacket and gathered himself together. He slammed the panel over the window and opened the door for his daughter to enter.

Elizabeth rushed in and set the food upon the serving table. She surveyed the study, most surely wanting to know where the loud noise came from. Gregory glanced towards her, commanding the familiar-do not dare ask- look, hardened and glaring. Elizabeth stared back. Her brows upraised, in her familiar curious stare.

"Father, you must eat quickly this fine meal, for Grandfather is here to speak to you." Elizabeth made herself busy setting his dining space.

"Now father, I told Grandfather to come and join you, but he said he preferred to spend this time visiting with Mother, so eat heartily and when you are finished, I shall fetch him for you." She said heading over to the window.

"Father why is the window closed on such a day? Snow is falling. All is fresh and new." Elizabeth struggled to unlock one of the latches that kept the panel firmly in place over the window.

"Leave it be, Elizabeth. Keep the window covered." Gregory said in an unusually gruff tone.

Elizabeth stopped fumbling with the latch and turned to face him. "I shall leave you alone today Father so you may finish quickly." Gregory could see the tears welling up in her eyes. If I offended her, then so be it, her adventurous spirit is not going to take her from me, he thought. Just as the thought passed his tired mind, he immediately regretted it.

"Elizabeth…it is just that…the wind is very strong this morn and the draft from the window, well it was causing the fire here to diminish." Gregory pointed to the hearth and the roaring fire.

"But I thought you liked the fresh air, Father." Elizabeth quietly left the room, her head down.

Gregory watched her go. He sat at his place and stared at the food. The smell of the roast sausage and hot apples spiced with cinnamon made him ill. This was not the smell he craved. Fresh sea air is what he needed. His body surged with rage. The devil of the open sea was taunting him and anger filled his being. He swiped his arm across the finely set table and sent the food flying. The devil was not the sea. The evil binding him and cutting him off from his own life force was his own doing. Standing up, he went to the cabinet where the crystal decanters glistened with the calming liquid. The carved wooden caravel caught his eye. He grabbed it and threw it into the fire. Pouring himself a hefty cup of his finest brandy, he watched as the dry wood burst into flames and disappeared into the roaring inferno. He gulped the fiery liquid and left his chamber to find the Duke of Winslow.

Gregory quietly entered his wife's bedchamber and stopped, out of sight, near the doorway. Charmaine was sitting up in a chair, a position that her father had most likely helped her into. The Duke was holding his daughter's hand, loudly speaking words of reassurance. He glanced around the room as he spoke surveying her chambers to be sure all was as he ordered it. Gregory was sure to hear of anything that needed fixing or cleaning. It was always that way. He shook his head and stared at the shell of a woman that was his wife. Charmaine slumped over, her head hung as if by a loose noose. The weight of her upper body closed in on her chest. How could she sustain her breath, in such a position, he wondered. Gregory stopped himself from rushing to help her. Taking a step forward, he remained hidden behind the thick curtain. Her head tossed slowly from side to side as her eyes opened and closed, fighting the slumber that engulfed her being. Gregory felt the burn of the whisky rise up into his throat. His wife looked pathetic and he could not stand to look upon her for one more moment. He turned to leave and that is when The Duke noticed him standing in the shadow.

"Son", he snickered with mock endearment. "Don't you think my lovely daughter is looking better today? You should come closer and give your wife a proper greeting." The Duke held up his daughter's hand, waiting for Gregory to take it.

Gregory's face burned red. He had absolutely no desire to touch his wife, let alone kiss her. The Duke did not waiver as he stared down Gregory, daring him to defy his suggestion. Gregory took Charmaine's hand and brought it up to his lips. It smelled of ointments and death. He brushed his lips across the frail, thin skin and gently held it out to the Duke.

"I have some business to attend to, my dear" cooed the Duke as he rubbed Charmaine's hand against his bearded face. "I will come say goodbye before I leave." Charmaine did not respond.

The Duke walked over to Gregory, put one hand upon his shoulder and the other on his elbow. "Come, Gregory. We have much to talk about and not a lot of time since the Yuletide festivities that you have planned for your household start this evening. It is a pity that I will not be in attendance."

The Duke was holding his arm tight, pushing him down the halls of his own home. Fierce anger welled up , yet he dare not release himself from the Duke's grasp. Not yet. The Duke guided Gregory down one corridor and the next until they were outside of the study. Before they entered the mahogany door, Gregory stopped and shook free from his father-in-law's grasp.

"Sir, allow me." Gregory retrieved his keys from his pocket and unlocked the double doors slowly. Pushing the doors, gaining composure, he motioned to the Duke to enter.

The deep sigh released from his body. The mess left in his fit of rage was nowhere to be seen. Once again all signs of turmoil were swept clean from the Cumberland Estate. When both men were inside Gregory closed the doors tightly. Sauntering to the newly filled crystal decanters and pouring himself another glass of spirits, Gregory turned to the Duke.

"Would you like a spot?" Knowing full well he would refuse, for the Duke never partook of spirits.

The Duke ignored the offer.

"What is it, you must discuss with me today?" asked Gregory feeling the bravado of the heavy wine full upon his lips.

The Duke stood eyeing Gregory, watching him drink yet another cup of brandy. "There are two orders of business, Gregory, and the first one is truly an opportunity…yes, a great opportunity for you…" He spoke slowly and methodically.

Gregory cringed. The Duke's voice weighed heavy upon his chest, for with every inflection another link was added to the already heavy chain of servitude.

"… I am sure you agree. Now that Elizabeth is of proper age, we must find someone to marry her, someone who will keep her close to home and someone who is worthy of the family reputation."

Gregory could not hide the disgust and outrage at what his father in law was proposing. To hear it come from this man's lips made the whole idea seem entirely outrageous. Gregory's earlier thoughts rang in his mind. Elizabeth had the spirit of adventure in her. She was not ready for marriage, no, not his Elizabeth, not yet. The Duke could never have his dear Elizabeth's best interest. She, like himself, was a mere commodity. Gregory's anger was about to burst forth, and he could put the whole lot of them in danger, if he dare say what crept up from the depths of his belly. Quickly, he poured himself another glass of brandy.

"Ah, you now know how I felt when I introduced my lovely Charmaine to you, Gregory. I see the look in your eyes. Only the finest gentleman will do, yes, only the finest. That is why we must act soon, for Elizabeth is a beauty…just as her mother, and I do not want her taken away by someone neither you nor I have approved of. I am sure you agree." The Duke interrupted Gregory's thoughts and Gregory made no comment. He tipped his head back and downed the sweet, hot liquid. The Duke did not wait for Gregory to respond. He never did. There was no need.

"And this leads me to the second issue on my agenda today, Gregory. It seems that the ship upon which we had our latest investments has been declared a lost vessel. I hold out no hope for us to see her treasures and this puts quite a strain on our financial partnership."

Gregory was startled at hearing the news of one of his ships. "Which ship have we lost? What are the details? The crew? Did they go down with her? Tell me Charles, I want to know all the details." Gregory never addressed his father-in-law by his first name unless it was during a business meeting regarding the shipping business. He still had much knowledge of all matters of the seas and this was where he felt on slightly equal footing with the Duke.

The Duke ignored Gregory's inquiry and continued. "I have asked James of Hartford to consider partnering with me in all future business ventures. He owns his estate outright and has no debts hidden in his closet." The Duke's eyes shone and his top lip curled upward as he continued throwing veiled insults at Gregory. "All of the Earl's business dealings with the banks in the city are extremely profitable. I have done business with him in the past. All has gone quite smoothly and that is why I believe he would also make a desirable son-in-law for you."

Gregory stood rigid. His concern for his ship and its crew cast aside with what the Duke had just suggested. James of Hartford was a liar and a cheat and everyone knew it. Gregory also surmised he was a leach who preyed on young innocents, yet he had not proof of any of the immoral and scandalous accusations. Gregory tried to force out these words of rebuttal, yet they would not emerge from his throat. He looked at the Duke and was immediately reminded of his own father's past transgressions. Shame surfaced and it was this that stood hard and firm between Gregory's fair and just character and the antics that the Duke had him involved in. Anger seethed within and had no place to go. Once more the Duke had backed him into the cage with thick bars of his own making.

"I am sure you will see to it that Elizabeth is made available to the Earl during the upcoming festivities." We would not want an unworthy lad to have any chance at her hand, for she has her mother's sense of passion. Need I remind you of how I had to steer Charmaine away from the many sailors who came calling and into the arms of you, my son." The Duke turned towards the door and opened it, bidding his farewell.

"So you say." Muttered Gregory.

"What say you?" Asked the Duke, his back to Gregory.

"As you say." Answered Gregory.

"I will call upon you in one week, to see how things are progressing. "The Duke quickly sauntered down the corridor leaving Gregory standing in his wake.

The Earl of Hartford will never have my daughter's hand. "Never!" Gregory said, slamming the mahogany doors. Courage welled up within for a long moment. Elizabeth was the only semblance of kindness, he had in his life; the only ray of hope in an increasingly dismal existence. He could not give her to a man, the likes of James Hartford. Elizabeth deserved so much more than to forever be the property of a deceptive swindler such as James. The thoughts flew through his mind like daggers until it all started to make sense. His morning remembrance ritual was bringing much sense to the once senseless events of his pitiful life. The Duke already knew everything about Gregory long before that fateful day. The Duke did not leave anything to chance, and fate was not a happenstance that likely, if ever occurred in the life of the Duke of Winslow. The urchins who were unlucky enough to fall under his prison of schemes and desires were puppets in his game of life and he, Gregory was one such puppet, locked in the maniacal prison with the deeds of his past. Perhaps the deeds of his past were never to be undone, yet from this moment on, the deeds of his present would fall under his own rule.

Gregory sat back at his desk and pulled out some parchment. He would write a letter to his good friend who still manned the trading vessels. He would ask him about the crew and the ship and inquire about Hartford, for it was not beneath that fraudulent Earl, to be a part of the downing of a vessel. Gregory started furiously writing, until a memory plunged through his mind. He remembered seeing James in town every time he had gone to do business with the Duke as of late. He always seemed to be there. Elizabeth was most likely already betrothed to James. It was a done deal and Gregory was the last to know as usual. He had no power here, it was all in the hands of the Duke of Winslow. He furiously crumbled the letter.

Gregory arose and poured himself a large bowl of brandy. He could not inquire, for his father-in-law was sure to find out, and what use would the truth be? Something must be done to deter the request of a courting invitation first right. The fate of his family had become increasingly precarious since the Duke was involving Elizabeth in his malevolent, greedy schemes. Gregory paced the room, the brandy swirling about in the bowl as he moved, spilling onto his shirt cuffs. Thoughts swirled in his mind, ripened by the brandy. He could not fathom how a grandfather could betroth his own flesh and blood to a man who would not love her and would most likely mistreat her in unspeakable ways. Gregory noticed how James looked at women. It was too much for him to think of. He threw his glass into the fireplace, shards of fine crystal and droplets of amber liquid hit the back of the hearth before landing deep into the fire.

Gregory stared for a long while into the burning embers, until he could stare no longer. He would not let the Duke have his way this time. He would figure out a way to keep his dear Elizabeth from succumbing to the wishes of her monstrous, omnipresent Grandfather.

Chapter Six

It was to be a fine gathering of about twenty of the area's wealthiest inhabitants. Elizabeth was full of anticipation, for she loved festivities and loved being in the center of the planning. The colder months had grown dismal and boring and the moon had not yet grown full. Elizabeth had since approached Madeline, the Spicer to help her chart the moon. She had overheard Madeline speak of such things to Eleanor, the confectioner.

A few days after she saw the women in the woods she had another similar dream. In the dream, she saw a woman who looked a lot like Madeline. She had a warm comfort about her and a wisdom that went beyond her young years, thus she sought out Madeline the very next day.

Elizabeth found her in the cellar grinding the spices that would be used for the pear wine. "It shall be full again on the last day of Christmas." answered Madeline, without stopping her work. Elizabeth sought to ask her if she knew the women of the forest, for her being emanated in a most similar way. She thought best not and instead thanked Madeline for the information and turned to leave.

"It matters not why you want to know, my lady, but I will tell you that I do see you."

Elizabeth stopped and turned to face Madeline. What did she mean by these words, wondered Elizabeth? She had not time to voice her inquiry, for Madeline's sparkling blue green eyes pulled her in and wrapped her in a blanket of love. She had not seemed so radiant before, thought Elizabeth. What has happened to Madeline? She questioned in the quiet of her own mind not wanting Madeline to know.

"I see you as the beautiful being that you are. It is you who have changed. You have been witness to true love." Madeline looked directly into Elizabeth's eyes as she spoke. Her gaze held still, until they heard someone scurrying about outside the cellar walls.

"Well, she continued, "it must just be that yee have grown into a woman. That is why you want to know the cycles of the moon, is it not? To help you remember your own bleeding time?" Madeline's words changed, but her demeanor did not. Elizabeth understood that it was not safe to talk of such things and that whatsoever was spoken here would remain between them.

"Yes, Madeline…yes." Elizabeth whispered. "Thank you."

Elizabeth hurried away. Being with Madeline touched awoke something inside that could not be explained. She continued to dream about the women each night. They showed themselves to her as brilliant colors and light that filled her eyes the moment she closed them. She found herself in their midst, in a type of school setting, or in a field of flowers dancing. The women spoke and they always said words similar to Madeline's. "You are beautiful…you are strong, you are brave, you are blessed." Elizabeth looked forward to finding the women again, when the time was right, yet for now she would allow the magic of the season to engulf her and bring her joy.

The days before the gathering on the first day of Christmas, were spent in busy preparation. Everyone from the bakers, to the stable men kept busy preparing. Smells of exotic spices that the brewers added to the wines and beers filled the air. Mounds of dariole lined the pantry shelves and the aroma of roasting meats had every stomach within the household growling with anticipation. The succulent stews simmered upon the fire pits and every ingredient used gave the estate the smell of goodness overflowing. The kitchen was full of activity and

Elizabeth and Henry were in the middle of it. On special occasions Cook would let both Elizabeth and Henry help in the kitchen. It was not proper for them to be helping the servants, but they loved it so. What was proper though was for the Lady of the estate to run the comings and goings of all of her staff. Elizabeth took on the responsibility the very year of the incident with Mother and by this point in time, she was quite adept at aiding wherever she could during the planning and preparation. She had not formally become the Lady of the Estate, yet she had taken on the duties this year as a welcome distraction. All was about done and Elizabeth was becoming increasingly restless.

"See here, mistress" said Cookie. "We stuff the pastries like so!" she said throwing a dollop of cod liver upon the perfect squares of dough that Henry had helped Priscilla, Cook's newest apprentice, assemble. Elizabeth scooped up a dollop of the smelly, creamy goop and she flung the concoction into the air and watched it splatter all over Henry's already stained shirt.

"Elizabeth, look what you did!" he exclaimed, wiping the greasy spots. "I smell like I fell into a barrel of eels!" Henry exclaimed, all the while eyeing Priscilla.

Priscilla turned up her nose and gave him a look fit for a measly hog herder as she continued rolling and cutting the soft, grain speckled dough. Elizabeth smiled at the sight and also felt a pang in her heart for her brother. She knew that Henry took a fancy to Priscilla and from the looks of it, Priscilla was not interested. Well, thought Elizabeth, she is older and a mere house servant at that. Henry would undoubtedly court and marry someone of their royal heritage, even though it may not be for some time yet, well after he had his education and roamed the world. He was encouraged to do such things, she was not. She felt a new sense of anger well up, the unfairness of it all! She took a deep breath and let out a sigh.

"You know, Henry, perhaps Priscilla will make you a special dinner for your sixteenth birthday. It is coming up soon. We could ask Eleanor to make you an eel cake!" She laughed, sure to get a rise out of her brother.

The look on Henry's face was exactly what Elizabeth wanted, red cheeks and all. Henry pouted. "Elizabeth stop with the jokes, please!"

"Serves you right, lad." reprimanded Cook. The women ignored his pleas and continued their work. They did enjoy Henry, he was easy to tease and he also had a way of keeping everyone entertained with his antics even when he carried them a bit too far as he was apt to do.

It was that very morning that his antics had gotten the best of him. Henry woke Elizabeth before the crow of the rooster and led her down the dark hallways, and into the kitchen before the first servant arrived.

"I have a plan, like we used to do as children…come!" exclaimed Henry, taking Elizabeth's hand. Elizabeth did not protest for she was as excited as he by the prospect of another adventure. When the two got to their destination Henry got to work while Elizabeth watched him and said not a word. Henry went to the hearth top and lifted up the large pot of duck fat. He carefully ladled scoops of the oily mixture over the floor boards and atop the rushes, winding his way from the doorway, back to the hearth.

"Come, "Henry whispered to Elizabeth, motioning towards the pantry. Henry and Elizabeth hid themselves in the pantry, cracked the door a bit and lay in wait for Cookie. She was always the first to come light the fire for the day's preparations. They could hear her whistling as she approached. Then they heard a voice. It was not Cookie's. They both looked at each other. Elizabeth shook Henry's arm.

"Good morning Cookie." Came the voice.

"Priscilla!" They both whispered to each other at the same time.

Henry quickly began making deals with God. "Not Priscilla." He whispered "Anyone but her." Elizabeth knew now that the only reason he stayed in the kitchen for so many an hour was so that he could be close to her. "Oh, no…" he whispered. Elizabeth grabbed Henry's arm to keep him from giving away their secret, but it was too late. He emerged from their hiding place, caught his slippers on the slippery wooden planks and started to fly across the kitchen, still upright.

"Please missy, don't be in such a hurry." Said Cookie as she pushed Priscilla back. "Don't you know I am always the first to enter this room each and every morn!" she said in a most stately tone. Cook then came prancing in, just in time to meet Henry head on. Elizabeth could hardly contain herself as she watched her brother slide and try to swerve out of the way of Cookie's massive body. Cookie landed with a thud, stopping Henry short. He went sailing over her and landed in the arms of Priscilla with such force that it threw them both to the ground. Cooks face turned a glorious shade of crimson as she frantically tried to pull her skirts down over her bounteous pantaloons, scrambling to right herself, not sure what had hit her. Henry lay in the arms of a greasy Priscilla. Elizabeth noticed the look of both panic and delight upon Henry's face. She also noticed how Priscilla smiled a soft seductive smile before she pulled herself out of his grasp.

"Young master, I beg you to get yourself up and remember that you are a gentleman!" she said in a most condescending tone. Henry scrambled up, completely embarrassed.

It took all three of them to lift Cookie up off the slippery, slimy floor, but once they managed to do so, she burst out laughing and soon all four were shaking with the deepest belly laughs they had ever had. They laughed and laughed until Cookie broke the trance.

"I do admire a clever lad at that!" she said, "My Jerome, God rest his soul, was a clever man. It is of great importance in this tragic life, that we find merriment where we can!"

The laughter subsided, for they had much work to do and duty called. Cookie had the last word as usual.

"I may admire the clever in you lad, but yee best be cleaning this floor before you do one more thing. You know where the bucket and the lye are. Get to work and do not stop until every last bit of fat is scrubbed clean and a new layer of rushes are put down. Now let's clean ourselves up, we have meals to prepare." And with that, they all went their separate ways to clean themselves up and prepare for the feast.

After the morning frolic, and after she brought Father his morning meal, Elizabeth retreated to her chambers. She wanted to spend as much time as possible readying herself for the evening and she also did not necessarily want to see her grandfather again that day. She would rather stay out of his way as much as possible, for he was always giving her an order. He did that with everyone; Henry, Father, the servants, everyone apart from Mother. He never talked with her, he merely told her what to do. That was it. No discussion. Perhaps he had to be so demanding, for he was a very important, wealthy man and he had much on his mind, yet she still did not prefer to be in his presence. She was glad he only came around about once per week, and he never stayed for more than one hour. He usually spent the time with Mother, so she stayed clear of him whenever she knew he was to be within the estate. Elizabeth put all thoughts of her grandfather out of her mind as she lay upon her bed thinking of who might attend the gathering this year. Although no one of exceptional intrigue had ever attended one of her family gatherings, she could still hope. Perhaps one of the ladies of the forest would make her way into the Cumberland's long gallery. Perhaps the beautiful lady dressed in white with the long flowing dark hair would walk right in and sit to the left of her father. The servants would act as if nothing unusual had taken place. They would serve the lovely lady first, as if she were the Lady of the manor. The Duke of Deveron would stare in amazement at her beauty and his wife, the Duchess would grab his face and reprimand him for forgetting his manners. Elizabeth laughed to herself. The lady would not say a word to anyone lest it be Elizabeth. Yes, that would be quite an evening she thought as she drifted to sleep. She awoke with a start to the pounding on her door.

"Elizabeth, are you ready?" yelled Henry, still banging on the door.

"Of course I am not ready." She said opening the door to find him standing there still dressed in his stained, dirty clothing from the morning. "And neither are you." She said shaking her head.

"Of course I am not ready, but you have been locked in here for hours. You must ready yourself and go talk to Priscilla for me." He nervously glanced around to make sure no one else heard him. He tried to walk past Elizabeth and into her bed chambers but she stopped him.

"Wait, little brother, I am going to bathe now and you must go get ready." She said, greatly annoyed at his self-absorbed attitude.

"Very well, sister, be that way!" he said backing out of the room. "I simply wanted you to speak to Priscilla and tell her how very sorry I am about this morning." Henry dropped his mouth at the corners which made him look so very sad and pathetic.

"I am sure she has forgotten the whole thing, Henry." Elizabeth would not let his pouty demeanor sway her just yet.

"I don't think she has, Elizabeth. You must speak to her tonight, for I will not be able to enjoy myself if she is angry with me." Elizabeth had never seen Henry so infatuated with a girl. She thought it quite funny, but she thought not to tease him, for the way he looked at her with those sullen pale blue eyes had her feeling quite sorry for him.

"Very well, Henry. Leave me be and I will speak with her as soon as I am ready. But Henry, I must warn you, she is much too old for you."

She is not too old. She is only eighteen." He answered still wearing his gloomy, woeful face.

Elizabeth was becoming so very annoyed with him, for she knew he would not take no for an answer, and she knew Priscilla would not be interested in the likes of her little brother, but far be it for her to disappoint him further. "As I said, very well, Henry, I will speak to her." She answered with a slam of the door.

"Tell her I am very, very sorry…and tell her I want a dance with her tonight, no, never mind do not tell her that". Henry kept talking from behind the heavy door.

Elizabeth walked towards her dressing table, shaking her head. Why on earth did Henry think it proper or even possible for him to dance with a servant woman at their Christmas gala. He had gone mad. It was then she heard the giggling coming from behind her press. It was not unusual for others to be milling about in her room, for as a maiden of noble heritage, she was not to have much privacy unless she insisted, a truth she learned long ago.

"I'm sorry, Lady Elizabeth." Said the voice. Out popped one of Elizabeth's dressing maids, Meg, holding an armful of washed petticoats.

Elizabeth knew that Henry's secret would now be the talk of the servants. She thought this was best, for then she would not have to do his bidding for him.

"No need to apologize Meg, but I do wish to dress alone for this evening's festivities."

"Yes, Lady Elizabeth, I shall put these freshly laundered garments in your chest here and be gone."

Meg, as well as the other servants, always looked at Elizabeth with a curious eye. Elizabeth knew that the staff talked about how odd her family was for they were unlike any other royal household of her day. Father did not have a Steward and Elizabeth was allowed to shoo away her help whenever she felt the need for privacy. This was unheard of according to others of royal heritage. Elizabeth had not known it to be any other way, for her whole existence was one of secrets and evasions. She did not like the looming secrets of some unknown origin, but she cherished the time she was allowed to be gloriously alone.

Meg had started her bath while Elizabeth lay dreaming of the evening's affair. The water was perfect. She added some drops of lavender and rose and entered into the cocoon of soft luxurious water. She washed her hair with the gentlest soap and combed it carefully, removing any knots with great ease. When she was complete with her bath, she wrapped herself in a silken robe and picked out a most handsome gown to compliment her natural beauty. She chose one of red and gold silk with a velvet damask overlay. Sitting very close to the fire, so her golden hair would dry, she smoothed lavender cream on her legs, arms and feet. Her legs were very long and a bit thin; she had recently grown much taller, nearly up to Father's chin. Once her hair was dry she carefully braided it, then swept the long braids up on her head and adorned them with holly berries. Her figure, now full in all the right places would not be stuffed into a corset. She had no need for one. She slipped into her ball gown. Buttons and ties were positioned on the sides of this particular dress, so she hadn't needed anyone's help after all. She stared at herself in the mirror and very much liked what she saw, well almost. Her lips were still a bit too full and her cheeks a bit red, but the gown helped with that., along with a slight dusting of Mother's face powder. She tied a golden sash around her shoulders and put one of mothers ruby rings on her finger. It was tight and pinched her and she decided not to wear it. Father would not approve anyway.

Elizabeth entered the long gallery and all eyes were upon her. She felt radiant and lovely this evening and carried her beauty with a shy assurance. Slowing her gait, she gazed out over the many guests. Panic started to rise up and her legs felt weak. Never before had she been met with so many stares and her cheeks flushed in response. Oh, how I wish I would have used more of Mother's white powder, she thought. She was sure she would have arrived before most of the guests. Had she not seen the correct time? Panic continued to course through her body as she scoured the room for her father. She spotted him a few yards away, just as he spotted her and she quickly strode over to him, her confident gait returning. As Elizabeth reached out for Father, she felt a firm hand land painfully upon her shoulder. The force pulled her entire body around and she stood face to face with James of Hartford. James locked into her and started to pull her into the deep black abyss of his gaze. He grabbed her hand and in a moments time had it up to his pale lips. Elizabeth tried to resist, but he held her hand tighter, digging his fingers into her delicate flesh. Elizabeth writhed in pain and prayed the same silent prayer that flew out of her being on the day she witnessed the five children's demise. "Great Mother, help me!" She looked around to see if she had actually said the words out loud. She had not. She had however unlocked from his piercing gaze.

"Good evening Elizabeth, you look quite lovely this fine evening." James said, bowing. He did not let go of her hand. Images of a horrific sea monster filled her mind. Yes, she thought, he wishes to take me into his very being and torture me. She jumped back when he momentarily looked away and freed her hand.

"Good evening James." Elizabeth coldly, yet politely replied, while curtsying, hiding her hands in the folds of the damask and begging for her father to come to her side. Father was so close, yet so far away. Arising from her curtsy, she looked directly at Father and his gaze caught hers, his face remained calm but his eyes turned to slate. A look Elizabeth knew well.

"Elizabeth come here." Father moved to her side, pulled her close and took hold of her hand. Elizabeth was sure he felt the tremble that shook her entire being. Shame and trepidation filled her completely. She felt weak and was grateful the Earl no longer touched her body. He was now far enough away that she could catch her breath. The very old widow Gramsely and her two almost as old, spinster nieces, surrounded James in a bevy of skirts and gloved hands. Elizabeth was so relieved, she thought she would faint.

"Father, that man greatly upsets me." She whispered up into her father's ear.

"What man upsets you, my dear?" Father asked feigning detachment.

"The Earl of Hartford! Did you not see him? Father, there is something extremely unnerving about him and he resides entirely too close to us!"

"Yes, I know you are not fond of him, but…ah, he is a fine citizen, and a wealthy businessman, besides his lineage traces back even farther than our own. You must give him that much." Elizabeth was sure she heard her father's voice choke and when she looked into his eyes, she was sure of what she saw. They turned from the usual pale slate color into a deep flaming blue. He then started coughing uncontrollably, in a way very much like Henry.

"Father, are you all right? Shall I fetch you some water?" Elizabeth was terrified. Never had her beloved father had a coughing spell!

"No water. Fetch me a large glass of spirits, my dear." Choked Father.

"Yes Father." Elizabeth turned in several directions, not sure where to go first. No sooner had she left her father's side as servant appeared with a large glass of amber liquid. He gently handed it to Elizabeth.

"Father, please drink slowly!"

But, Father did not listen to her, as usual. He took the glass and gulped down its entire contents. Gathering himself, he continued speaking very softly. The barely audible words did not get caught in his throat.

"Perhaps a fondness could grow, Elizabeth. You must give the man a chance."

"No father, he is evil." Said Elizabeth staring her father straight in the eyes. "He has a heart that is cold, I know this to be true." She turned her back on her father and continued. "I cannot believe that you intend on speaking to me about this, after your choking spell.

"How do you know this Elizabeth?" asked Father.

"I saw you choking just a moment ago. Have you lost your mind Father? Are you going to join Mother in the chamber of the dead?" Dread immediately filled her being. She could not believe that she had spoken such disrespectful cruelty to her own father. She stood in a pool of regret but would not step aside.

"I am well now Elizabeth. My breath has returned quite adequately and I mean to have you answer my questions." Father was not amused at her avoidance.

Elizabeth turned toward Father and took his hand in hers leading him to a quiet corner. She continued the conversation as they walked, hoping that somehow her anger would temper. "I know because I feel it each and every time I see him." She said walking with steady small steps.

She dared not tell father of her meeting with James in the forest, nor how she knew that she must protect not only herself, but the lovely women of the forest from that man's pernicious behavior. And she dared not confess to her father that she somehow knew of Grandfather's desire to have her marry James. Suddenly a mighty surge of courage rose up within her and she stopped to face down her father. "I know that he is wealthy and that for me to marry him would secure our fortunes. I know this Father. I am not a stupid girl. I also know that Grandfather put you up to this. And I will not be sold. I will not be sold." Elizabeth walked away from her father, vowing not speak to him for the rest of the night. She did not want to say such harsh words to him, yet she felt that she must. Father would listen to her, she was sure. He would come around, but she must remain steadfast in her disgust of the man who would never be her husband.

As the evening wore on and the guests had their fill of food and spirits, the dancing began in the south end of the long gallery. The guests would stay the night and the party would continue into the next day. Elizabeth said goodnight and was on her way to her bedchamber when she decided to see if the night was suitable for a stroll. She stepped outside and found it to be a calm and dry evening. She sat on one of the stone benches far from the crowd and the noise, amidst the barren gardens and thought of the evening's events and how disappointed she was at the sour start. The damage had followed her through the whole evening and she did not feel like dancing with anyone, let alone her father or brother. The night was about over and she would end it in the best way she knew, sitting under the sparkling sky, dreaming of the forest women. Elizabeth was lost in her thoughts and did not hear him approach until it was too late. James stood at her side and from the looks and smell emanating from his being, he had consumed much too much spirits for one evening.

"Hello, Elizabeth, how lucky I am to have found you out alone on this evening."

"I was just about to retire." She said coldly. A shiver ran up her spine as she stood up and turned away from him. He grabbed her arm before she had time to move out of his reach.

"I was talking to you and it is impolite for you to turn your back to me while I am speaking."

His grasp on her arm grew tighter and his hot breath burned her skin. She tried to writhe free, but as she pulled he tightened his grasp even more.

"Sir James, you are hurting me, please let go of my arm or I shall call out." spat Elizabeth, both annoyed and frightened.

"I wanted to tell you again how lovely you looked this evening Elizabeth" and I wanted to reassure you that I am interested in pursuing a very promising deal between your father and I regarding your future."

Elizabeth's annoyance and fright turned to anger and before she could censor her words, they flew from her mouth. "My father should not be discussing such things with you, Sir James. I am not, nor will I ever be interested in such an arrangement."

He tightened his grasp even harder and Elizabeth felt his rage shoot through her entire body.

"Elizabeth, I am surprised at your choice of words. You know that you may not speak to me in that way, that your father and I have every right to speak about you and plan your very existence." James twisted her arm ever so slightly behind her back as he reprimanded her, and it only served to make her all the more obstinate in her stance. She refused to acknowledge the pain she was feeling despite the fact that her bones were beginning to crush and bend beneath his strength.

"James, you must let me go at once and I will forget we ever had this meeting." She said, tears of pain welling in her eyes.

"There you go again Elizabeth telling me what is so. It is a no wonder you behave in such an unwomanly way, what with your mother being crazy and never teaching you the proper way to respect a man. Maybe those witches you meet in the forest have taught you some magic, some evil ways that might end you in the gallows instead of on my arm and in my bed, where you belong. Nevertheless, I shall be glad to teach you the proper way to treat a man. Since your father never had the nerve to deal with you, I will. I will be the one to show you how to respect a man and to be a proper wife. You will obey my wishes when we are wed. It is only a matter of time before it all comes to be." He sneered and hissed like the snake he is.

"It will never come to be, Sir James, this I know is true." Elizabeth shot back. His words about her father rang in her ears and she felt as if her whole being would burst in fiery anger.

James then bent down as if to kiss her mouth all the while still holding her arm tightly behind her back. She tried to break free of his grasp, but he had her in such a position that with any movement the pain was unbearable. She stared up at his face as his lips met hers. She allowed him to kiss her and as he did she bit down hard on the salty flesh of his mouth.

"Ah!" he jumped back in shock, but only for a brief moment before shoving her to the ground. He lay atop her full body, pulling up her ball gown and reaching to feel her flesh. His hands were hot and wet and strong. She writhed underneath the weight of his heavy body and heard herself screaming. She had to get out of here or something terrible was going to happen. Sir James covered her mouth with one hand and fervently fumbled under her skirts with the other. She would not succumb. Frantically she kicked and flailed her arms. Anything to get him to stop. He will not get what he wants from me, ever.

There was something nefarious about his needs, something altogether perverted and savage in the way he spoke, walked, and carried his being, and now he was trying to suck her into his whirlpool of evil. If he succeeded she would be lost forever. Elizabeth was now possessed by the resistance to being overtaken by this maniacal baneful monster. Please help me Mother God, she chanted within her mind, help me, help me! She felt a strange presence come over her and it was then that she remembered that a man's loins were a very vulnerable part of his body and maybe she could successfully injure him.

James was trying to free his loins from his trousers and she saw her opportunity to strike. She pulled both of her legs up together towards her chest and let out a mighty kick like she had seen the mares do to the stallions when they did not want to be mounted. James let out a yelp as his breath heaved in and out of his body. Elizabeth rolled out from under him, gathered herself up and ran as fast as she could for safety and did not stop until she had reached her bedchambers. Quickly locking the door she leaned against it with a great sigh of relief. She took off her dress and threw it under the bed. She did not ever want to see that ball gown again.

I shall burn it in the fire, she thought. As she was under the bed trying to retrieve her dress, the door opened. Matilda and Meg entered. Matilda set a tray of warm milk and custard on the table and Meg began tidying up. Elizabeth stared, trying to remember who these people were and why they were in her room. She pulled the dress out from under the bed and folded it in her arms, sitting on the cold floor. She did not move from her place and neither woman asked her a thing. Meg stoked the fire and turned down the bed. Matilda looked into her eyes and for a moment Elizabeth remembered this woman's gentleness and thought to tell her what occurred. Something held her back though, something deep and foreboding tightened the memory of the evening in place within her own mind. It shan't be spoken of. The women left and Elizabeth started sobbing. She crawled into her warm, inviting bed and slept for many, many hours, missing the next day's celebrations altogether.

****

Gregory had enough of the celebrations. He had smiled far too much that evening. His face was tired and a twitch set into his left cheek, most likely from the forcing of cheer. Many of his guests were retreating to the far end of the gallery to dance and continue to make merry. It was perfect time for an escape into his study, alone. Quickly and quietly he left the crowd as their attention turned to the music. As he walked briskly towards his study refuge, he was stopped in his tracks by a flush of terror as thoughts of Elizabeth flooded his mind.

"My child is in danger." He whispered, his own voice shooting up through his body. When was the last time he saw Elizabeth, he questioned? It had been awhile. He must find her.

Without another thought, his body propelled him into his study and immediately over to the large pane window. This window was also a door when need be. He pried it open and leapt out, landing a few feet below in the muddy window well. He found his footing quickly and proceeded to walk, quickly lunging forward with each step. He headed towards the maze, knowing this was a favorite spot of his daughters. Approaching a large grouping of olive trees, he stopped and scanned the surroundings, listening intently. He thought he heard something to his right, so he turned sharply, but was stopped from turning completely, by what felt like the tip of a blade digging into his back and the strong grip of a man digging into the flesh on his forearm. He heard it then, the screams of his daughter coming from ahead. The man's arm tightened around Gregory and the blade dug deeper into the flesh covering his ribs.

"You have gone far enough." Gregory was horrified, for the voice was that of the Duke of Winslow.

"What say you Duke? Why do you hold me hostage here? Elizabeth could be in danger, my daughter, your granddaughter! Let go of me this moment!" he fought the Duke, yet to no avail. The Duke had a weapon and the element of surprise to his advantage.

Gregory righted himself as he looked in the direction of the screams. They had stopped, but just ahead in the distance he could see what looked to be his daughter, lying on the ground with a man upon her.

"Do you not see? She is in danger. Give me your weapon and we shall help her." He pleaded, struggling to free himself from the devil's grip.

"I see nothing, except a man taking his soon to be wife. This is not our place Gregory, to be spying upon two lovers. Do you understand?" sneered the Duke.

Gregory did not understand. His daughter was in danger and the Duke was talking nonsense. Then he was flooded with the familiar feelings. Shame filled his belly. It fell upon him like a thousand pounds of jagged edged boulders. His chest caved in and he felt the blade of the knife go deeper still, feeling as if it was piercing his heart from behind.

"Yes, my son, now you understand." Spat the duke, still holding tightly onto Gregory, his hot rancid breath shooting down his neck. Gregory turned to face this monster and saw from where the baneful coward got his courage. The Duke was accompanied by two of his strongest henchmen, who stood like alabaster, their swords drawn and ready to cut Gregory if need be.

"What you witness is not your daughter in danger, but just a bit of pre wedding frolic with her soon to be husband and our newest business partner."

"I have not agreed to this! I am her father and she is not to wed James. What I witness is an attack on a young maiden. Now let me be, or…or…"

"Or what Gregory? What is it that you think you shall do?" The Duke released his hold and his two guards grabbed onto Gregory's arms and held him still while the Duke gave his rant. "Need I remind you, once more", snorted the Duke, feigning boredom, "that in a moment's notice I can have you attainted. All your rights and privileges will be revoked and you will be tried for treason. Your father saw to that and it is only by my good graces that you have remained of title. You and your children will perish without me. Therefore, you shall allow your daughter to marry whomever I say she is to marry." The Duke leaned in close to Gregory, his fleshy pale face shaking in its bid for unearthly power. Gregory could not bear to look upon such an offensive human and he turned his face away.

"And furthermore Gregory, it is my understanding that the Earl of Hartford quite fancies the young flesh, he takes great delight in capturing his women as if they were does on hunting day. Who are we to deny him such pleasure?"

Gregory could not stand the thought of his daughter as prey, his head hung low, shoulders upright to try and cover his ears from such words. The Duke poked Gregory's midsection with his dagger, egging him on. Gregory lurched forward and vomit spewed forth from his mouth, landing upon the Dukes fine leather boots. The Duke snickered. "Yes, just as I thought, your stomach is weak, just like the rest of you."

The Duke turned and walked back toward the estate. Gregory was dragged along by the henchman. He heard his daughter's pleas for help echo within his head for many a day to come.

Chapter Seven

Elizabeth counted the days until she could retreat into the forest once more. She waited desperately for her escape. The continuing festivities of the Christmas season simply made her uneasy and nervous this year. After her experience with James, she felt herself changed. Perhaps a bit edgy, yes, but there was a certain disdain that had settled into her being. Disparaging understanding took the place of the innate innocence of a young girl. She was never to feel safe and she would need to be on the lookout forevermore. The disdain was accompanied by a shrewd energy that created a need for her to walk the halls with even deeper care. If a maiden must endure the blatant violations from certain men, then she would have to be assured of her own safety in whatsoever way she was able. She took to listening intently to anything the adults were saying, for any information that would help her to avoid her father, grandfather and James would be of great use.

Finally, the last day of Christmas had arrived. There were no parties or celebrations slated for the entire day. It seemed to her that the whole estate was ready to rest. The season had taken its toll. Merriment can easily be overdone when one has the wealth and means to provide so. Elizabeth waited patiently until Henry was asleep. She wanted to be alone in her adventure and did not want to stir him. He had been giving her ample space over the holidays, or rather he was otherwise engaged. His interest in the Priscilla had consumed him and given her what she desperately needed. Time alone.

The night was cold and clear. Wrapping her cloak tightly did nothing to warm the chill of adventure alive within her heart. This evening her gate held a different air. She was older and braver than the last time she traveled the barely worn path and her new found bravado and certainty pushed her along. Walking quietly and carefully she soon reached the same area that she had seen the women praying during the last full moon. She knew it was the same place, for she found the same boulder in the path. There were no women in the clearing and she wondered what had happened to them. Was it too early? Was she too late? "No." she answered herself, this was the exact time as before, for the moon was once more high overhead. She knew it was time. Where could they have gone? Maybe they had moved to safety, somehow knowing the shire reeve and James were trying to find them. She felt her heart quicken at the thought of James being anywhere near her and thus decided to hide herself, just in case. The trees were barren and the bushes were thin and panic swelled within. There was nowhere to hide! Then she heard the unmistakable sound of horses approaching. She knew by the sound that more than one rider approached. She must hide now. Uttering the prayer of help, she ran in the same direction as whence she came. Nearly stumbling into its folds, she came upon a deep crevice formed by rocks and fallen trees. She slipped within its tight quarters. She was not afraid of any of the creatures that might inhabit this small cave; she only cared about hiding from the devil himself. Ever so quietly she waited, praying the riders would not see her tracks.

The sounds of dismounting men sent her body into a tremble. One of them cursed. It sounded like the shire. Then she recognized James booming voice.

"I thought they would be here. They were here every full moon. I know it. I have evidence, they were here. We must find these devil worshippers as soon as we can and purge their evil from our county." yelled James angrily.

"This will be the last time I follow you on your wild witch hunting escapades Sir James."

This man's voice comforted Elizabeth and her shaking subsided, ever so slightly. He once again seemed very annoyed at James for taking him away from his nightly brew.

"You and your men are useless, Reeve. I will get my own men and we will find the witch whores and burn every last one of them."

James voice unnerved her each time she heard it. He sounded much too calm and determined for her liking. She sighed deeply and sunk lower into her hiding place.

"Very well, Sir. I still say, what is the fuss all about, if there are women who dance in the forest, I would think you might enjoy the sight of such frivolity!" The men started laughing.

Shire reeve was being quite daring. He surely did not know the depths of depravity that James was capable of, she thought to herself. A tingle went up her spine as she remembered that she herself was indeed one of his targets. She and the women of the forest.

"I will have your heads you bunch of immoral heathens." James spat.

"Sir James, we shall simply disband and return to our nightly merriment. No need for such threats. If there is illegal and immoral activity in these parts, we will find them...eventually."

She heard not another word spoken as the band of unwilling men led by the wretched predator James, mounted their horses and rode off. Elizabeth slowly emerged from her hiding place, looking in every direction to make sure the danger was gone. It seemed she was safe and alone. The moon was still high in the hazy night sky, it was not yet time to return to the estate and now that the danger had passed, she would continue just a bit deeper into the wintry forest. Winding down the icy, muddy path, her new air of confidence returned and propelled her forward. It was not long, however until an odd sensation pulled at her. It felt as if someone were following close behind. Heart racing and fear rising, she dared not look back, yet the feeling was so intense she could hardly help herself. Turning, she caught a glimpse of a shadowy figure walking a good distance behind. Immediately she began running, sprinting faster and faster and deeper and deeper into the forest she went. Pure panic fueled her. She could not let this stranger get to her, and she hoped to dear God she was not leading him nearer to the women. Lost in a fluster of thoughts, she could see not an inch in front of her. One step farther and she was launched into the air, her footing no longer under her body. She did not travel far until landing face first into a pile of cold dead moss. Before she could right herself she felt a hand on her shoulder. A fierce chill ran up her spine, knowing for sure it was James after her again. But the hand was gentle and the voice speaking to her was not James.

"Are you hurt, maiden?" asked the gentle male voice. Elizabeth could scarcely move from the fear, so she lay and kept her face buried in the moss. Maybe he would think her dead and leave her be. "Maiden are you hurt?

A moment went by and she felt safe enough to respond and she picked her head up and pushed herself up on her elbows.

"I am fine, sir." She muttered. Turning her head around she saw who the kind voice belonged to. A most handsome and tender face of a young man stared down upon her. The moon's shimmer was shining so brightly on them both at that moment that she could make out the details of this helpful lad. He had a head of unruly blond hair, his features fine and fair. He looked to be of the same age as she and he stood tall and lithe. She knew at that moment he was not a threat, to the contrary, he looked to be a blessing. Gazing down, his smile broke into a full-fledged laugh. Ruckus laughter was contagious and soon she too started to laugh although she did not know what could be so humorous.

"What is so funny sir?' she asked of the stranger as she caught her breath from laughing.

"You are, maiden. You have moss and twigs in your hair and I do believe that is some of the finest dirt encrusting your pretty lips!"

Embarrassed at the thought of looking such a fright in front of this stranger, Elizabeth sat upright and fervently started pulling twigs, dirt and dried moss from her hair and face, but her hands were covered in mud and she was only making matters worse. She welled up with humiliation and that is when the young stranger knelt next to her and pulled out a clean white kerchief from his coat and started to help her wipe her face clean. He gently rubbed her cheeks, smiling all the while. The humiliation dissipated as she let him touch her as if she knew him. She was sure she did not know him, in spite of this feeling, for she would surely remember meeting this young man. Her humiliation turned to curiosity and then quickly to indignation.

"Thank you, kind sir, but I am quite capable of cleaning myself up. I will thank you for leaving me be so I may return home now." Elizabeth sprang up from her seat on the ground and walked away in the direction she hoped would lead her back to the estate. She seemed to be in fine condition, although her writing hand had an awful ache in it. She shook it off and continued walking. In her fright she had become hopelessly lost, but she was not going to ask this stranger for help just yet, for he had unnerved her with his kindness and familiarity. Her standoffishness did not deter him and he followed closely.

"You were looking for them weren't you?" he asked her.

She stopped and turned toward him, startled at his question. "Looking for who?" she posed, feigning innocence as she had so neatly perfected in a household now full of danger and secrets. For all she knew he could be one of the shire's men out looking for her heavenly friends and she would never give away any secret that could lead to their demise.

"For the women who pray in the woods each full moon, that's who!" He answered. "I saw you watching them last time. They moved their meeting place because of you, my lady. They knew you watched them and they let you, yet it was your presence, innocently enough, I am sure." The lad continued gently touching her arm. "When the men followed you and nearly caught them, they knew they had to leave and find a new place." He bluntly stated.

Elizabeth pulled her arm in and away from his touch. "I did not bring those men. I would never do that. They did not follow me either. They were surprised to find me. I told them nothing of what I saw." Elizabeth quickly regretted telling him so much.

"I mean... I mean..." she stuttered. Searching for something to say to take back what she had shared with him, left her stunningly silent. Staring at him, she tried to get a grasp on what he was thinking instead. Breathing deeply, she assessed the situation. Her newfound cunningness and necessary alertness was telling her that this young man was indeed familiar and she could trust him. Still she stayed silent stepping a safer distance away.

"I know you mean them no harm." The young man answered. "I can take you to them if you wish. I know where they meet. Follow me and we shall find them. It is not far from here. You were heading toward them the whole time."

Elizabeth decided in one instant that she could trust him. If he did anything, she would run as she had before. She did not have any other choice really for the pull to see the women was so very strong. The two began walking in a northerly direction and he continued.

"I followed you tonight; to be sure you were safe. I do not travel alone in these woods at night myself for fear of the wild dogs. You mustn't come out here without something or someone to protect you." He said as he walked beside her.

"Thank you, kind sir" she said with a contemptuous lilt, "but I have lived in this area all my life and I know these forests well." Her false bravado returned, for this was not true. She only knew the forest from within her dreams, yet she felt a need to boast to him and deny any thought that could provoke a sense of insecurity on her part. She would not trust him if and until she saw the women with her own eyes.

"Yes, maiden. The forest faeries surely look out for you. I can sense they follow you and they do protect you."

She was ready to pounce on him for she thought his words mocking, but instead she stopped, put her hand out and stared into his face, sizing him up. The lad seemed quite serious regarding his words and almost nonchalant in his gate. Maybe it was the magic of the forest or maybe it was the new found hope that this adventure brought forth. Whatever the reason, a sudden sense of excitement and passion and that uncommon familiarity took hold once more. The lad reached out for her muddy hand and took it in his own. She accepted and together they walked in silence. He led her to a small clearing just past a row of birch and there they found them.

The women were sitting in a circle, holding hands, a melodious hum rose up and Elizabeth smiled, remembering the songs of angels. This time it was she who grabbed his hand, sighed deeply and took in the healing magic. Within the circle sat a woman garbed in a most exquisite lavender robe. This woman was ripe with child and the others were blessing her with prayers for the health and well being of both mother and child. The mother- to-be rocked back and forth as the maidens touched her shoulders and put their hands on her belly. Elizabeth could almost see the prayers entering into the woman and caressing her large belly filling her with contentment and joy. A gentle smile lit up the soon-to-be mother's face with a love so deep and penetrating that Elizabeth could only imagine how loved she must feel. Time moved ever so slow and nothing beyond the forest mattered.

After what seemed like forever within the most delightful of moments, the women were finished and began to retreat. Elizabeth let out a fulfilled sigh and turned to her new friend who had been watching with the same intensity as she.

"Where are they going?" Elizabeth whispered." Are they real?"

"They go to their homes hidden deeply in the woods and yes they are as real as you and I. Come now and I will bring you back to your home. It is almost dawn and surely you will be missed."

Elizabeth arose and instinctively took the lad's hand. They headed back in the direction of the estate in silence. Elizabeth held his hand tight, clinging to the fluency and ease of their new found bond. Although she knew not his name, nor title, she knew she belonged by his side.

"Thank you, kind stranger," Elizabeth said as they stood before the gates. I do believe I trust you now, though I know not your name or how you came to be in the forest this evening.

"You are welcome maiden. You must hurry now, to your bed. The sun is almost up." The lad brought her dirty, sore hand up to his mouth and with closed eyes, he kissed it, ever so gently, yet firmly. He said not another word, turned and disappeared into the forest.

Elizabeth stood for one long second before she hurriedly found her way back into her bedchamber. The lad was right, for the sun was about rising and the estate would be bustling in a moments time. Elizabeth rested safely within the walls of her own private fortress, under the soft warm mound of blankets. The fire was only embers now, and despite the chill in the air, she was warmed. She stared into the red glow and thought of the night. It had started in fear and ended with the safest feeling she had ever experienced. Falling soundly asleep Elizabeth dreamt of the women and her handsome new friend. The lad was holding a beautiful new babe. He handed the babe to her and she held it close to her breast. Her body was full and so very alive in this dream, as if the babe was a part of her, and she had given it life. She could feel her breasts yearning for the child to suckle them. Looking into its eyes, she saw her own face looking back at her. Caressing its soft pink flesh she held the babe ever so close to her heart. This dream was so real that when she awoke at the crowing of the rooster she was surprised to find herself in her bed. She did not want the dream to end, and she forced herself to drift back into slumber with the magic of the shimmering moon on her face and the angels and faeries dancing behind every leaf on every tree in the forest.

Over the next few weeks, Elizabeth went outside the grounds every chance she could hoping to run into the kind stranger. Yet the days went by and she hadn't caught a glimpse of him again. Each day, after her studies and in the quiet of the afternoon, she would pretend she was in her room asleep and it was then that she made her escape. Most days, she succeeded, for she was not one to make her presence known in the estate. She preferred to be like a cat. Quiet and stealth. It was on one of those days that she happened upon a place that became her refuge. It was an abandoned store house barn and freezer about one hour walk in a westerly direction from the estate. No one had used the barn for years but it was still standing tall, as its base was made of stone. It was small and in the winter months it held its warmth and Elizabeth found she could snuggle safely inside its walls and sit and dream. On this day, she skipped through the forest, dancing and silently humming to herself.

"Soon it will be time, soon it will be time, soon it will be time, to set my heart forever free."

Elizabeth entered into the stone chamber and built herself a small fire. Sitting near the fire she watched the smoke curl up and out the large hole in the roof and dance with the filtered light of the mid afternoon sun. The antics made her sleepy and she lay down on the ground lazily following the flames dart back and forth. Languishing in the sheer pleasure of expansive aloneness, she did also come with a plan. Stay a few hours, assist her cat in giving birth to a litter of kittens and return home in time for the evening meal before anyone would realize she was away.

Cat, as Elizabeth affectionately named her, was a most beautiful calico breed and had welcomed her to this hideaway. A familiar companion. Apparently Cat had made its home within the walls of the old stone freezer long before Elizabeth found its hallowed space. Elizabeth knew about barn cats and when she realized Cat was pregnant on one of her last visits, she could tell her time was very near.

"Cat, cat, where are you? "She called.

Cat called back with a quiet meow. The sound came from what was sure to be a safe hiding place on the second story of the tiny barn. The timbers were weakened and Elizabeth didn't dare climb up to peek but she would stay and make sure the cat safely delivered her litter. Elizabeth drifted off, lulled by the sun, the fire's warmth and the waiting. Fairies and beautiful ladies danced within her head.

"Good day maiden!"

Elizabeth darted up, not quite sure if the salutation was part of her dream.

"Good day sir." She replied, instantly, shaking herself to make sure she was awake. Standing up, she was face to face with her friend, the handsome lad with no name. A mischievous grin lit up his face and it was easy for Elizabeth to stare back at him, for his presence was playful and good-natured. His tousled yellow hair and sparkling green eyes pulled her in, asking her to kindly take note of all that he was, lest she forget him. He was as she remembered him yet somehow better. He was real and so was she. She closed her eyes, and breathed in a deep breath. Once she was content to have taken in his presence, her demeanor turned playfully accusatory.

"What are you doing here?" she asked. Not waiting for his answer. "This is a place that only I come to. Oh, just my cat and me. She is about to give birth up there in the rafters at this very moment."

Elizabeth pointed upward and at the same time was struck with a thought both peculiar and familiar. How odd it was of her to trust this stranger again so readily. Lost in her thoughts,

Elizabeth tried desperately to acclimate herself to the feelings that were taking root within her. She somehow knew within the depth of her being that this man was to be trusted, just as she now knew within her very bones, that most others, most of whom she knew nearly the whole of her life, thus far, were not. Despite her readiness to accuse him of invading upon her privacy, she wanted more than anything for him to stay.

"Your cat you say?" said the lad smiling with all his might.

"Yes, I found her here and I have been caring for her." Elizabeth answered.

"Well that cat is a very smart cat, for it has tricked the both of us into being its master. I have been caring for the cat also. See here I brought scraps for her to eat." With that he opened a small sack and showed Elizabeth the left over morsels from what looked to be the carcass of a small bird.

"I didn't know she needed help with her meals. She seems to catch plenty of mice in this old freezer and she has a grand time doing it too!" cited Elizabeth. She really was a bit annoyed with him now, thinking her cat was actually his.

"I do not believe that we have been properly introduced to one another and yet we share or shall I say serve, the same feline?" the lad interjected.

Elizabeth continued. "Yes, this seems to be a dilemma and we shall right it this moment. What are you called Sir?" she inquired.

"My name is Demetri. Demetri La Peurta." He said bowing to her.

In one brief moment a shred of terror filled her being. This lad had a Spanish surname and Father possessed a dreadful hate for the Spanish. Elizabeth recalled a time a couple of years ago when Father cursed loudly and created a ruckus that ran throughout the estate. It had to do with Phillip II of Spain, taking control of the sea, as if it belonged to his country instead of to our Queen. Day in and day out, there was always talk of the bastard Spanish, until later that year the Queen's navy defeated them in the Spanish Armada. Was her new friend a spy for the army? The way he sneaks around and with such an unusual name, perhaps she could not trust him after all.

"My lady, what is your name?" He asked looking straight into her wandering gaze, interrupting her thoughts. Terror faded as she looked at him, slightly embarrassed. His eyes of green glistened translucent in the sun.

"I am Elizabeth Cumberland. My family owns the Cumberland Estate. My father Gregory is an influential trader on the high seas and he has many ties to Her Majesty." She hoped her words put him in his place, if he needed putting. "How is it that I know not of your family or who you are and yet you seem to make your home somewhere very near to my own? You are a mysterious man." She questioned him accusingly.

"Mysterious? Maybe I am but the truth is I am here doing work for my cousin who lives a quarter days walk from this barn. He is clearing some land for a farm and I do much of the labor for him. The Lord who owns the land was kind enough to allow my cousin to do so. My family is not from England."

"Are you Spanish?" She asked hesitantly. Coming right to the point was a strong suit. She had not time for banter or allusions. She needed to know. He didn't look the least bit like a Spaniard, nor speak like one, at least not like any of the Spanish traders she had seen visiting

Father, before the trouble all began. They were mostly dark and olive skinned and their command of the English language had an unusual flair. Demetri had a fair complexion and light green eyes and he spoke as if he was trained in the most upstanding schools. She stared at him waiting for his answer and then she began to blush, realizing how forward she had just been.

Demetri moved in very close and she could feel his breath upon her cheek as he explained himself. He whispered and the words rolled off his mouth and landed gently upon her cheeks, like a soft kiss.

"My mother is English and my father is Spanish. They fell in love despite their country's differences." He moved in closer still, his lips a mere inch from her own. "They went to his country to live." Demetri touched her cheek with his finger tip and then just as suddenly, turned quickly on his heels. "My first name comes from a distant relative, who lived among the Mediterranean Sea, for my mother thought I should have such a bold name. But, nevertheless, I do believe I have mostly English blood for I am mostly of the English persuasion. I love this countryside and the forests with all its richness and magic. I wish to live here and make this my home."

Demetri swept his hands up in a grand gesture before lowering them and returning to her side. Grabbing her hand, he looked straight into her eyes. She once again could feel his warm breath upon her face.

"But it seems that your family owns much of this land, you and the family Hartford."

The mere mention of James' family name sent a sharp jolt through her belly. Trembling, she pushed him away, her voice silent and try as she might, she could not speak, the words stuck in her throat.

"Lady Elizabeth, are you all right?"

Demetri had not seemed to notice her push and he kindly placed his hand upon her shoulder. As he touched her, a wave of relief washed over her body, clearing the pain in her midsection.

"Perhaps one day you may make this country your home?" The question was more of a request than inquiry.

Together they sat near the fire. Demetri did not answer. She knew why, for even if he wanted to come to her land and live, he would have to do so as a servant or laborer and it was highly unlikely that a man of his status would ever own land. One as young and handsome as he could hope, she thought. He looked at her solemnly and then it was she who comforted him. She lay her hand upon his leg and gently patted him.

"I shall check on the Cat!" Demetri jumped up with his natural vigor in tact. "Cat, Cat, how are you? We are here for you!" Demetri whispered in a most loving tone as he brought a rickety old ladder to where Cat hid. Carefully he checked each rung to see if the old thing would hold him. The first rung broke, then the second. Moving the ladder aside he peered up at Cat. "I do not see any newborn kittens yet, but she does not seem interested in these tasty treats either. I shall leave her be."

Demetri returned to his seat. They stared into the fire without a word for many a moment. "The women of the forest... Are they not the most intriguing beings you have ever seen?"

"Yes, Demetri, I love to watch them pray. They seem so full of life and yet if they were caught in their prayers they would surely be put to death. I have fear in my heart for their safety."

"They are safe where they reside. They know how to remain safe. A new babe was born to them this past eve, a healthy girl child."

"In the world I come from men with evil in their hearts want to kill the women of the forest. I hardly think they are safe!" she said. "And how do you know a babe was born to them?" she questioned, not quite believing him, yet excited at the thought.

"Because they are my friends and I have just come from visiting them. I, like you, saw them one night as I was out exploring the forest. They saw me watching them and they let me. They know who to fear and who to trust."

"Are they witches Demetri?" she asked in wonder.

"I don't know if they are witches or not, but I do know that what they want is to just live in peace. They mean no harm to anyone. It is the others who fear them, simply because they have different beliefs and do not see God as they do."

"Yes, but God is very clear about who He is and what is right and wrong, Demetri. At least that is what I am told." Elizabeth stopped as a deep sadness engulfed her. "I am saddened to think that God is so rigid and unloving as to condemn most everything as it exists in this world."

Elizabeth had just committed a crime with her words, yet she did not fear the consequences of her actions, instead she continued admitting to this stranger what was really true in her heart. She must trust him, she must. "I believe God is as a wholly loving deity, not a condemning man. And in my country as you right well know, we wage wars and kill those who are of another faith, the same faith that I once was. I really do not understand it at all. I ponder these thoughts many moments during my day."

Demetri took her hand and looking directly into her eyes. "Elizabeth, I ponder the same thoughts and I know not the answers to such questions. I know that I am here with you and that the beautiful ladies told me where to find you. I know they live in kindness and goodness and how could that possibly be wrong?"

"They told you to find me here in this old barn?" she asked.

Demetri moved in closer, so close that again she could feel his breath upon her. Gently he touched her face and kissed her mouth. "Yes." He whispered.

Elizabeth had no fear only a wave of precious bliss flowing through her body and then she boldly kissed him back, surprised that she knew how to return a kiss, for no lad had ever laid his lips upon hers before this moment. The spot on her bottom lip where James defiled her began to sear as if an open wound. Demetri touched the spot and then kissed it several times. No more pain, just sweet relief filled her whole being and she sighed deeply. Demetri pulled back and stood up.

"I must check Cat. I believe I hear mewing." said her new friend.

The only thing Elizabeth heard was the strong steady beat of her heart as it pounded through her ears and pulsated throughout her entire body. Demetri set the ladder against the stone wall, heaved his leg up onto the highest rungs and lifted his body up. Elizabeth watched his every move as if she were now a part of him. Demetri peered into the corner and jumped back down with a big grin on his face.

"She has three kittens, Elizabeth! Come see!"

 Elizabeth hurried over and stopped for a moment looking at the ladder.

"Come, I will lift you up to see." said Demetri gesturing to Elizabeth.

Demetri held her around her waist, tightly yet gently and lifted her with ease. Cat was laying atop the grasses, licking three slimy tiny, creatures that looked more like snails without the shells than kittens.

"I see them, Demetri. Do you think she shall have more?"

"I do not know, perhaps we can wait a while longer and see." Elizabeth was sure he kept his arms around her waist longer than necessary and she allowed him to do so, for his touch was ever so inviting.

She also allowed him to sit so very close to her as they joked and shared stories of their lives for the next hour. The light mood carried away the time and Cat eventually gave birth to one more, tiny kitten. It was however a sickly runt and died shortly thereafter. Demetri buried it in a small grave next to door and Elizabeth made a cross out of twigs to mark the grave. Together they said a prayer. Elizabeth looked up at Demetri as he gazed silently at the kitten's grave. It was at that very moment that she knew that he would be her friend forever. It mattered not whether he was a Spaniard or Englishman, a lord or a laborer, a Catholic or a recusant. None of that mattered after this day, for they shared an intimacy that went beyond the confusing boundaries of her life.

The week passed and Elizabeth went off to meet Demetri every chance she could. He was always at the barn at exact time as she. He stole away from his cousin's each day after he finished the grueling task of clearing the land. Elizabeth had a feeling he ran most of the way to meet her at the barn, for how could he get to her so quickly after such a hard day of work. He had large callouses on his hands and his body was quite raw from working through the damp winter months. Each day Elizabeth brought him delicacies that she stole from Cook's pantry. Pastries and meat pies, fruits and cinnamon crusted custard. She laughed as he gobbled down every morsel, her heart full as she cared for him in such a simple way. Demetri told her that it was she who warmed him and gave him reason to work hard. Elizabeth was very grateful for their time together, for it allowed her a freedom she had never before known. Gone were the frightening thoughts of caring for her brother. Father and grandfather's plans for her life seemed far removed from the lively and contented moments she shared with her new friend. Time went on like this through the winter. The days were her very best yet.

Chapter Eight

Spring was approaching and the weather had grown slightly warmer. Elizabeth dreamt most every night of the ladies of the forest. They came to her as angels and surrounded her with love. They did not say much to her in the way of words, instead they gave her feelings and fleeting thoughts wrapped in warm energy. Elizabeth was awaiting word as to when she could visit them next, yet no such words had come as of yet. Elizabeth had however received two distinct messages from the lovely ladies of the forest. The night that Cat gave birth she dreamt that she heard them singing these words, over and over in their beautiful, otherworldly melodic voices, *"When you follow your heart, you are following your soul, Goddess is alive in your heart and soul…"* Since this dream she oftentimes found herself singing the phrase as she went about her studies and especially when she ventured out. As she sang, she always felt a veil of protective calm come over her, different than anything she had ever experienced before. She felt the hands of the women, patting her back and urging her on, no matter what she was doing. The other message came from the woman in white and it went like this; *"Be true to yourself."* The woman appeared to her standing in an open field. Elizabeth had her arms outstretched and the woman was giving her extremely important instructions. Along with the words, the woman in white handed Elizabeth a book. Each time the book was handed to her, the woman spoke those words. *"Be true to yourself"*, and then disappeared. Immediately Elizabeth could see what looked to be groups of people coming towards her. The people were also familiar, yet not in a loving, kind way as with the women of the forest and Demetri. These were the people that wanted her to do what they pleased, what they insisted, and what they decided. Elizabeth did not quite know what it all meant, yet each time she met with Demetri, she was able to be calm and relaxed. There were no no pretenses and formality to interrupt the natural ease with which the conversations and actions between them flowed. There was a simple comfort and that unfamiliar, familiar ease and understanding. That must be what the woman meant. She did not know for sure, but she had made a vow to herself that she would find out what that meant if it took her to her dying day!

Elizabeth walked through the forest, searching for lady slippers on her way to meet Demetri. Although she knew they did not bloom until late spring she hoped to find some anyway. Her heart was light and she hummed as she went. *"I follow my heart and I am blessed...."* She spied a tiny mound of crocus and she sang, "thank you Goddess". Carefully picking the flowers, she made a tiny bouquet. She entered the barn as the sun was lowering past midday and was greeted by Demetri as he sat on the dirt floor with Cat in his lap. The kittens were happily playing with a sprig of green that popped up through the ground. Demetri stood up as she entered and cat went flying off his lap, landing perfectly on all fours as cats are apt to do.

"Hello my mistress", he said bowing to her. He knew her to be of noble heritage and he treated her just so.

"Hello, kind sir." This had become their ritual each time they saw one another again. They spoke as friends and equals when together and were quite informal, yet there was an air of importance between them. They were important to one another, thought Elizabeth, because of the love and friendship they shared. Unlike that of the bond between her father and brother and her, this was different. It was as if the bond they formed started many eons ago in a time neither of them remembered. Perhaps in my dreams, thought Elizabeth as she smiled at her friend.

"How are you today my fine maiden?" asked Demetri. He took her hand and gently kissed it.

"I am quite fine, thank you." She handed him the small bouquet and he pretended to be very impressed. I shall set them here and try to find a proper container for them. He looked around the barn to no avail. He started to walk outside, but she called to him.

"Demetri come here, do not waste any more time. I must go back to my home early today, for our family is having guests and I must attend to them." Elizabeth instantly became extremely uncomfortable as she spoke of the life beyond this barn. Demetri quickly went to her and put his arm around her shoulder.

"What is it Elizabeth, you seem disturbed. Is everyone well in your home?" he gently asked.

Elizabeth's panic faded and the calm protection that his touch lent, melted into her. She had told him almost everything about her family; Mother's illness, the attack, and Henry's illness. She told him about her father's worried, tired existence, how much she cherished Henry and how they spent their youth in constant companionship. Elizabeth told Demetri everything except for anything that had to do with James. She did not wish to confide in Demetri anything regarding James, for she was sure that if she did so it would hurt them both somehow. In spite of her comfort when with Demetri and their growing affection, Elizabeth's fear of James was growing stronger each day. What brought her the most fear was the truth. The truth of the obligation she held to her family to marry whoever would yield the greatest profit for them all, in both monetary gain and power. She thought Father would never force her to marry James, yet her grandfather was a different story altogether. Each week when it came time for Grandfather's visit, try as she might to avoid him, he cornered her, and each time he did so he would tell her the same thing.

"You are of marrying age, my dear and it will not be long until you are wed. I do hope you know that if you marry a gentleman who has his home close to yours, you will be able to see your brother and father regularly." He barked the words as if they were orders, rather than a suggestion.

Elizabeth did not like the tone of such a statement, yet she could never say such to her grandfather, for he was a Duke and had much power. Elizabeth would have agreed to this assumption, before she met Demetri. Now, even the promise of being close to her beloved father and brother after she wed did not sway her, not anymore, for she did not want to marry any nobleman of royalty no matter where it may land her. This she knew to be true. Demetri would be the man she would choose to marry, if she were allowed, if she lived in a different place, a different time.

Her mind was reeling with these thoughts as Demetri stood looking at her with concern in his eyes laced with a bit of skepticism. She did not lie to him and did not wish to withhold anything from him, yet she thought it best that she not speak of what she would go home to this evening. James of Hartford was to be the family's dinner guest and Grandfather would be in attendance.

"Nothing has happened of great importance. I dislike my father's choice of dinner guests and I would much rather spend the long afternoon with you and return home to take my evening meal in the kitchen with Henry and Priscilla. It is such a sight to see him ogle over her." said Elizabeth half-heartedly.

She tried to hide her sadness with a laugh. Demetri acted satisfied with her explanation for the moment, seemingly having other things on his mind. Looking at her intently he pulled her close and wrapped both his arms around her with gentle ease. Until this moment they had only kissed that one day many weeks ago, yet she had wanted to kiss him again so very many times since. Demetri stared into her eyes with such intensity that it took her breath away. Staring back, she pushed her body into his, or rather she was pulled into his strong torso, ever so quickly and easefully. A delightfully tantalizing force took hold of her as Demetri gently touched her face and kissed her mouth. Elizabeth was drawn into his lips, as the enticing power captivated and filled her body. She longed to be deeper in his embrace and she kissed him back with fervor. How very delicious he tasted and smelled and how very pleasing kissing him made her whole body tingle with sheer ecstasy, the likes of she had never imagined. His mouth moved slowly and gently from the bottom of her lips to the top, his tongue playfully exploring. Elizabeth continued to caresses his lips with her own. He lowered his mouth, moving slowly down her chin and onto her neck. The touch of his lips upon her neck sent sparks through her veins. His mouth was rough from the sun and wind and it caught on her skin, sending shudders deep into her body.

"I love you Elizabeth. I have felt as if I have known you for all of time." Demetri's hot breath made her body perspire in response. "I know we are not wed; yet I want to take you into my arms forever. I do not wish you any harm, only happiness and goodness. I do not wish to take you unless you are willing to be my wife." The words landed on every inch of her.

Elizabeth was not sure how to act or what to do with these words of love and affection, so she let them be true, let them fuel the feelings of intense pleasure that had awakened by this man's touch and by the arousing pleasure of his kisses. She pushed into his embrace and there was nothing she could do but let him continue to talk and kiss her and touch her. That was all she wanted and needed right now.

Demetri's hands ran up and down her backside, as he continued to kiss and speak deep words of regard for her. "Each day as I work the land, it is you who gives me the strength to continue. Meeting with you gives me all that I need. I spend hours upon hours thinking of you, your scent, your touch, your smile and your laugh." Demetri caressed Elizabeth's hair removing her combs and clips. Her golden tresses fell along her shoulders releasing a scent of lavender. Demetri breathed deeply as he continued. "I want to make you my wife, no matter what it is I must do. I know I am only a commoner and a Spaniard at that, but we will find a way, I know I must…we must…" He stopped talking and continued to kiss her lips, more forcefully with each moment. Elizabeth took each breath, each touch and each moment in fully. She was feeling the most incredible feelings and yet did not know what might be done to fill this deep and gaping opening that had been revealed to her by his touch and his words.

"I have talked to the woman of the forest about this, they told me to follow my heart and if I did so I would be blessed…"

When Elizabeth heard those words, her entire being grew vivid and strong, as if a large lantern inside of her was lit from above. She could not speak and instead she continued to kiss him as tears fell from her eyes. She could not stop them. Demetri kissed her wet cheeks and drank in her tears.

"I love you Elizabeth." He whispered. "The elder woman of the forest told me I would meet you and she told me we would fall in love. She also told me that it would be many lifetimes before we would be able to live fully our love. I think she is wrong. We can fully live our love now."

Elizabeth did not understand what Demetri was saying. Confusion set in and she was only able to take in the very last few words. "I love you Demetri, let us live true to our love now, true to our hearts." Her eyes were closed and she did not want to come out of the lovely trance she was in.

Demetri stroked her hair as she lay her head upon his chest. She searched for the beating sound of his heart. It was there, the rhythm of his heart, loud and clear. It must be moving with his love for me, she thought. I have the same love beating in my heart. A very warm sensation radiated through her body and a painful yearning to have him touch her in places that were warming and moist was taking over her entire being. He must have felt it too for his kiss grew stronger and his fingers moved deftly in between the buttons on her bodice. Her body danced with the touch of his fingers as they squeezed her flesh ever so tightly.

"You are my beloved, my true love." She whispered. Her heart was making sense of the world. Not the world outside, but this world, within. The world that contained only her and Demetri and this feeling beyond words. Demetri surrounded her with his breath, his touch, his being and she was taken in once more.

"Demetri I feel as if you must touch every part of me and never stop. What is this delightful yearning that is taking over my whole being?"

"I believe it is called lust my dear one." His kisses continued and his hands traveled inside her skirt gently stroking her bare legs.

"Lust! It is a sin…or so the church tells me." She continued, breathless as the lust overtook her. "If this feeling is a sin, then I wish to sin forevermore."

Demetri kissed her chest and lifted his hands up through her skirts and bodice and onto her bare breasts. She felt as if she would burst as her whole being ached for him to continue to do whatsoever it was that he was doing. She untied her dress and let it slip to the ground. He untied her petticoat and shift, fumbling with each loop as he went.

"I am so very glad that spring is upon us and you are no longer so heavily clad Elizabeth. It would be such a chore to remove yards and yards of undergarments when this lust is so overpowering." Demetri's familiar grin lit up his face. She smiled back at him.

When the last of the dressings were undone, Elizabeth stood naked feeling no shame at all. Demetri looked at her whole body, and said "you are so beautiful, so very, very beautiful." Elizabeth was surprised by those words, hearing them come from the mouth of the man she loved felt very different from any time she had ever heard them before. Of course, no one had ever exclaimed such compliments to her as she stood bare naked. Such comments were held for the loveliness of the garments she wore or the perfection of her hair braids, but now, she was being adored for that which lay beneath her coverings. Her long, lithesome silken legs, her curved hips, her slightly rounded belly and the soft roundness of her womanhood, her creamy golden skin and the pinkness of her nipples were being adored. It seemed so odd, yet so right and natural. She wanted him to undress so she could admire him too. Demetri reached out to her and pulled her close. He took her breasts in his hand and caressed them gently. He kissed the pink roundness and moved his lips down over her belly to her thighs. His fingers rolled ever so gently over the long jagged scar on the back of her thigh, inflicted by her own mother, as he pulled her closer and kissed her precisely between her legs. She could feel his warm tongue tickle her there too. What sensations he was creating for her, the likes of which she had never ever known. Demetri knelt down and gently turned her body around continuing to kiss the top of her leg, exactly where her scar was. As he did so, the sadness from that time dissipated. His lips continued to move gently up and over the curves of her body kissing her until she could no longer stand still.

"Demetri, I want to feel your whole body, naked and close to mine!" He pulled off his shirt and trousers and came to stand so very close to her. Now it was her turn to touch him. She put her palms upon his chest slowly gliding her hands up and down his torso. His skin was smooth and a light golden color, very similar to her own. She closed her eyes as her hands continued to travel his body, taking in each inch of him, his feel etching into her mind. She ran her hands around his shoulders and slid onto his upper back, his body, sweat soaked to the touch. Elizabeth leaned into Demetri and he caught her with his mouth.

Suddenly a bubble of laughter erupted within Elizabeth. She felt it rise up from her belly as Demetri tickled her with his soft whiskers. The laughter poured out and Elizabeth doubled over.

"What?" he demanded. "What is it that is so humorous?"

"You...ah, well..."Elizabeth could not contain her laughter and she continued giggling heartily. Demetri stood, saying not a word.

"You, your... well..." she continued with her warm laughter, pointing down to the area of his body that had suddenly protruded.

"Come close to me please, it is not at all polite to laugh at a man when he is in such a state." He said, pulling her into him. It was then Elizabeth realized why his body reacted so. The awareness bolted through her body, sending yet another array of pleasing sensations into places she did not know existed.

They both were full of such joy and mirth and nothing but this pleasure stood between them. No clothing, no title, no status, nothing. Elizabeth reeled in the truth of life at that moment. It was just she and her lover. It was just two people naked and alive within the ecstasy. "How did this happen, my love? How is it that you and I were brought together in such a perfect manner?"

He started to answer, but she put her finger over his mouth. "Shush, we shall talk no more." The laughter and joy had settled into her and now she felt her body pulsing to feel him touch her. Demetri responded by pulling her closer and closer, so she could feel the tightness of his muscles, the wet smoothness of his arms and legs against her own. She cast her gaze downward and allowed the sensations of longing mixed with great love overwhelm her and she found herself wanting to kiss him in all the places he had kissed her. She kissed his mouth and his neck and his chest. He pressed hard against her. She was safe and loved, desirous and desired beyond imagination.

"Let us sin all throughout the day and night Demetri. You must do something more to ease this ache, your body has created. She pulled his hand down to her aching and he readily touched her, ever so gently, his hand moved round and round her womanhood until she could stand it no more. Elizabeth was lost in the pleasures that were overwhelming her senses. She needed him to enter into her, to fill her. She took his hands and brought one to her mouth and kissed each of his rough calloused fingers. The scent and moisture was her own and she very much liked it. They stood together, her back up against the roughness of the side of the barn. "Enter me Demetri." The sensations pushed and pulled at her, making her desire a fulfillment that lay far beyond what she had ever known.

He took her hand, and led her to the pile of clothes scattered on the barn floor. He lay her down and opened her legs. She could barely contain herself from want as he lay his body atop hers and entered into her body with his. He moved himself deeper and deeper inside and she moved too, feverishly, for she was sure she would not ever have enough of this most potent and powerful urging.

"I am sorry that I laughed at you. I see why God has made you so." She said breathlessly. You fit into me so perfectly. You must always be within me Demetri." Elizabeth looked deeply into her lover's eyes as their bodies transcended all of time.

"I want to be with you forever and I give you my promise I will be. Whatever I must do … I give you my heart today and always, my love." Demetri whispered the words as he moved inside her body."

"I feel you touching my heart as we move together. Can you feel it Demetri? You are touching my heart with your very body," whispered Elizabeth, not knowing where these words were coming from.

"Yes Elizabeth, I am." He answered.

And with that they spoke no more, just moved together, their bodies taking her to places of wonder, thrill and bliss. The movements were so very natural even when the force of the intensity of the union brought her into waves and waves of delirious delight. Her voice called out to him and she feared she had awoken the dead with her shout out to the heavens. And yes, she cared not.

They lay together in complete contentment afterward for what seemed like hours yet the sun had not yet set. Elizabeth knew she had to leave very soon or explain her whereabouts to her father. She arose and began dressing. Demetri watched her and soon he was ready to fill her again, for she could tell by the way his body grew.

"Now I know why this funny thing happens to you and I do believe it is not funny at all, only quite wonderful." She bent down to kiss him and he quickly pulled her down onto the dirt floor next to him. She did not resist. He rolled atop her body lifted her skirts and found his way easily inside her body. She let out a deep sigh. Pleasure mounted. What power lay in this act of expressing love, she thought as her body arched upward, pulling him closer into her hips with the strength of her sinewy legs. A slight fear crept into her mind. What if this was the first and last time she was ever to be locked in such an embrace? What if… Demetri pushed himself deeper into her and held himself rigid and tight. Staring intently at her, his green eyes told her what she needed to know. A loud groan escaped her throat as he stared into her soul and released a thousand jolts of delightful warmth inside her. For many moments their bodies quivered in unison. She would not doubt. They were now forever bonded.

"Demetri, I must return home." She whispered softly in his ear, caressing the sweaty lobe with her tongue. "I will be out again tomorrow after the sun has past noon. We will meet then."

"Very well my love." He said, sliding out of her body. He lay next to her as she up to finish dressing. "You must go, I know. Remember I will make you my wife so you may never leave me alone and naked and laying on a dirt floor again." Demetri smiled and his green eyes sparkled.

Elizabeth smoothed her skirts and checked her hair, all the while smiling broadly. "Come, get dressed and you may walk me part of the way to my estate." She did not want their time together to end. They walked so very close to each other, as if they were no longer two people, but one. They were one, yet a bit more than that; an incredibly pleasing and gratifying more. It was hard to part that day, yet Elizabeth knew it would not be long until they were reunited. She had an important job to do now. She would be putting a stop to something that had been brewing a very, very long time.

When Elizabeth arrived back at the estate, she knew she must change her clothes quickly, for the meal would be served very soon. She flew through the hallways, beckoning her chamber maids to help her dress. James carriage was already outside and she did not want him, nor her father to see her with her hair in tangles, dress crumpled and dirt stained. Three very young maids rushed to her side, eager to finally assist their lady. They would do. She would be dressing to dissuade James and otherwise deter him from viewing her as a woman, suited in any way for marriage. The young servants would help her pick proper attire suited for a spinster, or very young maiden.

"Find me my most precious and innocent frock!" She commanded Molly, barely a decade old. The lass picked out the perfect garment; a pale blue frock with a high lace collar and lacey sleeves that covered her hands. Jane brushed the snarly clumps of Elizabeth's tresses, pulling out dried leaves and tiny twigs as she went. Elizabeth did not think the girls would suspect what she had been up to, for they were mere babes themselves and they would think that she must have been out laying in the gardens as she was apt to do. It was of utmost importance no one held any suspicion of her whereabouts and her activities. Her very life depended on it. Her life and Demetri's.

They all worked feverishly to complete their task and the result was as intended. Gazing at the craftsmanship in her silver hand mirror, she let out a mischievous squeal of delight and caught herself right away. She could not let on how very sensual and womanly she felt underneath the sweet and virtuous façade. Bringing the mirror closer, she continued the once over. Hair up in a tight bun, no wisps or curls anywhere to be found, no perfume, no rouge and certainly no jewels. The cornflower blue dress adorned with tiny dots of white fabric was suited for a babe's nursery. The dress did not fit her curves well, for it had been made at least two sizes too large by a seamstress who was long ago fired. Elizabeth stared at her reflection. Well, her cheeks were rosy and her eyes did sparkle, but she knew there was nothing she could do about that. She had lay with her lover today and that was most likely why she had the look and feel of joy bounding from her being. She could still taste his scent in her mouth and feel his body in the warm folds of her own. He had left her giddy and desiring more. She would just have to remember not to smile. She tried a few scowling faces out as she gazed into the mirror. She did not realize that all three of her maids were staring at her as she tried to look angry, puzzled and stern. Giggles erupted from each one, and Elizabeth started in with her own laughter.

"You are excused now." She said to them, walking past holding her kerchief to her mouth, trying to keep the laughter in and the most appropriate scowl on.

Entering the dining hall, the fully lit chandeliers caught her attention. Gazing up and into their glow she thought how lovely it would be to be standing in this very place with Demetri on her arm, bringing him to meet her father. Glancing at the long table covered with the fine white linen carpet she could not help but stare at the empty chair at the head of the table where her mother should sit. Perhaps Father would let her sit there this evening as he had at the Christmas festivities. She used to feel safe at her father's side, yet now she was not sure if this was still so. Watching the servants scurry as they set the silver platters upon the table she was brought back to the moment. She must stay aware and be very careful to avoid James. Slowly making her way through the room, she watched all, like a rabbit in the forest glen, she could not afford to be caught off guard. Nodding a greeting to the Marquis and Marquise of Deveron, she thought it best to avoid being in too close proximity to them. They were, as usual in a corner chatting amongst themselves in their familiar secretive manner. Those two were known to take in too much spirits, gossip incessantly and cause one form or another of an uproar at every gathering they attended. The Deveron's were always invited though, for their talents to entertain. The Marquise covered her mouth with her cheverill glove, eyes darting to and fro, most likely looking for their next victims, thought Elizabeth with a smile. They did not threaten her, she found them amusing, but tonight, there would be no banter with the likes of them. There was never before anything they could threaten her with. No scandal, no intrigue, until now that is. Elizabeth continued to span the room and spotted her uncle, the Earl of Winslow. Elizabeth was surprised to see him, for she had not seen her uncle since she was a very young girl and Father had not mentioned that he was to be among the guests. Dinner gatherings were quite rare in her household and when one occurred it was usually common knowledge among the household staff who would be attending. The earl was talking very quietly to James in another corner of the dining room. Many secrets going on here, this evening she thought and she was sure she had the most luscious one of all, one she would share with no one, at least not now. Just then James spotted her and she saw him give a knowing glance to her uncle. Strange, she thought, I did not know Uncle even knew that vile man. James rushed over to Elizabeth, so quickly she was sure he had wheels on his feet. She was not able to escape into conversation with anyone else before James was standing directly in front of her, grabbing her hand to bring it up to his mouth. She pulled her hand back, and he pulled her whole body forcefully toward his, kissing her hand with a deep slow languishing moist kiss. Elizabeth thought she would fly out of her lace covered tent dress.

"Good evening fair lady." He smiled a smile filled with wickedness directed entirely at Elizabeth as he held her hand tightly in his grip. She knew this game and did not like it any more now than she had before. "I hope you will sing for us this evening" he grinned.

As any proper lady of her day, Elizabeth was taught to sing a perfect melody, but she could never do so in front of an audience. The thought of performing made her extremely ill at ease and the kiss, sent her reeling. With an unfamiliar bravado, she had a thought. She must gather herself together and face this monster now. Elizabeth freed her hand and pulled out a fan from within the folds of the pale blue camouflage. She opened it with the flick of her wrist and shielded her face. I am not feeling very well just now and I hope to make it through dinner without having to retire. It very well may even be the plague by the way I am feeling, and to think of how you kissed my skin. I hope you will not fall ill." she lied.

"You look well to me. I think you jest, Elizabeth!" James said laughing a great booming laugh. All heads turned towards them. Elizabeth felt the stares like tiny daggers burning her skin.

The bravado was failing. The Marquise of Deveron nodded her head. Elizabeth could barely contain her outrage. The guests were thinking they were flirting. She had to do something. James continued his banter.

"You seem to have a certain glow about you and a certain familiar scent." He said, eying her with a look of both disdain and satisfaction. He lowered his head toward her, peering over her fan. Elizabeth backed away in a panic.

"Yes, I do believe it is lust that I smell." He said eerily, touching her cheek ever so gently.

She couldn't believe her ears. How could he know? Elizabeth fumbled with the fan, dropping it to the floor. James quickly reached for it and she remained upright, standing tall, knowing it was not proper for a lady to bend down to pick anything up. Elizabeth's eyes secretly darted in the same suspicious way she had witnessed from the Marquise just moments before. The guests stared back in her direction, her face burned where James touched her and the stares made it that much worse. James retrieved her golden fan, but did not give it to her, instead he held it tightly closed and stood staring directly into Elizabeth's pale blue eyes. Her mind was questioning and she looked directly at him, not wanting to shift her gaze away. She would face him down. She had to know. Could James had followed her. Could he know where she had been and what she was doing? Surely not! No, he could not have. She tried to console herself but now her entire face burned and fear filled her soul. She dropped her gaze. She was outwardly distressed and James was quite giddy.

He leaned in closer offering her the fan. "I am hoping that what I suspect is not true, my dear, I am hoping that you are still a virgin, for the way your father keeps you hidden away, I cannot imagine anything but. There are no men of title asking for your hand. This I know." His voice became low and barely audible as he continued. Elizabeth had to move in closer to be able to hear his words. What did he know? "No man of title…" he continued, "or perhaps it is a servant boy. Whomever it is I shall put an end to him, you can take my word as a promise." He handed her the fan and walked away.

No words would form upon Elizabeth's lips. She was crestfallen that this audacious man somehow had privy to her most sacred thoughts. She and Demetri had a blessed union. No, they were not yet officially wed, yet they had consummated the marriage, she was Demetri's wife, and up until this moment, her secret love affair was only between her and Demetri, blessed by the heavenly women of the forest. Knowing now that James somehow held knowledge of her love, left her incredibly unsettled and she knew not what to do. Her body was eerily light and feathery, her mind numb. She felt her life blood drain and she knew she was no longer carrying a glow. In her weakened state, she sailed through the rest of the evening like a ghost. Her spirit had left her being and had somehow become one with Demetri. She felt his touch and inhaled his scent. Yes, she was not here in the estate, she was with him, alone somewhere in the forest, safe, loved and protected. While her body greeted guests, turned her mouth up in an unnatural smile, sipped pear wine, felt the slither of the eels in puree slide down her throat, wiped the cinnamon sauce, with the napkin, her heart and soul were elsewhere. She cared not, for all evening long, she was held in the arms of her true love while the rest of the world made a fuss about the silver and the latest knight to be hung for treason and the gossip of the royal family. Nothing touched her that evening, for she was no longer present.

Sometime after dinner ended when the men retired to the study to discuss the true nature of this dinner, Elizabeth found herself heading to the kitchen. She heard a voice coming from somewhere deep within her, telling her firmly "come to the kitchen, we need you Mistress

Elizabeth, come now." The voice sounded like Cookie, and Elizabeth heeded its command. She excused herself, whispering to her father, that she going to the kitchen to check on the staff. As it was proper for the Lady of the Estate to do, her father nodded his approval, despite the glaring stares of both his father in law and James of Hartford. Elizabeth did not see the stares of the two men, but she did feel them, trying to get inside of her heart. They could do no such thing. Walking confidently into the kitchen, entering into the hustle and bustle put her immediately at ease and her spirit returned back to her body, causing her to heave a great sigh of relief. The tears fell immediately and she could do nothing to stop them. She quietly released thousands of tears onto the sleeves of her pale blue dress, soaking the fabric and lace into a sloppy mess.

Slowly items began appearing around her, first a cup of strong night brew, then a platter of dariole with cream piled so high, it looked like a mountain of clouds, then a fine linen napkin, with a gold pin in the shape of a swan. Elizabeth slowly drank the brew, put her fingers into the wisps of cream and tasted the delicate sweetness. She held the napkin in her hand, not bothering to pin it to her collar. She used it to dab the tears that continued to fall.

When she had her fill of love from her staff, she stood up and thought to speak her gratitude. Cookie stopped her, pulled her in close and spoke herself.

"Lady Elizabeth, Master Henry will now escort you to your room, for ya look like you have a might need to retire." Cookie gently hugged Elizabeth and handed her a small sack. "Go on now, I will see to it that your father knows you had to retire after you nearly fainted right into the platter of left over venison."

Elizabeth nodded. Henry took her hand and walked her to her bed chambers without a word. Elizabeth did not question Henry's absence of banter, for she was not in a state to wonder, nor converse. Elizabeth did not bother to undress, she had not the strength. She did however open the sack from Cookie and found within it several different small sachets of herbs. She knew this was from Madeline. Opening one sachet she put a few pinches of the herbs in her mouth chewing slowly and firmly, crushing the bits between her teeth. She chewed as she lay upon her bedcovers and until the sleep overcame her. She slept hard and dreamt of Demetri filling her and touching her heart once more.

Chapter Nine

Demetri came to the barn again the next day yet he did not arrive until near sundown. "I am very sorry Lady Elizabeth", he said as he bowed down to Elizabeth and took her hand. She smiled at him and pulled him into her arms. All the passion she had held in for the last day poured out to him. She desperately needed to feel his body around hers, to be held by him in this lifetime and not in the world of dreams or dread.

"You came to me my love! I have missed you so." She pulled him closer and closer, kissing him on his mouth, her tongue darting feverishly, taking in his taste. The need for him was consuming her, for her body and spirit came alive in his presence, by his touch, and with his love.

He kissed her fervently in return and soon they lay naked together making love as if they may never see one another again. Being apart would be agonizing for them both now. Elizabeth had felt each hour pass that afternoon as she waited in the barn for him, as if she were being dragged across a parched dirt roadway. She now lay full and moist, entwined with her lover. "I came to you last night. Did you feel me?" Elizabeth asked, as she stroked his cheek and kissed his smooth skin.

"I brought you home with me my love, for there is not a moment that I am not thinking of you and yearning for you to be near me." He whispered, lightly and playfully touching her breasts. "I think you are now my home. Your kiss, your lips, your womanhood." Demetri kissed her in all those places and entered her again. He pushed himself strongly into her and she immediately felt a new rise of bliss. She turned and moved atop him, never letting his body leave hers. Moving together, she pushed his manhood into her, churning and writhing in ways that made him groan and fill her with his release. Smiling at the perfection of the fit of their bodies, they were lost in the melodious dance. Together they had found the home they both longed for.

Elizabeth and Demetri continued to see each other most every day. Their love grew even stronger and they never spoke of a time when they would not be together. On the days he could not leave the planting of the crops, they would meet at sundown. Elizabeth always knew when Demetri was to come to her. A strong tingle would arise within her belly and a warmth would penetrate her heart. She then knew it would not be long before they would lie in each other's arms, wrapped in each other's naked bodies and enter into each other, becoming gloriously and passionately linked forever.

One warm evening in May, Elizabeth sat in wait for Demetri outside the barn. The sun was slowly setting and the nearly full moon was a misty outline on the horizon. She was excited to think of the prospect of seeing the women of the forest again soon. They had not yet come into her dreams to tell her, yet she knew in the same way she knew when to meet Demetri. She felt it in her heart.

Demetri strode up to his love with a bounce in his step. Without stopping he pulled her up to him. "I have a surprise for you, tonight, Elizabeth, come…come with me."

"Are we to dance together?" asked Elizabeth. "The way you pull me close and saunter has me desiring to dance with you!"

Demetri pretended to glide and mimicked the proper, orderly dancing of the nobility.

"No, no Demetri! I want to dance as my staff dances. We have no need for dance masters when we have love guiding us!" Elizabeth took both of Demetri's hands and moved her feet in a furious motion that made her tall body, bob up and down and her long curls swirl about her face. Demetri laughed and joined in, for he knew the dance of the common folk well.

"Come my lady, we shall dance all the way to my surprise. Let us go." They danced and walked for what seemed like a very long time and they were deep into the forest, a place she was sure they had not yet discovered. Their dancing and sauntering turned into a slow walk. Elizabeth was mesmerized by the beauty of the pristine woods. Humans do not come here much, she thought, for there was no path and there were no piles of stones, guiding the traveler as to which direction would lead to a destination. There were no destinations this far into the timber as far as she knew, but apparently Demetri knew different. She wondered how he knew which way to go, but she dared not ask. The magic and mystery of this journey did not lend itself to talk. The further they went the more she felt a strange presence. She sensed it with every step. Someone was watching them. But she was not afraid. Someone watched over them as they traveled. She was calm and safe, but grabbed Demetri's hand and pulled herself close to him, just to be sure.

They came to a small grove of pine trees and she saw a light in the distance. The evening sun had just set, so they had not traveled for as long as she thought. Peering ahead towards the light she recognized the shape of a cottage with small billows of smoke arising up from its chimney. This dwelling is inhabited, she thought and she pulled her hand away, just slightly in fear. Demetri simply squeezed tighter and kept walking right on up to the door. He knocked softly. Neither of them uttered a word, yet suddenly she knew who lived here. The door opened and there she stood. It was the beautiful woman in white who led the full moon prayers. Demetri had told her that her name was Sophia, but Elizabeth did not know her title, she only knew of the respect and honor this woman commanded simply by standing in her presence. She felt a similar way when she met Queen Elizabeth many years ago as a child. She had been in awe of the great mother of her country. The power Sophia held was different that the Queens. It radiated from within her being and shined outwards, emanating from her heart not from any outside source as the Queen's did. When Elizabeth met the queen from whom her name came, the powerful woman was seated upon a chair perched high on a stage, with finely armored soldiers and guards surrounding her. The Lady in White stood alone, the soft glow of candle light from within the cottage surrounded her, creating a golden halo. Elizabeth could not help but stare into this dark haired woman's deep chestnut eyes. She was taken in, engulfed in a mesmerizing stare. Sophia's hair was deep brown, almost black and it fell in many loose curls down her back. The lady did not tie it up or braid it, which was customary for a Lady in this day. She was not young but she did not look old either. Perhaps she was the age of her own mother, yet Mother did not look like this woman at all. The Lady in White's skin was creamy and naturally pale and fine lines were etched around her eyes. These lines seemed to add to the wisdom she held and did not make her look tired and sad as Mother did. Yes, this lady of the forest was the most beautiful woman Elizabeth had ever seen, for her beauty came from another time and another place. Elizabeth continued to stare forgetting her manners altogether until Sophia broke the spell and said.

"Come in you two. Welcome to my home." She gestured to them to enter the cottage.

"Sophia, this is Elizabeth Cumberland", said Demetri, introducing the two women.

Elizabeth curtsied a deep respectful curtsy although it was not necessary to do so. Sophia extended her hand to Elizabeth and when she reached out to take it, Sophia took both of

Elizabeth's hands in her own and held them together for a long moment and said, "May the forest spirits be with you and Demetri, and your child, forever. Remember the Goddess watches over you my children and she always protects you."

Elizabeth was still deeply caught in the woman's spell and stood for a long moment without moving, taking in all the blessings being bestowed upon her. She felt calm and still and full of a love she had never felt before, not even in the arms of Demetri. This love was an everlasting peaceful love borne of the world beyond, yet it came through this most lovely woman.

"Come and sit with us and drink some cider while we visit." Said Sophia. She offered them both a chair at the small table in the center of the room. The fire was in the corner and as was common to the ways of the peasants a large iron pot hung over the pit. Elizabeth had never been in a cottage of a commoner, but in that moment she decided she quite liked it. She had heard about the ways of the lowly from her servants, yet she did not ever think she would have opportunity to venture beyond her estate walls in such a way as she now had. Looking around she took in all the familiar and unfamiliar scents. Inhaling deeply, she recognized the exquisite fragrance of rose and lavender. Her eyes were caught by the bright and varied colors of the fabrics that adorned the walls and windows. Never before had she seen such elegant fabrics used in such a manner. The walls were made from knotty pine timbers and the scent of the pine wafted within. The floor was made of stone tiles and large colorful carpets with star shaped designs, that seemed oddly familiar, were strewn about. In one corner of the cottage was the kitchen area. It was small with a basin and cupboards, and many bundles of herbs and spices hung from the rafters. This was no commoner's home, she thought, taking in the colors, scents and distinction of this splendid abode. A loud noise caught their attention and broke the spell, if for a moment. It seemed to be coming from behind the richly embroidered curtains that were strung along the back wall. Sophia walked over to the curtains and pulled them back slightly allowing Elizabeth to see three large beds covered with more of the same brightly colored fabric. Three dark haired heads popped up from under the covers.

"You may come and greet our guests, children." Said Sophia.

One by one three figures emerged and took their places in proper greeting, standing directly in front of Elizabeth and Demetri.

"Are you a real princess?" asked the middle sized child. She looked up into Elizabeth's eyes and instantly Elizabeth felt a chill of recognition. Not only did the child look exactly like her mother, she had the same penetrating gaze, full of warmth and benevolence.

"I am not a princess. I am merely a Lady. "The words fell from her mouth as she found herself curtsying again to the little child.

"You are as pretty as a princess... well I think princesses must be pretty, they should be pretty, or maybe they could not be a princess if they were not pretty... well maybe they could be a princess even if they were very ugly..."

"Penny! That's enough little one." The oldest child scolded her sister and stepped forward, taking command of the situation. "Good evening and welcome to our home. I am Hyacinth and I am fourteen years old."

"Almost old enough to be a wife!" interrupted Penny." Only she doesn't even have a suitor, so..."

"This is Penny," Hyacinth continued, trying hard to emulate her mother's graceful presence. "And you must remember to only tell her things that you wish everyone to know of." said Hyacinth rolling her eyes. "And this is Maya". The littlest child peered out from behind Hyacinth's bed gown and stared wide-eyed at Elizabeth and Demetri.

Elizabeth took each one of their hands as they reached out to touch her. They all looked to be of the same mold as their mother with the same magical, mystical presence, although each seemed to have their own unique personality.

Elizabeth was enthralled at having the attention of these children. They scurried around her as they led her to the table to enjoy the refreshments their mother set out. Just as they were about to sit, the door opened and in strode a somber figure. The girls paid no attention, but Elizabeth was struck still as she watched a very old woman dressed in dark green robes hobble into Sophia's home. The woman was crippled and hunched over but she walked quite briskly despite the apparent deformities. Approaching Elizabeth she stuck out a bony hand.

"I am Malvina, Mother of Sophia." She then sat down with a thud, without waiting a moment for Elizabeth's response. Elizabeth stared at the woman, at a loss for words. She turned to the others and followed suit as they all took their places at the table. Malvina sat at the head of the table and poured herself what looked to be a strong brew. She never said another word the whole evening.

Sophia, Elizabeth, Demetri and the girls sat at the table drinking cider and eating bread with great dollops of berry jam. They each took turns sharing stories and the conversation flowed as if they were dear old friends. Elizabeth learned that there were many families that lived in the area, a village that had been here for hundreds of years. They hunted and farmed and prayed and worshipped as they wished, deep in the forest.

"Yes, we have lived quite nicely, away from the outer world for many a year. My mother is what you would call our leader, or Queen. We refer to our leaders as Priestess." Explained Sophia. Malvina grunted and took a long swig of her brew.

After a short while, the eldest girl stood up and offered to put the younger girls to bed. Sophia agreed and amidst a small amount of protest, the children retired for the evening. Sophia poured her guests hot tea and continued the visit.

"Demetri tells me that you two are deeply in love. I see it in your faces and I am assured that your union is blessed. I too had such a blessed union at one time, with my daughter's father." At that moment Malvina who had until now, been mostly silent, started sputtering and muttering. She folded the end of her long sleeve and used it as one would use a kerchief. She blew her nose, spat and made noises that sounded to be cursing. Elizabeth felt a strong laugh emerge and Demetri pinched her thigh. He stopped the laugh, all right, but out came a snort. Malvina did not seem to notice, Demetri's face turned red, Elizabeth sat wide-eyed and Sophia continued.

"My husband, my true love, was killed two years ago. We believe he was attacked by wild dogs." Again, Malvina muttered something and added a very clear belch on top of it. Once more, the group tried to ignore the old woman's rudeness.

"It was only recently that I came out of mourning." Sophia continued. "I did so because I must, for the Goddess came to me in a dream and told me it was time." Sophia rose and filled everyone's cups with scalding hot water from the kettle on the fire. "The Goddess told me to mourn no more, that it was time for me to lead the gatherings of women each full moon. It was time for me to take my proper place, that all was continuing as should be." Sophia took a long sip of her tea and sighed. "I am honored that you and Demetri have been partaking in the celebration of the moon. It is assured that as you were drawn to find us, you are also drawn together." She took both of their hands in hers and held them in a long gaze.

Elizabeth could feel the tingling energy rising up from her belly, stronger than she had ever felt. It rose up stronger and stronger and then burst into her heart. Demetri must have felt it too, for he reached out to her and put his hand over her heart.

Sophia continued her story. "Malvina passed the silver scepter to me, as the dream prophesized. I was assured that I must now lead the people, that I had much to give to the community and that I would now be the high priestess forevermore.

Elizabeth started to cry. She was in awe, for she knew that Sophia would never share with her such tales if she did not trust her. She felt to be the luckiest maiden alive to have been given this honor. Demetri offered her his kerchief and hugged her close. Sophia smiled a tender smile that hugged her with its warmth. Elizabeth could only wish to have a mother such as Sophia, a mother who was brave and strong and so full of wisdom. She so enjoyed the visit that she did not want to leave, but Demetri pulled on her sleeve repeatedly warning her of the approaching dawn.

They all said their goodbyes. Malvina stood silent, the girls giggled from behind the curtains and Sophia assured them that they were always welcome to return for a visit or to participate in the celebrations of the moon. She handed them a lantern to assure the way home in safety. Elizabeth was sure it was a magic lantern.

"I am so grateful to you Demetri, for taking me to meet the woman in white. I am without words to say about how my heart is bursting. I did not know that any woman, nor man for that matter, could be so kind, so pure and so full of love and wisdom. I did not know a person could be so."

"You are my love, you are so." Demetri answered. He turned to her on the dark path, in the middle of the deepest part of the forest. The moon light shone bright and the lantern flame flickered, as he took her chin in his hand and kissed her lips ever so lightly and ever so passionately. And onward they went.

Once again Elizabeth returned safely home just before the sun rose. She lay in her bed watching the bright orange hues seep in through the sliver of boards covering the windows. She thought of her lover and her new friends. With them in her life, she felt so safe, as if nothing could ever harm her now. She tossed and turned for a while wishing for some sleep. She instinctively rubbed the small roundness of her belly and she felt a stirring inside, ever so faint. I greatly soothed her and soon she was fast asleep.

Chapter Ten

Gregory knew something was different about his daughter as of late; although what exactly the difference was, he did not know, nor did he want to know. Knowing was Gregory's nemesis. If he sought to know more about his daughter, and what he found out was beyond his control, which it most likely was, the pain within would engulf him, for there was nothing he could do about such knowing. He was a trapped animal and it seemed so were his children. No gnashing or gnawing could destroy the claws of the traps on his soul.

There was something, however, he did need to know more about, and after much internal deliberation, he decided to seek answers about what had truly transpired with his ship and crew. However painful the insights might be, there was a way to use the information that would hopefully prove helpful and maybe, just maybe release the grip of the nightmare of his father-in-law, albeit slightly.

Gregory knew it would only be a matter of time before the Duke would have James completely entwined in the family business. Gregory also knew from dealings past that James was a liar and a cheat and would stop at nothing to rule. There must be a way to prove him to be the scoundrel he is. Gregory could not stop the betrothal of his daughter to this dark-hearted man, since his father-in-law made that clear, but perhaps he might come upon some information that would prove that James did not have his family's best interest with business dealings. Any information at all might delay or undermine in some small way, both unions. Perhaps it was James that was careless and allowed the ship to reach her doom. Gregory would find out and then would then give the information to the Duke. It was a chance he was more than willing to take. The restlessness could no longer be tolerated, his heart needed a reprieve from the prison of the estate. There was an opportunity for him to save his daughter and all of the Cumberland's from the combined wrath of the Earl of Hartford and the Duke of Winslow. Gregory shuddered at the mere suggestion of the two men together, ruling with the domination and tyranny that would bring sure death and destruction to all. Currently, James was on an expedition to Morocco, to secure a trade route. The Duke was enjoying a hawk and hound hunting expedition. Their absence was a boon as well as an opportunity and time was of the essence. Gregory would go into the city today and find out what had happened to his ship. His men, if any were still alive, would surely talk to him. There was very little possibility that he could do anything with such answers, but somehow, the mere seeking just might settle the growing unease that mounted within. This unease could no longer be tempered with his daily dose of spirits. His agitated impatience won out.

Gregory entered into the city on a blustery spring day. He did not take the carriage, for he did not want anyone to know he was traveling. He packed up one of his finest steads with saddle bags full of three day's supplies. His comings and goings must be kept private. He would sleep on the ground under the forest canopy if needed.

Gregory rode alongside the river, coming upon the London Bridge. He was sure to keep his gaze straight as to avoid looking at the remains of those who had dared defy her majesty and her army of knights, merchants and nobility. The severed heads of the unlucky folk dangled from the bridge, the stench of rotting flesh and dried blood reminiscent of death at sea. Gregory felt the tension in his throat increase as he entered the noisy city. The sun was high overhead now and the wind still. Waiting until he was well into the crowd, he dismounted and walked beside his horse in order to better navigate the narrow alleys that would take him to Brooker's Pub.

Brooker was a sailing companion of Gregory's from long ago and it had been many a year since he had last laid eyes on his feisty friend. If anyone or anyplace had remained intact, it would be Brooker, his pub and the sailors and sea merchants who frequented his establishment, if you could call it that. Gregory chuckled. The laughter loosened him into an unfamiliar momentary state. The pub was more of an indoor London alley, ripe with all the intrigue, gossip and stench. The closer he got to the pub, the more the need to be around his fellow seamen filled his being. Forgetting the brotherhood of his fellow sea mates was perhaps his worse sin to date. The sea and those who called her their home were the most noble, courageous group of disparate souls he ever met. What they lacked in commonality, they made up for in audacious bravado. He needed to be with his people, the men of the sea, and he was sure they would violently and vehemently remind him of where he had hidden his courage and gumption, if indeed he had any left at all.

Gregory turned down one alley and the next, stepping over the slime of refuge, careful not to fall. He did not mind the smells as much on this day, for the thrill of adventure and the long forgotten comradery, returned to his empty soul.

Gregory was sure not to dress in finery for he did not want to be known as nobility, nor recognized in any way. Today he was a mere commoner, blending in with the other common city rats. His horse, however was a different story and there would be much exaggerated talk of the man with the chestnut stallion worth a thousand pounds. This thought came to him, as he was trying to hold his stallion steady through the dingy alleyway. A bit late to think of this detail, he thought. He would surely be noticed, if he continued to walk his prize horse down the darkened alley ways of London.

"What have we here?" A raspy voice came from behind him. "A fine specimen of animal if I have ever seen one!" The sound of an authentic city rat gave Gregory a defining chill up his spine. He instantly knew he was in trouble and he was ready. He drew his foot-long dagger from its sheath and turned to face the scum.

"You best back away now! My weapon is ready to disembowel anyone who questions me!" The anger and rage that he had kept so safely inside, erupted quickly. The man and his counterpart backed away, but they were not finished with him yet.

"Such talk from a gentleman," the man continued, stepping farther out of Gregory's reach. "You are not among gentlemen and you do not have your knights to protect you now!" the man was swaying to and fro, his partner, trying to keep him from falling in the pile of sludge from an emptied chamber pot.

"Let me pass and I shall do you no harm." Answered Gregory, mustering all the decency he could. He so wanted to cut the man's bowels right then and there.

The man was inebriated and he did not recognize Gregory's demeanor. Instead, he kept up the banter. "You are but a coward, you and your fine horse! There is nothing inside of you but an empty hollow place where a man once lived."

Gregory felt the furry arise within his belly. Before he could stop himself, he lunged at the man, pointed dagger heading straight for his chest. The man stared at Gregory, eyes wide in an intoxicated stupor and he abruptly swayed. Gregory plunged the knife deep into the man's shoulder. The cracking of the man bones awoke Gregory from his fury and he quickly pulled his knife out, pushing the man to the ground. Jumping onto his horse he rode down the narrow alley, ducking and dodging the street urchins, the flying laundry, and various women of the night.

Gregory rode and rode until he found a quiet stable on the edge of the city. Here, he would board his horse for safe keeping and anonymity and be on his way to Brooker's Pub. The drunken alley rat could lay dead for all I care, he thought angrily. I came to this place to get information and I will not leave until he I have it. Gregory felt eerily alive again, for he had fought for his honor, and won. Albeit the man was a drunk street urchin, it mattered not. Gregory was fueled by this rush of rage and he was now ready to return to his roots once more.

Walking briskly, he kept his head down. Guided by instinct he found his way back through the streets and alleyways. Reaching out, he took hold of the large brass handle, stopping for a moment before entering Brooker's Pub with a new certainty.

The pub was crowded, smelled of stale ale, vomit and the sea. Gregory breathed deep this familiar scent and looked across the main room. Several groups of men loitered about. Some eating, drinking and laughing loudly, others seriously talking, heads hunched over maps and papers with orders. The men donned sailing uniforms, business attire and the rags of the poorest deck men. He fit in here. This was home and these were his people. Why had he stayed away so long?

"Well if it ain't the Cumberland himself, gracing us with his presence." Came the booming voice of Brooker as he entered the main room. Brooker carried two heaping platters of foul as he lumbered his way toward Gregory. Throwing the platters onto a table he sauntered over to greet his friend. Gregory reached out to embrace him. Brooker was quite a site, a large man standing nearly a foot taller than the average man, a crop of wiry red hair adorned his head and a large red beard covered a once boyish face. He had lost his foot to scurvy and he walked from side to side now, always trying to keep himself from tipping over.

Brooker took Gregory in with his burly arms and nearly picked him up off his feet. This was the welcome he had been craving. Brooker pulled Gregory by one arm to a corner table near the kitchen.

"Sit, eat…ale?" In no time, Gregory had a platter of food and a pint of ale. He devoured the meal, and whipped the greasy drippings clean with a large slab of brown bread.

Sitting back, digesting his meal, he watched the comings and goings of the patrons, taking it all in. Today that was his mission, to simply take it all in, survey and navigate the crowd, like he would the vast ocean, in order to find what he was looking for. Calm water, storms, schools of fish or the remains of a sunken ship. Brooker let him be until the crowd died down late into the evening.

"I have a room in the back for you to stay. I will not take no for an answer." Said Brooker as he sat with Gregory for the first time all day. Brooker called sweetly to a bar maid and she brought them both a large pint of brandy and more food. "I save this strong brew for my special guests, but hey…" Brooker said, slapping Gregory on the back, you ain't a guest, you are my brother. Once a brother of the sea, always a brother."

Gregory, could not smile, for he was overwhelmed with the truth of what his life had become. He had given up a life he loved, to have a life he loathed. He had to find a way out, but he knew deep within that it was never going to be so.

"What ails ye mate? I ain't ever seen ye so bunched up in a knot of rope." Brooker took a long swig of the brandy. I ain't seen ye in many a year, and last I here yee were livin in some fancy ass estate. Yep, I suppose ya got what I call the incurable disease of the maiden of the sea…yep, that must be what ye got." Brooker leaned in close, his face grew somber as he tried to reign in his boisterous spirit. "It's like this, ya see, the maiden of the sea is the most vicious of all lovers. She pulls you in, before ya know what hits ya, and ya fall, hard into her. Her scent, her flesh, she takes ya in and ya feel like ye are alive for the first time. She brought ya to life, she did. She knew where to touch ye and how to whisper to ye and then she's gone, and ye are never the same, until you ride upon her again. She swallowed ye whole she did. And ye ain't ever returned." Brooker seemed quite proud of himself for his sermon and he sat back and belched.

Gregory was caught in the words like a great fish caught in the nets of his fisherman brothers. The sea was his lover, and perhaps still is. "I did not come here to see you after all these years to pine over a lost lover."

"Well, maybe ye didn't, but ye still got the curse, I tell ye." With that Brooker left Gregory alone. There would be no more talk this eve.

Gregory slept fitfully that evening in the tiny room in the back of Brooker's Pub. Alley cats fought all night long and the sounds of drunken men and women of the night laughing loudly kept entering his dreams. He awoke to the crowing of a rooster, jumped from his resting place and headed out to find Brooker. He had to put his plan into action today. He found Brooker mopping the floors in one of the back rooms.

"Good morning to you, my friend," said Gregory, slapping Brooker on his broad back. This man is truly built like an ox, he thought, rubbing his hand where it hit upon Brooker's powerful muscular back. "I am ready to get down to business and you are the man who can help. No more talk of the wanderlust or the lack of lust or the sickness of lust for me. I made my peace with the tempestuous maiden of the sea, long ago. I have a job to do and I will see it done before tomorrow eve, for that is when I must return home to my family." Gregory shouted for all to hear, although no one except one lonely beggar was to be seen within Brooker's Pub at this early hour.

"What is it that you need, mate?" asked Brooker. Although Gregory was his captain on many a voyage, Brooker always addressed him as "mate." Gregory did not mind, for to have a man like Brooker as his friend and equal was an honor, a blessing and a sure manner of constant protection.

"I have had some business dealings gone wrong, and I must find out what happened. I was told one of my ships sunk. It was the Emerald Elizabeth. Do you know anything about this Brooker?" Gregory asked.

Brooker set down his mop and pushed the bucket aside, splashing dirty water on his cleaned floor. Ahh, some thatch will take care of that," he muttered, looking at Gregory. "I do know of the Emerald E. She was a fine vessel. Yes, I saw her me self before she sailed her fateful journey."

"Do you know what happened?" asked Gregory.

"I don't know mate. I don't know." Brooker turned away from Gregory then and stood up. "Let me get us some eggs, biscuits... morning brew." In a moment he was gone.

He returned a few minutes later with large trenches of eggs and meats and two large pints of ale. "Now we can talk." He muttered, setting the grub down with a thud.

He started in on his meal, one hand scooping the eggs, the other swigging his ale.

"Brooker!" yelled Gregory. "Do you know anything or not?" Gregory stood up and slammed his hand upon the table. Brooker didn't flinch.

"See, I am right, mate, ye need the love of a good woman or the sea to calm ye. What shall it be, I can arrange both." Brooker laughed a loud booming chorus of belching and snorts.

Gregory sat down and calmed himself. Perhaps his friend was right. He was too tense, too close to the matter. He must gather control if he was to find what he was looking for. "I just need to know what happened, and if a man named James of Hartford was involved." Gregory said. There he had said his name and now it was out. Whatever was to befall him and his family now, so be it.

Again Brooker didn't flinch. "I do believe he was." Brooker continued to shovel the food into his mouth, and when he was done with his serving, he started on Gregory's.

Gregory nodded and pushed his trench closer to Brooker. "I would bet my eldest born that the man you named was part of Lady E's demise. The man you name is scum...scum of the worse kind. He thinks he owns everyone and everything and believes he is protected by Satan himself." Brooker cleared his throat and spat a large wad onto his still wet floor. "No doubt. Does he own you too Cumberland? Is that why ye gave up your mistress and your true love?"

"No he doesn't own me and I want to see to it that he never does. What can you tell me? I need to know exactly what happened and I need proof."

"I see." Said Brooker. "Give me a bit of time here, I will find someone who will help you. But…" Brooker rose from his seat and Gregory rose to meet his gaze. "I want you to kill the bastard. Will you promise me that Cumberland? I give you what you want and you kill the bastard, Hartford for me and for everyone else he has run into the ground?"

It was Gregory's turn not to flinch. The thought of killing James, flooded his body with the now familiar and eerily calming wrath. "I promise you." He reached out to shake Brooker's hand. Brooker took Gregory's hand and pulled him in close to hug as two brothers would.

Later that day, as the sun was towards setting, Brooker's was full of sailors and whores, businessmen and captains. Gregory sat in the back room, alone, waiting. From where he sat he had a view of the main hall, separated by a low wall. This room was used for gaming and cock fights, but now it was Gregory's spot.

He did not drink another drop of ale, he just sat, waiting and staring at the shadows as they danced across the rushes that covered the newly mopped floor. There was one window in this back room, a small rectangular opening, high up near the ceiling. The window was covered with a ragged piece of burlap that blew with the blustery wind. Every so often Gregory could hear a bit of conversation coming from the alley. He kept his ears open for any mention of James. He was lost in his thoughts when he heard his name being called. Someone was calling to him from the window.

"Cumberland, I'm looking for Cumberland…are you he?" came the call.

Gregory went to the window and whispered loudly. "Why do you ask for this bloke named Cumberland?" Gregory spoke in his most convincing sea worthy manner.

"Brooker sent me. If you want to talk come out here and meet me." Gregory stepped away from the window scanning the room for his friend. Brooker was eyeing him from across the crowded main room, nodding an aye. Gregory quickly exited, turning sharply into the alley, keeping his hand firmly upon his dagger. There stood a lone man, a forlorn figure, bundled in many layers of rags which once may have been fine coats.

"What say you?" asked Gregory as he approached the man.

"I hear yee are looking for news of the Lady E. I might help ya, but I need somethin'," spat the man.

"I am prepared to pay…" started Gregory.

"I don't want yer money, I want revenge." With that the man sneered and smiled, drool coming from his rotted mouth.

Gregory stepped back and surmised the bloke. What kind of revenge could this slovenly character want and why? Could he trust him? He decided to find out. "Revenge is a personal matter, sir. What is it that you might tell me about the Lady Elizabeth and her crew?"

"James of Hartford is the devil's bastard son. The man is pure evil and I can personally attest to that, and so can me wife and me daughters and me brother. So, Sir revenge is not a personal matter, it is a family matter." The man stood suddenly taller and an air of importance radiated from him.

"Gregory decided to ask point blank, disregarding the street urchin his surly explanation. "Do you have information or do you just want to see the Earl of Hartford dead?"

The man looked around to be sure no one was in earshot and he leaned in close to Gregory. Gregory kept his hand on his dagger as the man proceeded to talk. The words poured out in painful dribbles as he told his tale of horror.

I was the captain of the Lady E. She was me ship, she was. I was under Lord Haverstat, and he trusted me like I was his brother. I been with the Lady E for ten long years. Hartford approached me a few years back giving me a might bit of gold and silver to be sure I sailed where he wanted. I knew him to be a scoundrel, but I didn't know of his ruthlessness. I had a family to feed. I may be small in stature but I know how to hold me own. I have a quick wit!" The man pointed to his head with his rag wrapped hand. "Thought the man was in some game to get to the top of the heap and win the Queen's good graces, just like all of them types." The man coughed and spat, his lungs sounding full and his face turning pale.

Gregory did not back away, he stared intently into the captain's watery eyes trying to listen to every word. This tale did indeed involve him and the words dripped with truth. Before the man begun again, Gregory lit up with recognition. Yes, he did know this pitiful sight of a man. He could not believe his eyes. This was the fellow he himself had commissioned to sail, many years ago. What had happened to him? He remembered his name. Dansville.

"Hartford was never happy with the returns on the ship. He always wanted more." The captain continued.

Gregory interrupted, realizing what he was saying, "But it was the Duke of Winslow and I who owned the Lady E. How did Hartford get his hands…?"

"Are ye a fool man, did you not hear what I said? I was bought by that bastard and he slowly took control over my ship and my men. Before I knew it, it was too late. He had his hooks in me and the last hook was the one that fell the Lady."

"I need to know details." Gregory fell into the disheveled captain's anger and sorrow and it awakened his own. He pulled out his dagger and held it to the man's throat. This creature was no longer the captain of any vessel, he was now his pawn in a game to win his soul back. The point of the dagger barely made its way through the layers of rags bound round his neck.

"I don't care if you are the captain, I don't care if I did put you in charge so long ago, and I don't care how much you hate Hartford. Give me something I can use to take him down and I won't put this knife into your sorry throat."

The captain started sobbing. Gregory was not prepared for this. He withdrew his dagger and decided to lead the man into Brooker's. A tankard of ale would do them both good.

"I can't be seen with you. I won't go in." the captain resisted but Gregory fought back.

"You are not recognizable and no one knows me here anymore. Brooker is to be trusted and he has his henchmen everywhere. We are going to drink and you are going to tell me everything. Now."

Gregory pushed the man through the door and led him to the still empty back room. They both sat with a thud and in walked the bar maid. She gently set two very large tankards of ale on the table. She left as quickly, and in her wake sat a very large, very menacing mastiff. The dog stood guard between Gregory, his guest, and the other patrons.

The captain took a long swig and his shoulders relaxed. "I have nothing left because of Hartford. They took it all. I may tell all, for I will be dead soon anyway. "Over the years I did the Earl's bidding. Hiring the crew members, he wanted assured that I would someday be rewarded. Hartford was in charge of everything having to do with The Lady E, as well as a half dozen other ships. Things seemed to go well, my children well fed, wife in finery…" he took a long swig of ale and winced. His lips were broken and bleeding, his mouth cracked deep in the corners. This man endures pain in each moment, just as I, thought Gregory. He is not just my sea mate, but a broken soul mate as well.

The captain continued but not before finishing the tankard clean. "Need I remind you of the war that raged on the seas between our majesty and her brother-in-law Prince Philip? Well, the damn devil himself Hartford, saw a way to gain control and profit from the deaths of many. He conspires with the Commander Medina Sidonia. The men he had me take on as crew were damn Spanish spies; every last one of them. I found out, it may have taken me awhile, but I found out…but it was too late. The Spaniards owned us, we were sailing for them. We were their whores and their spies."

"I understand. Bring us something stronger, now!" Gregory yelled to the barmaid. Brooker came barreling around the corner, and gave Gregory a ferocious look. Gregory did not waiver. He knew his friend feared for his safety, yet he did not care at this moment.

"So, what you say is that my ships were used by James of Hartford to win fortune for the Spanish?"

"Yes, but there is more." The barmaid brought the men a large bowl of brandywine. Gregory poured for them both.

"Hartford sold us out to the Spanish and then turned us in to our own people as traitors. Each and every one of my men were beheaded, the remains are still on the London Bridge." The captain suddenly stood up. "I must go now. I must go…"

Gregory also stood up, grabbed his dagger and then thought best to just set it down, for the threat of injury did not phase this man. He had been injured already beyond repair.

"How is it that you live Captain, for if what you say is true, the captain is the first to die?"

"This is my punishment, to live. To live to see the horror done unto me and my family, to live as if he had castrated me and disemboweled me and still I live…a ghost, a shell. Hartford does not want the power of the royalty, the riches of the world, he is not of this world, he is of the underworld, the most vile of all creatures. He is without soul, for God himself is in fear of such a man." The captain slouched and Gregory moved toward him, grasping his arms.

"Enough of the descriptions. I know this man to be of the devil. But, why am I to believe you? Give me reason, or I shall cut you right here."

"Can you not see me? I am almost dead, yet I must stay alive, if only for one thing…my youngest child. She is the only one left, the only one left. My crew is dead, my wife, my three eldest daughters, my son, all dead at the hands of Hartford. He did not want me dead, for a dead man will not do his bidding. Instead, he forced me to endure the torture of being forever in his debt."

Gregory felt incredibly nauseous, remembering the night he happened upon James trying to have his way with Elizabeth. The man was hurting his only daughter. He did nothing, he was held back, not in control, impotent.

These two broken men were forcefully locked in a death embrace as the truth of the Earl bound them together. The captain continued. "James forced me to watch him take my wife, beat her and rape her. He told me that if I did not do what he wished for the rest of my day, he would continue the rape. He then…then…did the same to each of my eldest daughters. Forcing both me and my son to watch the devil touch…the devil…penetrate…" the captain suddenly was filled with rage and broke free of Gregory's grip. He sat on the wooden bench with a heavy thud and wept. "Do you know what it is like to watch as your children are tortured? Do you know what it is like; to watch as he breaks them over and over and to see the face of a man as he delights in the taking of the flesh of your flesh? Do you know what it's like?"

The only thing Gregory could do was to keep hold of his composure as he listened to the Captain's gruesome tale. He knew now for certain he must stop James or this would be him some day. "You said they were dead. Did he kill them?"

"My son tried to stop Hartford. He was no match and he put a hot dagger through his heart. My wife died within days of this horror. She lay in my arms and told me she could not endure and she took her last breath. My three daughters all suffered the same fate, dying of their own accord, bleeding to death from broken spirits, blows and the touch of the son of Satan." My youngest daughter remains alive. She was spared, for she was not with us when the attacks began. I must stay alive to protect her. If I die, she will only be tortured and die too. It is the only reason I am still on earth. James will never get his filthy body near my Cicely."

The men sat in silence, completely still. Gregory did not want to take in the story, yet he thought of what evidence he might now have to convince his father-in-law of James' treason and sins. He was afraid to ask this next question, afraid of what he would hear. The answer would seal his family's fate and all future generations to come.

"I cannot fathom your misfortune, I grieve for the loss of your family, and all that James has taken from you. I am so very sorry, yet I must know Captain. Did he act alone?" The moments ticked on while both men emptied their tankards.

"He did not act alone. I know of one man who did give him funding as well as orders. This man showed up at my home once, he did not rape my daughters but he delighted in the watching. He is the devil's father, this man.

"Who is this man?" Gregory felt the blood drain from his body as he waited the answer.

This man was the Duke of Winslow. Yes, the Duke of Winslow and his henchman, the meanest son of a bitch I have ever worked with. His henchman is the only one spared from the Lady Elizabeth, besides myself. He is a pirate from the land of the ancient Celts."

The barmaid approached and Gregory shooed her away with a trembling hand. She did not retreat, instead she sat upon his lap. "No Master, you must listen to me." Her voice was low and husky. "I am here to warn ye. Brooker sent me over to tell you..." She laughed heartily and placed Gregory's hand upon her breast. "ye must flee out the back door and send this bloke on his way. Now." The barmaid pretended to flirt with the Captain drawing him in to her and straddling both men. "Follow me." She said as she sat up. "Is it fun ye want, both of ye? Well all righty, I shall oblige." The bar maid then led both men through the kitchen and behind the pub, taking them down the winding alley to the main street. The captain broke into a run and disappeared into the crowd.   The barmaid whispered to Gregory, "Leave the city, ye are not safe. Leave, quickly."

It was then that Gregory saw a foreboding figure of a man approach from the shadows of the alley. He was a giant of a man; taller than any man he had ever seen. Gregory recognized him immediately. He was the Duke's henchman, the pirate and crewmember the captain had just spoke of. They had conjured his evil presence by mere mention of him. The monster grabbed the barmaid and slammed her against the wall.

"Run, do not stop!" She yelled. Gregory wanted to help her but he knew he was no match for this man. He ran and did not stop until he arrived at the stable. He had evaded the henchman, for now. The stable boy was nowhere to be found, so he fed and groomed his horse and decided he had to return to Brooker's.

Brooker greeted Gregory the moment he walked in. He led him back in through the pub, past the darkened back room and into a tiny cubicle. He pushed back the rushes and uncovered the floor boards revealing a stone stairway leading into a darkened tunnel. Brooker disappeared into the hole and Gregory followed. He led him into another tunnel and yet another until they ended up in a small room.

"You are not right in the head Gregory. You are not safe anywhere in the city tonight. Word is out. I know not who the scoundrel is. Could be anyone, ye know the gold can buy so many! You can stay here for the night and leave in the morn. Hartford's men know you are here. The captain is already dead, his severed head delivered to me one hour ago. I ain't afraid Cumberland. I ain't afraid of no Earl or Duke, I ain't got a family, and for good reason. I belong to no one and gold don't buy me. But this business ye got yourself into, this ain't about no devil mothered Earl, this is about crossing two countries and now both want your head. Hartford set you up without you even knowing it."

Gregory listened to his fate being handed to him by his only friend. He shook his head. No words would form. He sat in stunned silence.

"I will come get ya when it is safe." Brooker turned to go, leaving Gregory with the demons of his newly discovered past and the destruction of any hope for his future.

Chapter Eleven

Elizabeth decided to venture on her own to see the beautiful ladies of the forest. She had many questions and knew that somehow these people held the answers. The gnawing of an uncertain future pulled her to visit. One night toward the end of summer, a few days before the moon was to be full, she found her way to Sophia's home. Excitement mixed with trepidation filled her being as she gently knocked upon the cottage door. Sophia opened the door, opening her arms wide and pulled Elizabeth in for a deep embrace.

"Hello my child." she said with great joy." We were so hoping to see you again. Come in and share our evening meal with us."

Elizabeth entered and saw that the table was set for six. Sophia's daughters came bounding into the main room when they heard Elizabeth's voice and the youngest one shouted.

"You were right grandmother! She did come to share supper with us!" Maya ran up to Elizabeth and hugged her tight around her knees, just as Henry used to do. She was no longer shy or afraid of the beautiful "princess". Malvina sat hunched near the cooking fire and she looked up at Elizabeth with a wry smile.

"Come help me up child and bring me to my meal." Malvina crowed. Elizabeth felt a bit frightened to speak to Malvina, yet she had spoken to her first so she thought it fine to ask her the question that was burning in her mind.

"Did you really know I was coming, Malvina? How can you know things before they happen? I did not know myself that I was coming here until late today." She spouted nervously.

"It is our way, my child." Malvina replied and sat herself down with a plunk. No one said another word until Sophia said the blessing. Her curious daughters started asking Elizabeth questions all at once.

"Is it true that you have servants to dress you? asked Hyacinth.

"Do you have knights guard your door and take you into town?" asked Penny.

"Well, I do have servants who want to dress me, but I rarely let them." smiled Elizabeth. "And on the rare occasion that I go into town, we are driven by our carriage driver. I actually live a very boring life except for the time I spend with my brother and when I have a chance to see Demetri. I also love my lessons," sighed Elizabeth.

"Lessons? What do you learn? Do you learn magic and prayers as we do?" asked Maya bouncing up and down on her chair." Malvina made a loud noise and flung her hand toward Maya. Maya, however did not seem to notice. The mere move of the old woman's hand, sent chills up Elizabeth's spine.

"It is not plain magic, little Maya, it is the ways of our God and we do learn important trades, too." said Hyacinth, proud and mature in her attitude.

"Well, I do learn many prayers, but none as beautiful as yours. I do not learn magic unless you consider learning another language magic." Elizabeth was delighted that the young maidens wanted her attention in such a generous and genuine way.

What language do you learn?" asked Hyacinth. "I want to learn a language."

"I learn French and Latin." Elizabeth smiled and took the platter of vegetables. In the exact moment that she took the tray a spell of dizziness hit her and the contents started to spill onto the table. Jumping up from her seat in shame, she caught a few falling morsels and muttered an apology.

"I am so sorry Sophia. I am feeling a bit ill. I think I must go outside for a breath of air." With that, Elizabeth set the platter down and walked out the door into the warm evening air.

The sun was setting and it was a beautiful pink and purple sky. Finding a seat upon a small bench just outside the cottage door, she sat and caught her breath. She did not know what came over her. She was feeling fine and suddenly the wave of dizzy nausea swept over her whole body and she felt so very hot and a bit faint. Was it Malvina's foreboding presence? Perhaps, but truth be told, this exact thing had been happening to her for many weeks. It was quite embarrassing and came over her without warning. This was a very different belly sickness than the malady that had brought her into the forest. It was hard to keep food down, her belly was swollen and she knew not what to make of it. It was her full intent to ask Sophia if she knew what could cause such sickness, for Demetri had told her that Sophia was renowned for her healing abilities and would surely know. Elizabeth sat on the bench amidst the lovely sky with head in hands and moaned. She was so enjoying her visit and hoped that she would not have to discuss anything of the sort.

"Drink this Elizabeth. It shall calm your stomach." Sophia stood over her and handed her a small bowl.

Elizabeth looked up at Sophia and instantly felt calmer. She peered into the bowl. It was a brew of some sort and did not have much of an odor and she was very thankful for that. Very slowly, Elizabeth sipped all of the contents.

"I am sorry to have interrupted your fine meal Sophia, but I know not what is wrong with me. I have felt ill for many weeks now and I seem to be so full and round. I fear I am dying and I do not know what to do." She looked sadly up at Sophia and continued.

"I did not come here to burden you with such talk but perhaps you might offer some advice, for Demetri told me you know about healing. I do know you have a great array of herbs, and by the way, about Demetri, do you see what might become of us? He also told me that you have the gift of foresight, and I suppose Malvina does too. What does that mean exactly?" Elizabeth could not stop talking, her heart burst open and all the fears and concerns she tried so hard to conceal tumbled forth. She was babbling like a frightened child.

"Calm yourself, my dear. Let us discuss one thing at a time. I know you came here seeking counsel and I have all the time in the world for you, unless perhaps a mother shall be immediately needing my attention with the birthing of a babe, then... you shall wait." Sophia smiled and patted Elizabeth on the shoulder. She then sat down and snuggled very close to Elizabeth. An immediate and gentle calm took hold, the nausea subsided and her head stopped spinning as she took in the wise woman's presence.

"Mothers? Babes? What do you mean Sophia?"

"Someone has to help the women of our village when it is their time to give birth. Someone also must tend to the health of these babes and mothers to be. This is my duty and gift, for I am a midwife."

"And a healer too, and a priestess, is that not so?" Elizabeth felt quite fortunate now, for this woman was so very wise and had so many gifts.

"I do what I am called to do." answered Sophia. And without skipping a beat, she continued to focus her whole attention on Elizabeth. "Now, let me address your questions, one at a time. What is it that makes you distraught over Demetri, my child?" asked Sophia, all the while gently rubbing Elizabeth's rounded belly. Elizabeth did not mind the healer's touch and she was feeling so much better moment by moment.

"We are so in love and yet given our family circumstances it is quite impossible for us to be wed in the given way. I want to be his wife and for the life of me I cannot think of any way to make this possible. The truth be, I fear I must marry another and be bound in humiliation for the rest of my days" she stopped and breathed a deep sigh.

"Elizabeth do you know how a child comes to be in the world?" asked Sophia.

Elizabeth was very surprised at this question but she pondered it for only a moment and came up with an answer for Sophia. "Well...I suppose when a man and woman are wed, God then gives them a child to love born of their love for one another." Elizabeth hesitantly answered. She was not sure about that, for no one had ever told her such things, but it seemed a logical explanation. She truly had not ever had chance to know of such things yet.

"Elizabeth, you are with child." said Sophia with her hand still on her belly.

Elizabeth pulled away stunned. No words came as she stared wide-eyed at the beautiful wise woman. Sophia began praying in her comforting way. The words were full of blessings and for the health of the babe growing inside. Elizabeth wept. "How do you know such a thing? I am not wed. How could this be so?"

Sophia put her arm around Elizabeth and explained in her gentle voice, "You and Demetri love one another as two people who are wed do and more so than many people who are wed ever will. You have joined your bodies together and from this union your child was created."

Elizabeth instantly knew of what Sophia spoke and felt the truth come alive in her body with a wave of joy. Looking up at Sophia, she allowed the loving gaze to enter into her heart and erase the fear and confusion. It was true; she was with child, Demetri's child. This was cause for celebration and joy. The child was conceived in the moments of ecstasy she shared with Demetri, when their bodies became one and they touched one another's hearts! This was as it should be and it all was making sense to her now. They loved one another and this child proved their love. The truth fueled her with indignation and she shot up from her seat. "I will marry my love and we shall have a family. I care not what my father wants, nor what the world tells us we must do any more. I will run far away with Demetri and I will be his wife."

Sophia put both hands upon Elizabeth's shoulders and set her back down upon the bench gently.

"Elizabeth, you must rest and be very careful for the next few months. I fear for your health and the health of your babe if you do not care for yourself." Sophia ordered, giving a stern, firm look.

"I do not want my child to be born into the prison I live in, Sophia! Whatever shall I do? Help me!"

"It is not wise for you to fret Elizabeth. Listen carefully and I shall share with you my thoughts. I have pondered this very moment for many weeks now and I shall help you, yet you must calm yourself, for the sake of your child's well-being."

"You do know the future. Are you a sorceress too? I am sure Malvina is. Is...Is she?

Sophia backed away and gazed upon Elizabeth with a look that stirred fright and reverence. "Elizabeth, what do you know of sorcery? I shall tell you that it is indeed our way to listen intently to what stirs within. Our thoughts and feelings meld nicely together with the voice of our God. We of the forest touch each other and connect with this forest in ways that allow us to know what is true and what is not, what is love and what is not. This gift gives us the power of wisdom and foresight, for when we are still we can hear the voices in the wind, the trees, and the moon and stars. We can hear the callings of our lovers, our children, our family near and far. We can hear the callings of the Goddess as she lives within each and every being and most importantly we are one with the beating of our own hearts. Our inner wisdom is strong and true for we live as one with the Mother God. She guides us and teaches us to be one with all. This ensures our safety and our abundance. If that is sorcery, so be it!"

Elizabeth did not quite know what to make of the words this woman of the forest had just spoken. Mouth agape, a stare froze upon her face. A deep breath, and sigh filled with a knowing relief flooded her body and expanded her chest. She felt mighty and words suddenly poured from her being like the rush of a river in spring.

"The Mother God?" asked Elizabeth. "Do you know the Mother God? I called to her long ago. Why did I call her? How did I know to do so?"

Sophia moved in closer, lowering her voice and softening her stare. "I do not know the reasons that you heard Her calling. That is for you to know." She moved in even closer and touched Elizabeth's cheek ever so gently. "I do know however that She brought you here to us and that I am to help you in any way that I am able. As I said, I have pondered this for many a week and here is what I have to tell you. Wait a short while before you and Demetri take any action. It may seem like eternity, but it shall pass and it is imperative that you hide your condition from your family and staff. It is not hard to do so for you say so yourself that your staff rarely helps you dress. Wear large clothing and please do not wear any binding fabrics, for that might limit your babe's growth. This babe needs to have freedom to grow…just as his mother." Sophia smiled and held both hands over Elizabeth's belly.

"I feel your hands as if they are caressing my babe, Sophia! I can feel the warmth and love."

"Yes, child. This is the love of the Mother God you feel. Take in Her love and let it soothe you as needed. Demetri will be able to care for you and your child when his work on the land is completed. He will have means and a way. It shan't be long before that time comes and you will then know where you will make your home. In the mean time you may come to me and I shall care for you and your babe. When it comes time for the birth, I will assist you. I shall teach you much about babes over the next few months. I shall take good care of you. You must however be very careful as to when you visit. Listen closely to the calling of your heart. When you know it is safe, you may come to us and not a minute before."

Elizabeth knew of what Sophia spoke and her directions seemed so very soothing and adequate. The voice of the Goddesses' call had been coming to her all along and trust it, she must. Her friend's lives as well as hers and her babes now truly did depend on it.

Sophia continued. "As you now know, we do not live as others do. You yourself thought us sorceresses. You know what happens to sorceresses and witches." Elizabeth nodded and Sophia continued.

"It will be a difficult journey ahead for you and Demetri. I promise you that I will do all in my power and through the power of the Great Mother, to help you travel the journey in safety."

"I am comforted by your words, my dear Sophia." Elizabeth shivered from the coolness of the evening. She so wanted to return to the warm cozy cottage and the delicious meal Sophia had prepared for her. She arose.

"Wait Elizabeth. Before we return to our meal, I must be sure that you understand." Sophia grabbed Elizabeth's hand and held on tightly staring directly into her face. Sophia looked different. For a moment, Sophia's face took on the features of Malvina staring her way through Sophia's soft sweet gaze. Sophia took Elizabeth's face into her hands and continued the eerie stare. Fear mixed with a sense of intense resolve pulse throughout her being as Sophia held her face in her hands. "If you and Demetri are to be together, you must remember to summon the Goddess to watch over you, guide you and protect you. Do not forget to summon the Goddess, for it is your life line."

"Yes, yes…I will remember, I will." Sophia nodded, dropped her grip and they both walked back into the cottage. Elizabeth shook the fear and dread from her being for this time was to be savored.

After enjoying the delicious meal and the company of her new friends, Elizabeth started back towards the estate with a new hope for her future. A packet of herbs from Sophia were tucked safely within the folds of her petticoats. These herbs, Sophia assured, would help her appetite and relieve her of the dreaded nausea. Walking away from Sophia's Elizabeth was caught in a trance of many thoughts and she did not notice the figure approaching her from behind a tree.

"Elizabeth, come here," said the voice.

Elizabeth wasn't frightened just startled a bit and she turned toward the gravelly voice. Catching a glimpse of what looked to be a green robe sparkling in the moonlight, she immediately realized that the voice belonged to Malvina. Sure enough, as Elizabeth approached the tree, out hobbled the old woman from the shadows.

"What is it Malvina?" asked Elizabeth calmly. She was sure she knew a lecture was coming.

"My old body will not make it to my cottage before sunup. Give me your help so I may move more quickly." Malvina crowed. Elizabeth gave her an arm with which to rest her weight upon.

"Lead the way and I will assist you to your cottage." Whispered Elizabeth.

Malvina did not seem to need her help, her gait was strong and sure. Elizabeth was not about to argue. This old woman was unsettling, for her way was uncomfortably mesmerizing. One could not help but be taken in, then shook up and left with an uncanny wise confusion. Malvina had been present at Sophia's that evening, yet had not said a word to her, not even after Sophia shared the news of Elizabeth's condition. The girls were overjoyed, but Malvina sat in silence. Perhaps Malvina did not like Demetri, or perhaps she did not think a commoner was good enough for one of noble blood. Whatsoever prompted her rude silences? Why did she even care what Malvina thought? Elizabeth walked faster. Malvina started to talk in a low but forceful voice.

"Elizabeth, do not worry about what I think. I am not your concern. I am however willing to help you. Do you know the elixir that your mother takes, in the green bottles?"

"Well, yes," said Elizabeth. "How did you know about…?" She stopped and stared at the old woman, sure she saw a piece of heaven and a piece of hell mixed in those eyes of gold.

Malvina cut off Elizabeth and continued.

"Elizabeth, *I* know many things. *You* need know only one thing, it doesn't matter how I know, I just know and what I know is to be heeded." Malvina pointed a bony finger right in her face. The point of which brushed against her cheek in the same place Sophia had so gently touched earlier. "If you find the need, take one bottle of the elixir and drink it all. That will stop your heartbeat and your babe's as well. You shall find peace in the green bottle of elixir, if and only if, the need arises." She stared into Elizabeth's eyes for a long moment and was gone.

Elizabeth stood alone transfixed and bewildered. The warning that Malvina had just imparted upon her was extremely odd and peculiar and in the way of Malvina, also contained a certain wisdom. The significance of such a wise warning was lost on her at the moment. She shook her head, removing the bewilderment and pushed all such thoughts of elixir and needed peace into the far recesses of her mind. She would not try to understand the warnings of this strange old woman now. She had other things on her mind and heart.

Elizabeth danced home, reveling in the most wonderful and joyous news of the eve. Exuberance and elation filled her soul and carried her home with splendid thoughts of when she would see Demetri again and how she would share the glorious news.

Their next meeting took place a few days later. Demetri came to Elizabeth at a clearing in the woods where they often met. As he approached her, she could see a look of despair on his face and although he tried to hide it with one of his whimsical smiles Elizabeth immediately knew that something was amiss. Her heart pounded in anticipation as she ran up to him. Hugging him fiercely she pulled him into her yet his trepidation did not fade. She pulled away and looked up at her love.

"What is it Demetri?" Why do you seem so distraught?" Elizabeth searched his eyes for an answer.

"I am not distraught my love, not at all." A forced smile barely moved his jaw.

"Demetri, please tell me what it is?" she begged, ignoring his response.

"You know me so well Elizabeth." Demetri cast his eyes down and held tight to her hands.

Impatience arose from her rounded belly. She just wanted to burst with the news and hold her love in her arms. Why must he be so sad today, she wondered.

"I must leave for a time Elizabeth." Demetri's face turned sullen and Elizabeth shuddered. "But it will only be for a short while. I was asked by my cousin to travel to Dover for some much needed supplies so we can finish with the clearing and planting of his land. I will be gone until the moon is full again, unless…unless… you come with me." He said, his forlorn look turning to a pleading glance.

Elizabeth felt relief fill her. This needed travel was not the terrible news that he thought it was. Her news would see to that!

"Must you truly go, my love? I do not know if I can last until the next full moon without you to fill me!" she started to tease.

"You see, Elizabeth, I cannot bear to leave you either, that is why I want you to come with me. We can be together on this trip and perhaps we will never return. I will find work and I will marry you." He said adamantly.

Elizabeth's mood turned serious. The words of Sophia reminded her what to do. She took a few breaths and listened to her heart. She said a silent prayer and asked the Mother God to help decide what to do. "No Demetri, not this trip. I must stay here. It is not an easy ride to the town of which you speak and I am with child so it would not be wise for me to travel." Elizabeth replied, smiling a haughty grin.

Demetri's eyes opened wide with surprise and he stepped back from her embrace.

"You are with child?" How could this be Elizabeth?" Demetri stared wide eyed.

She had not wanted to tell him in such a manner but it just slipped out. Pulling him close to her, she continued as she had planned and explained how this wonderful miracle happened. "I believe it was when you touched my heart with your very being Demetri. I believe that is when God gave us a child that is now growing inside of me. I feel it moving about in my belly. Here, feel it." Elizabeth placed Demetri's hand over the roundness of her belly.

"I know this is meant to be, and I know now that we shall be together forevermore. This child seals our fate!"

Demetri's eyes sparkled and she was pulled into the depth of his joy and affection. "I will care for you and our child." He exclaimed, picking her up and twirling her around. Elizabeth became nauseous and begged him to stop. Demetri set her down with a look of concern and she took his face in her hands, focusing on the twinkling in his sea green eyes and the love that radiated outward. She wanted to remember this moment forever in time, for it was a moment she was sure she was born to witness. The love of another, pouring out into her, reaching for her, pulling her in, embracing her and becoming one with her very soul was something so very deeply important.

"Remember Demetri when you and I met Sophia and she blessed us and the child I carried? She knew before I, that the babe was growing in me. I did not know such things about babe's growing inside. I did not know I was with child until Sophia told me…again." She kissed his lips softly, keeping her gaze upon him.

"Sophia told you? Did she come to you in a dream?"

"No, I ventured out just a few days ago. I went to see my friends and shared a meal with them. I wanted to ask her of this strange feeling I felt inside." Elizabeth blushed as she continued.   "I thought that I had caught an illness and that is why my belly was growing and my body felt so round and fat. But alas, Sophia kindly explained to me that when we came together in love, when our bodies became one, that is how we created this child that now grows in me." Explained Elizabeth, eyes still held firmly with her lovers.

"Yes, Elizabeth I am sure it is a babe that you carry and not a sickness that is making you fatter and fatter!" smiled Demetri. Demetri laughed and laughed as he swept her into his arms and hugged her with all his might, whispering words of endearment as he kissed her mouth. "There is no time for sadness now I shall leave on the right away so I may return to you, my love, and my child as soon, no sooner than I am able!"

"You are not leaving yet, for we must lay together before you depart. I want you to touch my heart and leave me with the memory of your scent and your touch and your gaze." She pulled him into her and could feel the strong urging of his body as it pressed against her round softness. Nothing enticed her more than to feel his want and need for her. He was touching her heart before he even entered her.

The two unlocked their embrace long enough to find a soft spot under a large pine tree, nestled safely out of sight of any traveler who might happen by. Elizabeth was trembling as Demetri gently lay her down. Her love for him was engulfing her mind, her heart and her soul. All of her being was wrapped and folded into his. Tears were falling from her face, or his, she knew not which. Demetri propped himself up on his side, put his face next to hers and gently kissed her tears away. She wrapped her arm through his and pulled his muscled strength close to her bosom. Here, he would enter her heart here, and down into her womanhood too, and here and here, she moved his hands over the length of her body, moving in perfect rhythm with him as she pushed his palms into her breasts and opened her legs to receive him. His tender touch sent her into a rush of tears and as the tears poured, they flushed out her fear of their unknown future.

Demetri continued to kiss her face and neck and rub her belly. He seemed in no hurry to enter her, as she so decidedly desired. He whispered to the babe as he lifted up her skirts and pushed them aside exposing her round soft bare belly. He kissed her skin, gently and uttered, "I love you little one. I love your beautiful mother too. So very, very much." Her lover's words and touch send her again to a place she had not yet known in his embrace. This was a far reaching place of binding and blinding love.

Demetri, kissed her belly and the soft place where he enters and it was here that she fell instantly into the bliss of his hot breath as it landed in drum beats inside the folds of her open body. She yearned for him to languish inside of her and to never stop touching, tasting and taking her in. She fell deeply into him as he entered her forcefully and tenderly. He moved into her again and again, intensely caressing her breasts and kissing her mouth, grabbing her lips with his own. The swollen lips of the place he entered were hot and ravenous. She craved his very being and would never let anyone else love her or enter her or, be this close to her and their babe. The three of them made a family, created and blessed in the deepest love that ever existed.

They made love for a very long time and lay in each other's arms not wanting to move, dare they break the spell. She could not get enough and the frenzy of her want lifted her up to sit upon him. She put him inside her, placed his hands upon her buttocks and insatiably rocked and moved in ways prior to this day, unknown. They now knew secrets, of how two people could touch souls, for the ecstasy would exist for eternity and keep them forever joined. The rapture led way to a quiet, satiated fatigue as they lay in each others arms, this time, they were both too spent too move. Her mind wandered to the other side of their fate. A dread crept in and the sickly, smoky cloud filled her heart and captured her joy. She pulled in closer to Demetri and lay her head upon his bare chest. She waited and waited to hear his heartbeat. When she heard it, she started to weep. Demetri turned to his love and looked at her in wonderment.

"Elizabeth, why do you cry?" he asked stroking her hair. "Is it the babe? Did we hurt him with our ferocious lovemaking? Tell me we did not." Elizabeth could hear his heartbeat pulsing faster and faster.

"No, my love." She whispered. "I do not think the joining of our souls disturbed our babe. Quite the contrary. This is why I weep. I can't be away from you for a day, let alone two days, or three…" Demetri interrupted her with a slight rise in his voice.

"I love you so and we shall be together forever more. Nothing can keep apart what our lovemaking has created. You said it yourself, in good words, nonetheless. We are connected in eternity. This is so." Demetri, lay himself gently atop her, yet did not enter her. She felt his words seep into their sweat soaked skin, and bond them again to a love so true.

"But I did not say such a wondrous thing in words, Demetri." She choked on a great well of tears trying to emerge. "My mind, or perhaps both of our minds, wrapped in the knowing of a love so true, spoke of our souls connected throughout eternity. I did not utter the knowing; I did not speak!" She pushed her ear closer to his heart, pulling him completely into her. Now she could hear the echoes of his life and her life, his body and hers together as one. The dread did not cease.

"I shall return from Devon and I shall bring you a gift. Perhaps I shall bring you a ring of gold. It is the symbol of eternity, my love. The eternity that somehow speaks loudly inside our heads and comes out of your mouth." Demetri smiled and playfully kissed her lips.

Elizabeth knew he was trying to make her feel better, but the dread was not leaving her being. "Or perhaps I shall not go and instead we leave together and marry." He continued.

Elizabeth smiled at the thought. He had found the right words to help her put the fears aside. Demetri slowly lifted himself up and lay his head down on her belly. A tear fell from his eye and Elizabeth could feel its warmth run down the side of her body and disappear into the earth below. Demetri gently kissed her skin where the tear had fallen. Her love and deep desire for their life together mixed with the fear of an unknown future. The fear was taking over her mind. It was then that she remembered the encouraging words Sophia had shared with her. She would pray to the Mother God, and thus she did. Ever so slowly, the dread moved aside and at last the darkness lifted.

She turned to her love and said. "Demetri, you must take your trip and when you return to me I will marry you. I do not wish to live another day without you as my husband so please hurry home to me and I promise you that when you return, I shall be fit and ready to start our life together. Take your trip and earn the last bit of money you can from your cousin and we shall then be together forevermore."

Demetri sat upright at hearing her words. He turned on his side and faced her. Putting his arm around her waist he leaned in close to her as he spoke.

"Elizabeth, I know we shall be together forever and I am filled with joy to hear you speak such words. Perhaps we can be wed under the fullness of the moon just as we met."

They sighed in unison and did not speak, for there was no need. They lay together in thought and when the sun was starting they arose, dressed and embraced.

"I love you my dear Elizabeth and I will return to you soon and take you as my wife."

"I love you my dear Demetri and I shall be honored to live my life forevermore as yours. Remember that we are linked in eternity. I do believe it to be so. Also…do not forget to pray to the Mother Goddess, she shall keep us both safe. Sophia told me so."

"Yes, my love, I shall be a good husband and do what my wife tells me." He smiled the mischievous grin that made her heart at ease. He would not let her go, until she pulled away first.

"Please be safe. Goodbye, my love." Elizabeth kissed him one last time. Holding her belly, she breathed deeply of his essence and painfully released herself from his embrace. She prayed to the Mother God all the way home, for his safety, for their love and for his swift return. They would be needing every bit of blessing from every God and Goddess, Priestess, Saint and Sage that ever existed.

Chapter Twelve

Henry hid safely behind one of the tallest and widest oak trees of the forest. A pang of guilt rattled his insides when he saw his sister with this man. His intent was to find Elizabeth on this day, yet he did not expect to find her with a man and in such a loving embrace. He had not really thought of what was occupying her time as of late, for he was consumed with his own troubles and if there ever was a time he needed his sister, her advice and expansive comfort, it was now. Yes, it was true that more times than not, during this long, warm summer, it was a common occurrence to be dismissed by his former best friend and confident. He would not stand for her insistent no, or her continuous evasiveness as cause for him to retreat any longer. He had no one else to turn to. Never was there another for him to turn to, he needed her now, and he was angry! How did she not understand what was going on in his life? She had always watched out for him, taken good care of him, knew his every need before even he knew. He was quite insistent, if only in his own mind, that he would indeed find his sister this very day and confront her regarding her expressed selfishness. She would surely apologize profusely, once she knew how she had been shirking her duties as his elder sister and offer her kind and sage advice. Now she had been found, yet he could not get himself to approach, so he lay waiting.

As he crouched in waiting, a stunning truth crept up from within. Out of all the places his sister could have been in this great and vast land outside the estate walls, how was it that he had found her? He had not followed her out of the gates, or past the secret exits, he had simply started walking into the forest. With a heart of sheer determination, he had just kept walking farther and farther away from the estate, his feet guiding him, as if he were in a dream. Is this a magic spell I am under? What shall I do next? He sought to answer his own question as his body grew still, compelling him to sit quietly, so he obliged. Whatsoever this odd, calm inner directive was he was at its mercy. He could not see Elizabeth from where he sat yet he did sense her. He could feel the familiar love and caring that his sister undoubtedly still had for him. He was comforted.

His mind drifted to the root of his problem. It was a woman. A woman who would not return his affection, or…would she? She was not a lass and not a maiden; she was a woman and was surely the cause of his suffering. Thoughts of her sent his mind reeling and his body quivering for she was so beautiful and he had in fact loved her for many a year. He had loved her since the day she arrived at the estate.

As he patiently waited under the oak for his sister, Henry went back in time to the fated day he met this woman. Sitting inside the back gate, behind the milk house, he laid in wait, much like he did now. Hidden, unobtrusive, silent and ever so observant, he sat as he had so many times before with Elizabeth, to watch the comings and goings of the servants. Always the new ones came carried within the walls of the tattered, old, menacing coach. It showed up without notice, sent by some unknown force. Elizabeth would tell stories about each new servant as they emerged from the belly of the dark coach and amuse him with thrilling fantasies who these people really were and why they were arriving at the Cumberland Estate. Some of the maids were actually princesses from faraway lands, in hiding, for fear of their lives, the stable boys, criminals escaping from the gallows. On this particular day, however, on this fated day, he sat alone. Elizabeth was otherwise detained. It was just he who bore witness when the young lass emerged from an unknown past and it was only he who was there to create a story of her beginnings. Her beauty immediately captivated him as she jumped down from the coach, every inch of her body, bouncing pleasingly from the journey. She landed but a few feet from where he lay in hiding, her tousled hair and uninhibited figure enticing beyond measure. His sister would surely have a tawdry tale to tell regarding this lass. She did not ride as a proper maiden would, safely tucked inside the coach, no she sat outside in the sun, next to the driver. Henry next sized up the driver as he sat like large bull in the grazing fields. The man looked to be of the same stock as the coach's horses, large and overbearing, muscles bulging in all the places a steed needs strength. The man threw down one large trunk, barely missing the fair lass, before sliding down after it. Henry sat as quiet as could be, completely enthralled by the tempestuous sight.

What happened next would forever be in his mind. The hefty, robust man grabbed the lass, lifted up her skirts, put his hands deep inside the folds of her petticoats and pulled her very close for what seemed to be a very long time. As Henry watched, he felt his body grow particularly aroused. The man was quite menacing with the same wild hair as the lass, a long beard and the looks of a pirate. Not that he himself had ever seen a pirate, but Father described these intimidating and gruesomely menacing characters many a time, for Father had encountered them on his many sea voyages. Perhaps he was such a bloke. It was mostly the lass's face and body that he would not forget. Her long hair was flowing outside of her cap, her cape flew open and her breasts exposed by her own hands. The look in her eyes was something he had never witnessed. It was as if she was in some faraway place, mesmerized by the man's touch. She wriggled and writhed as the man's hands moved eagerly underneath her skirts, lifting her up almost completely off the ground with his strength. The oddest sounds came from her bounteous lips and her voluptuous body writhed in waves of great motion. She caressed her own breasts and suppressed silent grunts as the show continued on for many a moment. Henry did not know what to make of this sight. He had never before thought such delight and deviousness could exist in one quick moment. He was indeed glad however that his sister was not witness to such a display. The man then said something to the lass that was forever etched in Henry's mind.

"You are mine forever, for no one else can make you feel as I do. Do your bidding here, you know what you must do. I shall return when you are finished. You are mine, forever…" The man spoke the words, with no mind to who might hear and her face flushed as she smiled at him a deep rich smile. She then kissed the man on his lips.

"I shall do your bidding." Said the lass.

The lass was Priscilla, Cookies kitchen maid of highest order. She is the one who stole his heart that day and now, he was in trouble deep.

The memory aroused his body, awakened his heart and pounded out the depth of his feelings for this intrepid woman. Priscilla had done some things that he feared might break her promise to the gargantuan pirate, and he was to blame. It was not long after she arrived that his fate with her was sealed. Henry was hopelessly in love with Priscilla.

His thoughts lingered backward in time. He was helping Cookie by bringing the heavy items for the week's meals from the ice house into the pantry. He wanted to be of service and since his own father was not teaching him the ways of a nobleman, then he would just have to help as he saw fit. Nobleman helped those who needed them, especially when it came to the women in the household, or so he had read somewhere. He knew that Cookie greatly appreciated his help too, she told him so. As he was about to enter the icehouse to gather the pork thighs Priscilla approached.

"Yes, Priscilla, is there something else that Cookie wants?" asked Henry, not wanting to look at her, for the stirrings she arose in him were so great as of late.

"No, Sir, there is nothing that she wants. I however do want something." Priscilla took Henry's hand and brought him around back of the icehouse. She pressed her body up close to him and put her hand upon his loins. She stared directly into his eyes, her look burned through his trousers. "I know what you want from me and I have decided it is time to give it to you." She rubbed his loins gently. He could barely contain himself, as the familiar pleasure arose. She was betrothed to the giant and yet this yearning would not cease. He found himself wanting to run from whatsoever Priscilla had become and also wanting more than anything to sink deep into her flesh. He squirmed and sought to release himself from her deeply penetrating gaze. She did not let him look away, nor move, for she held his face with one hand and furiously fondled his loins with the other. He was not at all sure what to do next, so he abandoned himself to the feelings she spurred in him, pulled at his trousers and freed himself. Priscilla just kept looking at him, her gaze fiery in its intent. The pleasures arose and then she was gone. Henry stood in shock, his trousers around his knees and shirttail wet.

Priscilla approached him many times over the following weeks. Each time, her stare took him in and she touched him in the exact way that made him want her body and soul, yet she never let him touch her. He was so confused. He loved her for making him feel such things, but she did not let him show her his love. There was never a time when the two were alone, unless she suddenly appeared and then he was at her command. After a time, humiliation grew, for he was not sure what to do or how to respond to her advances, but each time she held him, he did nothing but succumb.

Sitting back against the tree he aimlessly looked past the small growth of tiny saplings that protected him from discovery. He sighed long and hard. My sister seems to be in a similar situation, love has gotten a hold of her too. I long for the days when we were still children, he thought, holding his head in his hands and reminiscing. When we were children, all was much simpler. Simpler. He coughed himself into the present moment. A tightness erupted from deep within his chest. The panic to catch his breath started. He had not had a coughing spell in many a year and the familiar dread struck hard. It was upon him now and his breath became shallow and fast. He must retreat from his venture and find his way back home, to the estate. Now!

Henry arose and the air spun around him as if he fell into a whirlpool from the waist up. He righted himself against the tree and waited. He had to get control, he had to. The panic continued. Running to another tree, he fell hard against it and landed on his back. Counting would help. Yes, he would count to find his breath as Elizabeth taught him. Slowly he counted reaching deeper within for air and imagining his sister, holding his hand, soothing him. Time passed yet he did not know if it was an hour or two, or a mere moment. His chest relaxed and he drifted off into a memory from his youth remembering how the panic had welled up so often. As a child, he did not know how to stop the attacks but Elizabeth did. Mother did not, father did not. A faint memory of Mother burst into his mind. He could smell her; the stale stench of old bed linens and body odors. He could feel her frail, fleshy arms around him. Something sharp, stabbed him, his chest, his neck…the panic started once more, pulling at his ribs, jerking the life force out of him. Henry rolled over, stood up and ran, fast as he could back to the estate. He had to make it back, or he would be swallowed up by the thick heaviness within his chest.

Running and coughing and wheezing, he ran. He had to get to the vile, where was his vile of medicine? …oh, Elizabeth, why? He made it to the outside of the gatehouse. "I am here…here!" he shouted. Nothing came out, but a wisp of breath. He felt the ground hit his head. The vile of medicine crashed to the ground.

Voices, seemingly coming from far, far away stirred him awake. Someone touched his forehead, and he lifted up his arm in response. It did not move. His lips were burning…ah, he would lick them to soothe the burn, but his tongue was thick and heavy. He was breathing. He could feel his chest laboring. Up and down, it rose, up and down. He pried open his eyes. They too were heavy, too heavy for him to open.

"I told you, I will take care of him. I am in charge here now. Leave at once." He recognized Priscilla's husky voice, giving the command. Henry felt fear arise in him. He lay paralyzed, and love her as he did, he did not trust Priscilla. She was capable of anything. Betrayal, deceit. His mind drifted.

"Yes, ma'am, but I want to be with him. My duties are done for the day. I can stay by his side…please."

Annie. It was Annie's voice he heard. He tried with all his might to open his eyes, to glimpse his sweet friend. He saw her, through the crack in his lid. The light stung and he rested them shut. What was happening, he wondered.

"I brought you Master's medicine, I did what you asked, now please let me stay." Begged Annie.

"Oh, so you have taken a fancy to Master Henry have you? You are nothing but a whore!"

Henry stirred, he wanted to raise his hand in defense of Annie, but still it would not move. He could feel their presence come nearer and one of them touched him. It was Priscilla. He could sense her rough commanding presence. He was so afraid of how his body might react to her touch, with Annie present. Priscilla was touching his chest, pressing down…too hard.

"See here, Miss, he is fine now, and breathing without effort. I am sure he will come around soon and I will be the first face he sees. Do you understand? You are not going to ruin my plan…" Priscilla's hand was incredibly uncomfortable upon Henry's chest. He tried to move but the effort was so great.

"Plan? What plan do you speak of Priscilla? Does Dr. Fleish know of your plan?" asked Annie.

"You are a stupid girl. The Master and I are lovers. We plan to be wed." Priscilla hissed and ran her fingers along Henry's face.

Henry winced inside his thick coffin and Priscilla jumped back. He pried open his eyes once more and saw Priscilla's face threatening and menacing. She turned to Annie and whispered. "Quiet, you fool, you will awaken him before he has time to recover."

It's too late Priscilla, thought Henry. I am awake. His chest heaved. The immense effort it took to move was exhausting as was this conversation he was hearing. None of it made sense. They were lovers? Did she love him? What about the burly man? Priscilla was betrothed to him. How could she say they were to be wed when…and furthermore…. Annie was in trouble and Priscilla wanted to hurt her. He was a nobleman…he was in training…He must wake up; he must shake himself out of this stupor.

"I am not leaving my Master's side", said Annie. She stood next to Henry, her back to him. He wanted to reach out and touch her.

"You will leave now, stupid girl. I am in charge here, you are not." Priscilla grabbed Annie by the arm and flung her around. Priscilla was not only older than Annie, but she was bigger and stronger. She had years and weight on the young maiden. She pushed her out the door as Henry watched.

Annie, come back, he yelled loudly inside his own head. He knew where he was, he lay in Priscilla's bed in the servant's quarters. She had taken him there once before. Why did she take him here? He needed to be in his own bedchambers. Why was he not taken into his own bed? He moaned inside of his stupor and drifted in and out of sleep. Thoughts and demons, Priscilla and Annie danced within his mind. He was in love…with Priscilla…she was betrothed. He could not stop his desire for her...marry…I want you to love me! He screamed laying in Priscilla's bed, frozen.

He awoke to the feel of someone holding his hand. It did not seem to be Priscilla's strong grip. The hand was much smaller. This hand was cool and gentle. He then felt her breath upon his face, and the wisp of kisses, soft and light, upon his cheek, then his mouth. This was delightful.

"Master Henry, I love you. I want you to awaken, so I may lead you back to your room. Come, awaken."

Henry's entire body awakened with the sweet words from Annie the chamber maid. He felt the familiar pulling in areas that only Priscilla had formerly owned. Annie was with him since they were both small children, her mother and two sisters were their laundresses. They were more like playmates than servants then, yet Father would not allow such interactions. Lately, however, it seemed Annie was often about and he had taken notice of her, wondering when she had grown so beautiful. Her beauty was framed in a small and delicate body, her breasts full and face dotted with flecks of gold. She smelled of freshly laundered bed linens and the air of spring. She often made him smile, with a glance of delightful presence and he felt protective of her, a need to defend and honor his childhood friend. So very different than Priscilla, thought Henry. Annie is the one I should be kissing and touching, not Priscilla, the sultry woman who brought him to ecstasy over and over with her piercing gaze and firm touch. Priscilla was beautiful too, he thought, in a different sort of way. She was almost as tall as he, had sharp blue eyes and soft buttery skin. She smelled of wheat flour and roast duck, her body full and round, with breasts that protruded nicely from within her smock. His thoughts were of the pleasures of women now, not demons.

"Henry, wake up please, you are not safe here." Annie's voice woke him out of his thoughts of lust and lore, pretty maidens and feisty love.

"Annie…" he could speak.

Tightening her grip, she pressed her face closer. "Yes, Master Henry?" Her voice sent waves of comfort throughout his body as the delightful aroma of cinnamon and sweet cream poured from her lips and landed ever so gently upon his weary senses. Overwhelmed with gratitude that he was alive and could finally move, he had a sudden urge to kiss her. And so he did so, firmly on her delectable lips. Although his mouth was still swollen and dry, Annie kissed him back, effortlessly and with great affection.

"That is different." he exclaimed.

"What?" asked Annie as she continued kissing him, quite content without an answer. A faraway, yet loud noise startled them both back into the quarters. "Can you get up Master Henry?" she asked wrapping her slight arms around him and pulling him with all her might. She was a might bit stronger than he expected.

Henry wanted to continue to kiss her, but knew they must move fast. He took a deep breath and used all his strength to sit up. His head started to spin, but this he was used to, for the aftermath of a breathing spell never failed to leave his head in a spin. "Give me a moment Annie and I will be able to walk." She was smiling at him with a look of adoration and relief. Such a look sent him reeling with confusion and it was not from the aftermath of his breathing spell. Just this morn he thought he was in love with Priscilla and now, seeing how Annie gazed upon him…kissing him, well, he did not know what to make of such perplexity. He must find Elizabeth; she would know what to do!

"Come quickly, we must get you out of here before Priscilla returns. I fear she had taken a dislike to me and I do not want her to hurt you in any way." said Annie, stroking Henry's hair. "I have cared deeply for you since we were children. Please do not be angry with me, but I do feel, Master, that Priscilla does not mean well by you."

"Yes, Annie…let's get out of here…and please don't call me Master. I have not earned that title as of yet."

Henry escorted Annie out of the servant's quarters. He knew a secret way back to his bedchambers that he had not yet shown Priscilla. They safely entered the dark tunnel. He lit the hidden candle and led Annie back to the main hall and into his bed chambers. He was grateful that father kept a very small staff, for he did not want to see anyone at this time, especially not Priscilla.

"Annie, thank you for caring for me, I am grateful, you may leave now, for I must be a…a…alone." Henry suddenly felt nauseous and chilled to the bone. His head pounded. Annie stood looking up at him with her sparkly golden eyes. What did she want? What did Priscilla want? He ran to the basin and heaved. His body could not stop itself. Nothing came out, for he had not eaten in many an hour.

"Master, Henry, I shall go now and fetch you a warm coverlet… and shall I have Cookie make you a brew?" She did not wait for his answer. "Yes, I shall." Annie called from the doorway.

"No, no…wait!" Henry had to be very careful, this he knew. "Go to Madeline, the Spicer, ask her to make me a brew, you may tell her why. That is all." He called, trying to catch his breath as he heaved once more. The instructions to his servant had flown out from his being. He did not know as to why.

"Yes, Master, I shall do as you say, I will return quickly." With that she scurried out the door.

Henry felt relieved and supported in his words to Annie. He also felt upheld, as if an invisible being was surrounding him with a blanket of protection. He would not question this, it must be coming from Elizabeth, his trusted confident, friend and caregiver. She always knew. How could he have doubted her care? Henry lay on his bed. It had never felt so warm, and soft and inviting. He drifted off to sleep to images of Priscilla touching him and him entering into her as he so desired to do. She laughed at him, an uproarious and vengeful laugh.

"Master, Henry…Henry…I have the brew from Madeline, here, I shall set it on the bed table." He heard the soft whispers and then the feel of the warm coverlet surrounding his body and soft touches tucking him in around each inch of his torso. "I shall send Mistress Elizabeth in, as soon as she returns. All is well, all is well."

Henry tossed and turned, Priscilla and Annie were both pulling on him, wedging themselves into his bed, grabbing, groping. He felt as if he had no choice but to run, run, far, far away, and as he ran, he felt the tightness start, the pounding, the pulling, the heavy, heavy burden that made its home inside his chest. Priscilla and Annie stood in front of him, trying to stop him as he ran then they lay atop him, pushing him into the ground, shoveling dirt upon his face, burying him…alive.

Chapter Thirteen

"Henry, what have you gotten yourself into?" Elizabeth scolded rather than ask in a tone of sisterly compassion. All she wanted to do was to grieve Demetri's departure alone, but her brother needed her. "Wake up now and tell me what has transpired in my absence!" Hands on hips, Annie stood to her left and her brother slept soundly in his bed. She continued as if her persistence would wake him. "Annie has summoned me, so speak up." Henry was not waking, so she sat on his bed, and stroked his arm. He looked so pale. She had been summoned in a most peculiar way and her suspicions were alerted as she looked upon her brother. A wave of guilt overcame her.

Elizabeth had been heading ever so quickly across the Inner Court just moments before. She had no time to waste, for she stayed as long as she could in the arms of her love and now she was late for evening meal and she did not want to be caught off guard in case James made an appearance.

Annie jumped out of the shadows and stopped her. "Lady Cumberland, I need to speak to you, please."

Elizabeth was annoyed at the girl's sneaky manner. "Why do you hide Annie, and please call me Elizabeth."

"Yes ma'am, she curtsied." This infuriated Elizabeth. She had no patience for such protocols.

"Come with me for I am in need of rest before the evening meal." Elizabeth kept walking toward her chambers as a sudden waive of nausea came upon her. "What is it that I hear? Is that Father talking to someone?" Elizabeth then caught the unmistakable voice of James booming from somewhere in the distance.

"I must go; I don't have time." Elizabeth walked quickly toward her bedchambers, Annie scurrying behind.

Opening the door to her haven she stepped inside, turned to close it and nearly stumbled on Annie as she stood silently at Elizabeth's side.

"What do you want Annie?" Elizabeth was so very tired and had no energy left in her body to deal with the chamber maid.

"I blame you not for disliking the Earl of Hartford, Lady, for I find him quite offensive myself. "Annie covered her mouth, eyes wide with panic, looking as if she overstepped once more.

Elizabeth choked back vomit at the mere mention of his name. "Did you hear him too?" Elizabeth mumbled and headed over to the chamber pot. The nausea passed quickly and she spied a tray of stale biscuits and hardened cheese left from the midday meal. She devoured the biscuits, one by one before addressing Annie. Elizabeth's nausea completely disappeared along with any thought of the vile evil James, but the panic in Annie's face had not.

Elizabeth's demeanor gently lifted after consuming the much needed nourishment. "Annie, I have a great fondness for you and I am sure Henry does as well. You have been a part of our lives since we were wee tots in the nursery. I trust you. Tell me, what is it that you wish to speak of?"

"Henry took ill today and he wishes to see you." Annie's eyes were blurry with panic.

Elizabeth pushed herself up from the chair in a start and saw Annie eyeing her ever rounding belly. Quickly pulling her skirts to cover the evidence of her condition she charged towards the door. "We must go to him, what happened?" Rushing through the corridor in the direction of Henry's chambers they continued the conversation.

"He is much better now, resting well. He had a spell today and he was alone, I fear, when the spell began. Priscilla said she found him, but I do not believe a word…that witch…I am sorry Lady for the cursing. She said she found him and took him to her quarters instead of here. I know not why and it distresses me so. She has lay claim to him in a manner that is not of her right and there is something evil…" Annie trailed off in her description of her rival before continuing. "She did however call on me to find you and when I could not, I knew to get the vile of medicine. I knew where it was."

Now they both stood beside Henry's bed for what seemed an eternity. Henry did not seem to want to wake and Elizabeth could wait no longer. As much as the concern for her brother haunted her, the thought of James in the estate haunted her even more. She must go now and find out if he was afoot and if so how she could avoid him.

"Annie, he seems to be resting, which is what he is ought to do after a spell. You must stay here with him. I will see to it that Priscilla is kept busy and does not interfere with his sleep.

I will come to you later. Thank you for taking care of him. I am grateful." And with that Elizabeth left her brother's side, confident he would be just fine.

Elizabeth walked directly to her father's study. The door was open and she could see her father sitting near the fire, alone. Her belly churned and she felt the tingle of panic well up within her. Breathing deeply, she found herself heading to the kitchen to speak with Cookie. She had to trust her to help her for now, for Elizabeth was not ready to confront her father regarding James.

Elizabeth found Cookie stirring a big pot of broth. The staff was not scurrying about and this was a good sign. There would be no dinner guests tonight, this she was sure of. "Cookie, could you please do me a favor?" asked Elizabeth, standing next to the vat of broth and inhaling its aroma.

"Why yes, missy, is it some of this broth you crave? I can ladle ye up some right away." Cookie grabbed a bowl and spoon and filled it to the brim. Elizabeth sat and waited for it to cool.

"I need you to keep Priscilla occupied for a few days. Can you do so? "

Cookie nodded in agreement. Elizabeth then knew for sure something was amiss. It was not like Cookie to simply agree. She usually had much to say about her opinions.

"And, Cookie, the Earl of Hartford is not dining with us this evening is he?" Elizabeth peered into the broth, hoping the answer was no.

"No, missy, he is not. I don't like that bloke at all, and I am glad that he is not dining here tonight. I put a stop to it, I did. I told yer father that I had not time to prepare a meal for them that would suit the Earl. That is a lie of course, for I can whip up a fine meal in to time..." Cookie was laughing and her body jiggled in delight. "I just don't like the way he leers at me lasses. I don't like him, no not at all..." she wiped her hands on her apron and walked to the counter. She carved a few slices of bacon and set them in front of Elizabeth. "Here, child, eat this, it is good for yee and yer...just eat!"

"Thank you Cookie, and one more thing. If you find out that Father is planning to entertain the Earl, could you please give word to me?"

"Will do Mistress Elizabeth, will do." Cookie nodded her head with great conviction. Elizabeth felt safe in this woman's presence. She always felt that Cookie would defend her to the death, if she could, and it always seemed as if she could, at least inside of these kitchen walls.

Elizabeth was satiated with the nourishment that Cookie provided and she had the best night's sleep in many a month. She dreamt of Demetri and her babe, the women of the Forest and even Henry. They were all together. The dream seemed so very real, and she did not want to leave these people who loved her so, but morning came and with it, the pounding on her door.

"Elizabeth, open your door, it is I, your brother, let me in!" She had learned how to lock her door from the inside and had done so to protect her privacy. She did not want anyone entering without her knowledge as some were apt to do as of late.

Elizabeth arose from her bed, wrapped herself in her robe and let her brother in. Annie was behind him with a tray of biscuits and jam and hot morning brew. Henry did not even know she was there.

"Annie, uh...you are as quiet as a mouse." He moved out of her way and Elizabeth saw his face turn crimson. Elizabeth had a feeling Annie had not left his side all night long.

"Yes, Master Henry. I mean, Henry. Yes, I try to be."

"It is not a good thing, Annie. I need to know when you are about!" shouted Henry.

Elizabeth was surprised at Henry's outburst, especially toward, their friend, who had helped him just yesterday.

"Annie, I am sure Henry is still feeling the effects of his spell, please forgive him."

Henry did not heed Elizabeth's apology for him and continued in a rude manner.

"Annie, I need to talk to my sister alone…"

Elizabeth interrupted Henry, thanked Annie and told her to leave. "We will call you in a bit Annie." She ushered her out and watched her walk down the hall and out of sight before she returned to her brother.

"Henry, please tell me how you are feeling today and what on earth happened to you yesterday? I hear you had a terrible spell. Annie was quite worried. And what is this about Priscilla?" Elizabeth did not have time to deal her brother's vague rudeness.

"Now you want to know? Now you seem to care? Sister, I have hardly had a chance to see you over the last several months. You have been out and about, doing who knows what. I needed you and you were not to be found and how…how did you know about Priscilla?" Henry was sitting on one of the soft benches and looked as if he would burst open right into the cushiony fabric.

Elizabeth sat very close to him and put her arm around his shoulders. He was right. She had been so caught up in her new love that she had hardly paid attention to her brother. The time was right for her to once more spend her days with her beloved brother for his presence would not only keep her mind off of her traveling lover, but would give her opportunity to find solace and comfort in caring for her younger sibling. She knew well of her place as caregiver.

"Brother, I am sorry. I shall make it up to you." Elizabeth rubbed his shoulders and took in his posture. Always she knew if her brother was indeed feeling better for she knew him as well as she knew her own self, perhaps more so. As she consoled him an unfamiliar feeling came over her. She could not feel her brother's presence as much as that of her lover and her babe. She continued to press her hand upon his ribs and uttered a silent prayer. Mother God, help me care for my dear brother. Help me for I cannot do this alone.

Henry continued as if all was as it always had been. He was past the illness and his sister was there to console him. Yet all was not well and this Elizabeth knew.

"I am feeling much better today, but I must tell you that I fear for my future, and I need you to tell me what to do." Henry pushed out his bottom lip just as he had always done in order to gain her sympathy and attention.

"Tell you what to do? Well brother dear, you are near a man now, so I feel it is time for you to not need your sister to tell you what to do." Elizabeth felt the truth and the fear in this statement.

Henry started to wheeze and cough. "No, I need you…" Elizabeth immediately found the ointment in her dressing table coffer. She opened the container and rubbed it into his neck and chest. Henry took a deep breath and he was able to slow his breathing.

"Henry tell me what is on your mind. You have not had a spell in so very long."

"I am being haunted by a woman. She has stolen my heart and I know not what to do."
Henry looked so sad and forlorn.

Elizabeth almost burst out laughing. How could her little brother have such troubles? He
was a mere lad…was a lad…he is no longer young, she realized. He had grown into a young man
and she had not noticed. Staring at him in disbelief she noticed his pout. Still such a boy and he
did still need her even though they both had grown so much as of late. Both now had very
different needs than a mere season ago.

"The woman is older than I and she has ways…" Henry sat back and pushed Elizabeth's
hand away. His face contorted. Elizabeth sat solemnly, holding in her mirth at her brother's
dilemma.

"She has made me fall in love with her but she does not seem to want to return the favor
and then, she…I…heard her saying that she and I are to be married…I do not understand. Help
me please Elizabeth."

Elizabeth was a bit confused with his story. It had fallen so quickly out of his mouth that
she had trouble following. She did not however want to upset Henry, for she could see he could
not afford another spell so she patiently awaited his next thought to come tumbling forth.

"I do not know if I truly love Priscilla. I thought I did until yesterday when I saw you and
your lover. It was then that something deep within me awoke causing such a panic. I ran and ran
and ended up in Priscilla's bed asleep, yet awake and that is when I heard it…"

Elizabeth interrupted her face flushed red. "You saw me and my..." She could not say it, for she would not speak of Demetri inside the estate walls. To mention their world together within the confines of this world would surely cast a very terrible hex upon them both.

"Yes, I am sorry sister, but I had to find you. I searched for you for days. Each time you went out, I followed. You always lost me until yesterday. I listened to a voice that seemed to come from the deepest part of the forest. I thought it was you calling to me. Was it?" Not stopping for an answer Henry continued. "Well, I found you so it must have been. I saw you in the arms of a young man. You seemed happy, safe from harm. I did not want to disturb you. I am sorry I intruded. I just needed ..." Henry started to cry.

Elizabeth did not want anyone to know of her whereabouts, not even her brother. The sacredness of her union seemed tainted now.

Elizabeth consoled him, putting her arms around his shoulders and whispering soothing words. "It is all right now Henry I am here for you now. Your wish for my comfort has been granted. What is it that upsets you so?

"A spell came over me, I ran towards home and the next thing I knew I was in the servant's quarters and Priscilla was yelling at Annie, telling her that she and I were to be wed. I could not move, I could do nothing and I fell asleep and awoke to kisses but they were not from Priscilla, it was Annie, kissing me and telling me she loved me. I felt such feelings! None the likes that I ever felt with Priscilla, yet Priscilla...she..." he heaved a great sigh and sat waiting for Elizabeth's response.

Elizabeth sorted through his rambling words. Yes, Priscilla had a sort of uneasy control over Henry. It seemed a normal infatuation yet now her mind took her to remembrances of interactions with Priscilla. There was something malicious about her, yes, that was it. She pushed the thoughts in the background, not willing to reveal her concerns to her brother as of yet.

"I do believe you are caught between two loves. There is not a thing to do now. You need take time and ponder, you are a mere lad of sixteen and there should be no talk of marriage. You are the son of a noble man and you must quest. You have much to do, much to see. Do you not want to leave this estate and sail like Father? Or you could go to the finest school or…"

Henry interrupted. "Father does not want me to go anywhere. I am to stay here and run the estate. Grandfather has made it clear to me that running this place is my destiny. He has spoken to me many a time about what is expected of me and even told me who I was betrothed to. I will marry our cousin Margaret when she comes of age. I am betrothed already and I will live a life in my own father's footsteps, without will of my own, I accepted my fate… until Priscilla and Annie… "

Elizabeth stood up and started pacing. Staring at the fine Turkey rug, she followed the designs as she strode. She had not known of such things regarding her brother's future. She had not known he too was betrothed and that his life was also set according to the will of Grandfather. Elizabeth had always found solace in her heart at the thought of her brother being free to leave and set on whatsoever adventures his heart desired. This was what was expected of the men of royal heritage such as her brother. Now, he too was under the demands of her father and Grandfather. What was happening here? It was all wrong! The anger welled up within and she could not contain the hatred for her father and grandfather, and her mother. How could they do this to them? How could they do this to her brother, the one she protected and helped! They were born into wealth, they were not slaves or servants, but their very existence was determined by these two men and the illness that took over her mother. She was growing more and more angry by the moment. Her stomach tightened and her shoulders hunched upward as she drew her arms ready to strike. She brought her fist down hard on the table, shaking and spilling the morning brew and sending the biscuits flying across the room. She would not let them take away what she had so carefully protected. Her brother would know freedom; the same freedom she was planning for herself. It was his right. She wanted him to be well and to never, ever have to suffer the fate of Grandfather's or Father's or Mother's chosen destiny. She would not stand for this. They deserved a destiny of their own.

Henry sat wide eyed, never having seen his sister react with so much anger. "I am so very sorry to have angered you, sister. What have I done? I will take it all back. I need you to help me. I have now angered you."

Elizabeth continued pacing grinding the biscuits into the floor boards and carpet. Such a mess would attract rodents but she was so angry, she did not care. I will gladly live with the rodents if it means my happiness, she screamed inside of her own mind.

"You have not angered me Henry. It is Father and Grandfather and Mother who anger me. They treat us as if we are slaves to our inheritance, I shall not stand for it." Elizabeth knew there was nothing she could do and that infuriated her more. She was stopped dead in her tracks by her destiny. A destiny set out for her years before she was even born. She cursed God. "Damn the God who created this life. I see no rhyme, nor reason for it." She sat with a thud on the bench across from her brother.

After a few moments of complete silence, Henry spoke. "So, you are not angry with me? I have not ruined my life by falling in love with Priscilla, even though she threatened Annie and said that she and I were to wed? Priscilla has cast a deep spell on me, for I am not of right mind in her presence. Am I in love with her?"

Elizabeth shook herself out of her own stew realizing that her brother was not of the same mind as she. It is because I now know of another life and another way. I want that other life. Henry does not yet know. She would show him. Yes, the only answer to both of their dilemmas is to venture into the forest. They both must go into the forest, and as soon as possible. Tonight, in her dreams, she will ask the women if it is safe. A visit with the women in the forest would save them both.

Henry calmed when Elizabeth told him that she had a plan that would help him. When the time was right she would reveal her plan, she assured her brother. She knew he believed her by the way his face lit up and his body softened. His look reminded her of the times they were children and ventured into the maze or delighted in one of the many games they played within the estate walls. Her spirits lifted and carried her throughout the day. She was on her way to the kitchen in the late afternoon to see Cookie when she heard the voices again. His voice pierced her heart and she stopped dead in her tracks. Panic flooded her being and her belly reeled.

Annie approached her from out of the dark corner of the great hall, extended her hand and spoke gently.

"Lady Elizabeth, Cookie has asked me to tell you that the Earl of …Hart…Hartford is here and will dine with your father this eve. I am so sorry…" she whispered the last part with such an air of concern that Elizabeth started to weep. She felt the blow of having to be in his company harder than she had ever experienced. She did not want to see him ever. Not now, nor ever. She would be rid of him if it was the last thing she did.

"Thank you Annie that will be all." Elizabeth walked quietly toward her father's study and glanced around to be sure no one else was near. She stopped outside the door and listened. James was telling Father that he had tied up some very lucrative business deals while he was away and he was now ready to tie up the deal with him.

"I have two things to accomplish before the end of the year. One is to finalize our deal and the other is to see to it that our county is rid of the evil devil worshippers. On my most recent travels, I have learned that there is a handsome reward for anyone bringing to justice the idolaters and sorcerers who are sinning against God."

Her heart tightened and her head reeled but she continued to listen.

"I will tell you Gregory that I feel it my duty as a loyal Englishman to find them all and make sure they are hung or burned." James tone was ever so smug and condemning. She then heard her father's reply.

"A loyal Englishman? Is that what you say you are? I sincerely doubt..."

Elizabeth's heart pounded so loudly she thought for sure they would hear. What was Father doing? Why did he question James in such a manner? He could get himself killed in a moment for putting into question a man's loyalty to his country, especially such a nefarious man as James.

"I would be careful who you question about loyalty Gregory. I received word about you, while on my most recent travels. News of such sort could get a man hung immediately. Would you like to know what it is I heard?

Elizabeth moved in closer and James voice lowered a bit.

"I heard it was you using your old sea mates to run ships for the likes of Medina Sidonia." James laughter boomed through the corridor.

Elizabeth was enraged. James was accusing her father of being a traitor. Father never left the estate and if he did it was always under the tutelage of her Grandfather.

"And Gregory, if it was up to me you would suffer the same fate as the Captain of the Lady Elizabeth…and his crew…your family…his wife…his daughters…if it were up to me. Speaking of Elizabeth; how is the lovely maiden? Did you tell her of the betrothal yet? I hope so, for that would be a better use of your time that to gallivant into town…"

Elizabeth heard her father slam his cabinet door and then silence. She was sure he was procuring himself a brandy. She could use a bit of the spirits herself right now. Elizabeth cringed at the sound of her name rolling off the revolting tongue of James. She did not understand his words about the crew. What was he referring to? Elizabeth flung out her hand and was ready to open the door to her father's study to confront this preposterous tale coming from the vile man, head on. She stopped herself upon hearing his next sentence.

"Yes, I have heard of the great fervor regarding the capturing of the devil worshippers. I hope they are all found and brought to justice." Gregory spoke slowly and methodically.

"Father" She whispered his name under her breath. How could he side with James? The blood drained from her and she stood weak with shame and fear. What will this mean for her dearest friends, for her life and for the life of her babe? What was happening to them? Has everyone gone mad, as Mother? James laughed so loudly that Elizabeth fell backwards in the wake of the sound.

"Ah, then perhaps you shall help me. The women who practice witchcraft live in the forest not too far from our estates. These women are particularly dangerous, for they are all beautiful and they lull innocent men into their midst like lions leading their prey to certain death. Like the sirens of the sea. You know of such sirens, do you not Gregory? These women of the forest are the devil's lovers, indeed. I know of which I speak."

Father said not a word as James rolled on, telling a story of his cousin.

"He was hunting in the forest when he happened upon the most beautiful maiden. She lured him to her home with promises of a warm meal and the touch of a woman. He no sooner agreed as any man would and she turned on him, tried to rob him and when he resisted she cast a spell upon him. He narrowly escaped and ran and ran through the forest and was caught in a large briar patch for days until a hunter happened upon him. Alas, my poor cousin will never be the same, for I fear that the evil witches spell has turned him into a shadow of his former self. He is no longer brave and noble but weak and mild. They sucked his life blood from him. Took his manhood, they did!" James seemed quite proud of himself in the telling of this hideous tale. Elizabeth righted herself with defiance.

"If these women are not stopped Gregory, no man, woman or child will be safe within our county!" concluded James.

"I see James. From what you tell me, I am sure I can be of assistance to this noble cause."

Father's words seemed just as hideous. Noble cause; how is hunting innocent people a noble

cause? Why was her father going to help this corrupt man? Was her dear father also corrupt?

Corrupt or mad, yes it was one or the other. Father seemed caught in a malicious spell, unable to

see beyond the false pretense this man portrayed. If there was any evil befalling her country it

was brought about by him and men like him; fearful, vile men who wanted to destroy her dear

friends for the riches and reputation it would bring to them. She could not stand there another

moment and listen as her father sided with the most malevolent man who ever walked this earth,

but as she was about to go, she heard James start to speak again, this time mentioning her name.

"Yes, Gregory, we best fell these women as soon as possible, for I fear for your

Elizabeth's safety." He said smugly.

"Elizabeth? I assure you she is safe within the estate walls at all times. The only venturing

that my daughter does is with me when we attend Sunday services. What on earth are you

inferring James?" Elizabeth could hear the disdain in her father's voice.

"Well, you know I found her in the forest at an ungodly hour a few months ago. I thought

she would have told you that she is apt to take her walks out beyond the estate gate." James had

her father in his trap once more for she could hear it in his voice.

"She does no such thing James. Are you questioning my ability to keep my daughter

under my care and good eye?" stated Gregory. Elizabeth heard an unusual rage in the tone of her

father's voice.

"Do not worry, Cumberland as soon as you give your lovely Elizabeth's hand to me, she with be safe, for I will keep her properly busy."

Elizabeth dare not listen to this conversation a moment more. She had heard enough and more than she intended. The only knowledge she had hoped to attain was a bit of James' plan and now she had much more; much too much for a few moments of eavesdropping. The corridor started to spin and she leaned against the wall, knowing she had to get out of this spot quickly. Praying a common prayer of late she asked the Great Mother to help her. She ran into the kitchen and then up into Henry's room and then finally into her own bedchambers where she shut the door, locked it and started pacing. The Great Mother had surely given her feet wings. Father and James meant harm to her precious forest dwellers. Her mind reeled and body revolted. James had always wanted to persecute them and now it was clear that he would not stop until his deed was done. Worse of all he had somehow gotten to Father. If Father supported him in these efforts to kill Sophia, he would surely not support her when the time came to be rid of James and allow her to marry Demetri! She would have to do whatever she could to be sure James stayed far away from her until Demetri returned. It had come to be that both she and Henry needed help from the women of the forest and her dear friends needed her help as well. She had to warn Sophia.

Chapter Fourteen

"Elizabeth when will you tell me of the man who has stolen your heart?"

"No man has stolen my heart, Henry. There is no stealing involved. I have given freely of my love to a commoner and he has given freely of his love to me. We are together in love and we hold dear each other's hearts. I cannot explain the joy I feel inside." Elizabeth put her hand on her heart as they walked. It is as if all of me grew so very full with this love. I wish this for you too, my brother.

The two walked arm and arm through the forest. Henry was strong and tall in stature now. What he lacked in common sense, he had gained in physical strength. She felt safe on his arm. The time was finally right for them to see Sophia. It had been a very long two weeks but she could not go into the forest until she was sure it was safe. Dreaming each night of the women ensured her they were safe and now the time was right for them to meet. Cookie had kept Priscilla quite busy and Elizabeth did not see James. She did not question the grace period, but was extremely grateful. Perhaps the prayers worked.

"Wherever did you meet this commoner, for I have never seen him before and I do not know of anyone coming to court you, and I do not count that disgusting Earl of Hartford." Henry mocked the earl as he stood with his hands on his hips and nose in the air. "He is not a good match for you sister, this is true."

"Do not mention the evil man's name here in the forest. He is vicious and the mere mention of him sends my blood to boil. We must only talk of love here!" Elizabeth retrieved her bearings and they headed in a southerly direction.

"Well then, tell me of your love. I know of what you speak, this heart sharing. I feel that with Annie. There is a certain effortlessness and ease when we are together. I am grateful for your help sister. I know it is you who somehow has kept Priscilla away. I know not what you have done, but I am grateful." Henry sighed as he traversed through the twigs and fallen branches. They were not on a path any longer.

"There are certain servants we can trust and others that we cannot. It is a given and the sooner you learn of it the better." Elizabeth was now annoyed with her brother, for he was too innocent. Did he not know of the dangers that lurked within the hearts of most, even their own father? She had surely grown cynical since her eighteenth birthday. Perhaps it is just that she had grown up.

"Will you marry this man?" asked Henry. "Do you not want adventure as you seem to want it for me?"

"Yes, Henry, I shall marry this man. His name is Demetri. He is a commoner of Spanish and English descent. We are betrothed. He has gone on a journey for a short while and should return in a few weeks time, perhaps sooner."

"That will keep your heart happy, my dear sister and it seems it is your destiny."

"Yes it is Henry. A destiny that was not planned by Father or Grandfather, a destiny not set in the stone of our Mother's illness. This destiny is one of magic and mystery, of true love and is ushered in on the hand of the Mother God.

They traveled in silence then as Elizabeth listened intently to the soft wind. She looked to the stars on a moon filled cloudless night to lead them safely into this night's destiny.

The moment Henry saw them he stopped; dropping both hands to his side, his eyes popped wide. Elizabeth motioned for him to be quiet and to follow her. They found a comfortable spot and she and Henry sat speechless. They watched from afar safely hidden as the women began their worship. The women's songs and prayers for the Harvest mesmerized them both. Henry said not a word and that in itself was a miracle thought Elizabeth. After the prayers of the women young girls came from the mist. Their white gowns flowed as they moved and they looked like beautiful swans gliding on water. Henry held tightly onto Elizabeth, and whispered. "I feel I have fallen in love with each one of these beautiful creatures. This is the love of which you speak Sister. It is the free and true heart beating love!"

Elizabeth giggled. She was delighted to share the presence of the women with her brother. She knew that meeting them and seeing their ways would change him as it had her. Being in the mere presence of these women would inspire her little brother to make the choices that he needed to make in order to escape his fate. Her wish was coming true for he seemed to have fallen into their magic and fallen hard! "Henry come to your senses! I asked if you would like to meet them." Elizabeth shook his arm to awake him from his trance.

"Meet…them?" He stuttered. "Are they real?" Henry stammered again.

"Henry, come with me and we shall meet the beautiful women." He truly was quite amusing. Perhaps being innocent is not so bad she thought. It reminded her of days gone by. They sailed over to the group but the greeting was not what she expected. Every one of the women and girls stopped abruptly and turned towards their leader with terror in their eyes.

Elizabeth stood frozen. Sophia motioned to the group. "We are safe, for these outsiders are my friends. They mean no harm, there is no malice here. I know so." The women were shielding the girls and everyone was much too frightened to move. Elizabeth started to speak, to defend Sophia and tell of the nature of their visit, but Sophia stopped her.

"Malvina knows of these outsiders, she has given her blessing for them to know of us." said Sophia with a saddened look upon her face. "They may join us in celebration."

The women sighed a collective sigh and hurried back through the forest maze until they reached their village. Elizabeth and Henry followed in silence.

As soon as they approached what looked to be a green in the middle of several small cottages, the group was met by the elders, both male and female alike, young men, and many babes in tow. They gathered in the middle of the village green to eat and drink and sing. Elizabeth was taken in by everyone and almost forgot why she came. As the night wore on, she sought out the company of Sophia. Henry had not left the side of Hyacinth, Sophia's eldest daughter. He seemed quite taken by her and she by him. Elizabeth welcomed some time alone with her wise friend and confident.

"I am so grateful to you and your people for allowing us to partake in your celebration, Sophia."

"You are always welcome, my child." Sophia stared straight into Elizabeth's eyes, her gaze warming her heart and putting her completely at ease. "Tell me what has you worried?" Elizabeth told Sophia of the danger of James. Sophia nodded her head in a knowing gesture.

"We know of his threat Elizabeth, and that is why we do not worship in the same way as of late. We are more careful than ever, for if anyone with malice upon their heart should ever find us, we are all in grave danger. This has been the way of our people for many a year. Our ancestors knew of this day to come where we would not be safe to carry on our ways, and they also endowed us with powerful magic and ways to keep ourselves safe within the forest. We trust these ways of our heart, our forest and of our God, yet this is a time like no other. We must be very careful." She then led Elizabeth over to a group of women who were talking. The women fell silent as Sophia introduced Elizabeth. The woman named Rose stood to Elizabeth's side and began to speak as all listened on. Elizabeth instinctually took hold of Rose's hand.

"Sophia wishes me to share this story with you, Elizabeth. The others know of it already, but it is important that you hear this. I know not why, just that Sophia tells me so." Elizabeth then heard the story of the maiden who had met upon James cousin only this time it was the maiden herself telling the story. As was to be expected the young man was not so kind and gentle. Rose offered the man assistance. He turned on her with attack, hurt her and forced himself upon her. Sounds like James blood, thought Elizabeth with a feeling of bitterness rising up inside her belly.

Rose started to cry as she spoke of how frightened she was at the man's advances. Her plump bosom heaved as she shared the terror. "I am to be wed to Merton soon and I could not have him know if..."

Elizabeth understood Rose's tears. The fear and shame raged through her body as she remembered the night she lay beneath James. The stink of his breath lingered in the memories. Not even the touch of her true love Demetri could erase the shame. If James had entered her as she knew now he wanted to, she could never have loved Demetri, for James would have stolen a vital part of both her heart and soul.

Rose went on to explain how she got away. "It was all I could do to run from this man. I know not how I fought him for he was large and very strong. Not as strong as my man Merton. This man was full of the evil, he was! I will not be helping any more strangers until my powers of knowing have grown stronger." Rose cried as she spoke and Elizabeth dabbed the pretty girl's tears with her kerchief. The women all nodded their heads in agreement with Rose's promise to keep herself safe. Elizabeth thought it a wise lesson to heed. I shall remember to listen better to my powers of knowing too.

The dawn was quickly approaching and it was time to depart. Sophia held both Elizabeth and Henry in an embrace and told them to be very careful in their travels. "I give you my blessings and I know that you shall keep all that you have witnessed here tonight safely within your hearts." She whispered to them.

"They shall!" croaked Malvina. "I wish to talk to Elizabeth alone." Malvina glared at Henry and in an instant everyone retreated giving the two much room in which to converse.

Elizabeth came in close to Malvina, the night festivities gave her a sense of courage. There was something different about this old woman now. She could sense it as she stared into her golden eyes.

"It is not me who has changed. It is you. Here!" Malvina held up a bony finger and touched Elizabeth's brow.

Elizabeth felt a surge of warmth through her entire body and her babe moved furiously within her womb. She had to shut her eyes tightly for it seemed as if the light of the moon overhead was shining directly into her. It was entirely too bright.

"Open your eyes child. You are now able to see things much more clearly. You see things as they truly are rather than as you wish them to be. This seeing is a curse and a blessing." Malvina then held fast to Elizabeth's hand.

"I am not what you fear. What you fear is out there." She pointed beyond the forest walls. "You were born outside the forest walls and into the forest you were called. This is your destiny. You have awakened your sight and you have awakened your knowing. You cannot undo this. Do you understand?" Malvina stared into Elizabeth's eyes and instantly Elizabeth knew what she meant.

"I...I do." The words flew forth as if she were uttering an everlasting vow.

"I assure you that we of the forest will do all we can for you and your babe, for we are called to help when a soul such as you choses to see and to know. However, it may not be enough. This part of the journey is up to you. You must remember your own powers." Malvina spat.

Sophia walked quickly over to Elizabeth. "Thank you Mother. Your blessing is most welcome."

"Wait!" Said Elizabeth, pulling away from Sophia. "What are the powers of which you speak?" She did not like the sound of such a word.

Sophia and Malvina moved in close and each one held one of Elizabeth's hands. "You have the power of knowing, so use it well. You have the power of asking for help and being heard. You have the power of love, guiding your heart. You have the power of the Mother Goddess. You shall not falter." Explained Malvina.

Elizabeth received the blessings of Malvina and along with it a newfound sense of certainty. There were to be no more questions that evening. The certainty fueled her body and quickened the blood within her veins.

Before departing she took one more look around, scanning the people and the village green intensely. She had so hoped that Demetri would return home on this very night. The full moon celebration would be a most appropriate way to welcome him home. He had come to her in her dreams the last few nights. It was not clear if he would come to the celebration but she knew he was near. She felt his presence so very near. Holding her belly, she closed her eyes and saw him within her mind and felt him deeply within her heart. This seeing was what Malvina spoke of. She was sure he would arrive soon for the great storms of the last week were over and now he would have safe passage. She would not worry. She would trust her sight, her knowing and the Great Mother God.

Elizabeth and Henry left the women and headed back to the estate. Before leaving the forest Elizabeth found herself taking a detour to show Henry exactly where Sophia's cottage was. She did not know why she did so, she was so tired and wanted to go home to sleep and dream of Demetri, yet she felt pulled to show her brother. Henry danced along and did not seem tired at all.

"Hyacinth is the most beautiful girl I have ever seen. Her skin is so soft and her touch so gentle. She is even more beautiful than Annie and far more enticing than Priscilla." He continued to clumsily dance alongside her through the predawn forest. "I did not think that was possible. Did you see the yellow chrysanthemums she had in her hair? Did she not look beautiful?"

Elizabeth laughed to herself. Her plan had worked. Her brother was now formally introduced to that which would set him free. They both had a way to escape the life of servitude that Father and Grandfather expected them to submit to. Her brother now knew of another way, an altogether different choice, and it did not include the demeaning, vile, corrupt ways of her

ancestors.

Chapter Fifteen

Demetri did not come to her on harvest eve and he did not come the next full moon, nor the next. Day after day she went to the barn and day after day she prayed for his safe return and for protection for herself and the women of the forest. Venturing into the forest for a visit with her dearest friends, was much too risky. Sophia however did visit Elizabeth during her nighttime sleep and she shared much information with Elizabeth about how to continue caring for her burgeoning body, and what to do when it was time for the babe to come into the world. Sophia did not however give Elizabeth permission to enter into the forest yet and as much as it pained her to stay away she knew it was imperative.

"You might soon look like Cookie!" teased Henry one eve as the two sat in her bed chambers eating cakes. "Were you up at night stealing sweets from the pantry, Elizabeth? He joked with her, but she was not in a jovial mood. Her belly was becoming very uncomfortable and she felt a good deal of pressure whenever she walked. Going on her night strolls was becoming increasingly laborious. She had to go out, if only a short distance past the gates for it was the only way she would see Demetri upon his return.

"It has been many a month Elizabeth, when will I get to venture into the forest and see the women again?" asked Henry.

"Shush! How could her brother be so arrogant? Did he not remember that they were never to mention this inside the estate walls? Looking around nervously Elizabeth was relieved to know they were alone. One never knew if Annie or another nosey servant were in ear shot. She did not trust Annie anymore. Henry had shunned her since he met Hyacinth and Elizabeth saw how Annie had responded. She sulked around like a weasel, no longer the innocent mouse she had always been. Priscilla too had a different demeanor. Elizabeth noticed the welts and bruises on her arms and face that appeared each time Priscilla returned from town. She dared not question what was happening to Priscilla, for the answers would not be good. She did however surmise that it might have to do with the strange beast of a man they had seen her with last time they were in the city to attend Cathedral services.

"Henry, remember what Sophia told us, to be quiet and careful. I shall know when it is time to return and until then we must keep the talk of such, to times when we are safely out of the estate."

"Well, if we are not to venture into the forest, then perhaps we can talk without fear the next time we are in the city at Sunday services. That is far enough away from these walls." answered Henry.

"Henry, it is surely not safe there either, for remember what happened last time we were in the city. I fear we are not safe anywhere, except for in the depth of the forest and in the loving arms of the women of the forest." Elizabeth sighed a deep and lasting breath.

During their last jaunt into the city for Sunday services a few weeks prior, the most peculiar thing happened. All was going along smoothly and she was relieved that Father had not even glimpsed at her while she endured the rocky coach ride. Her belly ached, her back ached and her morning meal was about to be spilled, for the nausea that the coach ride caused was unbearable. Father was, as usual, lost in his own world. His frown was now a permanent fixture upon his once handsome, youthful face. Elizabeth had been so caught up in her thoughts of Demetri's return that she did not have the strength to share her rage toward Father. The coach lurched to a stop and all three Cumberland's tumbled from the dark smothering coach into the intensity of the morning sun. Blinded by the glaring glow they did not notice the group of city merchants selling their wares in the alley next to the cathedral until it was too late. Both Father and Elizabeth walked right into a cart handle and sent the wagon careening on its side. Henry took quick action and righted it before its contents spilled onto the grimy cobblestones. The merchant cursed loudly at them and onlookers stopped and stared at the raucous. That is when Elizabeth spotted Priscilla on the arms of a large burly man who from the back looked oddly familiar in his fierce and ominous presence. Priscilla turned and stared directly at her and then eyed Father and Henry. Elizabeth shook Henry's arm.

"Look" Elizabeth whispered to her brother and motioned in the direction of Priscilla. Henry saw her and his mouth dropped open.

Father too saw their servant girl. The blood drained from his face and Elizabeth could see his gaze catch and hold the gaze of the burly man who by this time had also turned in the direction of the commotion. Father reached inside his vest and pulled out his dagger pushed Elizabeth away and headed in the direction of Priscilla and the man. They quickly disappeared in the crowd, as Father was stopped by a large stallion crossing his path. Turning back to his children, the dagger blinded them both with its sunlight reflection. Father quickly hid the weapon and ushered them into the cathedral as if nothing out of the ordinary had just transpired.

Perhaps my sight is changing for I saw the look of revenge upon my father's face, she thought to herself as all three entered the cathedral without a word. That afternoon Henry sought out Elizabeth and told her that he recognized the man with Priscilla.

"He was the one I saw her with on the day she arrived here. That man told Priscilla that she was his forever. Do you think they are betrothed? If so, then why did she say she wants me?"

"Yes, Henry I do believe she is betrothed to him. I recognize him too, for he has brought many a servant to us here. He has a malicious look I shall never forget, much like …" She dared not utter his name.

Elizabeth was brought back to the present. They would not be going to Cathedral anytime soon and it was never safe to speak of the women of the forest in the city. The witch hunts had become the topic for many conversations as of late. Elizabeth even heard the servants speak of what was occurring out in the world. The pope had ruled them to be a menace and all over Europe the women, men and children were being killed for any such idle wrongdoing or for merely being a peasant, or a woman, or a midwife. It was not safe anywhere, except deep within the walls of the forest. Oh, how this distressed her. She was beside herself with an onslaught of worry. It was then that she knew she must go. She could wait no longer. She had to know if her friends were safe and she had to ask Sophia about Demetri. The decision was made.

"Meet me tonight in the maze and we shall venture out." Elizabeth whispered the directions to her brother.

"To see the…" Henry stopped himself before he said more.

"Just meet me in the maze at half past ten." Elizabeth gobbled up the last of the biscuits and napped the afternoon away. She put all thoughts of prayers and knowing and asking away.

The night was almost completely black and the only lights were those from the servant's quarters and the stable in the distance.

"We will travel into the forest this eve, come." Elizabeth led the way through the far southerly gates, down an invisible path and past the forest walls.

Soon the only light was the sliver of the crescent moon and the bright stars. Elizabeth removed a tiny lantern from within a satchel she carried and stopped to light it. "We will need this to help us find our way." She said to Henry.

"But Elizabeth is it safe? Did the women come to you in your dreams? Why did you not mention this today?" asked Henry.

Elizabeth ignored his questions. "We must go to them Henry. I fear it might be too late." Elizabeth bravely led the way. The lantern was so small that it barely gave light but it soothed her nonetheless to have something guiding her, besides her own inner longings. "I must go to Sophia and ask him of Demetri. She will know. He has been gone for much too long. I must know. I must go to him, wherever he may be. Sophia will help me! I cannot stay within the estate one more day. The forest is the only place we are truly safe."

"Sister, I will help, let me carry the lantern. You are distraught. I shall lead the way. I remember."

Elizabeth stopped as if she was knocked out of a dream. Her head was spinning with despair. "Wait, I know not what came over me. As we talked today I…I just have to see Sophia. But I did not ask the Mother God, I did not pray and I did not dream. I think we must return to the estate Henry. Now!" Elizabeth stopped walking but Henry did not.

"I am not turning around. We are going into the forest. You said it yourself, that it is the only place we are safe."

Elizabeth did not turn around, instead she kept on. "Let's pray as we walk, let us pray for the safety of the women, for Demetri's safe return, for you and for me and for my babe." linking her arm in Henry's made her feel a bit better for he was strong. Stronger than she realized.

"Yes, we will pray! What? You are with child?" Henry shook his head and kept walking. "I…I…" He turned to his sister and gave her a giant hug. "I will pray." That is all he said as the two made their way through the brush, brambles and thicket. They prayed silently and aloud, whispering in unison prayers that Sophia had uttered to Elizabeth many a time. The prayers led them to the clearing and then to Sophia's cottage. Sophia greeted them and ushered them in quickly. Elizabeth flung herself into Sophia's arms. Sophia tried her best to calm her. Elizabeth took in her love and felt better for a moment.

"Elizabeth, you are much too pale. Why did you come to us tonight? It is not safe for you and your babe. You must think of your babe and get more to eat and you must not worry yourself. She stroked her hair and set her down at the table and held her hand. Sophia's motherly love permeated Elizabeth and reached out to Henry as well.

"She is eating well, Sophia, I can attest to that." answered Henry. "She is missing Demetri. That is what is causing her great distress."

Sophia became very quiet and rose. Elizabeth felt a pang arise within her belly. She did not want to think of anything but her love at that moment. His smile, his touch and his sweet embrace filled her. She would not succumb to the deep foreboding fear that was always a part of her demeanor as of late.

Sophia fed them warm milk and sweet biscuits. "I have been praying that the Goddess and the forest fairies are watching over you and Demetri and Henry. I have been praying much of the day as of late. A great fear from the people of the city and towns has made its way to us. We all feel it. We keep you all in our prayers Elizabeth." Sophia's gaze penetrated Elizabeth. A sense of calm slowly made its way around her being like a halo of lightness and warmth.

"I fear for you." Elizabeth exclaimed.

"No my child, do not fear for us, for we will remain safe here. Nothing shall touch us."

Elizabeth sat with Sophia for a long while. Henry found Hyacinth and the two ran off chatting as if they had nary a care in the world. Malvina sat quietly in the corner and Elizabeth averted her gaze. A great fear arose within her as she felt Malvina's stare. Elizabeth knew she had not gained proper permission to enter into the forest that eve and the foreboding feeling would not leave. Malvina said nothing until it came time for Elizabeth to return to her estate.

"I must be heading back now. Thank you Sophia, I feel much better. I will continue to pray for Demetri's safe return. I shall take care of my babe and try not to worry." She realized that Sophia had not told her one way or the other of Demetri's whereabouts and she sought not to ask. The question could not be uttered. "I shall fetch Henry on the way out, thank you again Sophia, Malvina." Elizabeth was leaving when Malvina spoke.

"Remember the elixir." Malvina did not move an inch from her place of rest.

A chill ran down Elizabeth's spine. Brushing off Malvina's words did not help. The two began their travel back to the estate, she lost in thoughts of her love and Henry undoubtedly lost in thoughts of Hyacinth. The small lantern was not lit, for Sophia had warned them to go back in darkness.

Elizabeth was not listening nor praying and her heart was surely not looking in the direction of the estate walls and before she knew it, he was upon her. She was knocked off her feet and nearly trampled by his large black stallion. The horse was stopped by its rider moments before it would have killed her with its giant hooves. Elizabeth lay in a heap on the cold earth. Looking up she stared into the eyes of the Earl of Hartford.

"Lady Elizabeth, I did not see you. My apologies let me help you up. Are you hurt?" He grabbed her arm in a not so gentle effort to assist her.

"Sir James, I am fine." Elizabeth said in somewhat of a daze.

"What are you doing out here alone at so late an hour and why were you walking as if you were drunk? Is this what I must do to find you, come out to the forest late at night? How very odd." James smirked and smacked his horse's rump with his fist. The horse did not move an inch.

"James, I do not know of what you speak. I am merely out for an evening stroll with…Henry. He is my chaperone." Where is Henry she thought? Looking around she saw him lying prone on the ground a few feet from her. "You beast! You hurt my brother!" The terror flew through her as she rushed to her brother's side. A giant gash on his forehead oozed with blood.

"You mean your weak brother? A fine chaperone he is. He is nothing but a coward just like your father."

The terror turned to rage and boiled from within her belly. She thought better than to anger James though when both she and her brother were down.

"He is hurt, let me…" Elizabeth took some items from her satchel to bandage Henry's wound. She hid the herbs Sophia had given her in her cloak. She needed James to retreat lest the two be in grave danger and deep trouble. "Henry and I were merely enjoying a late evening stroll, please, leave us be."

"Elizabeth, do not lie to me. Do you take me for a fool?" he snapped as he helped her stand upright. Without releasing his grasp on her, he continued to speak. "I am finished with your antics and I am tired of you avoiding me. I am going to take you back to your estate tonight and insist upon seeing your father. He will give me your hand in marriage immediately. After I tell him how I found you once more within this forest, I am sure he will be relieved to have me take you off his hands."

"James, I do not wish to marry you, now leave me be." Elizabeth shouted, trying to break free from his grasp.

"Elizabeth my love, I do believe I have you exactly where I want you once again and you will not escape me this time." James tightened his grip and pulled her very close to him.

"No James, dare you touch me with my brother looking upon!" Elizabeth could see Henry standing, dazed at what had just occurred. She was relieved.

"I do not mind if he sees me taking you as my wife, for you will be soon enough and I rather fancy…"

"Henry run and fetch Father, now!" she yelled. "You will not try and force yourself upon me ever again." Elizabeth said in a low perfunctory voice.

Henry ran towards the estate. James did not follow, instead he turned to Elizabeth.

"And how do you plan to stop me? I am on to your tricks. What are you hiding under your cloak?" he asked ripping back the garment.

Elizabeth struggled, trying to close her coat and in attempting to do so the bag of herbs came spilling out at her feet.

"Ah, what have we here? asked James, picking up the contents of the bundle.

"Magic herbs I suppose? Were you going to cast a spell on me, Elizabeth?"

James shoved the bundle into his coat pocket and continued with his accusations. "Yes Elizabeth, I thought you might be one of them and now I have my evidence. Take off your cloak and let me see what else you are hiding."

James grabbed her cloak from around her neck and started to pull it off. Elizabeth tried with all her might to squirm her way out from under his grasp, but his hands and the cloak's tightness choked her.

"Stop James, you are hurting me." She coughed.

"I will do a lot more than that if you do not do exactly as I wish. I do not think you know the trouble you are in my Lady. Have you not heard of the many executions that are now taking place all over our great country, in fact all over the land? They burn witches like you in Germany!" he yelled into her face.

Elizabeth would not let James know he was frightening her. She stood tall in her defense. Her fear lay not in the truth of what he was saying but in the sheer evilness of his presence. She tried to keep herself calm as she countered his accusations.

"James, what you say is pure nonsense. I am not a witch and you know that I am not. You have nothing to prove that I am and that is that."

"Oh? On the contrary my dear Lady Elizabeth! I can prove to any Englishman that you are a witch. Lest you forget that you have not been at all kind to me. I have wanted to marry you for a long time now and you have shunned me and even tried to hurt me so I may never enjoy a woman's company again." He was spouting nonsense, she knew, but there was something in his voice that made her realize that she could not shun him this time. James continued. "Do you think I forget those things, Elizabeth? No I do not and you will pay for your sins. You will either pay by marrying me and being my wife forever or I will see to it that you are hung."

James pulled her closer and closer as he spoke. She looked directly into his black eyes and could see nothing in them. They were bottomless pools of evil. She tried to pull away, but his grip was like a vise. He was not going to be deterred this time, she thought. She had to think of something.

"Come with me Elizabeth, come lay with me now and you will see. Being my wife will be a pleasure you will surely want more of.

He dragged her in the direction of the stallion and Elizabeth tried with all her might to stop him, but it was no use. He was determined as ever and she knew she was in a very hopeless situation. He continued to drag her and her mind raced for a thought that perhaps could save her.

Her babe! "Mother Goddess help my babe!" Elizabeth did not realize she had said the words aloud. James did not seem to hear. She stopped resisting and James smiled.

"Ah, I see you might enjoy this after all." He sneered, his brandy soaked breath and spittle fell upon her face.

"Please James, you do not understand." pleaded Elizabeth.

"Understand? What is it? Do you have a lover Elizabeth? That would be good. Then perhaps you already know how to please a man. Or is your lover the devil himself? It matters not to me who you took as your lover, a mortal or Satan himself. You will forget him and I will have you now."

"No James, you may not!" Elizabeth bent down to grab for her only hope and once more uttered a prayer to the Goddess. This time he heard the petition. It angered him more and he pushed her down hard.

"You dare utter the name of the devil worshippers God." He tore off her coat and ripped at her gown, his hands ran over her whole body. It was dreadfully cold outside and the chill wind and his hands slashed at her body. As he continued mauling her, like a wild animal with it's prey, he noticed her swollen belly. He quickly pulled away as if his hands were burned at the sight.

"Oh my God, Elizabeth, you are with child. You are surely a witch. You have taken on a child from them. You are a whore, the devil's mistress. I knew I smelled lust on you that day; I was so stupid to think it was some servant boy! Now I know the truth. I will see to it that you are punished for this crime against our church and our country, our Queen…" He still lay atop her as he assaulted her with the vile words.

James is mad with hatred. He was going to enter her and steal her soul and take her babe! She must protect herself and her precious babe! Elizabeth lurched herself forward and found her only hope; a small blade, hidden in her gown. Sophia gave her the blade and told her what to do, in case of such encounters. She plunged the knife into James eye and pulled it out just as quickly going for a second attack and aiming straight at his heart. James was too quick and she was not able to make her mark. He rolled off her, holding his hand over his injured eye. Blood spurted from between his fingers. He stood up and started screaming at her.

"How could you do this you little whore? I shall make you pay."

Elizabeth had sufficiently wounded him and she saw this as her time to flee. Gathering her coat and gown and screaming to the Mother, she ran as fast as she could. Naked and terrified, she did not stop until she was safely inside the estate gates. She entered the estate through the hidden passageway, donned her ripped clothing and went directly to her bedchamber. The estate was eerily quiet and she did not see, nor hear Father or Henry. Perhaps they were out looking for James. She sat up in her bed waiting all the rest of the night for them but they did not come.

Chapter Sixteen

Sleep, sweet sleep. Finding the bitter balance of consumption always brought the sleep. Too much spirits and he would pass into the death throes of demons and monsters as the spirits invited them in to take over his mind, too little and he was wracked with bodily pain until dawn saw him up again. Sitting upright in his study he waited for the sleep to take him under. The footsteps were loud, heavy and hurried and they were coming towards his study. He wiped the delicious sleep from his face, reached for his dagger and stood ready.

"Father!" The door slowly opened and there stood Henry. What on earth did the lad want at this hour, he questioned. Panic started to flood his being. This was not good. He ushered his son in.

"Father, we must go now to Elizabeth! She is in the woods with James…he is hurting her." Gregory looked at his son for the first time in many a year. He stood eye to eye with his once spindly offspring. He noticed the gash across his son's forehead and grabbed a napkin from the table and pressed it on his bloody forehead. Henry grabbed the napkin and threw it down.

"We don't have time for this, I am fine, but Elizabeth is not. You must come!"

Gregory shook the haze from his body and followed his son. Before they left the study, Henry turned to him and locked into his gaze giving him orders. "I entered the estate with the utmost care, and I suggest we exit with silence. I fear that we are not safe among our staff or anyone for that matter. I was not sure if you could be trusted Father, but you are all we have now." Henry did not take his gaze away. Gregory felt the tears of shame well up and the blistering scars upon his hands burned in remembrance.

"Do we need to bring horses, son or is she near enough to go on foot?" he asked.

"On foot, hurry!" whispered Henry.

They left the estate grounds. "They are not too far out. Here!" Henry pointed in a southerly direction.

Gregory saw it coming but Henry did not. The arrow flew from a nearby thicket and missed his son's back by an inch. Gregory flew forward and pushed his son to the ground. Lying atop him they waited. He felt the hand upon his back, grabbing his coat and pulling him off Henry.

"Run, Henry, go…" he yelled. A hand hit him hard across his cheek, dazing him for a moment. Henry was furiously writhing to escape the grip of another man.

"You are coming with us. There will be no running." The man holding Gregory barked the orders. Gregory quickly assessed the situation. Three men no uniforms, faces covered with burlap clothes, they looked to be scoundrels.

"Is it money you want?" asked Gregory. "I shall give you money…"

The men said not a word as they wrapped Gregory and then Henry's hands behind their backs with thick ropes, a sharp blade pressed against his neck.

"You must let us go. I will give you all the money you want. My daughter is in danger and we must get to her. Surely you understand that a maiden is in danger." Gregory pleaded yet knew from within his being these men would not listen. The spirits could not deny the feeling in his belly. He knew who these men worked for.

The men mounted their horses and forced Gregory and Henry to walk next to them away from the direction of the estate.

Henry stopped walking in resistance and the men did not stop. They dragged him along until he found his footing again.

"We have to find my sister, she could lay dead, we must find her…"

"Shut up stupid fool." One of the bandits hit Henry hard on the back of his legs. Henry stumbled but did not fall. Gregory felt his son's pain in the likes of his own body.

Measuring the state of the situation he knew it best to go along with them for now. The way of these men made him recall interactions with pirates during his sailing days. The large burly man leading the way seemed to be their leader. His great mane of hair and long scraggly beard gave him away.

"I should have killed you on the streets of London while I had the chance!" Gregory yelled. "What do you want with my family?"

"Ah, it is not what I want, but what your family wants from me!"

Henry had no patience for riddles. "You have nothing I want."

"And you are not the man of this family. You are a mere puppet Cumberland!" The bearded man laughed and laughed as they approached the stables. The men jumped from their horses, gathered Henry and Gregory, pushed them into the stable and into an empty stall.

Where were the stable grooms, the blacksmith, wondered Gregory? What is going on here?

"Well, what have we here? Gregory, Henry." It was the voice of the Duke of Winslow. He strode in, sword drawn and back to the only exit.

"Grandfather, I am so glad you are here!" Help us, will you please. Elizabeth is in danger and we must help her, these men…"

"Quiet, stupid boy. Elizabeth is safe in her room." The Duke approached his prisoners. They stood huddled together with the three henchmen surrounding them. "Back off gentlemen" the Duke commanded. The three grunted in unison and backed away ever so slightly, their daggers and swords drawn stood upright in wait.

Gregory grew increasingly uncomfortable and his belly reared its rage. "Did you set this up?" asked Gregory, teeth grinding and temper boiling.

"Careful what you accuse me of, son. You would not want your own flesh and blood to hear something that could cause him to know the truth about his father, would you?" The Duke sneered and poked Gregory with the tip of his sword.

Gregory could see Henry's look of bewilderment and he thought it best to keep his mouth shut for now.

"It seems as if Elizabeth has angered her betrothed. She injured him in her resistance to his rightful desires. Sir James wants to press charges not only for her violent attempts to injure him but the gentleman deems it appropriate to charge her with the heinous crime of practicing witchcraft. These are serious accusations. Do I make myself clear Gregory?" asked the Duke.

Gregory's heart sank, deep into his being. This is the day he had feared would come, the day when the sins he tried to keep hidden would somehow erupt and his own flesh and blood would be paying the price.

"Did you hear me Gregory?" snapped the Duke.

"Yes…yes, I heard you."

Henry's jaw dropped. A look of horror and malaise came spewing out and landed upon Gregory's already sunken chest. "Father?" squeaked Henry.

Gregory hung his head low and did not respond.

"James is bringing the shire reeve here as we speak. We will meet with him and let him take Elizabeth. There will be no stopping this from happening. Your child must be taken to the jail to await her right punishment." He caroled.

"Grandfather, there must be something you can do, please…you are a powerful man and Elizabeth…is not a…witch." muttered Henry.

"Yes lad, I am a powerful man and so is Sir James of Hartford. It seems your father here is to blame for your sister's predicament, for if he would have taken the proper steps and given her hand to James sooner this would not have happened. That child was always quite independent. You on the other hand, have a chance…lest you be enjoying dalliances with the witches too." The Duke stopped and put the tip of his broadsword on Henry's shoulder." In fact, how did you come to be with Elizabeth tonight in the woods at such an ungodly hour?" The Duke dug the sword into his grandson's arm. Henry did not pull back. The Duke pressed harder. "I suggest you do not say anything about your whereabouts this fateful eve unless you want to meet with the same fate as your sister!" declared the Duke.

Gregory watched with pride as insolence rose up in his son. The pride fueled and awakened in him something that he had feared dead, long ago. He saw himself in his son, the innocent young lad he was before he sold his soul to this monster devil dressed as Duke.

"Stop!" yelled Gregory lunging toward the Duke. The bearded giant kicked the back of his knees and Gregory fell back with the giant's dagger at his throat.

"You should have cut me while you had the chance, Cumberland." The giant sneered and putrid droplets of sweat landed on Gregory's face.

"You have no power here Gregory, you never have. Perhaps it is time for your son to take over where you never could." The Duke motioned for the giant to step back. The hulk moved the dagger a smidgen and merely tightened his grip.

The Duke then looked directly at Henry. "There is something I can do to help Elizabeth, but alas it shall be up to you to see it through. Listen carefully. My instructions to you both are thus. You may not interfere with her arrest. We must see to it that James is placated. I shall see what I can do once she is taken into town. There may be something I can do, but it will depend…on you two…keeping your lowly mouths shut. About everything! Do you understand? Everything!"

Gregory spat. As usual his father in law's only concern was for himself. This man will stop at nothing to destroy everyone. Gregory wanted to plunge his dagger deep into the heart of the abhorrent monster who created this hell. He wanted nothing more than to watch him writhe in the pain he now felt as he imagined his daughter felt too. He wanted this man to writhe and beg for mercy as he himself had done on so many occasions.

Henry dropped down to his knees staunchly showing his alliance to his father. "You must help her Grandfather, please." Henry still believed pleading would help. "We will do as you say, but you must promise to do what you can."

Gregory said nothing. He looked at his son, the innocent bravado fearlessly poured forth from his eyes. He believed his Grandfather, for he had no reason not to. Gregory decided that he must do as this maniacal, monster wished. Just one more time he will give another bit of his soul, whatsoever is left of it to this man for one sliver of hope to save Elizabeth.

"Good boy." said the Duke, patting his grandson on the head. "I shall however make no promises. I make no promises to anyone who kneels prostrate at my feet and is bound. For yours is not a position to be demanding anything. Ask your father, he knows of this well." The Duke turned his back on his grandson and son-in-law and walked away shouting orders.

"Take them to the study and have them wait for the Earl. And call down Mistress Elizabeth. It is time she faces her just due."

***

James burst into the estate with the shire reeve and several of his men. "We've come to arrest Elizabeth Cumberland. She is a witch. We have come to take her to the gallows." shouted James as he let himself into their home. He entered through the Master's Lodging and bellowed as he strode through the kitchen, dining chamber and the great hall. Gregory listened, waited and stood transfixed on his son. Another son of the devil himself had arrived at the Cumberland Estate and his children's grandfather had invited him right on in.

Gregory found a slight bit of satisfaction as he glanced at the Duke. He was not happy that James had announced the reason for his untimely visit to the entire household. Charmaine probably heard his shouts as well. Perhaps we should invite her down for the show thought Gregory, for there would be no secrets about this morning's agenda.

"Where is she? Where is the harlot?" screeched James as he entered the study. He was met by Gregory, Henry, the Duke and the giant bearded man. They all stood and stared and for another slight moment, Gregory saw the look of alarm glint across James usually supercilious expression. He also noticed that his right eye was recently wounded and blood seeped through the bandage. This must be a wound from Elizabeth, thought Gregory; serves him right, if only I had the courage that she seems to have as of late. If only…As if he read his mind, the Duke interrupted his thoughts.

"Gregory, you are her father, what say you?" asked the Duke. "Will you defend your daughter or is it I who must do your bidding?"

Gregory was confused, he had never before knowingly played the game with his father-in-law. He had been conned and duped for years and always thought he was caring for his family in the only way he knew how. This time the game was involving his daughter and her fate, her life and her very future. What was he supposed to do to ensure his dear Elizabeth's safety now? He knew what he had learned at Brooker's Pub, that his father in law was a criminal, and a traitor, and so was James. He also knew that they had an army of men, just like the bearded giant that kept them safe and protected and informed. They were untouchable and he and his children were now in the middle. He said the only thing he knew how to say in the moment.

"I shall stand up for her here. I shall take the fall for her. She is but a child and I will pay any price for anything that you allege she did."

James pushed his way through the crowded room and stood directly in front of Gregory and started to speak when they were interrupted.

"I am here to face my attacker." said Elizabeth standing at the doorway. Gregory bent down in pain as if someone had cut his belly. She looked so calm and beautiful. How could his child have gotten herself into such a mess? He knew the answer was because of his failings. He had failed her.

"Arrest her!" shouted James as he walked over to Elizabeth.

The shire reeve stepped in between the two. "Wait, James, wait. We must have just cause. I must question her first. Protocol, you know."

"Damn, protocol! She is a witch, I found her with this! James drew the bag of herbs from his coat and threw them on Gregory's desk. They landed next to the brandy bowl.

"Patience, James." interrupted the shire. "I must ask her the questions first." The shire tried to take some type of command. "Elizabeth, were you using these herbs for magic?" Shire reeve asked as he grabbed the sachet from James.

"No, I was not." She quickly answered. Gregory noticed she had some cuts and scrapes on her face. His anger started to boil forth, the pain in his belly torturous. Elizabeth seemed much too calm, he noticed. This was unsettling and surreal.

"Very well then, where did you get them?" continued the shire.

"I gathered them in the woods." She answered, still keeping her calm.

"Liar, you are lying…you…" started James.

"That is enough James, I will ask the questions." The shire quipped. "I have not seen these herbs growing in any woods near us and I have never seen a pouch like this one Elizabeth. James claims this pouch came from a clan of witches that are known to inhabit our forest. I must believe James knows that of which he speaks." Said the shire reluctantly, glancing at James.

Gregory grew increasingly uncomfortable. He was realizing this was all a show put on for the benefit of …who? The estate staff? The sick perversion of the Duke? What was this insane drama that played out in his study? How had his life and his family come to this? He could see clearly where this was leading and he stepped forward. The bearded giant stepped on his foot and stuck a dagger in his side. Gregory stood still.

"Now, I will give you one more chance to answer me and you must think very carefully young maiden. Where did you get this from?" asked the shire, picking up the bag and shaking it in front of Elizabeth. The shire glanced at Gregory, urging him to say something. Gregory felt the knife go deeper into his side. He did not care about his life at this point, but if he were to object, this monster was going to wield a knife and his children would die right here on this day, in his study in plain view of their grandfather and Gregory would not allow that. The shire turned his stare from Gregory.

"Your own father is not defending you Elizabeth, perhaps you are guilty." He said softly.

Gregory glanced at his son. He could see how this was torturing him too. Then he saw the Duke's hand, holding a dagger, up against Henry's back.

"I told you I gathered them in the woods." Elizabeth answered as before.

"She will not tell you the truth. You are wasting your time. Take her to the jail!" yelled James.

"Elizabeth, please reconsider and tell us where you got these herbs." said the shire, patiently.

"Ask her about her child. Show them Elizabeth, show them that you are with child," said James as he walked over to her and lifted away her skirts to show her protruding belly. Gregory lurched forward to protect her child, and the bearded man held him back.

Elizabeth jumped back away from James hands but it was too late. Her secret had been exposed. Gregory saw her fill with sorrow and shame as this monster touched her. He lunged forward with his need to go to her and protect her, yet he could not. A great burly arm held him back and the dagger dug through his vest.

"Elizabeth my child is it true? Are you with child?" asked Father staring at James. He refused to even look at his daughter, the anguish was unbearable. Had James taken his daughter against her will? Was this James' child? He immediately felt a rush of distressing shame. The first words he spoke to her today were an accusation. How could he have failed her so miserably?

"Father it is true, I am with child. My babe shall be born in just two short months." Elizabeth's hands protectively rubbed her rounded belly. "I did not want you to find out in such a manner. I am so very sorry, Father, Grandfather." Elizabeth hung her head.

"And who is the father of this babe Elizabeth?" injected James.

"You do not deserve to know of a man so noble as my babe's father!" Elizabeth suddenly was seething with anger and looked to Gregory to say more.

"That is because there is no father, is there? This child is the child of the devil, isn't it Elizabeth?" James continued taking a step toward her.

"No James, my child was conceived in love, that of which you know nothing about." shouted Elizabeth.

"You were betrothed to me Elizabeth, you were to be my wife and look at what you have done. You have betrayed me! Furthermore, has anyone seen you with any man? No I think not Elizabeth! There is no father and that proves you are a witch, the mistress of the devil himself."

Gregory was relieved that the child was not James'. He was sure this evil man raped his daughter while he stood by and did nothing. The sword lanced his skin as he moved slowly toward his child.

"None of what you speak is true, James!" yelled Elizabeth. Gregory had never seen his daughter so angered before. Her face reddened and she held her hand over her heart.

"I have a love and we shall be married. He will return to me soon. And I was never betrothed to you!" she cried lifting her chin to James face and looking straight into it with no fear.

"Oh, go on Elizabeth, we want to hear more regarding this love of yours who does not exist except in the immoral mating rituals of the devil worshipper's." James seemed to be enjoying this fight, as was the Duke.

"Stop! You must stop saying such lies. I am not a devil worshipper and I have a love. I will prove it to you when he returns." James moved closer and reached out to touch her. She backed away from his grip.

"No, you stop Elizabeth! Your lies are not going to keep you from being tried and hung as a witch." He sneered rubbing his fingers along her cheek.

"Enough! Gregory interrupted James advances. "You shall not say such things in my home."

Elizabeth looked relieved. The sword was not going deeper and Gregory took this as a cue to keep talking. "You may not condemn my daughter. She has not been known to lie and I believe her."

"What would you know Cumberland? You spend most of your time here in this hell hole drinking your petty fortune away. You do not know anything. Your daughter is with child. Did you know? Your son and daughter gallivant in the woods with witches, did you know? You know nothing!" shouted James.

Gregory sought to speak and Elizabeth turned to the shire. "Please shire reeve, I have never done any harm to anyone." she pleaded. "Please! Can you not see that Sir James has taken offense to the fact that I will not marry him and that I love another? He is merely angry with me. I am not a witch."

"Never done harm to anyone? What do you think this is?" said James angrily pointing to his bandaged eye. "Do not forget that she attacked me in her rage." He added.

"She was a mad woman last night. I merely asked her if I could help her and she plunged the knife right into me. My eye is ruined. That is enough proof that she must be arrested." He shouted.

Elizabeth moved backwards slowly and sped out the door. She ran through the great hall and disappeared. The sire reeve, James and the men went after her.

Gregory stood stunned, his whole body wanting to run after his daughter, but he could not. He was held back by the giant bearded man, his heavy boot on his foot and sword in his side. He could not fight him, for he was no match.

Chapter Seventeen

Elizabeth ran as fast as she could through the kitchen and into the passage room. She opened the hidden door and entered the secret tunnel. She was terrified of James and she did not want him to touch her. She thought of nothing but running. Groping her way in the dark through the tunnel she saw the light that would lead her to the garden. A moments relief fell upon her like a whisper, as she entered the morning. James stood waiting. The shire reeve was close behind.

"You are not going anywhere, except with us to face your punishment!" said James

The shire approached. He walked over to Elizabeth and put out his hand. "Come with me Lady Elizabeth. I must take you into town and have you arrested. It is all I can do.

Elizabeth would surrender to him, if she had to, but not to James, never to James. She held out her hands thinking he would bind them. He did not. Instead the shire took her hand and whispered. "I do not believe you a witch, child but no one can prove otherwise now; the herbs, your condition. What trouble you have made for yourself. I am so very sorry for the Cumberland's on this day." He walked her slowly back towards the estate.

"Bind her hands, stupid fool." James screamed at the shire. She will run again and I don't want to chase her.

The shire said nothing and continued walking. James and his men followed. They walked to the estates gates and gathered their horses. Gregory and Henry were nowhere to be seen. Grandfather stood at the front door of the estate, watching.

"Father, do something!" Elizabeth yelled out, the words caught on her tears. "Please help me!" she pleaded one last time but her father did not come.

The slightly gleeful look on her grandfather's face stayed within Elizabeth's mind all the way to the jail. The shire had wanted to let her ride behind him on his horse, yet James insisted she be put into the cart, eerily similar to the one the dirty children rode in so many years ago. She had thought herself untouchable then. She was not. Transformed by a true love and now being taken to her death. Did love make you so? How could this be happening? Where was Demetri? Father, Sophia? Sobs of sadness released from the depths of her being and prayers to the Goddess Mother escaped her lips. When they arrived in the town, there was an angry mob awaiting them. The mob screamed obscenities at Elizabeth as she was taken off the cart and led into the jail. They hurled rotten food and chanted.

"To death with the witch! Rid our town of evil."

One woman spat on Elizabeth, "Because of you, I am barren. Your kind put a spell on me they did and now I am barren." The woman spat again.

Elizabeth could not believe what she was seeing and hearing. Why were these people treating her so? Had they all gone mad? She had done nothing, but they all believed she had. None of these people knew her, nor anything about her. She cried at their ignorance and intolerance as she was dragged along and led into a damp and barren room where she was stripped and searched. Her clothes were torn off of her and she was given some rags to wear. They even took her shoes before shoving her into an even damper, darker, colder cell. She again remembered the little children who were led to their death in the wooden cart so many years ago.

This was not supposed to be happening to her. A chosen one, was here to help the lowly, not become one. She curled up into a ball and wept.

The cell had one small window that faced east and looked out onto the town square. Two women stood inside the cell, under the window as Elizabeth was thrown into the dungeon. She did not notice them until she awoke from her slumber of escape a few hours later. She awoke with a start, shivering in the dampness. Remembering where she was, she rubbed her belly and whispered some reassuring words to her little one.

"Shsh." she said as she rocked back and forth. It will soon be over, for your papa will come for us. Shsh..." she said as she held back her tears.

"Here, you go young maiden" said one of the women handing a dirty cloak to Elizabeth. "They did not strip us of our clothing, it was not as fine as yours, I suppose." She said smiling a toothless grin.

"Put the cloak around your feet, child." The other woman said, helping Elizabeth wrap the fabric around her bare legs.

Elizabeth did as the old woman said and accepted her help. Her hands were soft and warm and she liked her touch. The other woman just stared and smiled her silly grin. The two women stood side by side staring. Elizabeth stared back in disbelief, for they looked identical to one another. They were very old and thin and had white stringy hair and no teeth. The one looked at Elizabeth with the most loving glances and the other kept laughing and smiling at nothing in particular. Elizabeth smiled at them both and thanked them for their care.

From that moment on the two sisters put a veil of protection over their new friend. They clothed her in kind words and stories and they gave her their bread and broth and tried to keep her from dying among the filth. There were puddles everywhere on the dirt floor and the rats and mice loved the cold damp mud. The days passed and no one came to see Elizabeth. She sat in the cell trying to keep warm and dry, waiting and waiting. She was sure Father would come to her and she would then tell him of Demetri. Perhaps Father might find him for her, she hoped. Thoughts of Demetri kept her alive. Some days she could picture him being there with her. She could feel his presence beside her as if he was really there. On those days she took great comfort knowing he was with her, but on most days she felt very ashamed thinking that she had let him and their babe down. The guilt would creep in just as the bitter cold slid under the walls of the prison and she would question her very existence. How could she allow herself to be put in jail? Her babe needed her to have a comfortable home and much good nourishment.

The guards ignored the three prisoners and for the most part this was a very good thing. Elizabeth could hear the torture of the other prisoners from her cell and she prayed and prayed it would never be her or the sisters. The three of them were being left alone and despite the wretched conditions she felt they were being looked after by her dear and beautiful friends of the forest; disguised as old crones. Perhaps Sophia had somehow saw to it? She did not know, but there was something about the sisters that reminded her of Sophia.

One day, after weeks and weeks of waiting Elizabeth drifted off to sleep. The dreams came suddenly and abruptly. Father watched as she was led to the gallows. He was watching her being led to the gallows. He stood and stared and said nothing. Henry was there too. He was pulling on his father's arm, begging him to stop them from hanging his sister. But Father just stood there. It seemed as if he could not see nor hear Henry. Elizabeth tried to scream at him.

"Father! Father!" She could hear the words in her chest, in her throat, but they did not come out. She tried with all her being to force the screams out but they were stuck inside. Her whole body racked with the screams. "Father help me! Father help me!" but once again the screams were held within her throat. Her father stood and stared as she was led up the wooden plank and onto the wooden box. The executioner put the noose around her neck. Still Father just stared. She continued screaming silent pleas for help. Just as the box opened up and she was about to drop down, she looked at her father and he smiled.

She awoke in a sweat. She tried to jump up but she was pulled down. She could not move. She was burning with a fever. Her body was limp and weak. The sisters had torn parts of their garments off and were using it to wipe Elizabeth's brow.

"Your sleep is so fitful, what horrors come upon you? You are too lovely of a woman to carry such a burden." Said one sister. "Yes, too lovely." agreed the other.

Elizabeth could hear them whispering; something about death, her babe... The two sisters did their best to make her feel better, but Elizabeth felt herself slipping out of this world, terrible visions of James and Grandfather, monsters and demons crowding her mind. She thought they heard the sisters mention herbs, medicine...Malvina. She could feel the old women's touch, wiping the sweat from her brow, their touch was hot and she saw a bright light enter into her where their hands touched her hot skin. She was suddenly pulled out of her delirium. She sat up and looked around.

"Please get the guard, I must talk to him." She said as clear as day. Elizabeth was being propelled by an unseen force that had taken her over. She knew she must get herself and her babe out of this cell now. The sisters jumped back smiling big toothless joyful smiles.

They quickly summoned the guard and he responded, much to their momentary amazement.

"What is it?" he asked, walking over to the cell door and peering in. Elizabeth looked at them and they knew exactly what to say.

"It is the maiden kind, sir, she has taken ill, and she is burning with fever." Said the gentle sister.

"She needs to be taken out of here at once. She could have the pox and we all will surely perish. Now go find someone to get her father. He is the Earl of Cumberland." said the smiley one.

The guard looked frightened. Elizabeth could see him out of the corner of her eye, she was sure he did not want the pox and she was sure he would not trust three accused witches. She was hoping that their magic would work now and he would do as they wished. It was her only hope. If they called her a witch, she may as well use the powers that she had. The guard hurried away and a few hours later another guard appeared.

"I am here to take the Lady Elizabeth out. Move out of my way old hags," he said as he entered the cell.

"He must have done something very wrong to be the one they picked to come in here and get the Lady Elizabeth." whispered the smiling sister to the other. They both laughed and Elizabeth had to hold in her mirth. She was going to leave! Her heart leapt with anticipation and fear. She suddenly began to panic, not sure of her plan to leave. How had this plan come upon her anyway? As if the sisters heard her thoughts, they both went to her and ever so gently held onto her hands. Once more, the light coursed through her body.

She reached out to them and called to them. She so wanted the sisters to be able to come with her. They had, after all helped her so much. They shared their story with her and she knew they too were as innocent as she. The sisters had lived a quiet existence until their neighbor had wanted their land. He accused them of holding sacrifices and stealing and killing his sheep and just as Elizabeth, they were wrongly accused and sat in jail. The guard had stopped near the jail door and watched the three women. He seemed frozen, allowing the women to have their say.

"We know now, my dear why we were sent here to jail. Do not worry, for we shall be freed." Said the smiley one, stroking Elizabeth's hair.

"We were sent to keep you safe, my dear. It was the day before you arrived and the sun was shining ever so brightly into our cell. She stood outside this very window, and told us of your coming. We have done our part."

"Who told you?" asked Elizabeth ever so quietly. She peered at the guard. He still stood frozen as a chunk of marble and as cold too.

"Why, Malvina of course," they both said in unison.

So that is how it came to be that they knew what they must do for her. It was all somehow making sense, somewhere deep within her heart. She knew what she must do now.

The guard came alive and walked over to the women. The sisters moved back and allowed him through. He covered Elizabeth in a blanket and picked her up. She curled up in his arms. He did not struggle with her weight, for he was a very strong man, but he did wince and whine as he hurried out of the cell. "I do not need to die of the pox," he muttered to himself. Elizabeth stayed quiet. She could sense when they were out of the cell, out of the jail and out into the light of day. She breathed in a big breath, and did not care that her lungs filled with the stench of this man who held her. She could feel the air upon her body and she tingled with joy. The guard threw her into the back of a cart and her bones felt the pain of the hard cold wood. The blanket was ever so thin, and Elizabeth started shivering uncontrollably as the cart slowly pulled away. In the distance, she heard the guard who held her curse at God again. She could make out each word he uttered.

"God cleanse me of any sickness that might befall me for having touched the devil maiden." She however did not care a bit. She was free.

The cart barreled through the forest. Elizabeth sensed two men riding in the cart in front and another beside the cart on horseback. She lay in a pool of protection and looked up at the sky. The sun shone brightly that cold winter day. She took the rays into her body and she could feel the heat fill her. She watched the clouds as the cart rolled along. Heaven seems a long way off, she thought, but I know it is out there, behind the clouds, behind the blue of the winter sky.

She felt the familiar callings of her forest as they rode, she felt the trees coming alive, welcoming her and giving her strength. She inhaled their fragrance, the tangy scent wafted upon the cool air. Her mind wandered and her fever broke. The forest fairies were with her, she could feel them too. They surrounded her and whispered to her on the wind. "You are home, you are home." She heard the gentle silence within and the messages from heaven called to her.

Chapter Eighteen

Henry watched as they took his dear sister away. He never felt so frustrated, angry and helpless. His anger was born of a deep sorrow as he watched the two men who could stop this from happening do nothing. In fact, his grandfather seemed almost glib and this angered Henry further. He had not known such wrath before now, for whenever he felt anything of the sort start to rumble within, his chest would tense and he would hear his sister say, "Henry, do not upset yourself." Now it rumbled and felt as if it would burst, but interestingly enough he did not utter one cough. Instead he knew what he must do.

Father stood to his side and Grandfather stood in front of both, bidding his granddaughter farewell. Henry glowered at the old man boring a hole in his back with his resolve. Grandfather quickly turned to face Henry but Henry would not back down. He stared Grandfather straight in the eye. Grandfather said nothing, just walked away and the bearded giant followed.

Henry and Father stood outside the gate and waited a few moments more. Elizabeth was out of sight and the crowd of angry onlookers was thin. Father started walking back towards the estate. Henry followed. He had no hope any longer in his father. What he would do, he would accomplish alone.

A week went by. The hush of death lay thick upon the Cumberland Estate. Father had not left his study for seven days. The maids brought him food and reported to Henry each day on whether or not he ate and how much he drank. It was not likely that Father would come around and help rescue Elizabeth, but Henry just needed to be reassured that his father was not going to die of grief before he had a chance to see Elizabeth again. He had to believe something, and he chose to believe that his sister would be coming home. As weak and pitiful Father was, Henry still loved him.

On the eight day of her absence, Henry could stand it no longer. It was time. He had to figure a way to get into town and see his sister. He had to be the one. He awoke before the rooster's crow and took a comforting seat in the kitchen waiting for Cookie. She might know what to do and if she did not, at least he could find solace in her presence.

"Aye, lad, hungry are ya?" asked Cookie as she entered her domain.

"Good morning Cookie. I am not hungry, have not been since they took…well you know…" I could use some words with you though." stammered Henry. He was not at all comfortable talking about his sister, for now every wall in the estate had ears.

"Good, I will fix you a good hearty meal and you can speak as much as you like. You can be sure your words will go no farther." Cookie held up a heavy iron pot and slammed it down on the stone table for emphasis.

"I must help Elizabeth, Cookie, and I need a way out of here. Can you help me?"

"What a minute…I …" Cookie stepped back, her face wrinkled up and she turned around as fast as such a large woman could. Priscilla was standing ever so silently in the back of the kitchen, near the door to the wine cellar.

"Here already missy?" she asked as she turned back to Henry, giving him a look to be quiet.

Henry stared at Priscilla and she stared back. He felt the familiar feeling welling up in his body. Since the day they saw her in town, he had only seen her from afar. He might catch a glimpse of her coming or going, but he had not looked at her, nor she at him since the day he had his attack in the woods. He sat very still, not wanting to move, for fear Cookie might see his reaction to Priscilla. He did not take his gaze from her until she slipped back into the wine cellar. Cookie fixed him a platter of venison and biscuits. They did not speak another word. Priscilla came and went as he ate, bringing Cookie the needed ingredients and supplies for the day's meals. When he finished he stood to leave, thanking Cookie. He would have to return later, at a time when Priscilla would not interrupt them.

The rest of the morning found him restless and agitated. He thought Priscilla was the enemy, yet why was she still there? Did she not love another and was she not betrothed? He still felt a deep yearning to be near her and that troubled him too. He impatiently paced the halls of the estate in his confusion.

"I must find a way..." he muttered to himself. The echo startled him and he looked up to see if anyone was near and stood staring at her again.

"Excuse me Master Henry, but perhaps I can help you." She said drawing closer to him. Henry did not back away.

"Help me with what?" he asked, his new found bravado meeting her.

"Forgive me, but it is not safe to talk here." She moved in so very close, her bosom rubbed against his arm. "I can help you get to Elizabeth. Meet me near the ice house at one hour past sundown." And she was gone.

Henry lifted his sleeve to his nose and inhaled. Her scent, smoky, and spicy, a mixture of braised game and cinnamon glaze. His body trembled and his hopes rose. Perhaps she could help me, he thought. What do I have to lose?

The hours passed ever so slowly. Henry spent them formulating his plan. He would somehow need a horse to ride into town and back, unseen. He must however have the help of someone in the stable. This was his best plan. If he went on foot, it could be too dangerous. He would be going either way, seen or unseen, but he could help his sister, he was sure if he could do so unseen.

Henry waited outside the icehouse. He arrived just as the sun was setting. He wanted to be sure absolutely no one was anywhere near. He listened intently and scouted the area several times. Leaning against the cold stone wall at the outer part of the structure, he thought of his sister and sent her prayers. Visions of the women of the forest danced before his eyes as the sun settled into the horizon.

"Please help Elizabeth!" he called to Sophia and Hyacinth. They nodded their heads and reassured him that they were doing what they could. He felt eerily calm, until she touched him. He had been lost in his thoughts of the women of the forest as Priscilla approached. He did not even hear her. That would not do, he thought. If I am to help Elizabeth, I must be a better knight.

"Henry, I have missed your comfort." said Priscilla, rubbing his hand gently. Henry fell into her and she sweetly kissed his lips. He kissed her back and she did not resist his kiss, nor his touch. He could not help himself as he put his arms around her waist and drew her close in to him. He needed to touch her everywhere, to go deep into her mouth, her breasts, her woman hood. He could not stop himself, for finally she was letting him into her. She dropped her cloak to the ground and untied her blouse. He held her all the while, not wanting to let go, lest she run before he had his fill. His eyes rested shut and he sensed his way through her body. He used his hands, and his mouth and his tongue. He kissed her breasts, her shoulders and the bare skin of her belly. He bent down and lifted her skirts and felt her warm soft legs. He found her womanhood and kissed it, taking in long deep breaths, filling himself with her scent. He lay her down on the ground and she obliged. Each moment his body moved faster, fearing she would put a stop to his touching her, his entering her, his coming to ecstasy inside of her. But she did not. He lay atop her and moved within the soft folds of her body, never wanting to stop, wanting to feel the ecstasy again and again.

"Henry, I can help you, lest you forget why I met you here." She whispered as he continued to push himself inside of her. Her words brought him to his senses. He lifted himself up and lay next to her. Guilt overcame him. What had he done? How could he seek pleasure with this woman who had caused him grief, when his sister was in jail? What had he done? He started to cry in his anguish.

Priscilla rolled atop him and kissed his tears. "Henry, do not cry. Lovemaking is a cure for the melancholy. It is why God made men and women this way." She said.

"No, I should not be partaking of such pleasures. Now, how can you help?" he asked. Priscilla continued to kiss him and he was once more pulled in. Before he knew it, he was inside of her again. She sat atop him, moving side to side, ever so gently. He felt her holding herself back and enticing him to push and pull himself into her, deeper and deeper. Henry thought he would go mad with the need he felt for her body. He grabbed onto her backside and was about to let out a cry, when she covered his mouth. He held her tight to him and released into her. He knew why she enticed him so, why he had to have her, for she took him to another time and place, a place like no other. Yes, he could live here inside of this woman, forever and ever. He lay under the weight of her body delirious from the pleasure. He forgot all for a moment.

"Henry, I hear someone coming. I must go. Meet me here, a quarter past midnight." Priscilla gathered her clothes and disappeared into the darkness. Henry lay still. He did not hear anything, but surely did not want to be caught half naked and looking like a fool. He retreated to his bedchambers to await their next meeting.

"Oh my, what time is it?" He jumped out of bed and realized he had heard the chiming of the clock at exactly twelve midnight. Priscilla would be waiting. He arrived and there she was, sitting quietly in the dark corner around back of the icehouse. He lifted her up and without a word, led her to a much safer spot, just outside the southerly wall of the estate. Through a break in the stone wall.

"Come, this is where Elizabeth and I ...I have found a quick way into the forest. You see, we have secret passageways in and around our estate. Look over yonder about ten yards", he said pointing in the dark of night. There is a small thicket and that is where the secret tunnel begins and ends." Henry was so excited to be in the presence of Priscilla.

"I see Master, perhaps you can show me on our way back." She said. "Where are you taking me now?" she asked, shyly.

"Somewhere where we will not be interrupted and can talk...and...in private." said Henry, turning to her and smiling. He led her to the abandoned barn.

Henry built a fire with the scattered wood. The light cast an eerie glow throughout the hollow belly of the old barn. He was suddenly overcome with sadness. He could feel his sister's presence here, and he saw remnants of her visits. A bunch of dried flowers, neatly stacked fire kindling. Yes, his sister was here. The sadness turned quickly into remorse, at his infidelity to her memory. Priscilla sat quietly and her body did not touch his.

"You said you could help. How so?" he asked.

Priscilla kept her head low and spoke slowly and quietly. "My brother is the new stable boy, been working here for a good part of a month. He will help me...us."

Henry noticed her tremble and he started to move towards her.

"No, wait!" she said holding up her hand." Henry immediately backed away and sat farther from her than before. They both sat crossed legged, still not touching, staring into the fire. "Let me finish." Priscilla said, brushing strands of stray hair up into her bonnet.

Henry was feeling the passion rising up in him, watching her frightened and so willing to help him. The way she sat showed off the perfect curves of her hips, her bosom was overflowing and he would not be able to wait much longer to touch her. He wanted to show her how much he appreciated everything about her.

"If you need a horse or coach my brother will arrange it. Is that what you need, Master?"

"Yes, Priscilla, how did...? Yes, I do need a horse. Can he have one for me on the morrow? And are you sure he can get me one without anyone knowing?" he asked, sure that his lover was now reading his mind.

"I will tell him what it is you need. I shall give you word as soon as I am able. If you show me the secret passageway to your bed chambers tonight, I shall be able to safely return to you with word. That is if you promise to stay put in your bed chambers until I return." Priscilla kept her head down, and gazed into the fire. Henry hardly heard what she said, for the rosiness of her warmed cheeks and the fullness of her lips had him mesmerized. It looked as if the flames danced upon her head and sent heat throughout his loins, the likes of which he had never before experienced.

"Yes, that is a plan, then." He said moving in to hold her. "I shall stay put in my bedchambers tomorrow and you shall bring me word when a horse is ready for me…yes, yes…" Henry lay her down and ran his fingers across her face. He pulled her bonnet off and untied the ribbons that held her deep auburn hair in place. He undressed her slowly, one garment at a time, until she was fully naked, lying open and waiting. He entered her again and again and it was not until the sun was just starting to peak above the forest floor that they headed back to the estate, through the secret tunnel, into the secret passageways and into his bedchambers, where he would wait for her return.

Henry waited seven long days and nights. Sleep did not come, neither did an appetite. Nerves on edge, it was all he could do to keep a breathing spell at bay. Finally, one tense week, she came back to him, entering into his chambers in the early morning dawn. He stood ready and waiting, still donning the clothing he wore seven days prior.

"Master, you must go now. Your horse is ready. Come now." Said Priscilla.

Henry approached her and drew her into him, holding her tightly in his arms, all panic ceased. "I first want to lay with you" he boldly announced.

Priscilla wriggled away and Henry felt the familiar blow to his midsection. He hung his head in shame. Priscilla stopped moving, still as the hush in Sunday services. Seeing this as an invitation, he opened her blouse and kissed her bosom. She did not writhe in pleasure as he tickled her nipples forcefully with his tongue. He stopped and looked at her. "What is it Priscilla?" he asked.

"Master, Henry, I want nothing more than to lay with you and enjoy the pleasures your body brings me, but I am told you must leave now, to avoid suspicion. I am sure you will agree." She whispered gently in his ear and planted a slight kiss on his cheek.

On any other day, he would have taken her demeanor as rejection, yet today, he must stay brave, for he had his sister to save. He took a deep breath of her scent before releasing his embrace. He would take Priscilla's intoxicating scent with him on his journey. It would give him courage. "Very well, I shall ready myself and go to the stable right away." Turning his back to Priscilla, he quickly threw on his finest riding clothes, suitable for a meeting with the powers that be. They were in still in neat array, upon his bed, where he had put them seven days prior. Muttering his disappointment at being denied the pleasures of her flesh, he thought to entice her one last time. Turning around he said. "I am ready! See it did not take me long, I am sure we can now…" Priscilla was nowhere to be seen. That is odd, he thought. She left without a good luck kiss. Being with Priscilla would have to wait. It was time to help Elizabeth. I am grateful to Priscilla and shall show her upon my return. Perhaps I shall buy her a trinket in the city, he thought. All thoughts dashed from his mind as he silently approached the stables. All was strangely quiet and a shiver ran up his spine. He was reminded of the meeting with his Grandfather that fateful day. Head down, he entered the stable. One young stable boy handed him the reigns of an unfamiliar horse. Grabbing the reigns, he slid atop easily. This horse was a charger, a war horse who knew it's way to battle. "I shall need you today." He declared as they rode off through the forest.

Henry found the destination easily. The Prison for Religious Offenders, the shabby sign stated. Heart racing, chest slightly tight, he called out his new found confidence in the job at hand to keep his nerves steady. He did not like the looks of this place, but what was he expecting? Beggars lined the streets, in hopes of scraps from the crowds that gathered to watch the latest executions. "Oh, dear sister, how did you get yourself here?" He asked to no one in particular. A beggar looked up and Henry turned away. It was Cookie who gave him explicit instructions as to where to find Elizabeth and who to speak to if he wanted to plead his case for her.

"Ya look for the prison and then find the Justice of the Peace, fancy word for someone who could care at all for the likes of the commoners, or peace, or justice." She sneered. "Those types usually listened to the nobles. They did not think kindly of common folk, but they did their deeds for the nobles. Please help our Elizabeth. I can't stand the thought of her…" Cookie took out a rag from within her skirt folds, dabbed her teary eyes and blew her nose loudly. "If she were to go to trial, there would be no good ending."

Cookies word pounded in his head. "No good ending." Shuddering, he jumped off the horse and walked into the building adjoining the prison, as instructed. So far no one noticed, as he strutted through the dark hall looking for the Justice. A booming voice threw him backward, knocking the breath away. He would recognize that voice anywhere. It was James of Hartford, and by the sound of it, he was close behind. The tightness returned to Henry's chest for a fleeting moment. He found his wits and entered into the nearest room. Hidden from sight, with a clean view, he leaned against the partially open door. There were two others with James. None of them seemed to care who heard their conversation, as their voices echoed from the ceilings and walls of the dingy prison office.

"What do you mean, you cannot put her on trial yet?" James screamed at the man he walked with. "This is outrageous. You must do so immediately." Boomed James.

Henry crouched watching as James drew his broadsword and held it to the man's neck. The man backed away, but held firm in his resolve. "I am ordered to wait, and my orders come from the Queen herself." He said. James lowered his sword, but did not return it to its sheath.

"The Queen, you say? Why would the Queen of England care about the likes of Elizabeth Cumberland?" Sword still exposed, James closed in on the man. "Give me reason not to kill you now."

"Need I remind you Sir Hartford, that you are not the only one who demands how things are to be handled?" questioned the man, not taking his eye off of James' sword. "Patience, patience. There are others who have an interest in Lady Cumberland's…shall I say predicament? You know of whom I speak. I take my orders from him. And the Queen. If you do not back away, it is he who you shall give reason to, as to why he should not kill you."

The man's face showed no sign of fear or fright. Henry smiled at the man's boldness toward the malevolent Earl of Hartford. He then shuddered realizing it was most likely his Grandfather who gave the orders.

"Don't patronize me Justice, we have the Cumberland estate under tight lock down, and I know all there is to know about Lady Cumberland's predicament. She is a damn whore witch and shall be hung." He backed away, returning broadsword to sheath. "If I find out that you are lying, you will die. You will die hanging, alongside the Lady Elizabeth." James stormed out of the building, leaving the Justice and the shire reeve standing alone.

Henry's heart sank, at the mention of his dear sister. Outrage fueled his soul.

"The Queen?" asked the other man. "Is it true Justice, the Queen is called on such matters? I shall say that would not look good for us, if we are not doing what the Queen…"

"Shut up, fool. I had to say something to get him to leave. Word is that the Cumberland lad is out and about, fishing for information and we are to…" The Justice stopped and looked around. Henry slowly shut the door with his boot and slid down against the wall, careful no glimpse of his presence would be seen, not even his shadow. They knew he was there? How could they know? He must be even more careful now. Surprise was a trusted element, or so Cookie, had led him to believe. He resumed listening, and searched for his next right move. The echo in the great building sent the men's voices in his direction.

"What say you Justice, I don't understand?" said the shire reeve.

"Come to my office and I shall tell you of the details."

The two men's heavy footsteps assured Henry that they were walking away. He stepped out of his hiding place and followed them. Seeing which door they entered, he stood outside waiting to hear of the details. There did not seem to be anyone coming or going in this wing of the building. Strange thought Henry, but he was so very relieved.

"By order of the Duke of Winchester, we are to keep Elizabeth for a time. He and only he can usher the orders to us. Besides, I do not like Hartford one least bit. He is ruthless. "said the Justice.

"And the Duke is not?" asked the shire. "I think they all are quite ruthless and I do not understand why the lovely young maiden Elizabeth must be held? She seems…"

"Stop! Our job is not to question the orders of those who feed us. If I stopped and looked at the accused with pity and remorse, I shall say, I would lose my mind! No…our job is to follow the instructions of those who, however they yield their power, instruct us, else wise our families and our very lives shall be in danger and we shall be the damned prisoners, us, and our families."

"I happen to think she is innocent." Said the shire.

"It does not matter what you think. It may however calm you to know that the longer we wait to bring her to trial, the better her chance is to escape her fate. The better chance for someone, or something to happen that shall change her destiny."

"What are you saying, Justice?"

"Let me tell you a story. Something peculiar happened to me recently."

"Is this going to be a story of one of your escapades Justice? I shall pass if it is." laughed the shire.

"No, no, this is different, this woman…" Let me tell you…

"Well, if you are going to go on, then do you have some brandy to share?" asked the shire.

Henry was sure he must stay to listen, and as of yet, no one had come upon him. Just in case, he had an escape planned, for there was what looked to be an empty room, adjacent to the Justice's office.

"Last night I stopped at the pub before heading home for the evening. I was enjoying a brew when in walked the most enchanting woman. She was lovely with dark hair that waved down past her shoulders in a provocative manner. Her eyes were deep smoldering embers set against skin with the look of the softest ivory treasure." The shire interrupted with a snort. The justice ignored him and continued. "She seemed to be a most refined lady. She did not look to be a harlot and I wondered what she was doing there, unaccompanied, in an establishment of that caliber? She sat down next to me and began to speak in the most melodious tone. We shared a pot of ale and the next thing I knew I was quite intoxicated. I thought it odd because I am not a man to become inebriated so easily. I am a careful man, a meticulous man, and after all I have a wife and eight children, and I do not want them to know of... Now, where was I?"

Henry was becoming annoyed at this man. He was telling a tale of his follies and he was the one in charge of his sister's destiny? Or was it his Grandfather, or James, or the Queen? Who was in charge of Elizabeth's fate? He was so irritated with the flippant story, it fueled his desire to barge into this Justice's chambers and take both he and the shire down. So angry was he that he held his hand upon his dagger, ready to cut these two men's throats, and it was at that moment when he was ready to pounce like a vicious wild dog that he sensed it. He inhaled deeply. Yes, it was the same distinct aroma that greeted him when he and Elizabeth visited the women of the forest. Lavender, rose, lilac; the scent brought Sophia and Hyacinth to the forefront of his mind. He heard the Justice continue his rant, but this time, the story drew him in.

"And there I was sitting with this most lovely woman feeling incredibly drunk and wanting nothing more than to take her to my bed. As if she read my mind she led me out of the pub and into a room a few doors down. I can barely recall a moment after the one in which we entered the small room. I was filled with her scent, the roses, the lavender. Ahh, need I say, I try to remember the night we spent together, for I am sure it would be a most intriguing memory, yet the only touch I remember is one soft luxurious kiss…that and a pounding headache and the worst belly ache the next morn!" he exclaimed.

"Forgive me, Justice, I do say, your reputation as a romantic is true, yet what does this have to do with Elizabeth and her fate?" asked the shire.

The Justice, did not answer him, just continued. "She had left a small pouch made of silk on the bedside table filled with the most wonderful smelling herbs and flowers. That is all I have left of the lovely lady of the night. I have it right here. Drawing in the scent of this magic potion gives me the most heavenly feeling. And dare I say it, but it is like I remember making love to her again and again as I inhale…"

"This is ridiculous, Justice." The shire had about enough of his foolery.

"Think what you will, but the lovely lady did tell me one thing, one thing I barely remember, but is brought to my mind whenever I inhale this. She said "do no harm to the Lady Elizabeth and no harm shall come to you. Do no harm."

Henry was mesmerized by the story and transported by the scent of Sophia's home and memories of Hyacinth. Someone was approaching. He had to leave this place on the right away. There was no time to loose. He had to retreat and make another plan. This he knew to be true. Elizabeth was safe for the time being. Sophia of the Forest was watching out for her.

Henry did return to the city one more time. He waited patiently for the knowing of when to return. Two weeks had passed and neither James nor Grandfather had made an appearance. Father was still inside his study and was of no use. The only thing that helped Henry through the weeks was Priscilla. She came into his bed most every night and let him do wondrous things to her body. It helped him keep his mind occupied and she always told him not to worry, and to stay put. He told her almost every detail of his visit. Except the part about the Justice and the Lady. He could not find words to tell this part, for he knew it was never to be uttered. He was concerned, yet not surprised that they knew of his entrance into the city. He knew that the estate had ears. He trusted no one, except for maybe Cookie and surely Priscilla. She had earned his trust, for how could she ever betray him now. He was her lover. She wanted him always.

"Goodbye, my love, safe travels." said Priscilla as he headed out before sun up that day. She had once more helped him to leave the estate unseen. He was so grateful.

He entered the city on a rainy cold winter day. No one was paying any attention to anyone, for they were all trying to keep warm and dry. Finding his way into the Justice's building he inquired with a clerk.

"How do I see a prisoner?" he asked.

"Are you a man of the law, a nobleman? What is your title?" the man did not look up from his ledger.

"I am Henry Cumberland, Sir Henry." He answered with the most authority he could muster.

"Cumberland you say?" the man stood up and immediately started shouting. "He is here, he is here. It is Cumberland!"

Henry shot out of that building as fast as he could. Like an arrow flying form the crossbow of the mightiest knight, he flew out of the prison, down the streets and did not stop until he was well outside the city limits. He had left his horse, but it did not matter. He had to get home. Once well into the forest, he zigzagged through the trees and thickets. He was so thankful that it was raining, for anyone on his trail would surely be confused. He prayed to God and he prayed to Sophia to help him find his way back home. He could not be captured, for who would help Elizabeth? What good would he be if he too was locked up in the Prison for Religious Offenders. He arrived at the estate unseen, took the secret entrances and did not stop until he was safely within the walls of his bedchambers. Soaked to the bone and shivering, he heaved great sighs of relief. The tears cascaded down his cheeks and he trembled with the fear of what could have been. Someone was rustling in his chambers, for he could hear it through the cracking of his chattering teeth. "Priscilla?" he whispered. He so needed her comfort and a hot bath.

He turned towards the noise and found Annie standing still and quiet. She held a large pitcher of steaming hot water.

"I shall draw your bath for you Master." She said, turning to fill the tub, that stood in the middle of the room.

Henry was so shocked to see Annie, yet he had no time to question her appearance. He needed the relief of the hot water and fast. Annie had not shown her face to him since Elizabeth disappeared. Her duties as his laundress continued, for it must have been her that left the fresh linens outside of his bedchambers each day.

"Annie, why…" he stammered, shivering so deeply, the words did not come clear.

"Shush, Master, if you do not take these soaking wet clothes off immediately, I fear you shall catch your death." Henry stood still, unable to move, except for the uncontrollable shaking. Annie peeled off his garments one by one and wrapped him in steaming warm blankets. She continued pouring the scalding water into the tub and beckoned he enter. He did not waste a moment, and was not timid in his nakedness. She was right, he must warm his bones, lest he perish.

Neither one said a word to the other. After today's fright, he did not want to speak of anything. For now, he soaked in the decadent lavender and rose scented water. Annie tended to him closely, keeping the water properly warm. Soon he calmed, his body stopped shaking, he stood up and she wrapped him in more warm towels and tucked him in his bed. She gently kissed his forehead and whispered.

"Rest well. I shall bring you your evening meal. You are safe now."

Henry drifted off and slept the soundest, deepest sleep since his sister was taken away.

"Wake up Master Henry, she is home!" Annie was shaking him and he sat up with a start.

"What? Who?" he did not know what day it was, what time. The words he heard coming from Annie's mouth were surely a dream. Annie? The light of the sun shone through the cracks in the window panels. He jumped out of bed, remembering that he had ventured into the city and that they were now after him.

"Here, put your fresh laundered clothes on. Elizabeth is home." said Annie, handing him his trousers and shirt. She stood and watched him as he dressed. She stared at every inch of his body. He could feel her watching. He did not care that she looked at him in this way. He rather liked it. And nothing could make this day any better than it was, for his sister was home!

"And Master, do not ever trust Priscilla again." Annie turned and walked out, Henry following behind and said not a word.

Chapter Nineteen

Elizabeth was delivered to the estate by two guards and the shire. One guard held Elizabeth's crumpled body in the crooks of his massive arms. The other pounded on the door of the estate leaving the shire hiding behind him. When the house maid answered the door the shire moved to the front and asked for the Master of the house. The maid stood staring at them with her mouth agape. Just then Gregory appeared. The shire shoved the official orders into his hands and told the guards to set Elizabeth down inside. Elizabeth was weak and fragile, but she was awake and the sight of her father put courage into her fading body. Father had not come to get her, but now she was home. She felt his presence as he held out his arms for her. She did not dare say anything, for she did not want the shire to know she was awake.

The shire began shouting at her father.

"It is by these orders signed by the magistrate that Elizabeth be allowed to return home until such time that her strength be regained. At that time, she shall be returned to prison to stand trial for assault and for the practice of witchcraft such that it brought harm to another. Guards will be posted outside the estate gates and at the door of her sleeping chambers at all times to ensure that she will not try and escape." He finished.

Gregory nodded his agreement. The guard dropped Elizabeth at her father's feet. He bent down to touch her, his breath foul with the stench of spirits. Still Elizabeth did not care. She was home. She could barely move her head, but she managed to look around as Father knelt down and took her in his arms. He barked orders to the maid to fetch Matilda. The maid did not need to fetch her at all for as soon as her name was mentioned Matilda was standing there. Father did not seem strong enough to lift her and Elizabeth nuzzled her head into his chest.

"Matilda, have someone call for Henry. He will help you get her to her room. Care for her with whatever means necessary. I…I…must get cleaned up myself." Said Father.

Henry was already running to greet her. She could hear him approaching.

"Elizabeth, Elizabeth!" he bent down to touch her face and jumped back in alarm. "She is so deathly pale, we must…Father…help her." Elizabeth did not want Henry to have a breathing spell and she reached out to touch him.

Father stood up and walked away, quickly. He did not return to his study, however. He was heading in the direction of his bedchambers for the first time since Elizabeth was taken away.

Henry picked up Elizabeth and carried her to her bedchambers. Matilda and Annie and several other maids followed, along with a guard who lagged behind, not wanting to breathe the air of a witch with the plague, no doubt, thought Elizabeth. Henry lay her gently on her bed.

Elizabeth soaked in the moment. She was home, her brother and father were near and she and her babe were safe. This was truly a miracle. She touched her belly and felt her babe move all about. "Demetri, we are safe now, we are home." She whispered.

"Not so sure about that." Snipped Matilda. "this place is anything but safe for you, lass." She must not think I am awake enough to hear her, thought Elizabeth. I am not going to respond to her. I need to stay still, in this moment…She is right though, there is more to do to ensure our safety and I will find a way to do so, after I rest.

The maids brought a giant bowl of steaming broth and another giant bowl of hot water and towels. Matilda started with the cloths, using them as compresses upon her grimy brow. She rubbed a healing balm on her chest and as she did so she started in again with her thoughts, aloud.

"I take absolutely no stock in any stories about witches. I do not believe for a minute in such creatures. I've lived with this family for years and nothing that happened here surprises me, no it does not." Elizabeth just listened, smiling to herself. Matilda did not care who heard her and who did not, she spoke, no matter what. And her speech was barely audible, and mumbled, just enough so that if anyone questioned what she said, she mumbled again. "Never mind, never mind."

Yes, thought Elizabeth, that is why Henry and I thought she had snakes in her bonnet. Always slithering in and out…she laughed inside at the thoughts and memories of her youth, she had no other choice for at this time, she was steeped in the miracle of being home.

Matilda continued as she washed Elizabeth from head to toe, careful not to give her the chill. She shouted orders to the maids and muttered her insights. "I know you got yourself into this trouble, Missy. This babe has nothing to do with magic or spells or sacrifices. No, you found a lad, that's it and I don't as well blame you! Not much in the way of love here. Except maybe your brother or your father…when the drink hasn't taken his good sense away. No, I take that back." Elizabeth cringed at the mention of her father. She tried to pull away from Matilda, but she was so very weak.

"There is nothing I can do to keep you from your fate lass, but I can nurse you back to health, and pray, but I don't take much stock in prayer. Maybe you do. Should pray then." Matilda covered Elizabeth soundly and tucked her in tight and touched her cheek with her rough hand. "You will have to wake soon and eat. Your babe will need nourishment."

Elizabeth felt a tear drop on her face Matilda's breath as she spoke words of healing. "I did not expect to see you again. Wouldn't let on how much I love you children, but I do, don't know why, but I do."

The words from her childhood nanny helped her drift into the space where all is well, the place of sleepy dreams. As she drifted she had a conversation with Matilda, or anyone who would care to listen. "I don't believe in witches either, dear Matilda, I do know that there are however, beautiful ladies in the forest, magical and mystical, and I know I am in love with the most wonderful young man in the land and I am not sorry. I also know that you love and care for me, more than my own mother ever did."

Elizabeth opened her eyes late into the next day. Henry was slumped over in a chair next to her, his head resting next to hers. She thought she was dead or that she was dreaming. She reached out to touch him and he jumped at the start and lifted his head up to look upon her.

"Elizabeth, you are alive!" whispered Henry not wanting to alert the guards.

"Am I Henry? I think I am dead, or dreaming. Why am I not in that dark cold cell any longer? Henry, talk to me!" Elizabeth cried out, choking on the words.

"Elizabeth, it is all right my sister." Henry said calming her with his touch." The justice and the shire let you come home for a while. You were quite ill and he allowed you to come home." He said with a calm reassuring tone.

Elizabeth did not like what she was feeling. The truth of her situation set in with a dangerous ovation. "Oh Henry, then my fate will still come to pass. I could still be hung. They only want me well so I may feel the pain and the humiliation of being punished for a crime I did not commit. They only want me awake and well so they may laugh at me and call me names, so they may make me the one they take all of their guilt and hatred out upon. Henry, this is not a good thing that I returned home. They should have left me in the cell to die." She cried sputtering and gagging on her words.

"No Elizabeth you are now home." consoled her brother. "You do not have to go back, for I will think of a way to keep you here with me."

"The only one who can really help me is Demetri." said Elizabeth. "If he came back to me he would tell them that this was all untrue. He could save me." She said closing her eyes and picturing her love.

"You do not need him, sister, for he is not a man of nobility, or he would never have left you to face this time alone." He said. "I will help you. I am a man now and I know of what I speak."

Elizabeth started to weep at her brother's words, for they cut deeply and opened her greatest fear. "How is it that you may speak of my love in such a way? You know not of his motives Henry. I know how he loves me for he has touched my heart as he held me near. He is a noble man and he would be here if something horrible had not befallen him." The weeping took hold and she could not contain it any longer.

Henry came close, but she pushed him away.

"Elizabeth, I am…so…sorry. What can I do for you?" he pleaded.

Elizabeth continued to weep, letting all of her sorrow and sadness fall. She could no longer keep it in, she missed Demetri so. It felt like a lifetime ago that he held her in his arms and told her he would make her his wife. She sobbed, for there was nothing else she could do.

"Elizabeth," Henry whispered. "Shsh, the guards, they will hear you and if they know you are awake they will want to take you back. Please, I will go find Demetri for you, whatever you need, whatever it is…please…" Henry was begging her and she knew she must quiet herself, but it was impossible, all the grief she had held in for years and years, months and months was let loose, broken from the dam of self-preservation.

"Tell me Henry, Elizabeth stammered. "Do you know? Father… he has…he never came to see me." She could barely say the words.

"Elizabeth" said Henry with great tenacity forcing the words from him. "I do not know what has come over Father. He cries all the time and is locked in his study for most of the day and night. He does not bathe or eat. I fear he has caught the same illness as mother. I fear he cannot help you at all," explained Henry, taking her hand in his. "only I am here for you now, sister, it is only me." He said starting to weep himself.

There was a knock on the door and it opened before Henry could answer it.

"Did I hear the maiden awake? The guard asked, peering in.

Elizabeth turned away from the door and lay very still.

"No sir, she has not awakened as of yet. I fear she may not awaken; she is still burning with the fever. Come here. Would you like to see?" asked Henry.

"No, I shall leave now." And with that he was gone.

"I knew he would not enter, for all the guards are so very afraid of you! I heard them say unspeakable things about what you would do to them if angered. Is it true, that witches can strike others ill or castrate men with their mere thoughts?" he asked.

"What has happened to everyone? Henry, I must tell you the truth. Witches are not real. The women of the forest are real and they have not forgotten their power. You know of what I speak. They are full of the power of love and no one tells them how to live and who to love. They are free. I want to live like them." Elizabeth lay back exhausted. She had no more fight in her and would not argue another moment about witches.

"Yes, sister, I believe it utterly ridiculous for these men to believe such things of you, but this is no ridiculous matter. I thought for sure I would never see my beloved sister again, but now you are back and I will never let you leave me again. I will stand by your side and I will go find Demetri for you, if that is what you desire."

Elizabeth nodded in agreement. This talk took the breath from her.

"And, we must think of a way to get you out of here and to safety very soon." Henry added.

Elizabeth was caught off guard at her brother's new found bravery. She gave him a good look over and even in her weakened state, she could tell that there was something different about him. He looked a bit older, a bit more like a man. Her incarceration had perhaps had this effect on him. She would trust her little brother to help her for he was the only one who could do so now.

"Yes, Henry, please find Demetri. Go to the barn, you know the one, the old icehouse barn, and his cousin's land. I shall tell you how to get there." Elizabeth slowly and precisely gave her brother directions to every one of their meeting places. Henry reassured her and left her with a kiss on the forehead. He would return in two days. The guards would not be forewarned. He would take measures.

Elizabeth heard him talk to the guards on the way out.

"It could very well be the pox, after all." warned Henry. "She had a wound, that is starting to form, right here on her neck." He hid his laugh. Elizabeth saw the guard jump back and Henry give a little wink in her direction. Now the guard would not want to be near Henry either.

Elizabeth lay in her bed hoping and praying that Henry would find Demetri. She slept fitfully, weeping and tossing and turning. At one point she saw Father, coming so very close, but as she went to touch him, he backed away. She fell back into her sleep, dreaming of her love and their babe, praying and dreaming, praying and dreaming.

Henry came back to report his news to Elizabeth late the next night. He had been to every one of the places she described, except Demetri's cousins. That would wait until the morrow. There was no sign of Demetri.

"But sister, I had so much time to think today, away from the estate. I have thought of a plan." Henry said staring at the floor. "You are feeling better are you not?" He asked walking closer to her as she lay in her bed. He took hold of Elizabeth's hand. "Well enough to travel? We will leave the estate and find shelter and I shall care for you and your babe." Henry had tears in his eyes and he was pleading with his sister. "Let me care for you. I can do it, for I am a man now."

Elizabeth reached up and hugged her brother and did not want to let him go. She looked at him and said "No Henry, I will not ask you to do such a thing. We could not live with or near the forest. They would surely find us and then your fate, as well as our dear friends of the forest, would be as mine. They would hang us all and I cannot have that on my conscience." Her voice was firm and strong as she finished speaking to him.

"You will go tomorrow to find Demetri for me and in the meantime let us pray that you find him." They held hands, she laying in her bed, and he sitting in a small wooden chair, body draped across his older sister for protection. They prayed for good news on the morrow.

Henry returned to Elizabeth from his day's travel with somber news. He had not found Demetri's cousin. He had found a farm in the vicinity of where Elizabeth had described. It had been abandoned. He had also seen something that greatly disturbed him and he did not want to share it with Elizabeth.

"Tell me brother, of what it is you do not want to tell me." She asked, knowing he was hiding something.

"I do not wish to alarm you and you know you do not believe in witches, but as I made my way back to the estate late this afternoon there was a group of townspeople gathering. They were carrying a doll made of rags and they had the doll hanging from a noose. They were yelling, 'kill the witch, kill the witch and shouting 'hanging is too good for the devil's wife.'" He sighed and said. "They named you."

Henry, I know my fate. You and I are the only ones who believe my innocence. I fear our own father, wants me hung."

"Elizabeth, how can you say..."

"He could save me. I am the daughter of a noble man and the Duke of Winslow is my grandfather. Why are they not helping me? If Demetri does not return, and Father does not defend me, then..." she cried out. The pain of her father's betrayal could not be contained anymore. She knew she came home to give father a chance to save her. And it had been three days and he had not shown his face to her, not come, nor talked, nor asked.

"Elizabeth, there is something you must know...about Father..." said Henry. "He cannot help because Grandfather will not let him."

"Whatever do you mean? Father does not want to help me. I have done something to him, shamed him, hurt him beyond repair."

"Grandfather and his men held both Father and I back from helping you, with fear of death and torture. He told me not to interfere, but I do not care. I will help you any way I can. Grandfather said he would help, but I do not see him doing so. He only cares of his money. I also think he has spies watching us, watching us all the time. I..." stammered Henry.

"I have done wrong by both Grandfather and Father. I have sought to love a commoner and rejected my betrothed. This is my sin and this is why Father will not help."

"Very well Elizabeth, believe what you will, but if I am to help you, we must leave here and soon. The townspeople were gathering and heading here, to our estate. It will soon be too dangerous for you to be here."

Henry left Elizabeth alone that evening. He would return again into the forest one last time, just to be sure. She protested, but he insisted, he must look again, there might be something he overlooked. She knew better, but sought to agree with her newly heroic and courageous brother.

The next day reached out long before her as Elizabeth waited. She was regaining her strength and the babe was wriggling about, cramped within its too small home. She could not rest, nor find relief from the terrors that awaited. She decided to pray to the Great Mother, and to Sophia. As she prayed she fell into a dream state with the women of the forest. She sought solace and answers, for in the depth of the forest, in the arms of the Mother, she would know. When she awoke, she decided to get up. Much to her surprise, she felt well rested and nourished. Better than she had in many a month.

The guard was not at the door. No one at all was about in the children's bedchamber wing. She would go now.

Elizabeth found her way to the outside of her father's study. She hid in the corner of the hallway, behind the panels that kept her from being seen, yet gave her a perfect view of any comings and goings. This was the same place she hid so very many times before, listening, waiting, wondering and trying to get close to the man who she would never know. Today she hid as a woman, a woman with child, hiding behind the panels outside her father's study, wondering and waiting, for what, she knew not. She could hear voices, muffled and dark. Who was her father talking to? What was it that…

Elizabeth almost lost her footing as the door to Father's study opened.

"There is nothing more for us to discuss. They will be here for her in two days. And Gregory, need I remind you…no one will believe you, you are nothing but a drunken fool." Hissed Grandfather.

Elizabeth felt the pull of her babe, tight and sharp. She doubled over and gasped for air. Grandfather turned toward the panels, as a large decanter of brandy flew out the door and hit him in the head. A large bearded man emerged from Father's study to see to Grandfather.

"I am fine, leave me be, go see to it that my son-in-law stays suitably incapacitated and we will be on our way." Said Grandfather, pushing the man off of him.

Another pain hit Elizabeth as she heard the bearded man hit Father. A few moments later he left the study. Grandfather closed and locked the door and tucked the key in his breast pocket.

"Come on now, leave him be, he's so drunk, he will be out til' morn." Said Grandfather as they left.

Father, however must not have been as drunk as Grandfather thought, for he yelled obscenities through the locked door, raging warnings at a man who simply spat and walked away.

Elizabeth left her hiding place, wanting to run far away from what she just witnessed. She went to the only place she knew, the maze. *Great Mother help us all.*

She lay on the hard dirt ground, under a large sculpted evergreen. How odd, she thought, as she lay looking at the rounded curves on the trees boughs. This is not how a tree grows in the forest. Trees grow straight and tall, reaching for the sun light, branches outstretched, meeting and intertwining with the others trees, saying come, join me in the dance of life, for it is in this beauty that I doth live! In the forest the trees met, embraced and formed small gatherings, everywhere you walked, were gatherings of trees. The trees of the forest grew wild and free, unencumbered by desires of grandiosity and glamour, untouched by the violence of the gardener's shears.

The trees of the forest held life in the midst of the chaos. Cherished life flourished in the mounds of dirt and moss, tangled branches held nests, and the bored holes fed birds. The maze was void of such chaos. Everything ordered and refined, cut and chopped to perfection. Each row took you somewhere, a journey already decided, steps carefully counted, turns in perfect sync with the destination. There was nothing alive here, nothing new. It no longer held for her what it did before. All was as it always was here. There was no way out of this maze, for it had been set in place by her grandfather's, grandfather. It was never to be so for her babe. She could make that happen now, and that perhaps was exactly how it was supposed to be.

"Where is the witch? We want justice, where is the witch?" she heard the chants, the shouts, from afar. They were so very close now. She rolled onto her side and sat upright, holding her belly.

"You are the child of my love and it is not to be that you will ever sit in this maze. It is not to be and for that I am grateful." Her babe did not move, but the pull of life wanting to enter into this world was so very strong within her body. She knew it would not be long and she knew she could not stop it. No one, not even a mother can stop the wild, the free, the passionate and the untamed. The forest, her love of Demetri, her babe, all of it was of that world. The world of the forest beckoned and lured and offered freely to any who dared enter. She answered it's call.

Before she would do what she knew she must, she had to see her mother, for Charmaine held the final key. Entering into her Mother's chambers, as she did so many times before, she was struck with her a solace unmistakably forlorn, and completely unavoidable.

"How I wished this was different, Mother. How I wished each time that I visited and rummaged, that my curiosity would wake you and cheer you, and that you would forgive me for saving Henry, or that you would tell me you love me. How I wished in the deep silence of my heart that you would be well and care for me. Perhaps if I was quiet and kind and good, you would do so. I was quiet and kind and good, yet that did not earn me your favor, or your love. I know not why you lay here. I know not why you can not love me. I know not why you have nothing to say, yet say so very much. "Elizabeth drew a deep breath, as if she were speaking to a priest, confessing her truths, knowing she would do penance, but not caring. The release of hoping and wishing things were different, cleansed her soul. Charmaine was so beautiful, and peaceful, yet she did not look real or alive, Elizabeth thought as she sat stiffly by her mother's side. Charmaine's breath was raspy. The only sign she was still among the living. Elizabeth sighed.

"I wondered how my own mother could sleep her life away, never feeling, never knowing of me, your child. You live a life void of all. What is the worse fate? To live a life that others call wrong and evil and to feel the pain of condemnation and injustice, or to allow others to tell you how you shall live and you obey, thus denying your own life? I choose my fate, for however it shall play out. I chose to love, to know the pull of my hearts longing and to follow it. I followed it into the forest and found true love, and others. Others, Mother, who live as I do.

Elizabeth stood up and paced around her mother's bed side and continued.

"I know Grandfather keeps you a prisoner here, just as he seeks to do so to me! I know Father cannot help you. I now know that you have sealed my fate in your everlasting slumber, so it no longer matters why. I choose my fate. I choose differently!"

The tears were falling from her face, she did not wipe them, but allowed them to fall into the embroidered roses, that adorned the neatly folded satin blanket that lay at the foot of the bed. Elizabeth stared at Mother through her angry tears. Mother did look like a corpse, a perfect porcelain face, with a small gentle smile, neatly packaged in a pure silk coverlet. There was no movement, no recognition, nothing. Elizabeth wanted to lash out, slap her mother, wake her out of this false death state that she lived in.

"I shall never live like you Mother. I have found another way, that shall free me forever, and my babe. My babe shall never know this life. I shall see to it."

Her soul was cleared, she spoke her peace, albeit to a half dead woman who claimed her right as Mother. She felt the release, flow through her being, cascading down her shoulders and crashing like a great heavy cape of knight's armor falling to the floor.

"I can bear the pain for it has purpose now. Thank you mother", Elizabeth whispered. She kissed her Mother on the forehead through a flurry of hot tears and returned to her bedchambers with exactly what she came for; a reason and a way.

Chapter Twenty

It was very late that evening when Henry entered Elizabeth's room with a huge tray of food. He did not want anyone interrupting this visit with his sister so he had waited until the estate was asleep. He did not find any sign of Demetri this day either and far be it for him to rush to remove his sister's last ray of hope. Returning from his travels, just as the sun set, he found his way to the kitchen for the comfort he so needed. Annie and Cookie greeted him and that in itself sent a chill of untold truth running through his body. There was to be no more hiding in his naiveté. Priscilla was nowhere to be seen or heard of, as where most of the servants of the household. They had all but vanished. He surmised that they had left the estate in fear for their own lives, for they did not want to be known as working for the devil's family, yet he knew that there was more to it than that. The future was grim for all within the Cumberland Estate and this was not something Henry wanted to be true just yet. He sat in silence while Cookie prepared the food for Elizabeth. Annie helped, throwing gentle glances his way. The tray was ready too soon. Cookie smiled and patted his hand and Annie offered her help.

"Would you like me to carry the tray, Master Henry? I could bring you two bowls of ale if you'd like."

Henry had his hands full with the platters of meat pie and sweet cream and biscuits. He beckoned Annie come close and kissed her on the cheek. "I shall go alone. I don't want to alarm the guards." With that.

"You would not believe it Elizabeth but the guard is still not outside your door." He said as he entered her bedchambers and placed the food on a small table next to her bed. "I believe he is so very scared that you will put a spell on him that he has gone into hiding and we will not find him until years later when one of us opens a closet door and out he falls, a mere skeleton!" joked Henry. He looked at his sister for her response, and found a faraway look upon her face. She seemed to be staring at nothing in particular yet looking intent on something of a serious nature. He searched her eyes to see what it was that held her attention. It was beside him to know, so he might as well sit and tempt her with delicious morsels of meat pie. Her favorite. Elizabeth let out a horrific cry and clutched her bedcovers. She writhed in pain and Henry jumped, panic-stricken. What could be the matter with her? Had she come down with fever again? He frantically felt her head but it was not hot, it was cool and moist.

Elizabeth looked up at him in between long deep breaths and started speaking to him in a calm, surreal manner. "The babe is coming now Henry. You must help me. "She once again stared pensively at nothing.

"The babe? Now? It cannot be sister! You said the time would be after the new year and that is a full month away!" he said quickly with wide eyed panic.

"Henry, it matters not what I said! The babe is coming now! The most unimaginable…. pain…Sophia told me it would be…" she breathed deeply and that seemed to help, for the moment.

Henry reached out for her, but she pushed his touch away. "No!" do not touch me, let me do this!"

"I shall fetch Matilda, Cookie…Dr.…." His offer futile, for he knew not if anyone except Cookie was still within the estate walls.

"No, Henry, it is just you and me now. They shall not know of this." She said calmly.

Henry did not want to ask his sister anything, nor touch her, nor, do whatever it is someone did to help a babe enter into this world. What could he do for her anyway, he wondered? He sat so very still, as not to interrupt her, lest she scream and call the whole house upon them. Not that it mattered, for no one seemed about, no one at all. His mind bounced from one thought to another and made no sense at all. "I will simply sit and watch then." He blurted.

"Henry, the babe will be born only with your help. I do need your help. I cannot do this alone." She was puffing herself up with breath now and her face was turning red and swollen.

"Pull off my bedcovers and help me to see if the babe is ready to come out." Henry pulled off the bedcovers and gasped at what he saw. Elizabeth was lying in a pool of blood.

"Please get clean bed linens Henry and put them underneath me." She ordered. Henry did as he was told. He went to the chest and pulled out all of the clean bedclothes he could find. He had never seen a babe being born, but he had seen a foal come into the world. Perhaps it was the same thing. Oh, he hoped not, he thought. He remembered seeing the stable master put his hands way up inside of the mare and pull the foal out. If this is what he had to do, he could not do it. He would not!

He handed Elizabeth the linens, no he threw them at her, as she was once again panting as if a dog after a long chase. Henry suddenly felt very strange, dizzy and weakened and the room seemed to spin around him. He sat down on a chair to keep from collapsing onto the floor. His mind bounced again. Elizabeth had been right to refuse his help, for he could never care for her and the babe, just look at him now, he could not even help her through this! "Oh, why am I such a fool?" he babbled. He had to help his sister. He had to be strong for Elizabeth now and he was very uncertain of how to do so. She had always helped him, and always seemed so sure. There must have been a time when she did not know how to stop his breathing spells. That was it! He mustered up all the courage he could, stood up and said. "Elizabeth, I will do whatever you need. Should I reach in now and get the babe?

"What are you talking about Henry? I am the one delirious with pain and you are the one acting like an imbecile!" shouted Elizabeth. Her sudden burst made him much more comfortable. His sister, was still in charge and she would guide him, yes, she would.

"I feel the babe coming Henry, this is more than I could ever have imagined..." she let out a great big grunt and curled her body in a ball, clutching and grabbing the bed covers. "Henry, help me now! The babe will be coming. Go to the foot of the bed and see that the babe is coming safely."

"What do you mean? What shall I do?" he asked as he went to the end of the bed, wanting her to scream at him again.

"Nothing Henry, just stand there and be quiet! Don't you dare do anything, I shall do the work, you keep quiet and give your hands to my babe when he emerges." Elizabeth pushed herself up and was trying to crawl off the bed, but then she stopped. She opened her legs and pulled up her bed gown, freeing herself from its bloody tangles. She stayed in this crawling position, staring once again at nothing. Henry stood wide-eyed and frozen with both fear and awe.

He could see the babes head coming out of his sister's body, its little face smashed and crinkled.

"He is coming out now, hold your hands under me, and guide him." She said. Henry reached out ever so gently, afraid to touch the babe, but he did not have time to be timid, for the next thing he knew, all manner of child and waters and blood were washing over his hands, arms and chest. He pulled up one of the bed linens and wrapped the babe, as to not lose hold of him.

Elizabeth collapsed and lay shivering. Henry nestled the babe next to her and covered her quickly. "Henry, is my babe…a girl child?" she asked, groggy, shivering and pale.

Henry thought for a moment, he did not think to look before, then he remembered. "Your babe is a boy child." said Henry sitting next to her upon the bed. "He is a fine boy, he looks healthy, although he is very messy, and it is hard to tell. I do not even know what a healthy babe looks like. He is breathing, that is for sure." He smiled shocked at himself. What had occurred overwhelmed him and he sighed loudly releasing the frenzy that had preceded this miracle.

"Shush Henry. He is beautiful." Elizabeth held her babe in her arms. She stared into his little reddened face and he at her. "Henry, go to the trunk at the foot of my bed and find the sewing scissors." Elizabeth said with a sudden fright in her voice. Henry leapt up, got the scissors and handed them to Elizabeth.

"What are going to do with them?" he asked worriedly.

"Please Henry you must cut this chord here, the one that gives him life separate from mine. Do it quickly and tie a knot in the end closest to him." Sophia instructed me Henry. I am so grateful to her, to the women of the forest, to you… Elizabeth breathed a deep sigh and sunk into the bed and started to drift off to sleep with her new babe lying comfortably next to her. She awoke for a moment, with a painful look upon her face. "Henry, one last push for the babe's life sack needs to…" Her face seemed ashen. The color of life was slowly draining from her. Henry noticed the sudden change and he became worried. He shook her arm and tried to wake her.

"Elizabeth, what say you, I am here to help. Wake up, your babe is hungry." He said, bewildered at her sudden pallor.

She opened her eyes and said, "No, Henry I shall never nurse my babe. He must not have my milk, for surely it is poison now."

"What are you speaking of Elizabeth? Your words do not make sense."

Elizabeth's eyes were heavy now, so very, very heavy. Henry could see she was trying to open them, and he wished he could do so for her. She spoke slowly and deliberately.

"Henry…I am at peace…I have done my job here well, yet not as I planned. You see, the babe came too quickly.

"Yes, yes, Elizabeth, but he is fine now…" answered Henry.

"No, listen. I did not want him to live, I must protect him from my fate. He must come with me. He will be murdered as the child of a witch, if he does not come." She whispered.

"He has to come with me and I need you to help me make it so." Elizabeth's eyes closed and two large tears slid from her eyes, down her cheeks and onto her babe.

"Henry, I took Mother's elixir a few hours ago. I shall die shortly. I will not allow my child nor myself to be tortured any longer. My beloved Demetri will never come for me and I cannot stay here and await my fate. I am not a witch Henry. My only crime is loving and being true to my heart and I do not regret it one bit."

"No, Elizabeth, don't say such things. You just had a babe and you do not know what it is you say. Mother's elixir will not kill you. She takes it every day."

"Henry, I drank the bottle empty. I will die."

"No Elizabeth, please stop saying that."

"Listen to me, dear brother." She whispered. "I have a... most important request of you...listen... carefully." Elizabeth could barely speak.

"Anything Elizabeth, I will do anything, just say you will not die." pleaded Henry.

"I will die Henry. It is coming upon me quickly."

Something in the very pit of Henry's belly told him that she was telling him the truth. He was completely distraught, yet he thought maybe he could still help her. "Tell me what I must do." He said standing over his sister and grasping her hand.

"If my child does not die with me now, you must give him the other bottle of elixir. I do not think I drank this bottle soon enough. He was supposed to die inside of me so we could be together in eternity. I do believe he was very anxious to be born, to see his father..." A small smile formed on her pale lips as her eyes closed shut.

She was leaving now. Henry sensed it. He shook her awake saying, "Elizabeth come back. I cannot kill your baby. Is that what you ask?"

She opened her eyes slowly and struggled with the last words she must speak to insure her promise to herself. "I cannot leave my babe here as our mother did to us. You will little brother. I have faith in you. If you do not do it, the mad townspeople will, or James will. I shall never rest in death, if you do not do as I ask. You must promise me…" She lifted her arm and he took it, touching his face with her cold fingers.

"We shared everything in this life, Henry, the sins of our mother and father shall not be passed on. Promise me," she whispered."

"I promise." cried Henry. He was sobbing uncontrollably. He felt so utterly helpless as he watched his sister fade away from him. How could he live without her? She was always there by his side, comforting him, caring for him, always making everything better. She always knew what to say and what to do to make life joyful and alive.

"Good, little brother." She whispered. "Now I shall leave you." She took one last breath and was gone. The babe stirred and snuggled back to sleep looking very comfortable in the crook of her arm.

Henry intermittently shook Elizabeth and paced the room. "Please awake sister, please!" He pleaded. "I cannot kill your babe." He said to her, hoping she would come back at those words. "I did not mean it Elizabeth. Please come back to me and tell me I do not have to do what you have asked." No Elizabeth, don't die, please do not leave me! He cried grabbing her, shaking her. Her little babe stirred and wriggled as Henry tried desperately to stop his sister from dying.

He knew he could never kill this babe. It was all that was left of Elizabeth. He had to do something. He checked one last time for any sign of life in Elizabeth. She had no breath. A brief sense of calm came over him as he pondered what to do next. Time stood still and he thought of the women of the forest. Sophia might know what to do. He started to pray as Elizabeth instructed him. He would take the babe to Sophia. She knew of babes and Elizabeth trusted her and so would he now. The estate was a ghost camp and the townspeople were asleep for the night, so now was the time.

He wrapped the child in one of Elizabeth's night- gowns and stole away to the small cottage in the woods. The bright full moon lit his way. Henry stood outside of Sophia's cottage and held his little nephew tight. He moved the wrap from around the babe and put his face close to his. "I hope your Mother will forgive me for this." He said as he kissed his warm face. Knocking softly, he felt a surge of love well up for this babe. Sophia opened the door a crack and peered out at him.

"What has happened, Henry?" She asked, ushering him into her warm cottage. "Tell me of your sister." Sophia said, her face saddened in her knowingness.

Henry thought of Elizabeth lying lifeless on her bed. "I believe my sister is dead, Sophia. I do not want to believe it is so, but she has no breath…" he started to stumble and Sophia caught him as he was about to collapse. She quickly grabbed the bundle from his arms.

"What have you here Henry?" Sophia asked as she put a loving hand on his to steady him. Henry opened the bundle as Sophia held it and she glimpsed at the child, so tiny and new. She uncovered him fully and lay him near the fire and looked him over head to toe. Placing her fingers gently on his chest, she made her decree. "His heart is beating rhythmically and wildly fast as healthy babes were supposed to do, he appears to be just perfect."

Henry sighed with relief. The elixir has not harmed him, good, well, good for the babe, he thought. "You must take him." said Henry quietly looking away toward the fire. "Hide him and keep him safe. No one must know he is here. He will be killed if you do not take him." He continued as if in a trance.

"I will Henry. I will keep Elizabeth's babe safe in my home but what of Elizabeth?" she asked.

"I told you", cried Henry. "She is dead. I am sure of it." He felt so guilty at not honoring Elizabeth's request that he would dare not ever breathe a word of the details of his sister's demise to anyone, not even Sophia.

"Where is she Henry?" asked Sophia calmly." I must go to her and see her now."

"She is at the estate. It is dangerous for you to go there, Sophia." said Henry.

"It is dangerous for all, if we do not take care of her remains. We must preserve the life of this child, as well as yours. Come, take me to her." Henry nodded in agreement, knowing he could never argue with this woman.

Sophia wrapped up the babe and brought him into the room behind the colorful curtains. She whispered instructions to her daughters. "Where is Elizabeth?" asked Hyacinth. "Shush, my child, I shall tell you later, for now, care for the babe, and I shall return shortly." Henry heard Hyacinth weeping softly and Maya and Penny cooing at the babe. Sophia emerged from behind the curtains, put on her wrap and hurried out the door. Henry followed close behind.

Dawn was nearing as they entered into the eerily quiet estate.

"Most everyone has all but vanished! Even the guards who were ordered to stand watch have been absent for the last two days." whispered Henry. "I don't understand why. They were ordered…?"

"Henry if those guards were still here Elizabeth would not have had safe passage to the other world." Answered Sophia, in her direct and knowing tone.

Her words were strange, thought Henry. "What do you mean Sophia?" he asked.

"Do you remember praying with Elizabeth for our help? We heard you. We heard her months ago when she needed the help of the Great Mother. We have been doing our best all along. We work with the Goddess, but there is only so much we can do. And only so much that we are allowed to do. We must be very careful not to interfere with true destiny. What we want and what is destiny's intent is not always the same." She said solemnly. Sophia spoke to him, yet it was as if she was also talking to many others. Her people maybe? Her children? He did not know, but her words were somehow comforting him.

"Do you think it was Elizabeth's destiny to die Sophia? I do not want to believe that she would leave me, us…her babe." Henry started to weep. They were winding their way through the narrow and dark passageways into her bedchambers. The cold, damp walls echoed with their steps, each sound vibrating the truth of his sister's passing within his bones.

The room was lit by the expanse of the full moon. Somehow the panels that covered the windows were wide open. The silver light danced into the room and surrounded his sister. Elizabeth was gone to another world now. She still looked lovely but the light of life had left her. She was merely an empty shell lying there.

"Her spirit has long since left. She is home with the Mother." Sophia motioned to Henry to come to her. "We must take a moment to bless her passage, albeit the time that has passed, she will need our prayers to ensure her safe travels.

"Mother God, we bid farewell to our sister Elizabeth. Take her gently into you and guide her safely to the light of your womb. Her life was a blessing to us and we shall miss her so. Godspeed Elizabeth. In Gratitude Mother.

There was something extremely soothing in this moment thought Henry. Gone is the panic and grief of losing my beloved sister. It feels like all is right with the horrific world I live in right now, in this moment.

"Why does the Goddess take such lovely goodness and leave the ugly evil?" asked Sophia. Henry was brought out of his momentary peace. Sophia continued. "With all of the wisdom of the ages, I shall never understand this." Sophia breathed a deep sigh. "I know this is your wish, Great Mother. Please help us to accept your way. May Elizabeth's love live on in our hearts for every day we are here on this earth now, and forevermore."

Sophia then started giving orders. Henry was ready. Whatsoever Sophia wanted him to do, he would do so. He trusted her implicitly.

"Henry, we must move her out of the bedchambers and out of the estate, for no one may find her here in this state. We will take her somewhere safe." Again Henry nodded and watched as Sophia cleaned up the room leaving nary a remnant or scrap of evidence that a birth and death had occurred hours earlier. She gathered the bedclothes and put them in a pile. She found the green bottles, one full, one empty. Henry's heart leapt at the thought of his betrayal and he was terrified Sophia would ask him of the bottles. She did not, but instead tucked them in her cloak pocket. Sophia did however look at Henry for a quick moment, and cast her eyes downward in respectful glance. Henry was grateful. When everything was clean she helped Henry lift Elizabeth into his arms. Despite his weariness, he had no trouble carrying his sister and they proceeded out into the clear dawn light.

"I know where we can take her", he whispered to Sophia. "To the barn in the woods. I will show you were it is. Sophia nodded. They arrived at the barn and entered. A cat darted out as they opened the door and Henry stopped abruptly to keep from tripping. Upon entering the barn, he looked around for a place to lay his sister to rest.

"Here" motioned Sophia. She gathered together the rushes that lay over the floor and made a comfortable heap for Elizabeth. Henry set his sister down and hugged her body close one last time, kissed her on the forehead and allowed his tears to flow as he thought of all that he would no longer share with his dear friend and beloved sister.

"We will make it look as if she birthed her child alone here and perished. They will believe the babe to have been taken by wild dogs." Said Sophia. This is how it must be." Sophia did an odd thing then. She pushed on Elizabeth's belly and pulled on the chord that he had cut. Out plopped something large and bloody. She wrapped it in a blanket. She then took out a small knife and cut some locks of Elizabeth's golden hair. This she tucked into her cloak with along with the knife. "Now we are finished." She said.

Henry could not speak. He had no words, only sorrow. He did not want this to be true. His sister was awaiting the return of her love. Demetri failed her, and now so had he. How could this be?

"Henry, the Goddess is with you. Never forget that." Said Sophia as she kissed him on both cheeks and hugged him close. "You are always welcome to come and live with us, for you are family."

Henry swiftly turned and fled the forest village. He would face both his and Elizabeth's fate with as much courage as possible. It was the least he could do for his dear sister. The Goddess was with him, though he did not deserve such a blessing.

Chapter Twenty-one

James arrived at the Cumberland estate just minutes after Henry returned. The Justice,

Magistrate and Shire were all in tow. Henry was not afraid. He went directly to Father's study a

few steps before the three. Here he found Father bound to a chair, head bobbing, and eyes

drooping. The stench told him, that Father had been there awhile. He quickly cut the chords of

rope to free him. Father tried to right himself and Henry grabbed his arm to hold him steady.

Father shook violently in his grasp, looking as if he were holding in his own vomit, but instead

he looked his son in the eye and shook again. All signs of intoxication seemed to vanish. The two

men stood ready, awaiting what would come next.

"Bring her to me now Gregory." boomed James as he pushed his way into Father's study.

"The time has come and we are here to bring our prisoner back."

Henry and Father stood steady, side by side, staring ahead at the man who threatened every

fiber of their being. Neither flinched.

"She is still ill and unable to travel" came a voice from behind James. It was Matilda

standing as firm and full of resolve as Henry. Where had she come from he thought? It had been

days since any of the staff were anywhere near.

James, the Magistrate and the Shire all turned at the same time and looked at Matilda,

parting their wall, they let her pass. Now it was she, the Nursemaid and Nanny who came to his

sister's aid. He almost lost his footing and felt father shiver. We must stand strong. It is all we

have, thought Henry. All five men stared at Matilda, waiting. Maybe she knew of Elizabeth's fate, and my betrayal of her wishes, he thought. His head bobbed for a moment and that is when Matilda looked directly into his eyes and ushered a direct and uncompromising stare. He knew that look. Matilda was now stepping in to take care of her charges. His gaze softened. Tears welled from his heart.

Guards started swarming Father's study. Still they stood firm. Matilda turned towards the group of overzealous heathens. "I have told you that she is not to be disturbed. And furthermore, each one of you should be ashamed of your illicit and disgraceful ways. How dare you barge into a man's home in this way." She continued. "I have raised Elizabeth since birth, and young Henry here too. I have raised no witch, and I take great offense to the scandal you..." She said poking at James' chest. "Yes, you, James Hartford have brought upon this upstanding family." Matilda stood her ground. Henry swore he heard Cookie's cheer in the echo's of the estate. "What say you?" she demanded.

A great silence fell upon the room. A deep and abiding silence took the voice and movement from each of the men who stood. Matilda created a moment of deep reverence and respect for his sister. This he knew. She could be hung for what she uttered.

James shook the reverence from his face within a moment's time, yet not before Henry saw a fleeting look of distress in his one eye. "I will get her myself, you stupid fools. She goes back today." James turned away from Matilda and pushed his way through the still silent lawmen.

A moment later, James was back from his search. "She is gone, where is she?" he yelled to anyone that would listen. "Magistrate, order your guards to search this estate, we must find her. Where were the guards ordered to guard her every move? Perhaps they wish to be hung alongside dear Elizabeth." He scowled at the Magistrate who seemed to not be listening at all.

"Magistrate, Shire!" yelled James. The two men slowly walked out the door and Henry could hear them calling for their men. "See if you can find the maiden." Was all Henry heard the Shire order.

All at once the house was full of guards going in and out, throwing items here and there and causing utter chaos. Henry sat Father down and Matilda fetched him some food. The three of them waited well into the evening for word.

It was almost midnight when one lone guard returned to Father's study to give them word. He had a deeply saddened look upon his face.

"We have found her. She is not alive. Seems that she died in childbirth, in an abandoned barn. The babe is nowhere to be found. Wild dogs, I am sure. They, uh…we…are taking her back to town." The guard bowed his head. "I am truly sorry, sir." He then turned and left.

Father broke down and sobbed, Henry brought him to his bedchambers and put him to bed. No words were spoken. Henry returned to his own bed. He lay awake all night long, sleep delaying its respite, his thoughts were but long, full stretches of loss.

Conclusion

Our souls wrap each other in warmth, returning home to share the goodness of each lifetime lived.

The days were so cold, so bitterly cold for Henry. It was the start of winter, the day before Christmas and the area had not seen such bitter cold in many years. For Henry the cold ran deeper than the feel of the air biting his face as he went about his chores. He had lived alone in this dismal cabin for eight of the fifteen years he had been gone. He was old beyond his years, thin from too little food, haggard and weary from inner turmoil and attacks. He had decided this year would be his last, for there was no more time left for him, no reason for his existence. Languishing in pain and sorrow would be ending soon.

A year after Elizabeth died he left the estate and never went back. His father had gone mad, for he never left his study and his mother, well she was completely despondent before Elizabeth's death. The few servants, along with Matilda, and Cookie, stayed on, continuing to care for Henry and Father. Annie left, along with any hope of him having a love in this lifetime. Missing Elizabeth eroded a hole in his heart, so deep, it felt an empty and bottomless well. His sister so bravely saved him, time and again, and from their own mother, no less. He knew now, of all of his childhood pain, for over the last fifteen years each and every memory rolled out from the confines of the darkened past, each one came out to play havoc on his gouged heart. He kept the memories out, in the light of day as a reminder to himself of his own destructive ways and how this life was unjust and tarnished.

The reasoning behind the hypocrisy, the love and the hate, the riches and the poverty, the betrayals and the loyalty, had to be his own sinning heart. Sophia's words rang in his head over and over as of late. "Why does the Goddess take the beautiful souls and leave the evil?"

He had tried so very hard to right his ways, to make up for his betrayal of his sister. He even joined the Queens army, hoping he might be able to save his countrymen, and bring honor to his Queen. Yet honor was not to be found, for he merely learned of battle and what he learned was that battles never end, they simply rage on and on, with neither side remembering why they were in the battle to begin with. Honor was negotiable, loyalty had a price and the highest bidder always won. The winners and thieves one in the same.

Now he found himself alone and lonely, barely living, in a cabin many day's travel from the grand estate of his youth. The grandness was left behind many, many years ago and replaced with a meager life. All thought of the life of leisure and fortune and pleasure, vanished when they burned his sister. Yes, it would be that James of Hartford had his way after all.

"They are going to burn her body." cried Annie.

Henry held her frail body close in comfort. He stroked her hair and caught her tears with his fingers. He took in her words, each one a dagger ripping and tearing any fabric of hope he had left that somehow his sister's memory might live with a shred of truth.

But it was not to be so. He had failed her twice. Once in life and once in death.

"I heard it today, they named her a witch, convicted of crimes against God. For that the punishment is burning. Her body would burn and she would be forever damned." Cried Annie.

Forever damned. If that was his sisters fate, then it shall be his too. All thoughts of life before his dear sister perished were now those of another man, in another time. That is how he came to live the last fifteen years; a long drawn out penance for the sins of his his life and his inabilities. His penance would soon be complete, he hoped.

The land around his cabin provided him with sustenance, just enough to get by, and more than most peasants of this day. Henry found it fitting, since he himself was responsible for losing his right to any sort of noble inheritance, squandered away by his inability to be the courageous man he ought.

Life had gone on far too long for him and far too short for his sister and it was now time to have it all be over, fifteen years almost to the day that his sister left him, would now be his last. He would take his life on the morrow, Christmas day. It seemed fitting, the birth day of the savior, would be his last day. He had a plan.

"Cat, you will be alone after tomorrow comes and goes. Will you miss me? I shall miss you." Cat purred her answer. The old calico had been his constant companion since the day he found this abandoned cabin. The cat never asked for much and did help keep his feet warm on the damp winter nights. "I hope you know how to care for yourself better than I could ever care for another. I will miss you a slight bit perhaps," he said softly as he drifted off to sleep.

As he was drifting off he felt a surge of warmth come over his face. He wanted to awake and see what had created such warmth around him. Had the fire suddenly caught a draft? He thought groggily. The sleep was heavy though, as if he had partaken in too many spirits and he did not awake. Instead he drifted into a dream, and it was there he saw her.

Elizabeth stood in front of him dressed in her lovely Christmas ball gown. The one she wore to the Christmas festivities the year before she died. She looked so lovely, just as she had on that night so long ago. He reached out to touch her hand.

"Hello Henry" she said placing his hand upon her cheek. Henry was flooded with memories as he held his sister's face in his palm. Her laughter the day he had Cook and Priscilla sliding across the pine floor rang within his head. Merriment filled his empty chest with a blithe he had not felt in years. His face turned upward to his beloved sister and his cheeks ached in a smile long forgotten.

"I am fine now you see." said Elizabeth still holding Henry's hand close to her face. Henry could not speak, for words would be a mere pittance of what he was feeling and he dare not break the spell.

"I am safe Henry." said Elizabeth. "And I am with my love, Demetri. He has always been with me here. He was waiting for me, here, all the while I waited for him to return to me and our babe, he was right here, awaiting my return." She smiled and laughed. Her joy entered into Henry's heart. "Into the depths of the forest, deeper than any one dare go in life!" she sang.

Henry was in a trance until he felt another presence, a heavy weight on his shoulder. The figure of a young man stood next to his sister. The man held out his hand too, and placed it upon Henry's shoulder. A reassuring pat, and a gesture of trust. This must be Demetri, he thought.

"He was returning to me and our babe, Henry, thus is true, yet the night was storming and his horse lost footing. They both fell far and fast and were killed as they hit the rocks below. He died a mere forth night from our estate. His remains lye their still." Elizabeth cast her eyes downward and bowed her head in respect as she spoke.

The three stood in a circle surrounded by a deep amber glow. Henry looked into the eyes of the man his sister could not marry in life, and what he saw was love, pure and simple. This love filled him too. There was nothing hindering it, no thoughts or feelings barring it, no raw pain and scarring upon his heart and soul, keeping the love forever at bay. It was gone and all that was left was the love. This is what it feels like to be free of this place and this time that has tortured my soul. I am so glad to know of the rightness of my decision." He thought to himself.

"Henry, I know you wish to take your life and I am here to ask you not to. I hold nothing against you, my dear brother. I know there was nothing you could have done to stop James and the evil men from prosecuting me. Father would never have listened to you either Henry. You know he would not have. Father was consumed by demons and his courage left him."

Henry hung his head low as she spoke these words. The feeling of bliss, gone as quickly as it came. Shame started to overcome him, and Elizabeth's touch once more warmed his face. She grabbed hold of his chin and lifted it unto her gaze. The amber light glowed still and Demetri's touch still comforted. He dared not look into their eyes. He did not want the pain to continue.

"There was nothing you could have done differently Henry. You must know this." She said staring sternly at him as she would so often do in life. "I should never have asked you to take my own child's life. It was foolish and selfish of me to ask you to give my babe the elixir. I was so very distraught over losing my love and I did not want the evil people to win or have anything of mine. I could not imagine how my child would be spared a certain brutal and painful death. But you see, Demetri has been here with me for all time and my babe has brought much joy to those who care for him; joy you could never imagine and it could be yours. If only… I am sorry Henry, please forgive me." She whispered, a tear falling from her face onto Henry's hand.

"I know you gave the babe to Sophia and I am forever grateful to you. You did the right thing Henry. What you did was so very brave. I hold nothing against you. On the contrary, I hold you as the most courageous man I had ever known." Elizabeth exclaimed, joy evident once more in her eyes of blue. Henry could not help but stare into them, as he took in her words.

"Our son has grown into a fine lad because of you, dear brother. A life was spared and flourishes because of you." With that she came closer to him, alive with light and warmth. He grabbed onto her and hugged her with all his might, not wanting to leave her, not wanting to remember the life that she spoke of, but instead to step gloriously into this other place with her and Demetri.

"I have another request of you Henry" pulling from his embrace. "And this request is one full of love, not sorrow and fear as my death bed request was. Henry, I beg you to heed it this time." He interrupted.

"No Elizabeth, I want to be with you now. I am done here on this cold dirty earth. I want what you have. I want to come be with you. I have decided."

"Please Henry, listen to my request. Then decide. You shall know your fate. I trust you will choose wisely." Henry did not say a word, he weighed hers instead. "Our child will come to you on the morrow. You will know him when you see him. He is looking for you. He needs you Henry as you need him and I am requesting that you greet him and spend time with him and then decide."

"I am so very tired, sister, and I have nothing left. I am sure I have nothing that could be of use to your child now." Henry was pulled. Again pulled, as he had so often felt in life. Pulled between his heart and duty. Pulled between his sister and his loud doubt. Pulling and pushing had left him shattered and weary.

"I have always been here watching you and forgiving you and praying you would know how I love you so. I had hoped that my prayers for you and our prayers for our son have strengthened you enough and kept you alive until this very time. Perhaps you might feel differently on the morrow." Elizabeth took her hand and lifted his face up so their gazes met. The same simple, intense love radiated through his being, calming his every fiber. She kissed him on his forehead just as he had done to her on her deathbed and then she was gone.

Henry sat up quickly and looked around the room. Cat jumped from his chest and landed with a thud, stretching as if she himself had decided to jump from Henry's still, warm chest at just that moment. The room was vibrantly hot but the fire was out. Henry sat perplexed and bewildered as the most curious feeling arose from within him. The most curious feeling was hope and it seeped through each crack and crevice of his immobilized heart. The hope lulled him and he could not fight it, there was no room for fight, no armor, no shields, no doors, no barricades. Before he surrendered completely to this feeling he lay back down, and reached his hand out for Cat.

"I shall determine what to do when the sun comes up." He told her before falling fast asleep.

The sun shone brightly on what was to be the day of Henry's death, so bright that its rays awoke him as they streamed in through the windows and cracks of the door. He sprung out of bed and started toward the fire to rake the embers. There was so much to do today. Get dressed, chop wood, start his breakfast and prepare his rickety shack for a guest. The floor boards would need sweeping, and new rushes thrown about. Perhaps he still had some herbs that would freshen the scent of his home, for the stench might offend a guest. He let Cat out and started on the sweeping. Tending to the hearth ash, he stopped frozen where he stood. What was he doing? This was to be his last day of life, what was this slight feeling of joy and where had it come from? Henry sat down to ponder what was happening to him, his thoughts fragmented bits of peace and hope, despair and sorrow. Could he be losing his mind as his mother had? He heard Cat meow and went to let her in.

"I'm coming my friend," he exclaimed, walking to the door. The hinges creaked loudly and the door flung open, sending a blast of chill air along with a dose of sunshine. A stirring heat, warmth and remembrance engulfed his being. Elizabeth, his beloved sister, had come to him. Maybe it was but a dream, yet the burden upon his brow was ever so light now. Lighter than it had been even a few moments ago. His head and heart were no longer fettered. Elizabeth forgave him. His heart swelled in the memory. She had come to let him know that she was happy, safe, loved. This knowing melted into him, the feeling of guilt, remorse, and shame, distant now. Cat darted in between his legs.

"I think we are to expect a visitor today, Cat. Let us prepare, for we shall see if Elizabeth truly appeared to me, or if I am going mad. I have nothing to lose now, haven't for many a year!" he laughed at himself heartily. Cat moved slowly toward Henry, sat and faced the door, where she stayed all morn.

Henry continued to ready the tiny cabin, cleaning, sweeping and even venturing out to gather greenery to adorn the small dining table. While he was out, he killed a fat pheasant for the midday meal. He was cleaning the pheasant outside the front of the cabin when he saw him, a lone figure approaching on horseback, riding slowly. Keeping his mirth in check, by remaining seated, his eyes strained to see who this could be.

"Hello!" shouted the lad. "May I approach?" The stranger asked, jumping down from a healthy grey gelding.

Henry noticed everything about this lad in a moment's time. His senses keen and unwavering, he registered a good heart, a strong and able body, and a familiar air of nobility. Could this be him; my nephew whom I have not seen since the day he was born? Henry remained seated and nodded to the stranger. He took his clipping shears and poked himself good and hard in the leg to be sure he was not dreaming this scene into being.

"Ouch" he whispered, jumping in his skin. "That was certainly a foolhardy thing to do!" Cat just looked up at him with her golden eyes, saying, "Yes, you are a fool" in her own cat language.

The young man strode over to Henry with his hand outstretched.

"Merry Christmas, sir." He said. "I am sorry to bother you on such an occasion, but I was passing by and was wondering if you might help me."

Henry merely stared at the stranger, and stayed seated, continuing to size him up. He looked to be the age that Elizabeth's babe would be, he was tall and lean and had light blond unruly hair, poking out from underneath his riding hat. He pulled his cap and gloves off in proper greeting.

"They call me Evan, kind sir." He said with a smile.

Henry then rose, took his hand and looked close into the lad's face, seeing something very familiar that he could not place. "Good day Evan." He said, holding the lads warm hand in his. Then it came to him in a wave of recognition. He had met this same face last night in his dream. It was the face of Elizabeth's Love. This was indeed her babe, grown into a fine young man, healthy and well bred. Henry pulled him close and hugged him fiercely.

"I do believe I have much to tell you young man." said Henry languishing in the embrace. Won't you come in and share the Christmas meal with me?" Henry could hardly contain his excitement as he pulled the lad indoors.

"I would be honored sir, but I just…just…needed some water for my horse, and I…and I do not mean to intrude on such a day. I know you must be sharing a Christmas meal with your family…

"Yes, I am at that, and you are just in time." answered Henry, feeling giddy and incredibly light hearted. This feeling he only remembered from when he and Elizabeth were children.

"I am looking for my uncle. He is from royal blood and lives on an estate close to here. Perhaps you know him and can direct me to him?" You seem a merry fellow, and perhaps you know many in this land."

"Yes, Evan, I can tell you where to find your uncle." replied Henry.

With that the two walked into the cabin with the pheasant in hand. They shared a fine meal and Henry shared story after story of Elizabeth's love for life and for all she touched.

"Your mother was a brave young woman, and she would be here with us, if she could." Said Henry as the evening wound down.

"You are the brave one Uncle, for if not for your quick thinking, I should not be here with you this eve, in celebration!" answered Evan. "Sophia, told me often of how you were the one who helped birth me. She makes the other's laugh with her tale of man become midwife." Evan looked upon Henry's face to see if this humored him. It did. "I always thought of you Uncle, as the young lad who defied authority and delivered me safely to be raised and loved. I am forever in your debt for saving my life and for ensuring the memory of my mother and father to live on."

Henry could not believe his ears as he sat and listened to his nephew speak of his gratefulness toward him. He had not thought of it that way at all, in fact quite the opposite truth had infested his soul for many a year.

"And so it came to be that I ventured to find you and tell you of my gratitude, for if I did not, I surely would not be able to go on. In fact, Mother came to me from beyond, she told me I must find you. I could not stop until I did so." Sighed Evan.

Henry could not help but cry. Big, deep tears fell from his eyes, cascading down his cheeks, falling as freely as his spirit felt. Cat jumped up on his lap and sat beneath the shower. Henry and Evan laughed and cried together throughout the evening and into the wee hours of the morn.

Both Henry and Evan were reborn that day. They brought each other to new life because of the life of their dear Elizabeth. Evan shared with Henry how he had become consumed with finding him, much to Sophia's dismay. "It is not safe to travel outside the forest, and especially not a lad of his years." He explained. "Of course you know this." Hanging his head in sadness, the young lad too cried. "My mother came into my dreams each night, telling me that I must find you. She would not let up. I thought she a demon!" he smiled through his tears and looked to Henry to be sure he knew he was saying such things in jest.

"Yes, my sister, your mother was very stubborn in life. I suppose it is how this day has come to pass." The mood turned somber once more as Evan continued.

"I was able to convince Sophia that I was ready to travel. She was distraught and I feel shame to bring pain upon her. My life in the village is so very good. I do believe you know of them. True?" He asked with a child's exuberance.

Yes, I know of them." Henry answered. Saddened that it was too late for him to enjoy the company of such a fine village of people. Evan continued with his stories. He told of how Sophia showed him the barn where his mother and father would meet. He would sneak to the barn often to talk to his parents. He always felt their presence there. He felt his mother's presence surrounding him often and he felt it ever so strong on the day he left. He did not know where he was going to go but Sophia had taught him to follow his instincts and pray to the Goddess, and that would always lead him to where he should be.

"I left it all behind on this search, Uncle. I had to learn where I came from and who I am. Mother insisted from the grave, at the same time I knew I had to find what was missing inside of me. Sophia has always cared for me as if I were her own, and I have three loving sisters and many others to guide and teach me. Yet none are my blood. Sophia told me everything she could about my dear Mother and Father. She told me of their great love for each other and of the reason they could not be together. I know of how and why my mother left the earth." He explained.

Henry listened in awe of the tales of this young man's life. Pride welled up within as he listened to his stories. He saw in him, his sister's spirit and his father's looks, and he also saw something he could not explain, but knew was of great importance. This child had come searching for him and this child, in his search had become a man. Perhaps it was time for Henry to become the man he too was destined to be. He is a man of royal blood, yet a man of his own making. A new man, born on this day. A Christmas gift of recognition and love, forgiveness and new life. It was a new day and a new life for both of them.

A few weeks later Henry lay in the throes of an afternoon nap, in his chair before the fire. Cat, sat contentedly on his lap. His thoughts drifted as the flames danced. Evan had stayed on, for how long, it was not clear. Neither of them spoke of a pending departure. He can not leave until spring, Henry demanded in his own mind. Each day they awoke and tended to the chores together, working side by side as he had so longed to do with his Father. Evan had a most promising life in the midst of the women of the forest. Hyacinth was his older sister, Sophia, his mother on earth. There was a man too who was a Father to him. None were his blood though, as Evan reminded him almost daily. He smiled at the thought. Evan told him many wondrous stories of the life he lived, of Sophia's teachings and the love that permeated their home. This is truly what my sister wanted for him, or perhaps it is much, much more than she could imagine.

The feelings and thoughts of what it would be like to live amidst such kindness, goodness and power soothed him and lulled him into a deep sleep.

The light of the fire burned bright and hot and Elizabeth once again appeared to him. She appeared as before, dressed in her Christmas ball gown, yet this time she stood alone, smiling her beautiful warm smile. She reached out her hand to him. Henry took it in his own, drawing in her light touch and warm presence. The amber glow rose up from their touch and once again held them in a tender hug.

"Henry, I see that you and my child have found one another. Thank you, thank you, dear brother. I have but one more request that I know you shall honor, for you are a most honorable man Henry." She said squeezing his hand.

Henry felt the wave of grace engulf him. He believed what his sister said to be true now. He believed it, yet he relished a chance to prove it once again. He wanted many chances to do so and he felt the hope alive in his heart that he would be given those opportunities to prove his bravado and his true nobility.

"You must go to a place three miles east of our estate. There you will find the rocky side of a cliff hidden from the road by four ash trees. It is there you will find the remains of Demetri. Please return them to Sophia and she will see to it that my Demetri has a proper burial."

Elizabeth's instructions sunk deep into his mind, etched in a place he would never forget. He nodded in agreement and Elizabeth's face shown brighter than before.

"Thank you Henry, I love you forever. Live your life in peace and happiness. I will be waiting for you, for when it is truly your time, we shall be reunited."

She was again gone as quickly as she appeared and Henry awoke. The room was still warm with her presence. He tried to fall back into slumber for she had left him so readily and it did not seem time yet. He rested his head for a moment yet sleep did not return. He arose and found a paper and writing quill. He wrote down exactly what Elizabeth had told him, lest he forget one detail. When he was satisfied that he had written all exactly as his sister requested, he got up from his seat and went to check on his nephew. Evan was sleeping soundly on the only bed in the cottage. Henry put his hand on his back, feeling the presence of Elizabeth in his nephew's dreams. She is visiting him too, no doubt. He smiled and blessed him with his words.

"Sleep well, nephew, for come sunrise, we shall ride and attend to an important matter, together. We will be the noble men that we were born to be. This is to now be so."

Henry then said a prayer of thanksgiving over Evan, thanking him for saving his life and for giving him a second chance.

Made in the USA
Las Vegas, NV
11 December 2020